The Ministry Witch

and other tales of perfidy

William Wilkin

Bell Street Publishing

Bell Street Publishing, LLC

Published by Bell Street Publishing, LLC,
7360 Middlebrook Cir
Nashville, TN 37221-6545

Copyright © 2019 by Bell Street Publishing, LLC

ISBN: 978-0-9903164-5-9

First Published in the United States, 2018

Contents

Acknowledgements

I owe an immense debt of gratitude to several people who have contributed substantially to this book's artistic integrity.

There are my two sons, James Wilkin and Matthew Stone.

James contributed the digital painting on the cover which captures, as I never could, my vision of the sense of the book. He also made a number of graphic design suggestions that are incorporated in the cover design and interior of the book.

He exhibited attention to detail and artistic consistency far beyond my capabiities.

My wife, Lou, contributed in both obvious and subtle ways to the completion of the book. She is a Spanish teacher and has extensive experience editing and correcting texts – both student and professional. Any remaining grammatical and spelling errors must not be accounted to her. They proceed from my eccentric ideas about the value of deviating from standards occasionally to accurately portray a state of mind or emotional content. A subtle way that she supported the completion of this book was her endless patience with those eccentric ideas.

In addition, she was willing to endure the many, many times that I worked into the early morning hours pursued by my characters who insisted on telling their stories at the most inconvenient hours.

She has always been emotionally constant in the shifting winds of our lives throughout the long thankless years of the struggle to bring these stories to print. Bravo Lou!

Preface

For those of you who have not read any of the preceding books, I will warn you that this preface contains spoilers. If you want to learn about the story line to the point where this book begins, you could read the stories in sequence—*In the Realm of the Blind, The Chessmaster,* and *The Spare Wizard.* However, reading the first book by itself would give you a good grounding in the Realm of the Blind.

This story takes place in the universe of the Realm of the Blind where Hogwarts School for Witchcraft and Wizardry exits. It is a residential finishing school for magical youth.

The main character James Wendt is an English Literature Professor and Muggle (non-magical). He has been hired by the Headmaster Albus Dumbledore to bring diversity to the school and the slightest touch of liberal arts education to an institution that is basically a vocational school.

He and the Assitant Headmistress Minerva McGonagall are "an item." However, the astronomy Professor Aurora Sinestra seems to have designs on Wendt.

The would-be despot Valdemort has a gang of followers who call themselves Deatheaters. Valdemort was permanently separated from his body but survived as a disembodied spirit. He had recently been gifted a new body and threatens the magical world order as he once had done. He and his followers are determined to enslave the Muggle population. Thus, Muggles like Professor Wendt are on their *persona non grata* list. They have been trying to kill Wendt for several years because of the effrontery of a Muggle in choosing to teach at one of the premier schools of magic.

The magical government of England is led by Minister Fudge who wishes to deny the survival of Valdemort and wishes to suppress anyone, such as the teachers at Hogwarts, who disagree with his prejudice. He has sent an assistant as an overseer to Hogwarts to enforce his prejudices. Her name is Dolores Umbrage, and she will teach Defense Against the Dark Arts.

Other teachers at Hogwarts include Rubeus Haggrid (Professor of Magical Creatures), Severus Snape (Potion-master), and Professor Flitwick (Professor of Charms). Other staff at Hogwarts include the Janitor, Filch; the Librarian, Ms. Pinz; and the Nurse, Madame Pomfrey.

Shrimp Gumbo

She thought a moment and said, "You want to do what on this date!" Her hackles were clearly up, and I could see that I had some explaining to do.

"Well, it's not really that strange. You know about the movies."

She snorted, "Yes, you go to a theater and squint at moving pictures on the wall at the back of the stage. It's like a play except that the actors aren't alive, and it seems like you only take me to them so that we can snog in the back row."

I laughed. "That's only the first time that we see one. When we go back the second time – which you have to do to understand the film, we pay close attention to the movie."

She giggled, "You mean that you pay close attention to the movie. I'm still hoping we'll get some serious snogging in. But, after the movie's over, we go to a restaurant and have a proper meal and talk. What I get out of this new idea of yours is that we go to your apartment, sit on the bed. . . "

I interrupted, "We could lie on the bed."

Her Scottish brogue surfaced, "AS I was saying, we sit on the bed and watch one of these movies on a tiny screen. Then after squinting for two hours, we . . . do . . . what?"

I smiled, "There's no reason that we couldn't go to a restaurant, but the beauty of watching a movie in the comfort of your own home is that you can order out. The best authorities suggest that pizza is the ideal meal for watching movies at home."

"I had your *pizza* once. What is it? Cheese on bread. What makes that so wonderful for watching movies?

"AND for that matter, what's so wonderful about watching them in the discomfort of your garret apartment, hmm?"

2

I stopped to assemble my forces, "Well. . . In the first place, there are lots of great movies that you can't watch in movie theaters."

"And why would it be that a great movie is not available in a theatre?"

This was turning out to be harder than I'd thought it would be, but I soldiered on, "There are far too many great movies for them all to be shown at the same time. That's true of plays too, you know. Can you just decide one day to watch Macbeth and just find a theater where it's playing, hmmm?"

She sniffed but didn't object, so I went on, "Great movies are available to rent from your neighborhood video store. I'll bet there's a video store near your sister's place."

There was no objection, so I went on, "The only way to watch a movie from a video store is to go to someone's home and watch it on a telly. *Quid Est Demonstratum.*"

She asked what the movie was that I wanted to see. I answered that she'd never heard of it, so she should just be patient and wait until date night. That wasn't a very long wait. Date night was that very night.

I had bought a television with a built-in VHS player. So, all we had to do was stop at the video store and order a pizza to be delivered. Voila, instant date night.

After I found the video and checked out, we walked home and the Muggle questions began.

How does a movie come in a little box?

I opened the box and revealed the VHS tape inside.

That doesn't look like a tape. Why do you call it a tape?

I gently pulled back the door that protects the tape when it's not being played. Minerva took the tape and pulled some tape out.

I exclaimed, "Wait, wait. Don't pull on that."

She said, "But it doesn't look like spell-o-tape at all."

"It certainly isn't spell-o-tape. There are many kinds of tape and this isn't spell-o-tape."

She sniffed but still held onto the tape. "The tape is black. How can it have a movie on it?"

I frowned. How was I going to explain? I retrieved the tape, rewound the tape back into the case and pondered. I made a list of the things that I'd have to explain to explain video tape. Let's see:

- Video capture in a TV camera

- Turning that into an electrical signal.
- Turning the signal into a magnetic field
- Magnetizing magnetic tape with the magnetic field
- Reading the magnetic field in a VHS player
- Turning the field into an electrical signal
- The electrical signal is amplified
- The amplified signal controls the flow of electrons to a phosphor-covered screen that glows due to the electrons hitting it. That makes the picture.

We were getting close to home, and she was getting impatient. "Well!"

I stopped walking, gazed into her eyes, and said, "Would you believe Scientific Magic?"

She just sneered, "I knew that there wasn't an explanation."

We reached my home away from Hogwarts.

The movie that I'd chosen was "Forest Gump". It was a long movie. Minerva had a million questions about it. I didn't hint to her that we could stop the movie at any point, talk and then start it again. We'd have been all night and well into the next day before we finished it.

When we did finish it, Minerva insisted that we go out to find a cup of decent coffee that we could have while talking over the movie. I thought to myself, "You mean a dozen coffees, don't you?"

There was a Starbucks about five blocks away, so we walked there. We both ordered tea. Then the questions began. "What is that story about?"

I was so happy that I knew the Socratic method that I asked her, "What do you think it was about?"

She pondered and then tried a series of ideas. It was about the conquest of optimism over pessimism. I had a thing or two to say about that, "So, do you think that Gump's optimism won the day?"

That made Minerva think hard, "Well, it seemed to work for everyone else around him."

"I agree. He saved his buddy in battle. He later gave him a reason to live. He rescued the love of his life from drug addiction.

"He helped the U.S. with its ping-pong diplomacy. That benefited the whole world."

Minerva knew me enough to know that I had a "but". She supplied it, "But?"

I obliged, "But did any of that give him happiness?"

She thought. "I don't know. Do you think he had any happiness out of all that?"

I thought about it trying to come up with an answer that made sense to me. I finally said, "Suppose that I had cancer and died in a week. Would you say that your life were happy?"

A determined look came over her face, "That will NOT happen."

"How can you know that?"

"That is such a sad story." Inadvertently (yes, I really think it was inadvertent), her hand fell on mine on the table, and she squeezed, "Do Muggles really not have a way to cure cancer?"

"No. It's like Forest says—Life is like a box of chocolates. You never know what you're going to find inside."

"And that man who lost both his legs. His story is happier than Forest's, don't you think?"

I had to think long about that. Forest's was coming a lot closer to mine than I was comfortable with, "I think Socrates was right. You just don't know whether a life is happy or not until the end. Even then, I suppose, it's too late to do anything about it."

Her hand squeezed tighter. "But, surely, we wizards can do things that make it better than this story."

I laughed internally at the way she'd said, "We wizards." None-the-less, I tried to answer as honestly as I could, "I don't know. Wizards have plenty of problems as well. You know that Potter's story is very sad, but his life is not over. On the other hand, Cedric seemed to have all the world at his feet, but who knows?"

She would not give up. She tried another theory. "Maybe the story shows that even the most crippled can recover a meaningful life."

I thought about that. "We really have to see another movie."

She sneered again, "What kind of answer is that?"

"Well, my answer is contained in another movie, 'Bang the Drum Slowly'."

She stared into my eyes, "Is that a joke?"

"Oh, no. Although one of the characters says of another character that the world had played the biggest joke on him and he was too dumb to realize it. It's another story about a man who is crippled by being 'plumb dumb'."

I went on, "But to answer your question, I think you are right. Even the crippled can come to a meaningful life."

She took my other hand in hers and said, "Well, you, at least, don't have to wait most of your life for the love of your life to come to you."

Requiem for a Wizard

I was surprised by an owl that dropped a letter at the door of my apartment. It was from the Diggory's. It was an announcement of a wake at their home. Minerva further surprised me by ringing me up shortly afterward. She invited me to go with her to the wake. I, of course, accepted.

A day later, she showed up on the sidewalk in front of my home. We disapparated there and I didn't even complain about the gut-wrenching experience. We entered their house and immediately, Mrs. Diggory ran up to Minerva and hugged her. Amos shook my hand. I expressed my sorrow, "You know that there are not many people who feel the tragedy of the death of your son more than I do."

He nodded and seemed at the point of tears, himself.

The living room was filled with people. Most I knew—students, their parents, teachers, and some others who were introduced to me. Most of those were relatives.

There were lots of stories of Cedric, his childhood, his time at Hogwarts. There was an aunt and uncle from Ireland who wanted to hear more about his chess exploits.

His aunt Susie asked, "Did he really win some international tournaments?"

I nodded, "Well, yes and no. He did win the last tournament that he played in. It wasn't the strongest tournament that he'd played in, but it was a good challenging tournament. He was ranked internationally in the top fifty in the world."

His uncle Mark asked, "Exactly where was he ranked?"

"Oh, positions change almost daily as the best players win, lose, draw. I didn't follow them particularly closely, but I think he reached 38th in the world at one point after that tournament."

"Really?"

"Yes. He was really talented. I don't think there was a player like him since Bobby Fischer."

They both looked puzzled so I explained, "Bobby Fischer was a largely self-taught American chess genius who eventually won the world chess championship. He was a genius, but he was very eccentric and never repeated although he was probably the greatest chess player in the world for a number of years.

"What made Cedric so amazing was that he was a much more rounded player than Fischer. I think he could have been world champion IF he'd wanted to. But maybe that's the key—not wanting it to the exclusion of everything else."

By this time a small crowd had accumulated around our discussion. I talked about how I'd "discovered" him and how his career advanced.

As the evening wore on, people began to say goodbye and eventually, there were only Minerva, Cedric's parents, couple of relatives and, I remaining.

His mom drew Minerva and me aside and Amos followed, "I just want to know how Ced died. Was he killed by. . .?" Suppressed tears choked her throat, and Amos finished for her.

"Was he killed by You-know-who?"

"I don't know. But I'll tell you what I believe. Either Riddle killed him directly, or he personally ordered someone else to do it. Potter says that it was Peter Pettigrew."

Amos asked, "Do you believe Potter?"

"I believe that he's right about Riddle being back. I haven't heard details directly from him, but what I've heard from people who've talked to him makes me believe that Riddle was present when it happened and at least directed it." I didn't dare tell them how I knew that Riddle was back.

Cedric's mom sobbed, and Amos said, "Well, it makes it a little more bearable that we know that it wasn't Ced's fault or an accident like the Ministry is saying."

I desperately wanted to know precisely what the Ministry had told them about Cedric's death. However, I thought it wouldn't be a good idea to try to get his parents to talk about things unless they really wanted to.

His mom thanked us for coming, "You know, nobody from the Ministry even came. Hogwarts teachers have been very kind."

I said, "You deserve far better than that. You know that I liked and respected your son very much. His friends won't forget him."

They both shook our hands and asked us to drop in again.

"I don't think that I've heard where you plan to bury him?"

"There's a family graveyard a few miles from here. We've buried him. You're welcome to visit it whenever you want."

We thanked them again and left.

A Little Underage Wizardry

The summer holiday had been particularly boring after all the excitement of the preceding couple of weeks. We'd returned to London, and Minerva had buried herself in some activity that she wouldn't talk about with me. I'd spent weeks trying to coax her out of her self-imposed exile from me.

Once in a while she would meet me somewhere for lunch. I tried to wheedle something out of her at those meetings, but she maintained silence. Finally, I decided that I had to force her hand.

"Minerva, why in the world won't you share your secret life with me? I know it's not because you've stopped liking me. I wouldn't see you at all if that were true. There must be something. Why are you holding out?"

She looked around as though she were afraid someone might be spying on us. "Do you promise not to tell anyone?"

I wasn't going to be caught in any word trap so I was cautious about promises, "As long as it is not illegal, immoral or fattening."

"I can promise not fattening."

"Oh, all right. I promise."

"And if an Auror asks you what I'm doing?"

"I'll tell the Auror nothing."

"Then, what has happened to your loyalty to the Ministry?"

"Nothing. I never had much, and if they put me through an inquisition, it would all be gone."

"Brave answer, but you can't get into trouble if you don't know anything."

I laughed out loud at that, "Now you know better than that. My ability to get into trouble is absolutely un-impaired by my ignorance. As a matter of fact, it's probably improved."

She frowned and said, "I suppose that you've got a point there. Your ignorance is practically unconquerable."

"Thanks. I think. But what am I ignorant of?"

Minerva looked around again as though the walls had ears. Then she hunched forward a little (I'm not kidding), "Well, where's your promise?"

"Oh, yes. You have it." She stared at me a bit more.

Then she went on, "All right. Here it is. Have you ever heard of the Order of the Phoenix?"

"Minerva, you are one of the few people I know who can answer a question with another question. No. I've not heard of the Order of the Phoenix. What is it?"

"Well, it was founded more than twenty years ago by Dumbledore. The purpose was to oppose Valdemort.

"At its peak it had more than fifty members—mostly friends of Dumbledore who were committed to preventing Valdemort from defeating the Ministry and taking over the government of Wizards.

"It seemed to be a losing proposition. There were more Deatheaters by far. We managed to identify and send some to Azkaban, but we were basically losing. Valdemort seemed to recruit Deatheaters and fellow travelers faster than we could detect and send them to Azkaban.

"A number of the members died or were severely injured. By the time that Valdemort disappeared, our numbers were reduced to a couple of dozen. Then, the strangest thing happened. Valdemort just disappeared from the scene.

"After that, we kept trying to find Deatheaters. We were somewhat successful. But, there were lots of former Deatheaters who claimed to have been under the Imperious Curse and the Order just dissolved.

"Well, at least until this year. When Potter reported that Valdemort had returned, Dumbledore re-activated the organization. We've been meeting on a daily basis. We're recruiting allies from non-human magical creatures, organizing opposition groups, and trying to figure out what Valdemort and his Deatheaters are doing.

11

I was surprised to say the least. "Wow. You've kept this really quiet. I'm impressed." Then, I added, "Can I join."

"That's exactly why I've kept it quiet. That is precisely what I was afraid of—you wanting to put yourself at more risk."

"Oh, yes. And you're not in any risk at all."

She grimaced, "Well, at least *I* can defend myself."

"Have you seen me practicing with my Glock? I've gotten to be a pretty good aim."

Minerva just rolled her eyes and shook her head—pretty hard to do at the same time. But then she was serious, "You'll have to talk to the Secret Keeper."

"The what?"

"The Secret Keeper—the person who knows where the Order of the Phoenix headquarters is and is the only person who can invite you in."

That was an interesting concept, "You've got an official 'Secret Keeper'?"

"Yes, we do. It's the only way that we can protect the location of the headquarters."

"OOOOKay. Just how does that work. You can't take me there yourself?"

She was insistent. "No, I can't."

"Then you don't know where it is?"

"Of course, I know where it is."

This was getting pretty strange. "OK. Suppose that we just take each other's hand and walk there from here. What's wrong with that?"

"Well, it sounds just marvelous if you want to go for a nice romantic walk, BUT the best that we could do would be to go to the block that the headquarters was on. I couldn't bring you closer."

"You mean that you wouldn't?"

"No! I couldn't. I don't know exactly what would happen from my point of view, but you would see that I just couldn't figure out where it was."

That was strange. So, I decided to tweak the situation a little. "OK. Suppose that you walk away by yourself and unbeknownst to you, I follow you and watch where you go."

12

"I don't know what would happen, but I'm pretty sure that I'd be able to find the place, but you wouldn't know better than what block it was on."

"But couldn't I just watch you enter one of the buildings?"

"You'd think so, but it just doesn't work that way."

"More magic?"

"Right."

"So, how does it work—from the inside?"

Minerva leaned back as though planning how to approach the question. Then she got up and paced for a minute, which seemed pretty unusual in a café. Then she sat again and leaned toward me, "OK. This is how it works. Let's say that you have a group of people that you want to share a secret with."

"OK. Sounds like a good start."

"Now, if you're all wizards and witches what you do is appoint one person to be the official Secret Keeper. That person is the gateway for people getting into the secret-keeping group. You can't share the secret or secrets until you're part of the group and then only with other members of the group. You can't show or tell anyone what the secret is. Becoming part of the secret-keeping group is rather like taking the unbreakable oath."

"Now, wait a minute! Do you die if you give up the secret?"

"No. No. It's not a matter of choice. You just can't do it."

"OK. Get me included in the group."

She eyed me and said, "I don't know. I just don't think that I'll do that."

I eyed her, "Why not?"

"It's dangerous."

"Practically everything we get involved with is dangerous, and is it dangerous for me but not for you?"

She frowned at me, "Look. I'm not going to argue this with you. You're not going to be part of the Order of the Phoenix."

"But you're not the Secret Keeper. Dumbledore is, isn't he! I've got it. He'll let me in and that's all there is to it."

She snorted, "We'll see."

△

I was early for breakfast that morning – at least early for me. That is to say that I got to the Head Table in the Great Hall a full half-hour before the end of breakfast. As usual before a term started, seating was informal. I sat with Minerva and this morning was no different. The one thing that was unusual this morning was that Dumbledore was not presiding as he normally did at all breakfasts and dinners when he was in the castle. Before a term started, it was a particularly nice thing because Dumbledore was at his most available then. The conversations that he was part of were always very interesting and could cover any topic from peculiarities of the Merlish language to a critique of the latest Chutley Cannons loss on the Quidditch Pitch.

But today was different: No Dumbledore. I asked Minerva about his absence and found her reply bizarre.

"Oh, he's at the Ministry. It seems that Potter has gotten himself in trouble for doing under-age wizardry—in front of a Muggle no less. The ministry is threatening to expel him from Hogwarts."

That reminded me that he'd been in a scrape like that at least a couple of times before, "So, what's the big deal. It happened the summer before last, and I think even earlier than that. No one cared two hoots about it."

"Well, yes. That was before he saw Lord Valdemort in the flesh."

"So. I have too."

"Yes, but you didn't make a big deal about it."

"Well, Potter beat me to it."

"Believe me, if you'd done it first, you'd be in as big trouble as he is."

I asked what he'd done that was so awful. She gave me the details that amounted to his saving his cousin, Dudley, from having his soul sucked out of him by a Dementor.

"Oh, yeah. I can see just how awful that is. They ought to throw the book at him."

Minerva frowned her This-isn't-funny look at me, "Well, the official line is that there weren't any Dementors around. But . . . "

"But why would Potter produce a patronus if there weren't Dementors around? There are other uses for patronuses but they are very sophisticated—communication at hundreds of kilometers and I suppose other things that I don't even know about."

"Right. Anyway, the trial is today and Dumbledore went to the Ministry to be Potter's defender."

This raised a sore point for me. "I don't understand this. In the first place, is Potter being tried as an adult?"

Minerva looked puzzled, "What do you mean—as an adult?"

"Well, where I come from, if you're a minor, you're tried in a special court, and any punishment you might get is child-sized, so to speak. The conviction doesn't stay with you after you become an adult. You get a *tabula rasa*."

"Really." Minerva seemed to be genuinely fascinated by the idea. "Is that true in Muggle courts, minors are treated differently than adults?"

"Well, duh, yes it is. I can't believe that wizards don't treat them differently."

That seemed to force Minerva to think. Finally, she said, "Well, you just don't understand how it was. For so long, years and years we were living under a state of siege and it was impossible to prove—REALLY prove—that someone was guilty of the heinous acts that we knew that they'd done. We were fighting a losing battle and there was no one who could think of a better way than to throw people into Azkaban on 'reasonable suspicion'. Then suddenly, Valdemort was gone. Well, it was just easy to keep going in the old way of putting people out of the way when there was 'reasonable suspicion'. "

"So, was the trial before breakfast?"

"Oh, no, it was supposed to be at 10 AM, but Dumbledore doesn't trust Fudge completely."

"I can guess why. Fudge might be a man who would unofficially try to execute someone he believed to be a mass murderer or a Deatheater, but I can't quite see him sending a minor to Azkaban."

Minerva nodded, "I agree. I think that there must be someone else behind this."

"Yes, someone who would send Dementors into Little Whinging to attack a Muggle or two and Harry Potter."

"Yes, but who?"

"It's obvious, isn't it?"

"Oh, just tell me who you think it is." She said with some exasperation.

"Valdemort."

"Don't be silly. Valdemort couldn't just walk up to Azkaban and ask to talk to a couple of Dementors."

"But someone from the Ministry could. Find out who has visited Azkaban recently from the Ministry, and you'll have a short list of likely suspects."

Minerva thought about that for a few minutes and then said, "Well, Dumbledore and everyone associated with him are pretty much *persona non grata* these days, you know. It's a good idea, but I don't know anyone who could make inquiries."

"Oh, come on. Do you mean to tell me that you don't have any contacts in the Ministry?"

"Nobody there would give me the time of night. You'd have a better chance of getting a straight answer from them."

That seemed like an idea that I might want to pursue sometime, but for now, I had more urgent things. I had lesson plans to put together. Also, it had been something of a tradition to ride up to Hogwarts on opening day, I needed to get back to London for the trip.

"Minerva, are you planning to ride the Express next week? And, if so, can I get a ride with you down to London."

She looked at me directly, making eye contact, "I would love to give you a lift to London, but I have to drop you off and then move on. I'll meet you at King's Cross to catch the Hogwarts express."

"You're going to your secret club meeting?"

She just looked away.

"What's your secret handshake?"

"Oh, don't be silly. We don't have a secret handshake."

"Then you must have a secret password."

"Oh, I know that you want to help. You just can't. Get over it." She rose and walked off without looking back.

I knew Minerva. I knew that I could not hope for her to change her mind. So, I went on to the next person whom I knew could override her. I approached Professor Dumbledore after breakfast one morning. He saw me approach and visibly sighed. Before I could say anything, he nodded at me and said, "Yes, yes. Come up to my office and we'll talk."

We went up to his office. This time the password for the Gargoyle was "Moon Pie". We reached the office. He sat and invited me to take a chair. "OK. Let's start with Minerva. She tells me that you want to be part of the Order of the Phoenix. True?"

"Yes, sir."

He nodded. "She doesn't want you to be part of the Order. She has her reasons, but I'd like to hear your reasons before we talk about hers."

"It's very simple. I have personal and philosophical reasons to want to defeat Valdemort. As a matter of fact, I want to kill him."

He nodded again to show that he understood that desire completely. "OK. First, if you feel that strongly, let's get one thing straight. His real name is Tom Marvolo Riddle. I think it might be better to use that name from now on. It takes away some of his mystique and his aura of invincibility. Oh, he's still extremely potent and dangerous and a force to be reckoned with, but not to be held in awe."

"Good. I think that I can handle that."

"Now, as I see it, you can't help the Order from the inside. Even if I made you a member by inducting you into the secrets that I keep, you couldn't even enter the headquarters on your own. You'd have to have help. You couldn't take any work assignment. Unlike Hagrid, . . . "

I interrupted, "Yes, where is Hagrid anyway? I thought he hardly ever left Hogwarts."

"He's on special assignment from me. You could never dream of taking on that assignment or any other that we are likely to have. Besides that, we'd have to divert someone else's efforts to protect you. As a matter of fact, I'm seriously considering firing you and sending you back to America to keep you from being such a nuisance."

I grimaced and declared, "That would be so unethical. You wouldn't!"

He shook his head, "No, I wouldn't. I ought to, but I wouldn't. On the other hand, I won't let you join the Order."

"OK. I guess we're done then. I know I can't convince you, but don't think that I'm done. I'll find the headquarters."

"Good luck." He looked down at his desk, and I understood that my interview was at an end. I got up and walked back to my office.

Then, I had another idea. I'd go see Snape, who was probably in the order. Maybe he would help. I was cheerily walking along to Snape's dungeon. I'd begun thinking of it as his because his office was there. The house he was head of was there and he just seemed to enjoy being there. When I got close to his office, I heard an argument going. I decided to get a little closer so that I could make out who was talking and what they were saying. As I approached, the voices calmed a bit but I heard Snape say, "Yes, I'm going to Grimmauld Place tomorrow. You know that I hate having to spend time in the same house with Black, but I suppose I can't avoid it."

Someone said something that I couldn't make out. But Snape replied, "Yes. Yes. You can count on me. I'll be there."

I immediately turned and went back up to the main level as quickly as I could without making noise.

There were still eight, maybe ten days before I had to be back to Hogwarts. I found Minerva and asked her to drop me off in London as soon as possible.

"Well, what are you up to? Do you want me to get you into Diagon Alley?"

I smiled. I hoped maddeningly, "No, you could just drop me off at King's Cross or any other train station that you like."

"Mysterious. What are you up to?"

"Oh, nothing special. I'm just doing a little research."

"Hmmm." She seemed not sure how to take it, but agreed, "I have to go into London myself tomorrow. I'll drop you off. When do you want to come back?"

I hadn't considered that question, but made a snap judgment, "I'll come back on the Hogwarts express with the kids."

She raised her eyebrows at that, "And you won't tell me what you're up to?"

"No. We all have our little secrets."

"Very well. I'm leaving tomorrow before breakfast. Too early?"

In point of fact it was certainly earlier than I wanted to go, but if she could be up and going, so could I. "No. That would be just fine."

"Well, you can't be trusted to get yourself up that early without help. Why don't you . . ." She had a definite twinkle in her eye as she said that.

"That sounds perfect. I'll drop by this evening."

She smiled broadly and agreed, "You be sure to do that, now."

⚠

Something poked me in the back. The first time, I barely noticed it. The next time, I noticed it and resented it. I forced an eye open a hair and decided it was late at night and closed it again.

18

It happened again. This time, it was really insistent and was accompanied by some sort of noise. The noise resolved into an irritating sound something like a screech owl. Then I realized it was a human voice, "Up you get, you layabout sluggard. If you want a lift to London, now's the time to be dressed."

I forced my eyes open and realized that it was actually beginning to get bright outside. That the poke in my back was actually a caress and the screech was actually—well, was actually pretty close to a screech that was intended to get me out of the bed that we shared. I looked around and found her leaning over me, her brown hair tumbling down over her left shoulder and down onto my neck. "Are you finally in the land of the living?"

"That's debatable, but I am awake if that's what you're driving at."

A hand reached into my pajamas and woke me up if anything would have. I reached up to convince her to join me in bed, but she was fully awake and too quick to be trapped, "Come on. I have to be gone in fifteen minutes. Are you going to go with me or not?"

"Yes, yes. I'm on my way." It was not as impossible as it might have seemed. I'd already packed last night. My duffel was light. I was planning on living in the minimum clothes that I could manage. With the pleasant weather, it was really quite easy. Two pairs of jeans, daily changes of underwear and socks. One pair of sneakers. A few light shirts. Battery powered razor. I could never use it at Hogwarts, but for travel, it was great. It was a Christmas gift of my Aunt Nell. She always had a way of coming up with wonderfully useful gifts.

Thus equipped, all I had to do was to put on my jeans, underwear, socks, shirt, and sneakers, and I was ready to travel. I actually managed that in eight minutes. Then, I was able to sit down in Minerva's office to wait for her. When she left her living quarters, I could smile, "Any time."

"How do you manage to be ready to travel soooo quickly?"

"It's virtuous living. Minimalist wardrobe. Hard choices." I could hardly keep back the laughter.

"You needn't be so smug. Let's go." She walked back to the fireplace, took a handful of floo powder in one hand and held out her other hand for me. I joined her and asked her, 'How is it that you go without luggage?"

"This is only a day trip for me."

We walked through the fireplace, and after having my stomach wrenched for the latest in an uncountable number of times, staggered into the dining area of the Cauldron. Tom, the barman, was always cheery. He waved at us, and we parted company. She headed for the back door that led to Diagon Alley and I turned the opposite direction that led to the city street.

Azkaban Revisited

I wanted to investigate Grimold Place but before I did that, there was something that was bothering me that I wanted to look into before working on Grimold Place. I needed help, so the first thing I needed to do was get in touch with someone to help me.

I went to the nearest post office and bought an envelope. I got parchment out of my duffel and a quill. I addressed the inner envelope with the address that I knew almost as well as my rooming house address. It was a quick note. Then, I bought a larger envelope and wrote a general delivery address on it. At the counter, I had it weighed, bought appropriate postage, and it was in Her Majesty's post.

From there I made my way to my summer apartment. It had been a pretty exhausting day although it was early in the afternoon by then. A nap and dinner finished the day for me.

The next day, I took up my habit of walking for exercise. I went to the park and got in a good brisk walk. Those walks usually exercised my brain more than they exercised my body. I stopped in the mid-morning for a rest on a park bench. As I sat there, something fell on my head. At first I thought it might be bird dropping. I tentatively reached up to my head to discover if my guess were true. In a way it was. What I found was an envelope. It was addressed to James Wendt, Hyde Park, The Serpentine, Park Bench 238.

I quickly ripped it open and pulled out the single small sheet of parchment. It simply read, "Meet me at the barrier to track 9 ¾ King's Cross for lunch." There was no signature, but I knew perfectly well whom it was from. I jogged home as quickly as I could. I reached my apartment just in time to take a quick shower, change into casual dress, and reach the nearest tube station. From there, I made my way to King's Cross. I reached track 9 and sat on a bench near the barrier.

Mr. Weasley walked through the barrier and without breaking stride headed directly for me. We shook hands and he suggested our next step, "Rather than disapparating here, let's go through the barrier and we can disapparate from the other side conveniently."

I stared and asked, "And going through the barrier will attract less attention that disapparating?"

"Yes." He took me by the arm and led me to the barrier and we were through. I had to admit that it was much less disruptive than any other magical means of transport that I'd ever taken.

He rubbed his palms together in obvious anticipation, "What are we going to do? Break into Gringotts? Steal one of those 'new clear' weapons that I hear Muggles talk about?"

"I hate to disappoint you. All I want you to do is to take me to The Ministry and drop me off at the Auror Office."

He squinted at me, "OK. OK. That's the cover. But what are we really going to do?"

"Just that."

He sagged, "Really? I was hoping for something at least a little exciting. What are you going to do at the Auror Office?"

It was obvious that he really wanted to have an adventure. I thought about it. "Well, you can tag along. But you may not want to do what I'm planning on doing there."

He brightened a little. "Well, I can't imagine your not doing something at least interesting—if not exciting. Yes. I'm in."

"OK. Just remember, you can drop out any time you like."

So, it was that we first disapparated to a deserted street beside the apparently disintegrating department store that housed The Ministry. He led me over to a red telephone box. "This is the visitor entrance. It takes us directly to the Visitor Desk in the Atrium."

He opened the door and we both crowded in. He picked up the phone receiver and talked to the Visitor Desk Witch. She set some mechanism into motion that lowered the box into the great Atrium of the Ministry. We landed next to the Visitor's Desk. The ministry witch asked us our business. Arthur showed her his ID and explained that I wanted to visit the Auror Office. She nodded and filled out my name on a temporary guest badge. It listed my purpose as visiting the Auror Office.

I thanked her and she said, "We don't get many visitors wanting to go TO the Auror Office." She smiled, and I smiled wanly.

"Yes. I don't intend on staying long term."

We started to walk off when she called after us, "Oh, Mr. Wendt, don't forget that you need to return the badge before you leave."

"Thanks, ma'am."

She interrupted me again and said, "That's MISS Hopkins."

"I'll not forget to return it to you."

She smiled at that.

We turned and Mr. Weasley led me to an elevator. When we got on, he said, "Fourth Floor please."

We arrived. When the door opened, we found a large double door with a strange symbol on it. I asked Arthur what it was.

"Oh, it's just the Auror symbol."

I shrugged an OK.

The door opened as we approached and disclosed a large Waiting Room with another Visitor Desk. We walked over and the witch behind the desk asked our business.

I replied, "I want to apply to visit a prisoner at Azkaban."

Mr. Weasley did a double take and stared at me. The witch was a blonde with long hair up in a sort of French twist. She was completely unaffected, saying, "Please sit, I'll have someone from the Prison Ministry come to help you with that."

We sat and Weasley whispered to me, "I take back what I said about 'new clear' weapons."

It was at least fifteen minutes before someone showed up. The wizard was middle-aged but completely fit. He looked like he'd just come off the running track where he'd done a half-marathon on one foot. "Gentlemen, I hear that you want to visit Azkaban Prison. Are you concerned about the conditions of the prison or the security?"

We stood and introduced ourselves and I answered, "No, not really. I want to visit a prisoner."

That seemed to surprise him, but he nodded, "Come with me. You'll have to fill out a form."

The Auror, whose name was Smithe, turned to lead us back to his office. Under my breath to Weasley, I said, "What a surprise."

We walked back through a long corridor lined with offices and turned a corner to find an elevator, which took us up two floors. When we arrived, he led us down another corridor, around a corner and into his office. He opened the door for us and we found that it was a window office with a large window that looked out on the main Atrium of the Ministry.

I couldn't help complimenting him on the nice office. He nodded humbly. He went behind his desk and motioned to a couple of chairs that a flick of his wand sent flying next to the desk behind us. We sat but he remained standing. He rummaged through one of the drawers of his desk and pulled out a piece of parchment. "You'll have to fill this out, but I'll ask you the main questions just to save you some time in case your answers would preclude you from doing the visit."

He kept it in his hand as he sat. He scanned down the parchment nodding occasionally. He started off, "OK. First, who are you?"

Mr. Weasley started off, telling him his name and office. Smith nodded and said, "I think I've seen you around." He turned to me.

"I'm James Wendt, a Squibb. I work for Dumbledore at Hogwarts."

Smith looked at me quizzically, "Really? I had a couple of kids who went to Hogwarts. They graduated about ten years ago. I don't remember you."

"Right. I didn't work for Dumbledore then. I suppose I don't look as young as I am. This term will be the beginning of my sixth year."

"What do you do at Hogwarts."

"I'm a teacher."

His eyes widened at that, "How does a Squibb teach magic?"

"Oh, I don't. I teach. . "

Mr. Weasley interrupted, "He teaches English. A couple of my kids have taken his class. They like him a lot."

I made a mental note that I owed him big time.

Smith went on, "Now, who is it that you want to visit?"

Weasley looked at me with as much curiosity as Smith, "I want to visit Belletrix LeStrange."

Both stared at me incredulously. And both asked, almost in unison, "Merlin's Beard, why do you want to visit her?" Smithe recovered from his surprise first and placed the parchment on the desk and set himself to write. "Again."

"I want to ask her a question."

"Just what question do you want to ask?"

"It's a personal question."

Smithe just gazed at me. "What is the question?"

"I won't tell you."

Smith looked up to the heavens. "You may not be able to see her then."

"Then, maybe I won't."

He stood and threw the quill down, "You won't tell me?"

"I won't."

His lips tightened to a thin straight line and then he said, "All right, but you may not be able to see her alone."

I shrugged. "That's all right."

He sat and quickly filled in the application. He got a stamp out of his desk and stamped it. Then he signed the document. "Come with me," he said.

We got up and walked out of his office and down the corridor to another office where he took out his wand and applied it to the hinges. He then opened the door, and we found another wizard behind a desk. He handed this wizard the application and said, "When they're ready, send them to Azkaban."

The wizard stood and Smithe left the room. Then the wizard said, "Are you ready to go?"

I looked at Mr. Weasley, who nodded. I then turned to the other wizard and said, "We're ready."

The wizard took his wand and ran it along the apparently blank wall. The outlines of a fireplace appeared, solidified and became a fully working fireplace. "It's part of a very special subset of the floo network. It connects only to a fireplace in Azkaban." He handed the application back to us. "You may go through. They'll help you on the other side."

I held out my hand to Weasley. He took it, and we walked through. When we re-appeared in the world, I had one overwhelming feeling—utter depression. I looked to Weasley. He appeared to be turning green. Thankfully, a wizard approached us along with a patronus. The world turned livable again.

Weasley held the application out to the wizard. Who glanced at it and his eyes turned as wide as platters. He looked from one to the other of us. "Wait here. I'll send someone to get the LeStrange woman. We'll take her to an interview room. But first, we've got to search you. Ever since that Black escaped, we've doubled and re-doubled security."

He left, and in a minute returned with another wizard, who led us to a small room with a table. He turned and said, "You'll have to sign in to the Visitor Book." He opened a large ledger book and handed Weasley a quill. He wrote, "Arthur Weasley, Ottery St. Catchpole, England, August 17, 1995."

I slowly wrote my information in a fine fair hand, as I scanned the visitors this year—all listed on a single page of the ledger. They didn't get many visitors in here.

"OK. Everything out of all your pockets onto the table."

We turned out our pockets. Weasley had a wand and a money purse, which the wizard opened and dumped out. He had a pocket knife, a few scraps of parchment, and a mini-quill. I had nothing but my purse, a small moleskin notebook, and a conventional pen. The wizard tried to open the mokeskin purse and, of course, couldn't. "I'll have to ask you to remove everything and put it on the table." I'd expected that so when I opened it and emptied it out, there were only some galleons and a few assorted smaller coins. The wizard examined them. "They'll be returned to you after you've finished your visit. Now, strip."

Weasley asked, "How far?"

"Everything. The quicker you strip, the sooner we can move on."

We stripped down. Weasley was a lot slower, and I guess shyer. There was the obligatory probity probe up the, well, into a body cavity. Then we got to dress again. The wizard took us on to another corridor. We went along it and up a flight of stairs. At the top, there was another corridor and several doors. One labeled "Q" opened, and the guard wizard motioned us in, "She'll be there in a minute. I'm scared to death of her, myself. If you need help, just shout out."

We went in and I said to Weasley, "Encouraging, eh?"

There was a table and four chairs—two on each side. I walked over to the table and put my hands on it. Just then, the door on the opposite side of the room opened, and a black-haired shrew in a prison uniform entered. There was a wild cast to her eyes. They seemed to take in the whole room at a glance. She laughed a shrill frightening cackle. "Well, Arthur Weasley, what brings you and your friend." Here she turned her attention to me and a look of wonder came into her eyes, "A Squibb, isn't it. Yes. What would a Squibb want here?"

I invited her to sit. "We seem to be your hosts. Why don't we sit and discuss it?"

She stared at me, and a strange smile came over her face. "We're going to be civil, are we?"

"Yes."

She pulled a chair out and sat. Weasley and I sat. "I'm afraid I can't offer you anything to drink," she said. "What do you want?" Her eyes kept roving over the small room, looking for what, I knew not.

I waited for her attention to drift back to us. "I have a question."

"Which is?"

"When is Riddle coming to spring you out of here?"

A sly smile came over her face. "If the master of the house had known at what hour the thief was coming, he would not have left his house to be broken into."

"Oh, I'm not the master of the house and the master wouldn't listen to me even if I knew at what hour it was to happen."

She cackled and her smile was, if anything, seductive. Her voice was almost sexy as she said, "You're clever. You could join us. You could be in the top ten."

"Is it better to be in the top ten of the losing side or at the bottom of the winners?"

She spit at me and sprung up, toppling her chair backwards. She turned and went to the door, banging on it as she shouted, "Let me out of this hell-hole." The door opened immediately, and she strode out without a backward glance.

For the first time, I turned to Weasley, who was staring at me with the sort of expression that I might have expected from Bellatrix. "You didn't really expect her to answer you, did you?"

"Oh, I got what I wanted."

"Spit in the face?"

"No, but sometimes you luck out." That broke the tension.

By this time, the door on our side had opened and we left. We picked up our things and returned through the special floo connection to the Auror Office. The wizard there took the application, passed his wand over the fireplace, which dissolved back to blank wall, and took us to the front office.

We signed out and left the Auror Office. Weasley offered to give me a tour of his office. I decided that I owed him and I went for the tour. It turned out to be a good idea.

First, it was pretty quick! Second, it was fascinating to see the things that he found interesting. His office was a little museum. He had several of his prize Muggle artifacts. He showed me a small glass bowl that was full of ball bearings. They were polished till they almost glowed.

He had a chain from a chain saw. He held it gingerly and asked me if I had seen such a work of art. It was coiled up and I had to admit that it could have passed for a work of art. I didn't have the heart to show him how it was intended to be used.

Finally, he brought out of a drawer something that must have been his pride and joy. It was delicate, and I could see why he kept it protected. He explained, "I think this must be a portable totem of some sort. I know that the Indians of the northwest states made something like this–but much larger–as religious objects, but this is made from a material that I think is called plastique. Do you know anything about this?"

I looked at it and had a really hard time keeping from laughing. When I could trust myself to control my voice, I said, "It's called a PEZ Dispenser."

He rubbed his chin and said contemplatively, "PEZ? I wonder if that is some kind of religious dispensation?"

I admitted that I didn't know what PEZ was.

He nodded wisely, "But someday I'll find out."

△

We then went back to the main Visitor's Desk where I handed my visitor's badge over to Miss Hopkins. But she didn't take it. "Mr. Wendt, please keep that. There's a message for you to report to the Minister of Magic's office."

"Do you know why?" Weasley asked.

"No, he's just to go there. Would you mind showing him the way up there?"

"No problem."

So, I kept the badge, and Weasley led me back to the elevators. We arrived on the third floor and were greeted at another Visitor's Desk.

The witch there said, "Good. Glad you could make it. Please take this badge."

She handed me a badge that had a head-shot photo of me and my name printed in large letters. It was some sort of metal with a gold surface. I pinned it on my shirt. "Thank you, Mr. Weasley for showing Mr. Wendt up."

It was apparently a dismissal. Weasel nodded and asked if I needed someone to show me out. Both the witch and I said, almost in union, "No." I then added, "I can find my way out."

She turned to me and said that someone would be there in a few minutes, "In the mean time, would you like something to drink—coffee, tea, pumpkin juice?"

I declined with thanks and sat. That was just as well because a wizard immediately came through from an inner door to get me. We walked down another interior corridor and turned a corner. At the end of that corridor was a grand door, gilded and carved ornately. My guide opened the door, but I walked in by myself. There was a figure looking out a grand window onto the Atrium. At my entry he turned and said, "Mr. Wendt?"

"Yes, sir."

He held out his hand, and we shook. "It's lunch time. I'm having a working lunch here. I've taken the liberty of ordering for you. It ought to arrive any moment."

"Thanks. What can I do for you?"

"Oh, please sit." He took his chair behind the desk, and I sat in a plush velvet chair that had been placed next the desk.

"Well, that was easy."

He looked puzzled and then got the joke. "Well, Mr. Wendt. They tell me that you visited Azkaban today."

It was not really a question, but I thought that I needed to make some response, "Yes, I did. I have to admit that your security there is extremely thorough."

Fudge chuckled, "Yes. I had to go through it once myself. Even I am not immune from the gods of security."

"It's gratifying to know that they are that thorough."

"They also tell me that you visited Bellatrix LeStrange."

Another non-question that I felt compelled to answer, "Yes, sir. I did."

He stared at me as though he expected more. Eventually he went on, "And what did you talk about?"

I was tempted to ask him if he didn't know that already, but I decided it would be more politic not to, "I asked her about Tom Riddle."

Fudge was puzzled again, "Who. Oh, yes. You mean He-Who-Must-Not-Be-Named."

"I prefer Riddle. It's less . . oh . . I don't know, grandiose."

Fudge frowned at that. "Why in the world would you ask her about Valde. . that is, Riddle? He's gone for good."

"I would have said that he's gone for bad." I quickly added, "But I take your meaning.

"I wanted to see if she thought that he were gone for good."

Fudge seemed uncomfortable, "You're not one of these people who have been fooled by Potter's lies."

"I like to think that I'm rarely fooled by anyone. I don't take him or anyone at their word on serious issues. I wanted a second opinion."

"So, you asked her if Riddle were still around?"

"Not precisely, I asked her when he was coming to break her out of Azkaban."

Fudge laughed, "You didn't really?"

"I did."

"You didn't expect a serious answer to that?"

"Regardless what I expected, I got a serious answer."

Fudge's brows knit in concentration, "You did? What did she say?"

"I can't quote her exactly, but she basically said that if the guards at Gringotts knew when the robber were coming, they wouldn't let there be a withdrawal."

"She's mad you know."

"Yes." Just then lunch arrived. Fudge apparently didn't want the delivery woman to overhear our conversation, so he changed the topic to lunch.

"I hope you like my choices. We've got corned beef on rye and chicken salad on whole wheat. Which do you prefer?"

I took the chicken salad. There was also potato salad and fruit cups. Fudge went on, "We've got hot tea, pumpkin juice." At that point, he smiled roguishly, "I understand that you like American soda. I had them pack a can of Cola Coca."

"Thanks, Minister. Yes, I like Coke, as we call it in the States." I didn't, but I wanted to be companionable.

We each finished a sandwich, and Fudge wiped his lips and went on, "As I was saying, LeStrange is crazy."

"Yes, but when you get both of two enemies agreeing on something, you have to wonder if there isn't something there."

Fudge was triumphant, "You certainly do. When two crazy people agree, you know the idea is crazy."

I had to admire the point, "Touche."

"Exactly. Now," He bent toward me conspiratorially, "Where do you stand politically?"

That took me a bit by surprise. "Do you mean am I a Republican or a Democrat?"

Fudge looked puzzled and I quickly explained, "Those are Muggle political parties in the States."

"OH, no, I mean wizarding politics here."

"Well, let me tell you a story. A true story.

"I went to graduate school in the States at Stanford University. I went to live there in Palo Alto, California. Shortly after I arrived and got settled into an apartment, a political worker paid me a visit.

"She asked if I intended to vote locally. She was really trying to convince me not to. My response was that my voting residence was still in Ohio, and that I would vote by absentee ballot there. She was very gratified that I wasn't going to poke my nose into local politics. That's the way I feel here."

Fudge smiled broadly and said that he approved. Then he took an unexpected turn. "Good. I think that Dumbledore wants my job."

I'm afraid my eyes bulged out a bit in surprise, "Your job! Why would he want your job?"

Fudge was now surprised, "Well, it's the most powerful position in the country. He's a powerful wizard. Why wouldn't he want it?"

"Well, I think he feels like he has a very important position himself. He's the headmaster of a great school of Wizardy. He helps shape the future of nearly every wizard that comes to prominence in the country."

Fudge's hand banged down on the desk. "That's just it. He has got the makings of a powerful army. He could lead an uprising to put himself in power."

I stared at Fudge, "I think you've got Dumbledore confused with another powerful wizard."

"There, you see. He's got you thinking that Valdemort is still around. What better guise to stage a takeover than to raise hysteria about He-Who-Must-Not-Be-Named!"

"But what if Riddle really is still around? Why are you so sure that he's not?"

Fudge's face changed. When he spoke it sounded almost as though he were pleading, "Don't you see what a tragedy it would be if he were. He just can't be back!"

"Well, back where I come from we have an expression about that. For me, that's a dog that won't hunt. I can't do anything about it one way or another. I'm just a Squibb."

Fudge's face brightened a bit, "But you can. You could help by being my eyes and ears at Hogwarts."

"What do you mean?"

"Oh, nothing hard or dangerous. Just keep your eyes open and your ears. If Dumbledore leaves the school, make a note of when he goes, for how long, and, of course, if you could find out where he goes, it would be great. Just look for little signs that he's putting together a . . uh . . an army. You know the Defense Against the Dark Arts course would be a perfect place to do that. They practice real defensive magic." He hesitated and added, "And sometimes offensive magic, you know. That teacher that Dumbledore hired last year, Moody uh Crouch. I think that he even did some of the Unforgivable Curses. Crazy Deatheater. He believed that He-Who-Must-Not-Be-Named was back too."

I looked at Fudge wondering who was the crazy old man. I finally answered, "You know that Dumbledore hired me when I couldn't find a teaching job anywhere. I really can't do something to undermine him."

"Come now, you don't really believe that He-Who-Must-Not-Be-Named is back, do you? What evidence do you have?"

I didn't even consider telling him that I'd seen Riddle less than a couple of months ago. "Well, I just can't see why Potter would lie about that."

Fudge pounded the desk again, "Potter. Always Potter. He's got Riddle on the brain, and who could blame him. Both his parents killed by him. Potter desperately wants Valdemort to be around still. He needs for him to be around. He wants revenge, and he doesn't care who gets hurt."

I got up and said, "I'm afraid I can't help you Minister. I have to be on my way."

Fudge looked surprised, "But you're not leaving without finishing lunch."

"I've lost my appetite."

Fudge held up a sandwich and motioned toward me. "At least take along a little snack."

"Oh, I'm afraid I couldn't. Besides, you have a lean and hungry look. I think you need it more than I do."

"Well, that's uncommonly generous, thank you."

I turned and left the office. I found my way out to the reception desk. "Do you need this badge back?"

"No, you keep it as a memento of your visit with the Minister. Did you like lunch?"

"Lunch was fine."

"Do you want help finding your way out?"

"No thanks. I'll be fine. I have a good sense of direction."

I left the office, found my way back to the elevator, and down to the Atrium. I went to the main Visitor Desk. I asked Hopkins how I got out. She pressed a button on her desk. "Did you have a good meeting with the Minister?"

"Yes, I guess you could say so. We had lunch."

She took in a gulp of air and leaned over toward me, "Really?"

I shrugged, "Really."

She leaned a little closer, "Would you like to have dinner with me?"

I smiled faintly, "As appealing as that would be, I'm afraid that I have business that I have to get on to. I'll probably not be in town later."

Her face drooped a bit, "Oh, that is sad." Then she brightened a bit, "The next time that you're in the Ministry, please look me up—even if I'm not at the desk." She opened her purse and pulled out a card holder, pulled a card out and handed it to me.

I casually put it in a pocket without glancing at it, "Thanks. I'll keep that in mind. Have a good afternoon."

She sighed, "Oh, you too. Have the best afternoon."

By this time the phone booth elevator had arrived, and I got in and ascended.

Grimmauld Place

I had some things that I needed to get as soon as I left the Ministry, but they were easy to do. I needed a new copy of *Collins* Greater London. I needed a pair of good binoculars. I didn't trust the pair of omni-occulars that I'd gotten at the World Quidditch Cup. I wasn't sure that they'd work without magical folk around. So, I went to the first bookstore that I ran across. I knew it pretty well after years of wandering the streets near the Cauldron. After picking up a copy of *Collins*, I consulted the phone directory and found a store fairly close where I could find a decent pair of binoculars.

I entered the shop and found the glass display case with the binoculars. Almost immediately, the proprietor came over. I suppose he sensed a sale. He was a thin graying man, wearing a cardigan sweater. Before speaking, he seemed to size me up visually and then asked, "Can I help you select a pair?"

"I hope so."

He seemed to have decided that I was a "newbie" to binoculars. He asked how I was planning on using them. Well, I wasn't about to admit that the real reason that I wanted them, so I said, "I'm thinking of doing some bird-watching."

His gaze narrowed, and he asked, "Then you're perhaps hoping to see a blue tanager this fall?"

I started to say, "Yes." Then, I realized that there was no point in attempting to convince him that I was really a bird-fancier. So, I decided to tell as much of the truth as I could manage. "Well, I don't think that I can confund you with an excuse in place of the truth. The truth is that I think that my girl friend is being unfaithful to me. Frankly, I want to follow her and find out if she's cheating when I'm not around."

He frowned, "That's not a good idea, you know. If she's unfaithful, then there's nothing you can do about it. And if she's not, she'll probably discover you spying, and then you will be in trouble."

I frowned myself and said, "I can't help it. I've just got to know." There was some of the real desperation that I'd been feeling since the end of the last term that still hid in my voice and the salesman noticed it.

"Well, if you've got to do it, I guess I can't prevent you. I suppose that I should refuse to sell to you, but you'd just go somewhere else. OK." He thought a minute and said, "I think that you'll want fairly high power so that you can watch from a long distance. You'll want one with as much light collecting power as you can get for night work. If you're doing that, then you might as well have variable magnification as well."

He opened the display cabinet and brought out an Olympus pair of binoculars. "Give a go with these." I turned around with the binoculars and looked through the display window at the front of the store. I varied the magnification and was impressed with how much detail I could see across the street.

"I have to admit these are really good. How much will these set me back?"

He gave a little bark of a laugh and said, "In the cause of true Love is there any price that's too much?"

My severe frown gave him an idea that there probably was a price that was too much. So, he answered flatly, "Three hundred fifteen, ninety-three, tax included."

I gulped but decided that I'd probably use these for many years. "OK. That's fine." I got out my credit card.

But he wasn't done, "The box includes a simple cleaning kit, but for a fine pair like those, you'll want something better. We've got a couple of very nice kits over here."

I convinced him that a very nice kit would be something for a later purchase. He rang up the sale and gave me my receipt. I stuffed the box into my duffel and headed on for my next destination.

It was an Avis Car Hire at Victoria Station. I found the office and mercifully it was fairly empty. There was an American family—my guess was mom, dad, daughter, about ten or eleven, and grandmother—finishing up a car rental, and there was someone else in line ahead of me.

When I arrived at the front of the queue, I found a cheery, twenty-something working the line.

He asked me what kind of car I was looking for. I was easy. "I want the smallest, cheapest car you've got."

He made a face and looked down a list on his computer screen. He hesitated, "Well, we've got a Yugo that will supposedly seat four and has room for baggage for two. But, I'm sure that won't suit."

"That will be just fine. There's only me." I lifted my duffel, "And this is all the luggage that I've got."

Still trying to upsell me, he went on, "It's not got any performance to speak of."

"I just want to get from point A, here, to point B and I'm not dying to get there in record time."

"Well," he still was uncertain, "If you're sure. . ."

"Yes, I'm very sure."

He took my international Driver's license (renewed in the summer in Ohio), my passport, and my credit card. He made conversation as he went, "Are you here for business or pleasure?"

That stumped me for a moment. It sure wasn't pleasure that I was contemplating, but on the other hand, it wasn't exactly business either. Suppose he asked what business I was in. So, I settled on pleasure. He asked where I was from, how I could be reached.

My answers: Ohio, my cell phone number, and I would be traveling around, finding bed & breakfasts as I went.

"You seem to have a bit of an accent. have you spent a lot of time in England?"

Yes. There was a question. Had I spent a lot of time here? It seemed like I had spent three lifetimes since the Tri-wizard tournament and before that? Surely another life when I first met Minerva and then before that, still another life-time. I was tempted to say "Five lifetimes, at least." But, of course, I didn't. Instead, I said, "Over the last five or so years, I've been in and out a lot."

"You must like it here then?"

Anywhere would be bliss that had Minerva in it, but I couldn't quite say that either. "There's a lot to like here. And a few people whom I like a lot." And one of them dead now.

That answer was a little too far off the beaten path for him.

He eventually completed the rental agreement. I initialed on half a dozen spots and signed three times. I was finally assigned a car in a specific parking spot in the for-hire lot and went out to it with many wishes that I find my visit pleasant.

I thought, "Pleasant.- interesting word." I was pretty sure that I wouldn't find it pleasant. However, I just glanced over my shoulder, waved and went out to the car park. I found the Yugo after some false starts down aisles. The keys were in the ignition. I got in, tossed my duffel into the passenger seat and worked the car controls without starting the engine. Lights, brakes, hand brake, windows, radio and so on.

I opened the duffel and got out the *Collins*. I needed the index to find Gimmauld Place. It was a little cul-de-sac with what might be generously counted as a couple of blocks and a little park. I spent some time plotting a course there from the car park.

Then, I opened the binoculars box and tossed all the packing material into the back seat. Just then, there was a knock on the driver's side window. I looked up and rolled down the window. "Sir, are you having trouble?"

The Avis car park attendant was trying to be helpful. I just smiled, "Oh, I'm trying to decide how to get to my destination from here." I held up *Collins* and he chuckled.

"New to London, I guess?"

I honestly answered, "This is my first time to try driving in London."

"Can I help you with directions?"

This was becoming tedious, but I asked, "Do you know Grimmauld Place?"

"Afraid I can't say's as I do."

"Never mind. I've found it on the map, and I think I can get myself there, thanks. I'll be leaving the car park in a few minutes. Thanks again for the offer of help."

He turned and walked away back to the kiosk where I'd have to check out. I returned to the binoculars. I brought them to my eyes and focused on the receding back of the attendant. I could easily see the hairs on the back of his neck. I nestled the binoculars into the clothes in my open duffel beside me, hesitantly pulled out of the slot, and headed for the exit kiosk.

An hour of exasperating driving later, I was only a few blocks from Grimmauld Place. I hadn't quite decided whether to park and walk onto the street or simply drive through the first time. I mentally flipped a coin and chose: drive through. I drove into Grimmauld Place. It was narrow, short block followed by a small square with a park in the center followed by another short block. It was immediately clear that I couldn't find a spot to park the car that wouldn't be immediately the center of attention.

When I hit the other end of Grimmault Place, I turned around and went back to the entrance of the cul-de-sac. I found a small car park there. I could park for eight pounds per day or two pounds per hour. There were a couple of spots that actually had an unobstructed view down the length of Grimmault Place. I decided to take one of those parking slots for an hour and see how it worked as an observation post.

Once I was parked, I pulled out the binoculars and worked them. I focused on the near end, the far end, the middle. I could see a little of the small park in the middle. I settled in to watch for an hour. There was not a lot to see. Every now and then, someone would leave one of the houses along the street. The houses would have been called brownstones had they been in New York. They had several steps up to a small entryway with a door.

Once while I was watching, a Fed-ex delivery truck squeezed into the street, stopped, and delivered a package. I wondered for a moment if the Order would ship something by Fed-ex. Then I slapped my head. What was I thinking? They'd deliver things by owl. Or would they? Would they use a method that no wizard would guess? I finally decided that they wouldn't. If they thought that Valdemort couldn't find it, how would they ever think that Fed-ex could find it?

The foot traffic was small but was almost always there. After all, there were probably around 60 or 70 families on that short street. I saw nearly fifty people coming and going during that hour. I could see the faces clearly enough to recognize people that I had seen before on the street. After a while when I saw someone, I recognized him at least half of the time—maybe three quarters of the time. The binoculars were good. It was actually kind of fun. Being in London I couldn't help thinking of James Bond.

So far I hadn't seen anyone who looked at all like any wizard that I knew. That wasn't surprising. I probably hadn't seen a quarter of the people who lived on that street. But I was rather satisfied with myself. So far, I'd done everything that I needed to set up surveillance. I drove back to my summer villa—as I sometimes thought about my attic flat. It took nearly two hours to get there. It was, after all, only a little after rush hour.

I hadn't prepared for the necessity of finding a parking spot. I circled the blocks in my neighborhood for a good fifteen minutes before something opened up. I blessed the tiny Yugo. I could park it anywhere that was legal.

When I reached my rooming house, I entered and found a few people in the living room watching TV. I rarely did that. Today, there were four people watching. I stuck my head in to see if I recognized anyone. There was the student whom I'd met earlier in the summer. He was a first year graduate student in French Literature. He seemed to have a girl friend whom I'd not seen before. She was a short blonde with short blonde hair. They were whispering—it seemed like it was French, though I couldn't be sure. She wore a light tan sweater with a short skirt that was somewhat longer than a miniskirt. The other two were older than school age—even graduate school. I guessed that they, like me, were working odd jobs, trying to find the break that would lead them somewhere better than here. They lived here, but I had never introduced myself. They were watching a "Benny Hill" rerun.

A wave of nostalgia swept over me for the old days when I'd lived below the attic and the amazing blonde who was attending design school had lived across the hall. I knew all the residents in at least a passing way then and some quite well. Now, I was just a transient—the oddball who taught somewhere in the "North" and spent his summers in London. I was standing in the doorway that didn't have a door, and no one had noticed me. I went on up to my room, trying not to disturb them.

The night was long. In the old days, I could look forward to seeing Minerva the next day or at latest in a couple of days. We didn't have secrets from each other—at least, most of the time. I wasn't spending my days in a cheap car in a car park watching the street to catch a glimpse of where she went during the day.

The next day, I got up, had some breakfast, and prepared for the day's surveillance. I found the French Lit student and his girlfriend (who'd apparently spent the night) finishing their breakfast when I came down.

The French Lit student, Frank, said hi and his girlfriend wanted to be introduced. "This is Jim—proof positive that there is life in Literature after degree. Where is it you teach?"

I shrugged, "In a small finishing school in Scotland—far away from any big towns. It's called Hogwarts."

She spoke and revealed that her native tongue was not English—or American, "You kid, do you not?"

"About the school name. No. That's it. It's taken I think from the small nearby town—Hogsmeade."

"Vraiment. What is it like living up there near the Arctic Circle?"

"Oh, you know, when the sun sets, you enter the long tunnel and don't emerge for four months."

"You pull my limb. Er Leg?"

"Yes, I do. It is pretty and it is also far from most of the civilizing influences of the great cities, like London."

"Why izz it that you choose to live there?"

"It was the only place I could get a job."

Her eyes widened and her jaw dropped. Frank assured her that I was making a joke.

I agreed. "It's not quite that bad, but I probably wouldn't have stayed on as long as I have if I hadn't met a fellow teacher who makes every day glow."

She laughed, "Yes, it izz l'amour that conquers all, n'est-ce pas?"

"I suppose. Sometimes I wonder, though."

I poured some cereal into a bowl with milk and Clarisse (that turned out to be her name) tsched her tongue, "Would you eat that, that board-card?"

"Card-board. Yes, it contains plenty of bulk and is a pretty good diet food."

She made some sort of trilling sound with her tongue that was probably meant to sound unpleasant. They left.

I had brought down my duffel with nothing but a change of clothes and the binoc's in it. After eating, I went to a local convenience shop, bought a couple of sandwiches—for lunch and supper, a bananna, an orange, a carton of milk, a package of baby carrots and a Times of London. I found my Yugo and drove across town to my car park. It must have been used mainly by residents of the area, because it was almost always empty when I arrived in the morning and full by the time I left at night.

I always had my choice of slots, and I always chose the same one. On this first real day, I settled in with my binoculars, the duffel on the floor of the passenger seat, the lunch/dinner box in the passenger seat and *The Times* on the back seat. I wasn't quite sure what I would do with that. I couldn't read it AND watch the street through Binocs. I'd have to see how it worked out.

I got myself settled in. It was 9:30 by then, but I intended to rise earlier and get here earlier tomorrow. I watched the street intently for what seemed to me to be an hour and a half at least. There had been few people entering or leaving the street. I glanced down at my watch to see that the time was barely 10. I looked at the watch two times to be sure that I'd made that big a mistake.

I asked myself how I could have done an hour yesterday and it seemed to have passed like a moment and now half an hour seemed much longer. I realized two things: It's a lot easier to spend time watching a street when there are actually people moving about on it. When you are looking forward to twelve hours, it's a lot harder to do one hour than if you're looking forward to only one hour.

I started thinking about how to pass the time without taking my eyes off the street. I glanced around the car—at lunch, at my duffel bag, at the seat controls. Maybe I could get into a more—or less—comfortable position. Then, I noticed the car radio. Of course, I could turn it on, listen to news, weather, music. I could do that without taking my eyes off the street.

So, I turned on the radio and searched around randomly. I quickly found a news program. I discovered very quickly that there just isn't that much new that happens in the course of an hour. After you've heard twenty minutes or a half-hour, you've heard it.

I twiddled with the dial as I watched the street without binoculars. I decided that I'd see how quickly I could get my binoculars up and focused from the time I first noticed someone walking on the street. I found a classic rock station and settled there for a while. They were playing Pink Floyd, which seemed like a good place to stop for a while. They played a couple of Pink Floyd cuts and then moved on to someone else. So did I.

Through the rest of the morning, I kept scanning the FM band randomly, stopping here and there. Then a little after 11, activity picked up on The Street. A mother and two children left their apartment building. An older couple arrived and went into a different building. I made a break of lunch and ate while only off and on watching the street. I also did some more systematic scanning of the radio spectrum. I found a couple of classical music stations and entered a couple of classical stations, a couple of classic rock stations, and a news station into preset push-button memory. Lunch was very pleasant. Then I went back to watching.

In the late afternoon, a flood of people returned to the street. I decided that they were commuters returning from work, but, I thought I recognized a face. I thought it was Snape. There were several people on times the street and he had disappeared before I could decide whether he had disapparated or entered a building.

After dinner, the traffic slowed but didn't stop entirely. But there were no more suspicious people arriving or leaving.

The next couple of days were much the same. At the busiest times I saw one or two people who looked familiar. One might have been Molly Weasley. Another might have been Fleur Delacourt. You'd think it would be hard to mistake her for someone else, but I couldn't be sure.

I was running out of time. Then there was a day that had been very slow. No one that I recognized appeared, but in the late evening, something very strange happened. I couldn't believe my eyes. There was suddenly a group of people who appeared seemingly from nowhere. They were all carrying brooms. I'd laid down my binoculars and had almost decided to call it a night.

I scrambled in the seat next to me, trying to find the binoculars as I strained to identify the wizards and witches there. I finally got my hands on it, lifted it to my eyes and focused on the group. Yes, there was Mad-Eye. I'd been sure about him from the moment that I'd seen them appear. There were some others that I didn't recognize, but there was Harry Potter himself. No doubt they had to be bound for the Order headquarters. It was dark, but I tried to identify what landmarks they were next to.

They seemed to be climbing stairs, but they were becoming fuzzy and I couldn't really see the stairs and then they disappeared one by one, as though walking through a solid brick wall. This was definitely it. I watched the last ones disappear. Then, still holding my binocs, I fumbled out of the car, closed it, and locked it hastily and trotted across the street and into Grimmault Place. I didn't know whether running would attract too much attention or not. I thought that I'd seen a tree in the small park next to where they'd arrived. They'd crossed the street almost perpendicularly. I found the tree.

I looked across the street and decided that they must have gone into #10, #12, #14 or maybe #16. I stood and thought long about whether I should try to enter any of them then or wait till daylight tomorrow. I finally decided to wait until tomorrow. By then, maybe I could invent a cover story for the entrances that had ordinary Muggles living in them.

I went back to the car and headed for home. It seemed like I was fewer than 24 hours away from uncovering the location of the headquarters. As I drove, I thought about a cover story. An inspiration was forming in my mind. Yes. It would take a little research, but it could work.

The night was almost too exciting to allow me to get to sleep, but I did manage it. The next morning, I visited a book store where I bought a copy of *The Times* and borrowed their phone directory. I found a couple of the entries that would do. I called them and found one that was reasonably close and open. I went then and found them very helpful. They had more than enough of what I was looking for.

I went back to my apartment and changed into a suit – the only one that I owned. Then, I went to Grimmauld Place. As before, I parked in my usual parking spot. I walked across the street into Grimmauld Place and walked resolutely down to #10—the first that I would approach.

I took a deep breath and realized that I'd not thought out thoroughly what I'd say, so I took a moment to rehearse my lines and walked up the stairs. I rang the bell several times. No one answered. I had seriously considered that possibility, but I'd begun, I had to continue.

I walked up to the next, #12. I rang the doorbell. Once. Twice. I hesitated a moment and reached to ring the third time, but the door opened a crack and a voice escaped the crack, "Who is it? And what do you want?"

Well, at least, I'd found someone home and willing to open the door—a crack. I quickly repeated my rehearsed line, "My name is James Thomas. I'm a volunteer for the Church of the Latter Day Saints. I'd like to talk with you briefly and give you a small gift."

The voice considered a moment and said, somewhat more boldly, "I'm not religious."

I smiled. This was like debating. I'd enjoyed debating class or "Dialectic" as we'd called it when I took it. "Well, ma'am, strictly speaking, I'm not religious either. It's almost universally true that those who love God, are rarely 'religious'. We can talk through the door if you like, but a cup'o would go very well, thank you."

I couldn't believe it. She actually opened the door and was inviting me in. She appeared to be in late middle age. Her hair had been raven black, but now had streaks of dirty gray going through it. Somehow, it was not unappealing. She led me back a long narrow hall to a small kitchen. There was already a kettle on the stove. She turned it on and retrieved a couple of fine china cups from the cupboard beside her refrigerator.

By the time that she had put some loose tea into a metal ball, the kettle was whistling. She took it off the stove and put it on a trivet beside the stove that said, "Ve get too soon oldt und too late schmart."

I smiled at the motto and said, "Isn't that the truth."

She stared at me, but I quickly said, "The motto on your trivet. I had an aunt who had a trivet with that motto. She never used it. It was decoration on the wall of her kitchen."

Her face relaxed into a smile and she said, "Ain't it so."

"Yes, ma'am."

She poured me and then herself some hot tea and asked if I liked cream or sugar.

"Neither"

She put a little milk in her tea and took a sip. "Now, what do you want to talk about?"

"I'm here because the Church is concerned for the souls of all people. We want to bring redemption to all people and all of Creation."

She looked at me, assessing, "Do you think that I need redemption?"

"I think everyone needs redemption. Have you been happy about everything you've done in your life?"

"No, of course, not." she snapped out

"Would you take some of it back if you could?"

She was slower to answer, "That's not possible."

"That's what redemption's about—finding a way to make things right that people can't take back."

"Oh, that's just silly."

"I think it works."

She looked at me long before speaking. "Well, what do you want?"

"You've already given it me."

"What are you talking about?"

I raised the cup and tipped it slightly toward her. She laughed at that. "Come on, you want something else. The church didn't send you here to get a cup of tea from me."

I thought a moment. "I think it did. But, I can give you something. I'd like to leave some reading material. And if you don't like it, it makes good kindling."

She laughed again and started to rise. But I decided that there was something she could give me. "Wait a moment, please." She returned to her chair.

"Could you tell me a little bit about your neighbors? It's always nice to know something before you meet someone?"

She looked at me with narrowed eyes, "You mean gossip."

Then I had to laugh, "No. No. I just want to know very basic things. For example, #10, I tried to see them today, but no one answered the door. Are they off to work, or do they just not open the door to strangers?"

She puzzled for a moment and then said, "Yes, I suppose I could tell you that. They're a young couple and are off to work. They'll be back in early evening."

She didn't stop there but went on telling me about # 8 (married with a son), # 12 (single man who partied a lot), # 14 (older couple with three kids, one in college, one barely old enough for school and one in between). She didn't know anything about # 16, besides the fact that there were lots of guests there, coming and going a lot.

That interested me very much. I thanked her, left a couple of tracts and walked with her back to her front door. As I started down the steps, she stopped me with a word, "What if I want to attend your church?"

That was the last question that I expected but I glanced at the tracts left in my hand and noticed that there was an address and phone # stamped on it, "Oh, the address and phone # of the church is stamped on it, like this." I showed her a tract. "Please call and ask about directions to get there."

"Thanks again. It was very nice talking to you." She waved, turned, and went back in the house.

I now felt sure that # 16 must be it, and certainly none of the others was. So I plucked up my courage (after all, everyone in the Order were all friends, right?) and walked on to # 16. I slowly mounted the steps and rang the doorbell. Nothing happened after a few seconds, so I rang again. Some more time elapsed. I was about to ring for the third and last time when the door opened.

A young blonde looked out through the door and asked what she could do for me.

I had to think very fast. Was she in the Order? If she weren't, what should I do? If she were in the order, what should I do?

Fortunately, my mouth just started talking and what came out was my prepared spiel about the church. Her slight smile drooped, "Oh, another evangelist?"

I quickly answered, "What do you mean, 'another evangelist'? Has another church member already been here?"

She smiled at that, "No. No. Thank God, No. I just meant that you're everywhere—on the Telly, on the radio, in the newspapers."

"Wow, I get around a whole lot more than I realized."

She laughed at that, "Not you, personally. I just meant. . ."

"Oh, I know what you meant. We're all boring with our constant talk about sin and how you can get forgiveness if you just send five quid to the address at the bottom of the screen."

"And you don't do that?"

"No, I'm not selling anything. I'm not asking for anything—except a cup o' tea if you've got it?"

She scrutinized me again, "OK. What's your gig? Do you give salvation away and 'oh, yes, if you want to. Only if you really want to, you know, you could send five quid to the address at the bottom. . . "

I finished it for her, "of the screen? No, I'm not the man to give salvation away. No man is that man."

"Well, you just want a cup of tea?"

"If you want to." I hesitated, "Only if you really want to, you know."

She laughed again, "OK. It will be interesting to see how long it will be before you ask."

She led me back a long corridor. All these houses must be designed along the same lines, I reflected. The kitchen was small, but had bright fresh paint. The cabinets had been replaced and were a light wood, recently finished. She took two cups, filled them with water from a water bottle, put them in her microwave, and turned it on. She got out a box of tea bags and pulled two.

The microwave dinged, she took the hot cups out, put tea bags in both, and put one in front of me. "Now, what do you want?"

I looked around for signs of anything that would let me know if there were a dozen wizards holed up somewhere. All the signs were negative—no strange clocks, no potato peelers going on their own, only recessed lights in the ceiling.

She noticed my interest in the kitchen. "Are you thinking of offering me redecorating tips?"

"Oh, no. I was just admiring your taste. Re-decorated recently, right?"

"Sure. Is that a sin?"

"Not at all. Well, the reason that I'm here is to talk about redemption."

She got up and opened a cabinet, asking over her shoulder, "I forgot to offer. Do you want cream or sugar? I never use them myself, and I always assume that no one else does."

"No thanks."

She closed the cabinet without saying anything, but just stared, "Do you think I need redemption?"

"Everyone and everything needs redemption."

"Does this kitchen need redemption?"

"That was what I was trying to figure out before." I took a glance around and said, "I guess I'd have to say that it does. The wood came from a forest somewhere—probably needs redemption."

She stared at me even harder. "Are you one of these green evangelists?"

I pursed my lips and then said, "I think we all are—or should be."

"What do you think I need redeemed?"

I looked around the room again and still facing away from her tried to say the next thing as casually as I could, "Has the owl post come yet?"

She stared at me again, "Did you say owl post?" No other reaction.

"Yes."

"What in the world is that?" Then she had an inspiration. She laughed, almost bending over in hysterics, "It's a hitching post for owls right?" She just managed to gasp that out.

"Right."

"Well, how is it that I can get redeemed, and where does it happen?"

I decided that she was at least half serious, so I pulled out a couple of tracts. I handed them to her. "The address is stamped on these. There's a phone number too, if you want more information."

"The information that I want is whether you'll be there?"

I shook my head, "Sorry. I know that you'll be devastated, but I'm from the States. It's part of our duty to be an itinerant missionary in a foreign country. I'll be on to Little Babblington shortly."

"Oh. I was hoping that I might get to hear you preach."

"You just heard it." I rose and thanked her for the tea. I started out to the front door. When I almost had reached the door, a hand caught my arm. I turned.

She asked, "If you're still in the neighborhood at dinner time, you could come back for a bite."

"Thanks. But it's against my principles."

"Eating?"

"No. Giving in to temptation. Have a good day."

She frowned, and I left. As I walked down to the street level I wondered if I could have been mistaken about the house that they'd gone into. I was walking down the street toward my car. Along the way, I was staring at the sidewalk lost in thought. I bumped into someone, looked up, and excused myself. As I did that, I noticed a sign in a window across the park. I walked closer and was able to read it. It said, "Room for Let."

Why had I not seen it before! I stared at it. And then, I realized. I'd been driving through the street and hadn't wanted to be recognized. I was in a hurry, but now, I wasn't. I walked over to the house and rang the doorbell. A voice almost immediately said through the door, "I saw you going into the other houses. I don't want any."

"Do you want someone to let your room to?"

There was a lengthening silence. "It's fifty quid a week. And there's kitchen privileges." Still the door was shut.

"Can I see it?"

There was another lengthy silence. Then I could hear the lock click. The door opened in and I said, "Thanks."

The woman was the oldest that I'd seen so far on the street. She had stringy gray hair that was slightly longer than shoulder length, but her face was almost unlined. Her hands had some age spots, but she didn't seem as old as her hair suggested. She led me up the stairs silently. We reached the third floor, and she unlocked a door. She opened it and motioned me in. I entered a large room with a bed, a fairly nice roll top desk, a couple of chairs and a small sofa.

I hmmmed and said, "Nice." The nicest part was immediately commented on by the owner.

"There's a nice view of the park."

There certainly was. I walked over to the window, pulled the half-transparent drapes aside, and saw that all the houses that I'd visited were easily visible as well as a number on either side. "Very nice view. I'd like to rent it."

She smiled and started to say something, but I interrupted, "But there's a catch."

She frowned, "There always is. What is it? You can't make the first week's rent?"

"Oh, no. I'll pay you the first week's rent and the last week's rent right now, BUT, I won't be staying longer than that."

She stared at me. "That's really unusual."

"Yes, it is."

We were both silent for a while. "Would you like to tell me why?"

"Sure." Another opportunity to think fast. "I'm a photographer, and I'm doing a cityscape exhibition. I want to do some photos in this area, and I think I'll do a good many in Grimmauld Place."

That seemed to impress her, "Good. It's a nice little Place. But, I'm going to leave the sign up, and if someone comes along who wants it for longer than you, you'll have to move out. No refund."

"That would be all right."

"Hey, where's your equipment?"

"I don't have it with me. I don't have my luggage with me either. I do a walking tour of places that I want to photograph before I bring equipment." She nodded wisely. We went downstairs, and she gave me two keys—one for the front door and the other for my room.

It was still early afternoon, so I went back to the store where I bought the binocs. I bought an inexpensive 35 mm. Camera, a tripod, a cheap gadget bag, and some film. I went back to my real apartment, packed a few days' worth of clothes in the duffel and headed back to the Place. I parked as usual and dragged all of my stuff to the room that I'd rented.

That night I set up the tripod and the camera and took a couple of test photos. There was a fair amount of light from the street lights, but I had to open the aperture of the camera all the way and use a long shutter speed to get an acceptable exposure. I watched the street. No binocs were necessary as this was much closer to the subject locale. I kept them close to hand if anyone showed up that I thought I might be interesting.

The street was pretty quiet. The houses that I'd visited showed no action other than the return from work of families—apparently not wizards or witches.

The next day, I was watching again. This time I was up pretty early—before 8 AM. I had a breakfast bar and a banana as I watched. I saw with amazement a pair appear from nowhere outside the house. I was seeing them from their backs, and they were wearing cloaks, but I grabbed the binoculars—just in case they turned my way. I had it on them and followed them as they crossed the street between #12 and #14. Then, they disappeared. Had they disapparated? I didn't know. Maybe they had.

A little later that day, I saw another four appear. This time, I caught a glance at one of the faces. I was sure that it was one of the Weasley twins, and I was sure that their mom was in the number. This time I decreased the magnification of the binoculars and watched carefully. The building seemed to turn hazy, out of focus for a moment, and the four disappeared. I was pretty sure that it wasn't disapparation.

I decided that I'd try photographing the process. Maybe the camera would catch something I didn't. In the early evening, several people just appeared again, walked a few steps away and disapparated. They did that from the other side of the street, and I was pretty sure that was disapparation. I'd not been fast enough to catch it on film. I got out the camera manual and tried to see if there were a way to take several photos quickly.

It turned out that there was an automatic photo mode that required a drive motor. Fortunately, it was an optional piece of equipment that I could add to the camera. I decided to try to do it without the drive. The next day, a couple of wizards appeared, and I started taking photos as fast as I could. I probably shot six of the twenty exposures on the film. Even though the roll was not complete, I took the roll out and loaded a new one. I left immediately and found a chemist's where they would develop the film overnight. I bought a couple of more rolls of film and went back to my bird's nest.

The rest of the day was quiet including the night. I was down to having only a few days left. So, I had high hopes when I returned to the chemists, the next morning. I had to wait a couple of hours before the overnight delivery truck arrived. I hurriedly paid for the photos. I didn't even want to look at them there. I went out to the car and opened the packet of photos. I went through them. Three were badly focused, but there were two clearly focused. One showed the wizards in mid-stride. The next showed nothing. I was disgusted. OK. I thought that I'd have to break down and buy the motor drive.

I set it up in the afternoon and tried it as soon as someone walked down the street. I composed the photo and turned on the auto mode. It shot the whole roll of twenty in less than seven seconds. Impressive. I changed rolls and waited for something to happen. That evening, several wizards left headquarters, crossed the street, and disappeared. I got the auto drive going but only barely before they disapparated. It just wouldn't work when they left. I'd have to catch them coming.

The next morning, I made sure I had a fresh roll in the camera and three other rolls ready to load. This time, only two wizards appeared. I had the camera pointed in almost the right place. I corrected the position and set the motor drive going. I shot through the entire roll even though, the last five or six would have nothing on them, I was sure. I immediately left for the chemist's and dropped the roll off. I returned and was rewarded with another arrival a little before noon. They were having lunch I decided.

I shot a roll of them too and got it to the chemists in time for overnight service. I could hardly wait for the next morning, but that night, against form, I slept the sleep of the righteous. The next morning, another group arrived before I left for the chemists, and I shot a roll of them as well.

When I got to the chemists, they had the photos back, and I paid for them with shaking hands. I didn't dare open the packages there, but drove back to my parking spot and went up to my room. I opened the envelope and took them out slowly one at a time. The first eight photos were completely normal—just a small group of people crossing the street, but the next ones were fascinating.

The first showed the strange de-focused, haziness that I'd seen. The next showed #12 and #14, seemingly distorted. They were bent out as though they were seen through a fun-house mirror, and there was something between them.

The next photo was very unfocused, but it had a strange shadow —like a doorway with a number above it between #12 and #14. I couldn't quite read the number, but I laughed, thinking about it. It must be #13.

I walked down to the street, strolled through the little park, approached #14. I walked up to it, but not up the steps. Instead, I walked to the wall below the door. I felt the brick wall as I slowly walked from #14 to #12. The brick wall was continuous—no sign of break or discontinuity. I couldn't find any vestige of #13—if that was what it was. I turned back to my rented room. There was nothing to distort the view from there to this spot.

I walked back to my room, sat at the roll-top desk and pondered. It really looked like I couldn't break in. I couldn't knock on the door. I couldn't even see the slightest hint of it except via a photo. And only barely at that.

Well, that was it. I was done. I got up, packed my few belongings, put my duffel strap over my shoulder and walked out the door, which I left open. I went down to the living room where my landlady was She looked up as I entered. "Ma'am, I'm leaving. I've finished with your room. I tried to leave it at least as clean as I found it."

She seemed surprised, "But you've not even finished your first week."

"That's OK. I'm finished. You should keep all the rent that I've paid. I wish you good luck."

Her face still showed the shock that she apparently felt. I had warned her that I'd only be here briefly. But she wasn't quite ready to accept it.

I placed the two keys on a small table in the living room. "Thanks again."

I left the living room and then went out the front door, down the steps and headed for my rent car. I drove to the car rental agency, thought to return it but decided that since it was located in the Victoria station, I'd just keep it for the couple of days until the trip back to Hogwarts.

So, I went to my apartment. I unpacked and re-packed what I didn't need for the next couple of days—which wasn't much. I actually could lay back and rest. Of course, that didn't last long. Within 24 hours, I was working my way through lesson plans.

The Hogwarts Express

I got up especially early on the day of the trip—well pretty early. I threw my dirty clothes into the duffel with the clean and dropped off my keys in the kitchen. I drove to the car rental agency, turned in the car and took the Tube to King's Cross and walked from there to track 9, waiting for someone that I recognized to show up. I didn't have to cross the barrier with Minerva, although I almost always did. She showed up about a half hour before the scheduled departure time.

There was no one around on the Muggle side of the barrier, so she gave me a heart-warming kiss, and we linked arms as we crossed the barrier to track 9 ¾. I took my duffel onboard after we dropped Minerva's trunk in one of the freight cars. We boarded the teacher's car. There was no one else there today. That wasn't unusual this early. Even when the train left, there were usually only teachers who were assigned to ride the rail and Minerva and I, of course.

She had a pert smile on her face, "Well, how was your little stay the last week?"

I was wearing a pretty self-confident smile, myself. "It was very instructive."

Her smile broadened, "Then, you aren't going to pester me about joining the Order?"

"Right. I won't. My experiences this past week showed me that I shouldn't. After all, why do I need to join when I know where the headquarters are?"

She gaped for a second or so, "Don't kid me. I know perfectly well that you don't. Just stop being a silly goose."

My smile didn't fade. Instead I said, trying to be as casual as possible, "Does Grimmauld Place mean anything to you."

Her face froze in a mask of surprise which just began to unfreeze when I added, 'Number 13 Grimmauld Place." It was a guess, but I thought a pretty shrewd one. I watched her face. The mouth distorted into an O that was held for a minute.

I was about to drop the subject, victorious, when a realization struck me. "You can't say anything, can you? You're not the Secret Keeper. You can't do or say anything that would reveal whether I were right!" My smile turned broad and beaming. Her face seemed to collapse.

She seemed to be stuck for words, or more likely, she was trying out various things to say to see if she could actually utter them. It led to some unusual distortions of her face, but she did manage to say, "Interesting idea."

I laughed. "OK. But I was serious. I'm sold. I tried to break into the Headquarters. I even just tried to knock on the door, but I couldn't. I'm sold. You're defended, and I can't do anything about it, So I won't be a nuisance any more."

Her face relaxed into a smile, and she said, "Good."

By this time there were kids boarding the train, and we decided to start our patrol of the cars. This early, we helped the younger kids stow their gear that they were carrying on into the overheads.

When we got back to the Teacher's Lounge once the train had started, I brought up another topic, "I learned something else since you dropped me off."

"Really, you have been a very busy boy." She waited and then, "Well, don't be shy. What is it?"

I thought about whether or not to tell her now and decided that I wanted a broader audience for this revelation. "No, I think that we should discuss this with Dumbledore. I'm going to wait to see him and let him decide whom should be included."

She made a face of exasperation, "Well, why did you mention it then?"

"I didn't decide until I was about to say it. It can wait."

She sniffed her disapproval.

A Ministry Witch at Hogwarts

The opening feast was its normal high-spirited self. Most students are actually somewhat happy for school to start after a summer holiday that has begun to cloy. Of course, after the first couple of days of real classes, that exuberance usually gets rubbed off, but the first feast is, after all, a feast. No one has responsibilities, at least away from the raised dais that the teachers sit on. Dumbledore can always be counted on for a few brief (very important) and amusing remarks. So, the feast normally comes off quite well, and there's entertainment—the sorting of first years. There's something about witnessing others in distress that makes your case seem fairly decent by comparison.

So, it was with some mounting dismay when at the end of the sorting, and while Dumbledore was still introducing new staff, that one of the new staff rose to make her own comments.

I hadn't noticed her until Dumbledore called her name, which was already familiar to me. Dolores Jane Umbrage, in fact, made a little speech that probably doubled the length of time normally devoted to speeches at the opening feast.

This speech was not notable as an exemplar of the oratory arts. If examined semantically, it would be found to be almost completely devoid of information except for one point. As a matter of fact, I'd have had a difficult time keeping my composure and keeping myself from laughing if it weren't for that one point. That point was that she intended to make changes at Hogwarts. The fact that Dumbledore hadn't sent her packing that moment said that she had a great deal of real power. It made the meeting that I intended to have with Minerva, Dumbledore, and whomever else he wanted present all the more important.

The feast ended dully. Most of the teachers, except for Heads of House went directly to the Teacher's Lounge for the normal beginning of term teachers' meeting. The Heads of House would be along fairly quickly, we knew.

The Teacher's Lounge filled rapidly. This was something that no one had witnessed at Hogwarts in living memory—someone had challenged Professor Dumbledore directly and before everyone on the opening day of term, no less. Half of the staff was looking for Dumbledore to put her in her place. They figured that he would not set out the dirty laundry to air before students. The other half were expecting the opposite. They expected her to bring the full weight of the Ministry to bear on him. It looked to be an exciting evening whatever happened.

I personally was of the Dumbledore-smashes-Umbrage camp, but that wasn't because I really expected it to happen—I was just hoping it would happen. Whatever happened, it was my intention to fly under the radar—not that it was easy to do that when the staff could almost be counted on your fingers and toes. So, I sat in the next to last row of hastily improvised seating. I knew the trick that the ones on the last row got called on first.

Minerva had decided that she wanted to be at the front to show support for Dumbledore. I told her that that was fine. If it got down to a pitched battle, I'd be there in the trenches right beside her. But, if a pitched battle could be avoided, I'd just as soon do it, thanks. Besides that, I was actually a Muggle, impersonating a Squibb, which was a little bit like a maggot impersonating an inchworm, in most Wizarding circles. It would be better all-round if no more attention were paid to me than was absolutely necessary–for my sake, for Minerva's sake, and even (or especially) for Dumbledore's sake.

So I was in the back of the Teacher's Lounge watching the last stragglers file in. I guess Filch figured that we Squibbs needed to hang together, because he found a seat next to me and engaged me in conversation. "I see how the wind is blowing. It'll be the supporters of Dumbledore against the supporters of Umbrage. I've decided that Umbrage is going to come out on top. She's got Fudge behind her, and Fudge has got most wizards behind him. Nobody wants anyone scaring people with the idea of 'You-Know-Who' returning. 'The bad luck of the day is more than enough for the day', I say and everybody else out there says too. So, I'm going to help Umbrage in this fight. What about you, Wendt?"

"I'm trying to stay beneath everyone's attention. That's why I'm sitting back here."

"Well, at least come down after the show and have a drink."

"I think I can do that."

At that point, Umbrage entered the lounge followed by Dumbledore. He came to the fireplace (the traditional spot to speak from during these meetings) and said, "Good evening. I hope you all had a good meal.

"I've already introduced Ms. Umbrage. Her position was created by the Ministry itself, not the Board of Governors of the school," Filch jabbed me in the ribs. "She", Dumbledore continued, "is to help us improve the education at Hogwarts by pruning un-useful practices. I think that I should allow Ms. Umbrage to speak for herself."

She walked to the fireplace. Dumbledore stepped back, and she began, "Professor Dumbledore has spoken correctly, but he has left out a minor point or two. My purpose is also to evaluate teachers and help them improve." She hesitated for effect, "OR leave Hogwarts.

"'I hope that I'll receive full cooperation from you all."

I'd been listening carefully. No one seemed to have any questions, so I raised my hand. She almost didn't notice me, but Dumbledore did.

"Ms. Umbrage, I believe there is a question in the back."

She scanned the room and noticed my hand. She asked me to stand, and then she said, "Yes. Is that a question in the back?"

I rose, "Yes. Ma'am, it is. I was just wondering if you could give us a quick review of how this process of evaluation will happen?" I could see plenty of opportunity for cronyism. Also, it would be a good way to get people whose political philosophy you didn't like out of the way to declare them bad teachers and fire them.

She was prepared for this question, so she quickly snapped off, "I'll visit classes at random times and observe the teaching techniques of all teachers. I'll formulate recommendations based on those observations. In some cases, I'll commend the teacher. In others, I'll require remediation of shortcomings, and in some cases, I'll have to remove the teacher and find a substitute."

She turned as if to leave. It was at that instant that I made a decision. I decided that it would be necessary to oppose her. So, I asked a follow-up question, "Ma'am, a follow-up question?"

She stared at me as though she had never heard the word and asked, "Follow-up?"

"Yes, ma'am."

She didn't say anything, so I proceeded. "Let me say that I am thrilled that you're going to do evaluations of teachers." With those words, there were murmurs from the rest of those seated, but there were smiles on both Umbrage's and Dumbledore's lips.

"I've wanted to suggest that we have evaluation of teachers for a long time. It's so good to hear that it's actually going to happen." When I said that Umbrage seemed to be in shock. And Filch had been tugging on the sleeve of my robe ever more insistently, probably trying to warn me of the dangerous path that I'd been taking.

None-the-less I was not to be diverted. The glint of a plan had formed in my mind's eye, and I intended to follow it as far as I could, It might not be very far, as an inner sense warned me, but I proceeded. Umbrage was probably too stunned to speak. I was determined to go with this hunch as far as I could.

"I can see it now—a dream of a far off land that is seen but vaguely as in vision. Of course, we'll have evaluations. How can we improve without them? You will, of course, write up specifications for teaching standards.

"There'll be standards for the material taught in each course. You'll specify the teachings to be pruned back and the teachings to be emphasized specifically for each course.

"You'll specify the techniques to be used in each and every course.

"You'll specify the standard for student achievement for every course. These will include the number of owls that should be achieved, the average grade point average for every course, the number of newts that should be achieved. These will be metrics that you'll use later in the process.

"You'll publish these, and then you'll teach these standards in a series of in-service days.

"And then, after that, you'll visit every classroom and observe teachers to evaluate them. This will be for a baseline to compare how teachers are improving or not.

"You'll do the evaluations each term, and then you can determine how the teacher is improving from term to term and from the baseline.

"Then the next year, you set goals for teachers in terms of your standard teacher metrics.

"Finally, then, you're ready to base salary changes on how well the teacher met or exceeded the goals you set the previous year."

Professor Umbrage's mouth was gaping wide, and she said, "That's not how I'm doing it."

"Oh, but it should be. That's the process that the Six Sigma organization approves for reaching excellence in teaching." I was making that up, of course.

She seemed a bit dazed and asked, "Six Stigma?"

"Oh, yes. That's the organization that sets as its goal only one error in 100,000 opportunities."

She had begun regaining her equilibrium, "And you want us to do all that?"

"Oh, yes. It will improve teaching and make sure that the people who do well are rewarded."

She just stared at me, as though she weren't sure whether I was making some hideous joke or was completely serious. What made it hard for her to judge was that I was just giving her the standard procedure that the undergraduate instructors at Stanford were judged by. It was a good standard, but it required a lot of work. I'd never advocated it here because the staff was so small and everyone knew everyone else's strengths and weaknesses. So, an elaborate formal structure wasn't necessary.

Of course, Umbrage didn't know any of that. I was looking forward to pushing it as far as I could.

Dumbledore saw what I was doing and played along. "Yes, Dolores, I've often thought of instituting a system like that. But I've always been too busy for it. It's a real blessing that you've arrived and want to do it. I can't thank you enough."

Umbrage's face fell, and then she apparently had an idea. "We need to get together to discuss this further when I have the opportunity. I'd like to hear more about this."

Dumbledore took the initiative and dismissed everyone with wishes for a successful term.

As the teachers filed out of the lounge, I hung back to talk with Dumbledore. I hoped that Umbrage would leave as well. Normally, the Heads of House would stick around too. Sometimes there was further discussion among the heads and sometimes not. In the end, there were the heads, Dumbledore, Umbrage and I.

I'd rather not talk to Dumbledore with Umbrage present, but we were all there and Dumbledore was not an easy person to reach. And what I wanted to talk with him about was really quite urgent. So, in for a knut, in for a galleon.

"Headmaster," I'd rather have not called him that, but I thought that it was important to assert his primacy here, "I'd like to talk with you about something."

Dumbledore smiled, winked, and said, "Go right ahead, my boy. Anything that you have to say to me, you may say to Dolores."

I looked daggers at him. "Well, it's just that I'm going to be working rather closely with Ms. Umbrage." She cleared her throat. "Sorry, that is, Professor Umbrage and I thought perhaps we should share an office."

Umbrage coughed and fluttered her eyelids, "Well, well," she said with an upward inflection, "That's very flattering, but I really feel that I must have an office of my own."

She'd been speaking to Dumbledore, but then she turned to me and touched my arm as she said, "I appreciate the thought behind that." Here she tittered softly. "But, I really must insist on my own PRIVATE office, since that would be more appropriate for my role at the school. But, of course, you can come to work at my office whenever that would be appropriate." She fluttered her eyes again and smiled as broadly as her mouth seemed to permit.

I so much wanted to tell her what the proper role for her at the school would be, but I resisted the temptation. Meanwhile Minerva and the other teachers were staring at me as though I were crackerbox. Only Dumbledore nodded slightly. He concluded the impromptu meeting,

"Well, I think that covers everything that I want to talk about." We all separated in little groups.

When we were out of earshot, Minerva cleared her throat in a decent imitation of Umbrage, "Well, that was entertaining. What could you possibly have in mind?"

"Well, I was going to ask Dumbledore to put a meeting together. Probably if Umbrage hadn't been there, we could have done it right then, but she was there. And then Dumbledore insisted on me talking to me right there in front of Umbrage, so I had to make up something on the spot. It was the best I could do."

She harrumphed and said that she could suggest some things that I could have said.

"Yes, yes. I thought of some of those myself later, but you can't blame me for not saying them.

"Could YOU get in touch with Dumbledore and have him set up a meeting."

"About what?"

"Oh, just tell him that it's about the person who set the Dementors on Potter."

She perked up at that. "That was what you didn't want to talk about in front of Umbrage?"

"Yes."

She thought about that a moment and then said, "Sure. I think he'd want Snape there as well."

"Sounds good to me."

"I'll get in touch with him and we'll have a meeting before the week's out."

I took her arm and stopped us walking. "Sooner would be much better than later."

She nodded.

I hadn't forgotten my promise to join Filch for a drink. I arrived at his office and found him pouring what was evidently not the first drink of the night for himself. He looked up as I entered his office and a smile broke over his face. He reached into one of his desk drawers and pulled out a grimy glass. It probably hadn't been used (or washed) since the last time that I'd drunk with him in his office. Without asking me, he poured from his bottle into that glass and pushed it across his desk toward me.

"Well, Wendt, I congratulate you. You did what I wouldn't have done myself without a whole lot of this. . ." Here he paused and raised his bottle toward me, "in me."

"I'm glad you gave me the idea. I might not have thought of cozying up to her on my own."

He turned a gimlet eye toward me and said, "Well, I wasn't exactly thinking of cozying up like you seemed to be thinking of. But if you can stomach it, more power to you."

I took a shallow sip of the paint remover that he called fire whiskey and tried to keep from gagging. "I assure you, she thinks far too much of herself to ever consider being seen publicly outside school with a Squib like me."

Filch nodded a little too violently. I was afraid he might fall out of his chair, but he didn't. Instead, after steadying himself, he said, "It wasn't what happens in public that would scare me – if you know what I mean."

I forced down another sip and said, "I know exactly what you mean. Don't worry about me."

△

It was actually the day after the next that the meeting happened in Dumbledore's office. Minerva's guess about the attendees was spot on. When we were all there Dumbledore asked me to start. "Well, Wendt, this is your party. Why don't you start it?"

"Sure. First, Albus, are you quite sure that this conversation can't be overheard?"

He stared at me, "This is MY office. You must be aware of what that means."

"OK. OK. When you hear what I have to say, you'll see why I want to be absolutely sure that we can't be overheard."

He paused and looked down toward his left foot for a moment, "Yes. I'm pretty sure that even Riddle couldn't overhear us.

"OK. I think I've discovered who ordered the Dementor attack on Potter." As Snape looked like he was about to object I anticipated him, "OH, I know that ultimately it was Riddle, but I'm talking about the person who delivered the order."

Snape jumped up and said, "How can you possibly know that? I've been using every contact that I could to find that out. I haven't succeeded."

"Just calm down. I'll tell you.

"First, I asked myself who could possibly relay that order to the Dementors—prisoners at Azkaban, staff at Azkaban, somebody else?

"I started off with the realization that security in Azkaban, already strong, was undoubtedly improved immensely after the escape of a supposed DeathEater—Sirius Black. As a matter of fact I have dramatic evidence of that.

"I came to the conclusion that nobody actually in Azkaban could do that. Whether it were prisoners or guards, they would have to have instructions. They couldn't get them by owl post because that is undoubtedly scrutinized—maybe even copied over—so that nothing physical could reach them from the outside. I have evidence that that's true. When copies are made, if they're very clever, even the wording of notes might be changed to frustrate codes being used to transmit secret messages without changing the superficial meaning.

"Guards are triply hard to pass messages through. First, as part of security, their backgrounds are checked thoroughly. Second, they are like the crews of nuclear submarines. . . "

Snape interrupted with a laconic question, "Here's a puzzler. What do nuclear submarine crews and guards at Azkaban have in common? "

Minerva interrupted Snape, "What's a nuclear submarine?"

Snape looked at her as though she'd just crawled out from under a rock, "Do you mean that you're dating a Muggle and you don't know what a submarine is?"

Minerva bristled, "Well, it's not something that comes up in everyday conversation – even with Muggles."

I smiled and ended the little spat, "They both have long tours of duty away from family and friends. In the case of nuclear submarines, it's around three months. In the case of guards and staff at Azkaban, it's three months. I guess the administration figures it's easier to recruit people to work in that god-awful place if they know they'll have six months of vacation every year."

"So, how could a message come in? Only by visitor."

Snape said in a bored voice, "Yes, yes. You've said that much before. So what?"

"I now know who passed that message."

Everyone perked up at that. Snape spoke for all, "Just how can you possibly know that?"

"I found out by visiting Azkaban."

Dumbledore smiled for the first time, "Just how did you do that?"

"It actually wasn't so hard. I just asked."

Minerva stared at me. Then she said, "Of course, you asked to visit a prisoner? What prisoner of Azkaban did you visit?"

"Bellatrix LeStrange."

Minerva gasped, "You didn't?"

"I certainly did. I had a very instructive conversation with her."

Snape snickered, "As someone who has had conversations with Bellatrix, I find that rather hard to believe."

Minerva was surprised, "You asked to visit Bellatrix LeStrange, and they just let you waltz in and visit her?"

"Not exactly, there was a rather sticky point involving probity probes, but basically, yes, they just let me visit her. Why not? It's not exactly as though she has lots of visitors."

Snape laughed at that.

"And, well, she was a bit manic, but buried under the mania was some truth."

Dumbledore wanted to know what I asked her, "I asked her when Riddle was going to break her out of Azkaban."

Snape was surprised, "And she told you?"

"No, but her calm confidence told me that she did expect to be rescued. She wouldn't reveal the time. I doubt that she knows."

Minerva asked, "But she also told you who had brought the message in to the Dementors?"

"No, but I didn't ask her that. Asking that would have poisoned the well for the other question."

Snape asked wonderingly, "Would you care to share how you found out who it was? And, of course, the identity?"

"Of course. All visitors to Azkaban have to sign the guest book. ALL visitors. The page that I signed had names stretching back to last year. The prisoners don't get many visits."

Minerva shivered, "Who could blame people. It's really unpleasant just being there."

"Yes. Anyway, there was only one name that showed up in the last two months."

The tension in the room was palpable. I went on, "Dolores Jane Umbridge."

Dumbledore dropped back in his chair, "I knew she was Fudge's man er woman, but Riddles' too?"

"I also had lunch with Fudge. Do you know that he thinks that you're planning to lead an armed revolt?"

Dumbledore made a dismissive wave of his hand, "Oh, yes. That doesn't surprise me at all."

I speculated, "I wonder if she hasn't been poisoning the well of Fudge's thoughts with suggestions that you want his position."

Minerva chuckled, "It's not a very deep well."

She went on, "Well, it's good to know for sure how things lie, but we basically knew that she was a spy for Fudge. It doesn't add a lot to know that she's a spy for Riddle too."

Dumbledore said, "You're right. I don't think there's anything that we can do more than we were all determined to do anyway."

I asked, "So, what do you think she's here to do? Replace all teachers with toadies of Fudge and/or Riddle?"

Snape said, "Possibly more than that."

Dumbledore said, "Yes. For one thing, there's a new text for the Defense Against the Dark Arts. It was thrown together hastily. I didn't get a look at it sooner than the students. It's basically a political diatribe. It's got pretty much all the theory of defensive spells but it calls for no practice. I'm sure the Owl and Newt exams will all be done on paper with no practical demonstrations."

Minerva was scandalized, "You're surely joking? Even if Riddle weren't around, there are plenty of criminals who would attack unprepared youth."

Dumbledore rummaged on his desk and pulled a thin book out of a stack and tossed it to Minerva, "Take a look at this."

She thumbed it open at a random page and her eyes slowly grew as large as pie plates. "This is criminal."

Dumbledore sighed, "Yes, I suppose it is."

I had an idea, "Surely, most parents would be as shocked as Minerva. Can't we appeal to them?"

Minerva said, "You obviously haven't been reading much of the *Prophet*. They've subtly suggested that Dumbledore isn't fit to lead a school that teaches potentially dangerous spells."

I wished that I had a hat or something to throw to the ground, "Dangerous spells! I wish you'd show me one that isn't."

Dumbledore said, "That's a demonstration for another day. For now, can anyone think of anything we can do?"

"How about non-violent civil disobedience?" I asked.

Dumbledore asked, "You mean like Ghandi?"

"Well, actually, I was thinking of Martin Luther King Jr. but, come to think of it, I like Ghandi better. He didn't get shot."

Snape asked, "So how does that work out practically?"

"Well, for one thing, anyone who teaches a course that's got spell work teaches a defensive spell along with the rest."

Snape laughed, "Well, that leaves me out."

Minerva answered, "No, it doesn't. You have spells that you use when brewing some potions, don't you."

Snape just mumbled.

Minerva went on, "Of course, she's going to visit classes. You just leave off doing the defensive spells from your lesson plans when she's around. BUT she will eventually find out. There will be some tattle-tale, probably a Slytherin, who will let her know."

I answered, "That's where the disobedience comes in. I don't think she'd fire any of the main teachers. The parents may not trust Dumbledore, but most of the parents were taught by you, right?"

No one said anything, "I'll take silence as consent. I can't believe that if there were mass firings that they'd stand still for it long."

"Oh, you don't know what parents will stand for." Snape shook his head as he spoke.

"Well, that's all that I can offer."

There was some more discussion, but we finally departed without any further useful points being made.

Civil Disobedience

The next week, I went to Umbrage's office to start my part of civil disobedience. I couldn't teach defensive spells or any kind of spells, but I could get in Umbrage's way.

I knocked on her door. It took a couple of minutes for her to answer. When she finally did, she opened the door only a sliver, slipped out into the hall and closed the door behind her. "I'm afraid Mr. Wendt, my office is occupied. I'm supervising detention. Perhaps another time?"

"Detention? Who?"

"Harry Potter."

"Really? What has he done?"

"He has been lying."

"What about?"

"About He-Who-Must-Not-Be-Named returning."

"He's said that he hasn't?"

She thought about that a moment and said, "No. No. He's saying that Valdemort has returned."

"I see. Oh, of course. You're singling him out for punishment to prove to people that he's right, because he's willing to undergo detention to prove his point?"

She shook her head in confusion, "No. No. I'm forcing him to take back what he's said."

"Let's see. You punish him to get him to recant, and everybody's going to figure that he was lying?"

"No. No. It's to keep him from talking about it."

"How's that working for you?"

She didn't say anything. Then she said, "I'll get him to change his mind."

"Right. Just keep telling yourself that. It's sure to convince someone."

"Well, what would you do?" She asked in an exasperated tone.

"I'd pay absolutely no attention to him. Don't encourage people to think about what he says."

"But he keeps asking embarrassing questions."

"Just don't answer them."

"But what if he disrupts the class?"

"Easy. Expel him from class."

She seemed to ponder that. "Maybe."

But, I was pretty sure that she wouldn't.

△

She didn't, but after a few weeks a funny thing started happening. Potter stopped objecting in class. It was like he had found another way to protest. That allowed me to get some time in with her.

I insisted on having her review my English Literature characteristics and goals. She was a reluctant student.

"Why do I have to review details? I trust you.'

'But you need to use it as a template. And you can't suggest improvements if you aren't familiar with it."

I authored a performance appraisal document and pushed her to read it and comment. She found a bunch of problems, but I didn't care. I didn't care if she changed every single word. As a matter of fact, the more changes, the better.

She began to suspect Potter's quiet meant that he was doing something in secret—probably as part of an organization. She started banning organizations.

I was furious—at least publicly. Privately, I was delighted. The more innocuous past-times she made illegal, the more people would despise her—maybe enough to protest to parents.

One day, I showed up at her office. We'd always met in my office or her classroom. It was the strangest office I'd ever seen. The walls were covered with cameos of cats—really kittens. The decor was pink, and the windows had lace curtains.

After I'd gotten over gawking, she inquired, "Yes, Mr. Wendt."

"Right. What in the world do you have against wizard's chess?"

"Why, nothing."

"Then, why is my chess club banned?"

"Oh, it's not your chess club."

"Well, it sure seems like it's my chess club."

"No. No. It's all clubs."

"Yeah. That includes chess. What's wrong with chess?"

"Well, nothing—per se."

"Do you think we're plotting to take over the school?"

"No."

"Then un-ban it."

"I couldn't do that." she said with a cloying sweetness, "Then people would want all the other clubs un-banned."

"What about the gob-stones club? Why can't you un-ban it?"

"I told you, Mr. Wendt. It's the principle."

"The principle is that you can't allow harmless clubs?"

"No. We don't know which clubs are harmless."

"Do you agree that mine is?"

"Oh, of course." She seemed to be losing her temper.

"What about the glee club?"

"Well, no problem there."

"Then un-ban us!"

She stopped talking. I think because she wanted to consider something radical. "I can't. Potter definitely has a secret society. He's training students to oppose the Ministry. I can't un-ban any societies as long as Potter's is still active."

"And you know this because?"

"I just know it. Get out."

"OK. Good luck with that."

She snarled at me. Better and better.

Halloween

There was a knock at the door. I invited the knocker in. The door opened, and Professor Sinistra entered, took the red leather chair and made her annual proposition. "You want to irritate Umbrage, right?"

I had gotten to the point where I understood how she thought pretty well, but I didn't anticipate that she'd have an anti-umbrage pitch.

"I might quibble about choice of word, but, yes."

She leaned forward, "Then I've got a plan for you."

"You know, I swore the last time that I'd never listen to you again."

"Oh, but this is your civic duty. You can make a difference for Hogwarts!"

"I know I'll regret this. What's your idea?"

"It's very simple. You go disguised as Sirius Black."

That was the stupidest idea that I'd heard yet. Was she crazy? "Look. If I go as Sirius Black, and I do assume that you mean by using Polyjuice potion, then Umbrage will know: One, that Sirius Black is around not too far away and two, that I almost certainly know where he is. That's pretty bad."

"Oh, no. We found some of his hairs where he was hiding out when he was here two years ago—the Shrieking Shack."

"How do we know that they were his hairs? How do we know that they weren't Hermione Grangers' or some bum who was just taking refuge there?"

"Are you kidding, the Shrieking Shack has had a bad reputation for a very long time. Who else would camp out there besides someone like Sirius Black?"

I had to admit that the idea of putting a Sirius Black look-alike into the Halloween Ball was really appealing. Also, she made it sound like a plausible proposition, but there were some problems. "Look, what if Umbrage or even somebody else uses the Petrificus Totalis spell on him and sends for Dementors to apply the kiss before the polyjuice potion wears off? You know that almost happened a year ago. I don't think I'd look that good without a brain."

"Oh, you might look just the same."

"Very funny. Well, no one is going to step up to that job without a better back-out plan if things go south."

She thought about that and raised this possibility, "What if you take only very small doses of PolyJuice potion, sort of the way that the fake Moody did. A small swallow at a time when you begin to revert would be unnoticeable, but would keep you disguised indefinitely."

I swore that I would never let her talk me into something like this again, but here we were. I wanted to do everything to make life at Hogwarts unbearable for Umbrage, and here was a real opportunity. "I can't believe that I'm saying this, but I'm tempted by your idea."

Sinistra clapped her hands together enthusiastically. I was beginning to have a bad feeling about it, but I would do things differently this time. I started to talk about just how that would work. "Well, provisionally, let's start by assuming that I'll go along with this. There are a few conditions that I insist on.

"For one, we have to test this potion thoroughly to make sure that we can time what a sip will do."

She nodded and said, "Good. I'll get to work making the potion right away. You might just try to get some hairs from Black."

"Just how do you think I can do that?"

"Oh, that should be easy," she said with a casual flip of her hand. "Black must be a member of the Order. Ms. McGonagall ought to be willing to get a few locks of hair for her sweetie." She ended the sentence with a light uplifted lilt that made me grimace.

"I'll talk to her. But for now, we're done with our talk."

"What about your other point?"

"I'll think of one."

I watched her leave the office while I mulled over my misgivings.

The next day, I invited Minerva to my office. She showed up, and I worked hard to be upbeat.

She was in a foul mood. She flopped down in the red leather chair. I asked, "What's your problem?"

"Having a hard time with Umbrage?"

"That foul hag has been using torture on students in detention. I could just . . . " She didn't finish the thought, but I got the general idea.

"It sort of makes you long for the time when Moody was turning students into ferrets."

Her frown broke for a moment of relief, "Yes, I could almost wish to have that faux Moody back. You know, when he was imitating the real Moody, he was a decent teacher. No, better. He was a really good teacher. In a different life, he might have been in the Order."

That seemed to provide me with as good a lead-in as I was going to get, "That brings me to the reason that I wanted to see you tonight."

"You mean besides wanting to snog on the sofa?"

"Well, snogging and the other thing. You see, I've been thinking about making Umbrage regret that she'd ever come here."

"And just how would you do that?" her eyes narrowed, the way they do when she smells a student planning to get away with something.

I tried hard to prevent myself from using one of my "tells" before I make a suggestion that is kind of dicey. When I'm about to make that kind of suggestion, I normally release a long sigh. This time I didn't, "I've got a great idea for irritating Umbrage. You know that the Halloween Feast and Ball are coming up soon."

"Wait!" She held out a hand with the flat of the palm pointed at me, "Tell me this doesn't have anything to do with that witch, Sinistra."

"It was an idea that she had."

"You promised me that you would never again fall for one of her stupid ideas." She got up and paced one way, turned around, came back and stared at me again. "You know those ideas always get you in trouble."

"This is an idea that you'll like. She wants to give Umbrage fits."

Minerva dropped into the chair again and, being resigned to what was coming, said, "OK. Tell me about this brilliant idea."

"Well, it's really simple. She hates rule-breakers doesn't she? At least people who break her rules."

In a tired voice, Minerva agreed, "I suppose."

"Well, suppose that one of the people that showed up at the party were Sirius Black?"

She sat bolt upright at that. "Are the both of you crazy? Sirius can't come." And then she stopped a moment for thought. "It wouldn't be Sirius, would it? It would be someone using Polyjuice Potion." Her mouth then got a really foul expression, "It would be you, wouldn't it?"

"It could be me."

"Sure, it could be you and it could be the Man in the Moon, but it WOULD be you."

"OK. That was the original idea, but it wouldn't have to be me and it WOULD be a good idea. Umbrage would go crazy."

"Yeh, crazy and maybe would kill you on the spot."

"We could prove it was me. I could drink it in front of her. I'd have a glass of pumpkin juice laced with the Polyjuice, and I would drink it in front of her. Then I'd. . . "

"Then you'd be in big trouble. Who knows what she'd do?"

I had to admit that Umbrage didn't strike me as having a very stable personality. She might just do anything. Then I had an idea. "What if there were more than one set of Weasley twins wandering around? That would make her day, and she couldn't very well do anything to a student—at least more than she already has."

Minerva thought about that a minute. "There's something there. Fred and George are as irritating as you get. Can you image four of them at a party? It would just serve them right if there were another pair of them running around doing stupid things. It would be a two-fer—a send-up of both Umbrage and the twins."

"Sounds good to me."

"Yeh. I know. That's not a good sign, but I kind of like it."

"I'm pretty sure that Sinistra already has Polyjuice Potion."

"I don't doubt it. I think she must start brewing it every summer in anticipation of Halloween."

Then MInerva's eyes began to shine. "If two pairs are good, wouldn't three be better?"

"Just what are you driving at?"

Minerva leaned forward as though trying to prevent anyone overhearing the idea, "What if you, Sinistra, Snape and I all went as twins? Four of us—or four of the Weasleys—should be a real shock to her."

It was just crazy enough to work.

The next day, I stopped by Sinistra at breakfast and whispered, "Tonight, 7, my office." I could swear that I could hear a purr as I walked away. At noon, I casually walked by Snape's place, but he was in a conversation with Professor Sprout and I was forced to visit his office later in the afternoon. He was in as foul a mood as most teachers were.

"What's your good mood about?" I asked.

"Do you know that Umbrage has started evaluating teachers?"

"I suppose I could only hold her off so long."

"That, that," I'd never heard Snape stutter before but this was unique provocation, "ADMINISTRATOR, who doesn't know anything about teaching and much less about doing, critiqued my class today.

"She doesn't know the difference between a poultice and a poltergeist but she thinks that she can tell me how to teach potions."

I suggested, "Perhaps we could enlist Peeves to help with her education about poltergeists."

"Don't be facetious. This is serious. She'd replace me with some moron who pulls the party line about Voldemort, like Methilda Hopkirk, who couldn't brew a cup of tea if her life depended on it.

"And just to add insult to injury, she demands that I brew her a gigantic supply of Veritas serum. I was so tempted to give her access to my classroom and tell her to brew it if she wanted it."

He stopped and chuckled, "I'd insist on that if I weren't afraid that she'd blow the classroom up." He hesitated, "Still, if I could be assured that she'd be there when it happened, I just might do it yet."

With encouragement like that, I went ahead with my invitation, "Well, I've got an idea about making her life a bit more unhappy. If you're interested, show up at my office tonight at 7PM."

"Serious?"

"As serious as Sirius Black."

He frowned at that, but said, "I'll be there."

That night, MInerva showed up immediately after I left the Great Hall. That was twenty minutes before 7PM. About five minutes later, Sinistra made an appearance. She was rather flabbergasted to find Minerva sitting in the red leather chair.

Minerva beat her to making a comment, "You'll have to show up earlier than this to win the red leather chair."

Sinistra simply looked daggers at her and took one of the yellow chairs. After a bit she asked, "I suppose we're waiting for someone else. Can we have a guessing game?"

Minerva chuckled again, "It wouldn't be much of a guessing game since you're the only one here who doesn't know who it is." It was "catty", but I couldn't blame Minerva.

A little later, Snape arrived. "Well, if it isn't the Halloween Party gang. I didn't know that the three of you had gotten together to have fun."

The two women were looking daggers at him. I invited him to sit, "Look. Let me assure you, this is not for fun—unless you think that driving Umbrage crazy is fun."

Snape looked from one to the other of us and smiled, "Well, it's worth hearing even if it's crazy, as I expect it will be." He leaned back and laughed dryly.

I knew it would be a volatile combination, the four of us. So, I took a deep breath and began, "Who are the most irritating students?"

Snape said, "Hands down, the Weasley twins. They even beat Potter."

Sinistra said, "They only took my classes when absolutely required, but I'd agree."

"Right. Do you think that Umbrage finds them irritating?"

Snape answered, "I know she does. She's been trying to figure out a Ministry decree to ban them from the school, but she doesn't want it to name them specifically. That would be a bit too blatant even for her."

"Well, then, suppose she were faced with a half-dozen Weasley twins at the Halloween Ball?"

Sinistra laughed raucously, "You mean for the four of us to use Polyjuice Potion to impersonate Fred and George! What a joke. Do we have their co-operation in this?"

Minerva shook her head emphatically, "I think that we should keep them out of the planning for this. They're most effective when they're working on the spur of the moment."

Snape wanted to know who would provide the PolyJuice potion. Sinistra admitted, "I only brewed enough for two doses. That could maybe be stretched to three, but I don't have enough for all of us."

Snape admitted that he had a private stash, "I can contribute enough for two for the night."

Minerva summed it up, "Well, that seems good. I have my own contribution."

I was pleasantly surprised, "What would that be?"

"Oh, I confiscated some of the stores of skiving potions from the two dear boys. Not a lot, puking pastilles and fainting fancies. We can make a certain witch pretty uncomfortable if the mere irritation factor of the Weasleys isn't enough. I shouldn't have much trouble getting some hair from them for the Polyjuice potion too."

I offered, "I'll get us some appropriately sized clothes for the night."

Snape suggested that we meet the day before to assemble all the props for the party and do a little rehearsal of the required steps for the evening. It turned out to be a rather exquisite ballet of steps that required precise timing to achieve the results that we wanted. By the end, I was convinced that it was beyond the typical practical jokes that the twins play.

Christmas at Gringott's

The next weekend Minerva and I continued a tradition that we had been developing over the last couple of years—shopping for Christmas early. We met for breakfast on Saturday prepared to go directly from breakfast to Diagon Alley. We had a policy of not disapparating or traveling by floo or portkey together in plain view of Hogwarts students. It was not because we were trying to hide the fact that we had an extra-curricular relationship. As a matter of fact, practically everyone at school knew that we did. It was just that we didn't want to seem to flaunt that fact. We didn't want to hint that it was all right for students to have a relationship dominate their school experience. Students were going to have relationships with other students. We couldn't prevent that, and it was probably not a good idea to try. Those relationships should be secondary or even tertiary if possible.

So it was that we went up to her office after breakfast and took the floo network from there to the Cauldron. As usual Tom was behind the bar and gave us what was for him a cheery welcome. We answered in kind, and I said, "Keep a table warm for us. We'll be back later for lunch."

He smiled and thanked us. This little bit of pleasantry was necessary to keep the wheels of commerce oiled and running smoothly. It was unfair to use an establishment's connection to the floo network and not repay in some way. Just what was considered adequate depended on a number of things—how many people used the connection, what the long term relationship between the flooer (I'd never heard an adequate term for people who have used the floo network to travel. You'd think that there would have been a slang term, at least, but no one seemed to have invented one.). Other variables concerned whether the flooer could do a small transaction in the place of business. If the least you could do was buy something, say a shirt (like at Madame Malkin's), no one would use the connection unless they were certain that they would do that. So generally, where it was possible to do a small transaction—like buy a drink—that was expected, but where only larger transactions were possible, it was OK to use a floo connection if you had a regular business relationship and it was normal for you to periodically buy things at the business.

In this case, we had both. We regularly had meals there and even on rare occasions stayed the night. We also usually would have a drink and pass a little time in gossip with Tom. Today, we had delayed our custom till later. That was perfectly fine with Tom.

On these trips to Diagon Alley, my first business was usually to stop by Gringotts to get some gold out of my vault and check on my business interests. Minerva opened the magic passage to Diagon Alley from the back entrance to The Leaky Cauldron. We walked to Gringotts and agreed that we would meet for lunch at the Cauldron around 12:30. That gave me plenty of time to do business at Gringotts and maybe do a little shopping as well.

I entered Gringotts and was greeted with the usual frowns that greeted even the best customers of Gringotts. I went to the Concierge and requested to have a meeting with a bank officer about my special account with Gringotts. He took my name and asked me to wait.

"I have a little business in my vault. I'll go do that first if that's all right."

The goblin frowned especially deeply and said, "When the officer is ready, he'll be ready, and if you're not here, you'll miss your chance."

I smiled especially broadly. "I don't mean to be difficult, but I've never waited for less than an hour to meet with an officer. I think your excellent customer service will get me to my vault and back long before then."

He nodded, and I went off to find an open teller. I was right. I arrived at my small vault in ten minutes, pulled out 750 galleons, and was back to the Waiting Area in less than a half hour. About twenty minutes after that, a goblin disturbed my reading of the *Daily Prophet* and summoned me to a back room. There was an older goblin and a younger assistant. The assistant was dismissed without introductions, but the officer introduced himself as Slubagg. He started rapidly by pulling out a sheet of parchment with a summary of activity on my special account. Business had been good. My account's balance was over ten thousand pounds. They kept accounts for it in English money and only converted it to galleons when I wanted to withdraw some. I did that periodically because I wanted to keep most of my funds in galleons. I prepared a request to withdraw three thousand pounds to be transferred as galleons to my vault. The officer accepted the order, "That will be executed before the day is out." Then he added what he thought was just a sort of courtesy, "And will there be anything else, sir?"

I actually had another item, "Yes, I do have something else."

Slubagg stared unbelieving for a moment before regaining his composure, "Of course, sir. What can I do for you?"

"I have a sort of business proposition for you."

I saw an expression on Slubagg's face that I don't think that I'd seen before on a goblin's face. My guess was that it was surprise, "Yes, sir." It was quickly replaced by the sort of expression that I had come to associate with avarice in goblins.

"I think that you could increase your profit by opening a few more branches. I'd suggest one, at least, at the Ministry of Magic."

His face reverted to one that might have been amusement, "Don't you think that we've thought of that? There are lots of our customers at the Ministry, and it would probably be more convenient for them—some of the time. However, there are many problems.

"The ministry is not always open when all of our branches are— like weekends. We'd have to do extensive construction work to install vaults. Just getting permission to do that would be horrendous. It might even not be permitted."

I nodded complacently, "Oh, I wouldn't suggest going to all that trouble. I have something entirely different in mind."

He leaned forward and the expression on his face changed again to one I'd not seen before. "Just what would that be?"

"Well, I have a 'special account'. What that really amounts to is that you keep my pounds sterling in Gringott's company vault, but you keep track of how many of those pounds belong to me and how many belong to the bank. Whenever I want any, I don't go down to my vault. You just scratch out my old total and decrease it by the amount that I want out. Then, you hand it to me from the money that you keep in the lobby for small transactions. You replenish that from Gringott's business vault, right?"

"Well, that's not exactly the process, but its close enough. So what?"

"Well, maybe wizards would like to have an account like that. They just walk into the bank. Fill out a form like I just did and you give them galleons from the lobby that get replenished from the customer's vault."

The goblin smiled, "Yes, we could do that, but how does that help with starting a branch in the Ministry?"

"Well, if you want to know that, you'll have to give me a cut of the profits."

The frown returned. "Just how much of a cut would you want?"

"Oh, say 5%. I'm not greedy."

The goblin scratched its nose on top. "That's too much. How about one percent?"

"Three."

The goblin said, "Are you satisfied with a verbal agreement before we go on?"

"Goblins are well known for keeping AND enforcing the terms of verbal agreements. Sure."

"Then two percent."

"Two and one half."

The goblin stared at me as though he could force me to change my mind by force of will. None-the-less, I didn't say anything.

"All right two and one half it is. Now, what's your brilliant idea?"

"Customers open a special account. You charge a maintenance fee every month—whether they use the account at all or not. You pick the maintenance fee. I'd advise you to not be too greedy if you want to maximize profits.

"When they sign up, they tell you how many galleons to keep in their account from their vault. At the end of each day, every bank sends an owl with a list of all the transactions—both debits and credits from the accounts that happened at their branch. Overnight, adjustments are made to the account by either taking galleons from customer vaults or returning galleons to customer vaults. Then owls are sent back to each branch with a list of accounts and how many galleons are in them.

"The next day customers come into the branch and do transactions—either depositing galleons or withdrawing them. Every now and then the branch ends up with more galleons than it needs or not enough. You can adjust the number of galleons at each branch so that you don't have to ship galleons more often than once a month, probably.

"That way, branches can have no vaults at all and they can be quite compact—taking up only the size of a small store—like Mr. Olivander's. There doesn't have to be a vault at all—although if you want one for the Gringotts galleons, you could do that."

Slubagg had been writing furiously on a parchment as I spoke and kept writing for some time after I'd finished. When he finished, he said, "Very well. We'll consider this, and if the bank decides to do something like this, you'll be notified, and we'll start depositing your share of the profits in your 'special account' if that's OK."

"Perfectly fine."

"And you trust us?"

"I know that you goblins are afraid to break the rules of business. Some people might call it a superstition, but it doesn't matter whether it is or not. What's important is whether you honor those rules. Some people do and some don't. The Muggles have an expression. 'Breaking those rules is bad Karma'. They mean that it has consequences."

Slubagg got up and extended his hand, which I readily took. He said, "Yes. Bad Karma."

I left the bank with my purse bulging (if it could bulge) with galleons. A few months later there was a front page article in the *Prophet* about Gringotts opening a new branch—actually in the Ministry of Magic itself. More amazingly, the branch would not have vaults. It would only do business with customers who had a special kind of new account that Gringotts had invented for the branch but that would be available at any branch. It was called a "virtual vault" account. Anyone interested in using the new branch at the Ministry were urged to visit that branch or any branch to get literature on how the new account worked. One of the bank officers, a Slubagg, had been quoted as saying, "Everyone will want to have one of these accounts. It's as though you have a vault at every Gringott's branch."

English Lessons

It was a few days later that I had a visit from the Grand Inquisitor. That was the name that the teachers had begun using for Umbrage. Strangely it was one that she later adopted for herself.

I was in my class of Sixth years. Our main project for the term was the play, "The Merchant of Venice." As preparation for actually performing the play, we'd studied some Muggle European history, including the historic place of Jews in Europe of the Middle Ages. We'd finished that a week or so before, and we'd begun the task of preparing to present ACT IV. It contains the culmination and most of the memorable quotations from the *Merchant*. For that purpose we'd started rehearsing in class.

We had just begun when I heard someone clear her throat behind me. I swung around but was quite sure of whom it would be. I didn't know anyone at Hogwarts who would sneak up on a class in progress besides Umbrage. Besides that I saw her in my reflective surface framed picture of Dumbledore.

So, even before I turned, I said, "Professor Umbrage, what can I do for you?" Of course, I knew perfectly well why she was in my class.

"Mr. Wendt, please proceed with your class. I've just come to observe."

I turned back to the class and asked the class to proceed from where we had left off. Jim Rockford, a Hufflepuff, playing the Duke spoke the next lines:

"I am sorry for thee: thou art come to answer
A stony adversary, an inhuman wretch
uncapable of pity, void and empty
From any dram of mercy."

Just then the class was interrupted again by a cleared throat. I was determined to maintain my equilibrium and present an equable visage. I turned and asked if she needed a lozenge. I kept a supply in my desk in case an actor had a sore throat.

"No, professor, I don't understand."

I interrupted before she could go on, "Oh, I"m sorry, I should have introduced the scene for your sake. The speaker is the Duke of Venice who is sitting in judgment of Antonio, the Merchant of Venice. The Duke is referring to Shylock, the Jew."

She cleared her throat again, interrupting my exposition. So I offered help, "Oh, I am sorry. You should really take a lozenge. That throat sounds very bad."

"No, Professor. I meant that I don't understand how you could be rehearsing a play. I disbanded all extracurricular groups, including your drama club. How is it that your drama group is still going?"

I smiled, "Oh, but this isn't a drama club. This is my 6th year English Lit class. We're studying the play, 'The Merchant of Venice.' As a class project, we are going to present the fourth act of the play at the end of term. I think we'll do it during the Yule party. The class will be graded on the quality of the production."

She harrumphed but couldn't seem to come up with an objection to that.

I instructed the class to proceed with the play. We went along for a while. The student prompter was not too busy doing her job a few times. I was impressed by how well the students had learned their lines in the sometimes difficult Elizabethan English, but Umbrage was unimpressed.

After one of her interruptions signaled by the classic cleared throat, she asked, 'Don't your students know their lines any better than this?"

My eyes narrowed as they concentrated on her. I could tolerate critiques of me, but these students had done well and I was angry with her for criticism of what I thought were nice performances for the most part. I restrained my temptation to snap at her but instead said, "Professor Umbrage, I think the students are doing quite well. They've not had much time to learn their lines and I am enjoying this class's handling of the play."

Umbrage's face betrayed some shock, and she snapped back at me. "Well, perhaps your standards are lax." She hesitated and then challenged me directly, 'Can YOU recite any lines of the play?"

I turned from her to the class, whom I regarded as the proper and qualified judges of my performance and said, "Portia's speech from later in this act,

"The quality of mercy is not strain'd,
It droppeth as the gentle rain from heaven
Upon the place beneath: it is twice blest;
It blesseth him that gives and him that takes:
'Tis mightiest in the mightiest: it becomes
The throned monarch better than his crown;
His sceptre shows the force of temporal power,
The attribute to awe and majesty,
Wherein doth sit the dread and fear of kings;
But mercy is above this sceptred sway;
It is enthroned in the hearts of kings,
It is an attribute to God himself;
And earthly power doth then show likest God's
When mercy seasons justice. Therefore, Jew,
Though justice be thy plea, consider this,
That, in the course of justice, none of us
Should see salvation: we do pray for mercy;
And that same prayer doth teach us all to render
The deeds of mercy. I have spoke thus much
To mitigate the justice of thy plea;
Which if thou follow, this strict court of Venice
Must needs give sentence 'gainst the merchant there."

Umbrage cleared her throat again but had nothing more to say. I remained facing the class and told them to proceed. They picked up, and we went a little further in act IV. Then, I stopped them.

"Very well. We've listened to some of the play. So, let's talk about the social milieu that it is embedded in. Who can tell me something about Shylock?"

June Avril's hand shot up. She was a Ravenclaw and frequently had answers. I tried to avoid her whenever someone else raised a hand, but this time hers was the only hand. I nodded at her bobbing ponytail. She said, "Shylock was a Jew. His business was lending money."

"Correct. Jews had a reputation as money-lenders. You would think that they would be popular people, no? And, incidentally, five points for Ravenclaw."

A Hufflepuff whose name I couldn't remember had his hand raised along with Jill's. I recognized the Hufflepuff, "Well, sir. Jews weren't liked any more than the goblins of Gringott's are."

There was general laughter, and I had to reign it in a bit, "OK. That's worth five points for Hufflepuff." I had a sheet of parchment listing my points. Regular magical teachers could wave their wands, and the points would show up in the hourglasses in the main hall. I had to record them on parchment and find a helpful teacher to tote them up for me in the hourglasses.

I went on, "Then, whenever you hear Shylock speaking, let's imagine that he's a Gringott's goblin. Do people like the goblins of Gringott's?"

Someone called out, "No. The moneygrubbers. Sell you for a silver sickle."

I heard Umbrage behind me say, "Right." emphatically.

"Well. Let's talk about Jews and Goblins. Is it fair to feel dislike for all Goblins—or Jews?"

There was a fairly strong chorus of "Yeh's."

"Well, most of us think so. I want you to keep that question in mind as we go through the rest of the play. Shylock has some points that he wants to make in his favor. And you would do well to listen to them carefully. We'll discuss this question again later."

The play proceeded. Before we reached my next planned stopping point, Umbrage had noisily gotten up, and walked out the door, calling over her shoulder, "Thanks, Professor Wendt. I'll see you later to discuss your rating."

The class ended. As I was putting papers into my briefcase, I found Ms. Avril standing in front of my desk, "Professor?"

"Yes, Ms. Avril, what can I do for you?"

"Are you going to get canned?"

"You mean the way that Professor Umbrage is reviewing all teachers?"

She nodded.

"I don't know. I don't think so. I think Professor Dumbledore has something to say about it. I don't think that he'll approve that."

"But she seems to have so much power—all these decrees. I'm worried that you'll be gone next year."

I smiled. "Well, you aren't eligible for my class next year, so you'll be OK."

"Don't joke about it. It's serious."

"Maybe it is serious and maybe it isn't, but I don't think I can do much to affect it. So I'm going to try not to worry about it, and neither should you."

She continued to stare at me. I asked her if she didn't have a class to go to, and she reluctantly left. As she left the room, I shook my head. I was afraid that she might be working on a little crush. I'd have to be very careful.

Weasleys to the Rescue

Halloween happened on a Thursday this year, so it was decided to move the Ball to Friday—All Saints Day this year. In preparation, I'd ordered from Madame Malkins four men's robes. I'd not wanted to spend a lot of money, but it seemed like it was not possible to avoid it. I suppose the reality of being fairly rich hadn't sunk in yet, but I forced myself to pony up for the costumes.

I'd sent a note to Madame Malkin, explaining that I had a little practical joke to play on the Weasley twins, and that we need four sets of dress robes of the appropriate sizes for Fred and George, two each. I implored her to provide them without informing anyone. This was really the weak point of the plan. It depended on getting properly sized robes because it was clear that they were tall, and we couldn't just pull anyone's dress robes out and use them.

A few days before the party, a tap tap tapping sounded at the window of my office. I opened it and discovered not just a single owl, but five. Four were carrying large boxes and the fifth, a note. The owls flew in, deposited the boxes and the note on my desk and flew out.

I had a strong suspicion that I knew what was in the boxes, but the note confirmed it. It was from Madame Malkin. Her note expressed surprise at my unusual request but pleasure that we would be playing a practical joke on the Weasley twins. She confessed that they were the customers that she least liked to see come into her shop. It wasn't that they were bad tempered, but they were constantly playing little jokes on her—like the time they'd made robes shrink on another customer who was monopolizing her time. She'd sent two sets of robes each for the two Weasley twins. The boxes were marked as to which robes were for which twin.

I wondered why there was any difference between them, but when I opened the boxes I understood. They had subtle differences in design. I doubted that anyone besides the twins would notice the differences, but who knew.

We had the meeting in Snape's office the evening of the official Halloween. Minerva had brought her confiscated Weasley Wizard Weezes products, and everyone else had brought their contributions.

The next day, the ballet began early—before breakfast. Minerva called an early inspection of the boys' part of the dorm. Nominally, it was to discover contraband (Weasley Wizard Wheezes), but actually, it was an excuse to get access to their hairbrushes. She succeeded in retrieving a good sample of hair from both the twins. She met with Snape, and they worked on completing the Polyjuice Potion. That was quick but it had to be in order to fit in-between her classes.

In the meantime, Sinistra came and pestered me. She showed up in my office between classes. She barged in as though she were expected, and maybe I should have expected her. She'd been unusually agreeable throughout so far.

She walked up and took a seat in the red leather chair. "OK. We need to meet tonight to get into costume. I volunteer my office."

"I think that was pretty well established as my office. I have the costumes. Snape and Minerva have the Polyjuice Potion. There's nothing in your office."

She pouted, "I'm in my office."

"Like I said, there's nothing in your office."

"Oh, don't be boring. You've got to allow me my part of this joke."

"You'll have plenty to do once we're costumed. Don't be a nuisance. I've got papers to grade. Surely, you've got things to do? I mean other than pester me?"

She got up and pouted off. I should have expected trouble, but I was counting on our common disgust with Umbrage to keep it directed at her.

I had a hard time forcing food down at lunch. Somehow despite the heavenly things that the house elves came up with, I just couldn't conjure up an appetite. I knew it was nervousness, but it seemed almost criminal not to enjoy some of the sandwiches on the platters on the table. I don't know how the elves managed it, but even simple BLT sandwiches were incomparably better than the best fare that I'd had at any Muggle sandwich shop.

The afternoon classes were as much a burden for me as they were for the students. I finally dismissed the last class after half an hour. Nobody was getting anything accomplished other than the notes being passed back and forth between May Proctor and Henrietta Gamble. Everyone was overjoyed to be released. The two fourth years were somewhat downcast that they didn't have an excuse to be in the same room and share their secrets.

The evening meal was strange. No meal where Umbrage was could be an unalloyed pleasure, but there was so much anticipation of the party that everyone seemed willing to let her bizarre pronouncements and rules pass unheeded. She was in rare form. She had announced that there was a new "educational" decree that male and female students could not be closer than 25 cm. at any time. There was a small sigh that arose from the audience but that was all. The one announcement that did come close to sparking indignation was that the party must end by 11 PM.

After everyone was dismissed, there was a general exodus to hurry to dress for the party. The four of us made our way to my office. When we'd all arrived, I handed out the boxes containing the dress robes and shoes. We'd decided that there had to be pairs of twins—a male pair and a female pair. So, I drew George and Snape got Fred. Likewise, much to Sinistra chagrin, Minerva got Fred and Sinistra, George. That way, Minerva and I could be paired together. And also, Snape and I could be paired together. Not that there were that many people who could tell the difference between Fred and George.

As we were going over that, Minerva commented, "Of course, it's obvious who's George and who's Fred."

I was curious, "Oh, yeh? How in the world can you tell them apart?"

Minerva looked at me as though I were speaking nonsense. "Why, it's obvious. Just look at the colors."

Snape and I stared at the robes and then at each other. Snape simply said, "They're red."

"No. No." Sinistra said, "Fred's robes are dusky rose, and George's are more of a ruby, wouldn't you say, Minerva?"

Minerva looked at them assessingly and agreed, "Yesss, but I think what you call ruby is more like crimson."

"You may be right, Minerva. It depends on how the light hits it."

"OK. OK. We've got to get going. We're running out of time". Sinistra brought out her flask of Polyjuice Potion and Minerva put the sample of George's hair in it. Then Snape brought out his flask and Minerva put Fred's in.

I drank half of the George Polyjuice Potion and handed it to Sinistra, who commented, "Good. We get to share a cup."

I thought to myself, I've got a bad feeling about this. In the meantime, Minerva had two small bags. "These are the fainting fancies and these, the puking pastilles." She handed one bag to Sinistra, and she and Sinistra went into my bedroom to change into their robes. Snape and I stayed in my office to change into ours.

George was a lot taller than I. The distortions my body went through as it changed were bizarre. My fingers lengthened faster than my hands. For a while, I had grotesquely long fingers. My vision blurred as my eyes grew unevenly and the world seemed to swim about me. I was trying to work my clothes on as I changed, worried that the girls would finish first and come in before I was dressed.

After we had transformed and changed, we went down to the Great Hall. It had been transformed into a ballroom. The band had set up. More important, most of the attendees had arrived, and some people were dancing. We could sneak in two at a time and, with a little luck, not many might notice a superabundance of twins – at first.

Snape and I were first. Our job was to keep Umbrage's attention engaged for the rest of the party. Although the physical change that the Polyjuice Potion causes makes the vocal cords just like those of the copied person, it's necessary to control the tension in the cords to really mimic the voice. We decided that the best idea would be to have men do most of the talking—especially with Umbrage.

She was posted near the table of refreshments. We went directly to her and engaged her in conversation. I said. "Well, Professor Umbrage, it's good to see you this evening. Are you enjoying the party?"

She stared at the two of us, "I can't believe that you are choosing to talk with me."

Fred said, "Oh, certainly Professor. Sometimes we crave adult conversation. You don't often get that with the likes of Potter or Ron."

She stared even more incredulously and asked suspiciously, "What do you two want?"

Fred and I looked at each other and managed to say in a pretty good imitation of the twin's unison voice, "Whatever do you mean?"

She stopped being suspicious and simply stated outright, "I know that you want something. Let's just drop the pretense and get down to cases. What is it?"

I said with the greatest candor, "How can you possibly believe that? There's nothing in the world that we want from you."

Fred agreed heartily. She began to simply wish that we were pestering someone else and began walking away. That was precisely what we wanted, so we followed her. She walked a couple more paces and asked, "Why are you following me?"

"We just like being in your company, Professor," Fred said

"Right!" She said incredulously, "Just go sell your wares somewhere else!"

"Professor!" Fred and I agreed, 'You don't mean that. We don't have anything to sell!"

I added, "Especially after Professor McGonagall confiscated our stash!"

"Did she? Well, that's certainly good! It serves you right! All those nasty potions that you two make."

"Now, you misjudge us. We only supply the market for jokes and fun-filled products. They're strictly for use by and upon the purchaser. You just need to read the fine print on the labels."

We kept walking with her and talking to her, keeping her attention away from Minerva and Sinistra who were giving away free samples of Weasley Wizard Wheezes. They were mixed in among the other refreshments on the table.

Who got affected by them was completely random. Sometimes it was a student and sometimes a teacher. At first, there were only a few people who were faint or had to run to the bathroom because of a sudden urge to evacuate their stomachs.

Meanwhile, Umbrage was beginning to be hoarse from talking with us. So, she went to the refreshment table for something to drink but didn't have any solid food. While we were there Professor Dumbledore dropped by.

"Well, Professor, and Misters Weasley, I hope you are enjoying the party. It seems like I just keep on running into you two. I could have sworn that I saw you talking to Ms. Grainger a moment ago.

Fred said, "Optical illusion."

While we were talking with Dumbledore, Umbrage took a pastille from a tray, and Fred and I crossed our fingers. But nothing happened. Just then, a third year girl fainted right in front of us. Fred caught her, and Umbrage sent us to take her to the hospital wing. When we got there, we found several students in bed and Madame Pomfrey just said, "Oh, lay her in one of those beds. I don't understand what's going on at that party, but it's lucky that no one seems to be seriously ill."

When we got back to the party, we found that another pair of Weasleys had accosted Umbrage. We overhead the end of her saying, "don't understand how you two got back so quickly."

We came into view, and she made a double take. I said, "Well, Fred, George, good to see that you make it to the party."

Umbrage took another pastille off a tray and started to bite into it. Just then another Fred and George (it must have been the real ones) entered the room. One of the other pair waved her hands at the newcomers and shouted, "Fred, George, over here. Come join us."

Just then Umbrage's eyes rolled up, and she said, "Urrppp!" and threw up right there in the Great Hall.

I said, "Why don't you take poor Professor Umbrage up to the hospital wing?"

The real Fried (I think) said, "No problem. George and I will be happy to accompany her up there. Right Georgy-Porgy?"

"Right-Oh, Fred."

They each took an arm and seemed to be doing a three-legged race out of the Great Hall. Just then, Dumbledore strolled by and with a wave of his wand made the vomit disappear. "You know, I think that it would be good for whoever is responsible for this outbreak of stomach flu to remove the evidence and make their way back to their offices."

None of us needed more in the way of hints, so we meandered off after clearing all the pastilles and fainting fancies from the table.

Back in my office, we still had not begun transforming back. Snape said that we would just have to wait for the effect to wear off— which would probably be more than an hour. One of the others suggested that we could play spin the bottle. I figured that was Sinistra. I couldn't even tell the other George from the Fred's. I suggested that we play a card game. Someone suggested Cribbage, so I got out my cribbage board, and we played a couple of games.

Finally, we started transforming, and by the end of the third game, we were all pretty much returned to our original forms. Sinistra still had some red in her hair, but we decided to change back into our normal clothes because our costumes were by now way too big. We were tripping over our robes with every step.

I could tell that Sinistra was frustrated that she hadn't been able to turn the situation to her advantage, but Minerva and I were happy. We hustled Snape and Sinistra off and we finished the evening in each other's arms.

△

The next day, at breakfast, which was very lightly attended, Dumbledore announced that there had been several unaccountable cases of twenty-hour flu, but that everyone would be well recovered before the day was over. He said that the flu accounted both for the unusual incidence of nausea and several cases of fainting.

No one saw Professor Umbrage before the next Monday in class. It was my suspicion that the Weasley twins—the real Weasley twins—had snuck some of their potions into the trays for Umbrage in the hospital wing. She was the only one who had not returned from the hospital wing by Saturday afternoon.

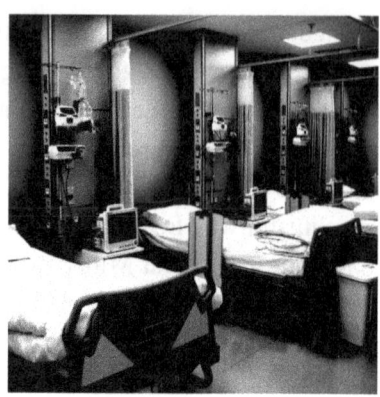

Saint Mongo's

A couple of weeks later, I was beginning to wish that the term would just come to an end. All my students had Christmas fever and some of the teachers as well. But one Friday, Minerva came to my office and asked, "You know about Mr. Weasley?"

"I know him, but I don't think I know ABOUT him. You do mean the father, right?"

She agreed that was who she meant.

"Why, has something happened to him?"

She stared at me and asked, "You've not heard that he's in Saint Mongo's?"

I admitted that I hadn't. She informed me that he'd been working late on a hush-hush project when he'd been injured and he was in St. Mongo's.

"By hush-hush, I presume you mean Order of the Phoenix."

She hushed me and nodded.

"I'm sorry to hear that. How's he doing?"

She admitted that she didn't know, but she intended to pay him a visit the next day. She wanted to know if I'd like to come along.

"Of course, he's one of my favorite wizards. We've had many a deep discussion on Muggle artifacts."

So, it was that the next day, after breakfast, I was in Minerva's office lamenting the fact that there wasn't a better way of reaching St. Mongo's than the floo system. I'd gotten to the point where I was almost comfortable with the floo system. From my perspective, it beat disapparation and traveling by broom easily. It still was a step behind hot air balloons, but at least was faster. Minerva took those comments to be facetious.

"Not at all, I'm perfectly serious. As a matter of fact, I'm considering writing a monograph on wizardly travel. I'm thinking of calling it, 'Magical Means of Motion: A Study in Nausea'. It's my objective to suggest the least uncomfortable technique of traveling between any two places."

I suppose that you think that I was joking, but I was perfectly serious. I hoped that some enterprising young wizard would invent a better means of travel, by which I mean a less painful one. I doubted that anyone would but I could always hope.

In any case, she held out her hand and I walked to her beside the fireplace, and resolutely took her hand. We walked into the fireplace, the green fire rose up around us and I spun merrily as I tried to hold down my stomach's contents. We walked into what could have passed for the Waiting Room of any Emergency Room in the States. Any Waiting Room that had a twelve-year-old with an engorged purple tongue sticking out, a centaur with an arrow stuck in its foot, and a goblin speaking gobbledygook to its neighbor.

We went to the reception desk and asked where Mr. Arthur Weasley was. She informed us that he had just been moved from the intensive care unit to a general ward on the third floor Room 332. Minerva led me to the bank of elevators. We boarded, Minerva pressed the #3 button, and we lurched up. I had begun to wonder if any conveyance built by wizards was comfortable to ride. We reached the third floor and started looking for 332.

We entered and found that although it was designed to have four occupants, Mr. Weasley was the only one occupying it. Mr. Weasley immediately greeted us, and we shook hands.

"I hope that you're feeling better, Arthur." Minerva said, as she opened her purse and drew out a large potted palm.

"Thanks, Minerva, but you didn't have to. . ."

I interjected, "Oh, yes, she did, and I wish that I could say that I'd come up with the idea. How are they treating you here?"

Weasley smiled immediately, "Oh, they're very good to me. As a matter of fact, there's a healer here who is rather taken with the idea of trying some Muggle techniques—just as a minor research project."

Minerva frowned and Weasley immediately interrupted, "Don't you give me a hard time about it. Molly is just as prejudiced as most wizards are about Muggle healing, but I think they may have some good ideas."

"Just what is your ailment?"

Weasley frowned, "Oh, I was attacked by a snake. I was bitten several places, and the wounds are not healing very well, despite all that the healers can do. So, my healer and I have the idea of trying a Muggle technique in these circumstances. They sew the wound shut."

Minerva grimaced and took me by the arm, leaned over so that she wouldn't be heard and said, "Oh, James, don't let him do this crazy scheme."

I, of course, objected, "What can I do about it?"

She frowned at me and kicked me in the shin. I just frowned and thought. "You know, Weasley, I don't have anything against Muggles." With that he gave me a conspiratorial wink. He knew that I am a Muggle, but I suppose he didn't know that Minerva knew. "Anyway, I'm not prejudiced, but my understanding of Muggle healing is that in the vast majority of cases, the patient's body has to heal itself. All the doctor, uh, Muggle healer can do, is help to keep the illness from taking too much of a toll before the body starts curing itself.

"Anyway, as I see it, Magical Maladies and cursed wounds are things that the body can't heal without serious help. Help that only magical healers can provide. So, I think that you'd really be better off if you worked in the normal magical means."

Minerva patted me on the arm in encouragement, I suppose, of my little speech. Weasley was clearly disappointed that I hadn't supported him in his desire.

I wanted to change the subject and find out more about the source of this injury. "You say that you were attacked by a snake? How did it happen?"

Weasley seemed disturbed by the idea of talking about it. "I can't really talk about it. All that I can tell you is that I was on guard duty for the Order and I was attacked by a snake."

I thought about it a minute, trying to figure a way to weasel out some more information. "I suppose that you can't tell me what you were guarding? Or where you were guarding it?"

"No. And No."

"Since we know that Riddle is a parsal-tongue, can we suppose that it was Riddle himself who sent the snake after you?"

He looked at me warily, "I don't know who sent it, but your deduction sounds reasonable to me."

I turned to Minerva, "Is there anything else that YOU can tell me?"

She shook her head, "No. I don't really know anything that Arthur doesn't,and he's told you pretty much everything that we can say."

I was beginning to be frustrated, "Well, is there any extra security here, considering that Riddle attempted to kill you, Weasley?"

"No. I think that everyone thinks that now that I'm out of the way, so to speak, there's no reason to attack me."

"I hope so. You'd think not." Minerva was kicking me in the shins. I supposed that she thought that this was too disturbing a topic to be talking over with a sick man.

She said, "Well, Arthur. I'm sure that the healers will get the bleeding under control,and you'll be back home before too long. Wendt and I have to get going." She turned to me and aimed a blistering stare at me.

"Oh, yes. We've got to go before I encourage you any more."

We left. As we walked down the hall, I heard a voice that I thought that I recognized. I stuck my head in a ward and discovered Gilderoy Lockhart. "Minerva, let's go in and say hello to Gilderoy."

I found that the former author seemed to be in good spirits, "Oh, do come in. I'm so glad to see you. I'm sure you must be fans of my books. I'm sure that you're great fans. I've probably signed books for you." He stared hard at both of us and said, "No, just give me a minute. My name is on the tip of my tongue. I almost had it yesterday."

Minerva opened her mouth to speak, and he said, "No. NO. I'll have it here in just a minute. No hints. No hints." We stayed and watched him struggle for a minute and then said, "Sorry. I almost had it there. But I'm sure, I'll remember soon. Now, which of my books did you like the best?"

Minerva was struck speechless. But Lockhart wasn't, "Oh, now, dear woman. I know that it's hard to pick but I'm sure you have one. There's no reason to be shy. Just go ahead and speak it out loud."

I decided that I'd save Minerva further embarrassment. "I personally prefer your story of ridding the Castle Hogwart of the dread Monster of Slytherin."

"Oh, of course. It's one of my personal favorites." He looked on a large bookshelf that was filled with multiple copies of his books. "I don't seem to have one in my personal collection. I suppose it's too popular to keep it in stock. But, if you bring your copy the next time you come to visit, I'll be sure to autograph it for you."

He leaned closer to us and said in a stage whisper, "I've almost got the knack of cursive writing down pat. Maybe you'll want to wait for that, but I can always do block letters if you're in a hurry."

I studied him for a minute and said, "You are an amazing case. I wouldn't believe that you could have that much memory loss and still be able to hold a conversation."

He smiled gamely, "Oh, I am always up for the round or two of verbal repartee.

"Now, what can you do for me?"

Minerva had been staring at him all through the conversation and she said, "Oh, we've already done everything for you that I think we can."

"Yes, I suppose so." Lockhart said magnanimously, "It's so hard to do things for the very privileged."

I took his hand and shook it, 'It's been a pleasure for you to meet us. Please keep up the good work, and I'm sure you'll have cursive mastered before the summer."

He beamed happily and waved as we left the ward. I turned to Minerva and said, "I suppose that we should either feel sorry for him or feel that he's got it far easier than he deserves. I suppose that he may never leave this institution. How do you feel about him?"

Minerva shook her head sadly. "I don't know. He deserves to spend a good long time in Azkaban but here he is, as happy as a lark. Still, can you even say that he's survived? He's so different from the old Lockhart."

"I don't know. In the States if someone is insane, the theory is that he should be treated and cured to return him to sanity so that he can stand trial for the crimes that he committed.

"Who knows? If his memory were restored, would the realization of what he'd done be punishment enough? Should he be tried and sent to Azkaban for stealing people's memories? That's what he's done. Is that illegal?"

Minerva's eyes dropped to her feet, trying to remember something, "I think that technically it's considered aggravated assault and battery."

$$\triangle$$

We returned to Hogwarts, and both of us felt somewhat forlorn after the visits of the day. After supper, we retreated to my office and sat before the fire with drinks, mostly musing. Minerva asked, "If your memories of me were stolen, do you think you'd fall in love with someone else?"

"I think that I'd be the saddest man in the world, and I wouldn't even know why I was sad."

She shuddered and hugged me tighter. "Don't ever forget me."

"I won't."

That evening, we both felt that we wanted to be sure that we made love at least once more before the fall of the magic of light.

$$\triangle\triangle$$

It took some time, but it was inevitable. The first sacking of a professor happened in the run-up to Christmas. It was Professor Trelawny. As a matter of fact, I was surprised that she hadn't lost her job before. She was a fish out of water—wherever she was. She taught Divination. I suppose that she had been adept at it at some time in history, but the gift must be very fickle. I don't think that I ever heard anyone give more predictions —none of which ever came true.

I'm sure that it was a case of overcompensation. She had no reliable—perhaps we should say, predictable—ability to forecast the future, and she used every opportunity to display the talent, hoping at least a few would strike home. One time at lunch, she had come over to sit beside me toward the end of the meal when people were leaving for afternoon classes. I didn't have to leave for a class. She started a conversation that would have been a normal conversation of introduction if she hadn't tried to take both sides of the conversation.

It went something like this, "Ah, Professor Trelawney, we've never really talked. I'm glad that you've dropped by."

"Oh, yes, dear boy. But then, I really don't need to get introduced to you. My 'inner eye' tells me that you come from a prominent American magical family, who have disowned you because you are a Squibb.

"I'm so sorry. But you may yet win yourself back into the good graces of your family." She seemed to swell up and stare off into the heights of the cloudless sky visible through the ceiling of the Great Hall. "Indeed, I see yourself returning in triumph to your ancestral halls."

She took my hand in both hers, exposed my palm and ran her finger down the Life Line or the Health Line or the Love Line or maybe the Help Line or something and she went on, "Yes. You will regain your reputation, but it will be at the cost of the love of your life."

At this, I started, "What do you know about the love of my life?"

"Oh, you haven't gotten together with her yet, but I have a feeling that she is someone here amongst us, perhaps this moment."

Minerva had come over to see what was happening and was standing behind Trelawney. She cleared her throat and said, "Yes. Yes. Please go on. What do you see in the sands of time for Wendt here?"

"Oh, I see a lovely, shy young woman with long lustrous hair that some have described as 'mousy' but which is a rich luxurious brown." She was looking far away but was caressing my hand, completely oblivious of my Life Line.

Minerva smiled but took care to extricate my left hand from Sybill's hands. She snuggled in between us and said, "Sybill, all this is fascinating, but Professor Wendt and I have some things to discuss."

Sybill's attention returned completely to the here and now and tried to regain my hand. Unfortunately for her, my hand was firmly in Minerva's hand. Minerva rose and said, "We, both of us, look forward to talking with you again."

When we were out of earshot Minerva commented, "She is completely clueless. I wonder if she even was aware of what she was doing . . ." She hesitated in thought and said, "But I really think that she will lose her job if she's not terribly careful.

"I don't have any great love for her, but I really don't know what would happen to her if she lost her job."

I glanced back at Trelawney, still sitting next to where I was. She was gazing off with what I have heard described as a thousand meter stare. "You know the expression—those who can't do, teach?"

"Yes. I've heard you use it before."

"Well, she is a perfect example. Do you suppose she could get a job teaching somewhere else, if she lost her job here?"

Minerva stopped walking and turned to stare directly at me, 'You mean like at Durmstrang or maybe Beau Batons?"

"Well—maybe somewhere in the States or Canada?"

She shook her head and sighed sadly, "I think that kind of second chance is one that only Professor Dumbledore would give her."

"Now, he loves magic and wants it to be taught well. Why do you suppose that he lets her keep teaching?"

Minerva laughed, "Well, the truth is that Dumbledore possibly believes in prophecy but he, like me, doesn't believe that it can be cultivated or controlled. When it happens, it happens. And that's it.

"Do you know that there is some sort of prophecy that Sybil made that is in the Hall of Prophecy at the Ministry that Dumbledore thinks is important? As a matter of . . ." She suddenly broke off and said nothing more.

I tried to urge her on, "You were going to say something about prophecy."

Minerva turned to look at me and said very definitely, "No. I wasn't. And if I ever seem to be about to say something along those lines, you're to interrupt me immediately."

I thought to myself, "Fat chance of my doing that."

In any case, I was thinking about that when a few weeks later, Minerva came to me and, gulping, asked, "Do you know what happened to Sybil?"

"Sure, she got sacked. So?"

Minerva was puzzled, "How did you find that out? I came directly from seeing it happen. You weren't there, and no one could have seen you since." She thought a minute, "Do you have the gift of prophecy?"

"No, I have the gift of Deduction. What else could excite you so much about Sybil other than her getting sacked and what was more likely to happen concerning her?"

She looked down at her feet, "I can think of one thing, but, no, you're right. She was sacked. Umbrage was in the process of ejecting her from the castle, when Dumbledore intervened. He's letting her stay on in her tower. I don't know who he'll get to replace her."

"I'm glad that she's still got a place to stay. I'll bet Umbrage took that well."

"Dumbledore is on the verge of getting sacked himself."

Christmas

As the first term ended, I had the feeling that we were standing on the edge of a cliff. Once we crossed that brink, there would be a quick descent to whatever it was that we were heading for. None the less, the Christmas season was full of joy. For me, it really began when I boarded the train from Hogwarts back to Kings Cross and platform 9 ¾. The ride was uneventful. Minerva and I took turns patrolling the cars along with Snape who hadn't taken a turn on the train in quite some time.

Everyone's spirits were too good for there to be contention. Everyone, including the Slytherins, was so happy to be away from Umbrage that there were even a few small groups of Slytherins and students from other houses talking together about what they were doing for Christmas.

I spent time in the teacher's car working on lesson plans. I wanted to be finished with my lesson plans before Christmas for the first couple of weeks of the new term.

We arrived in King's Cross and saw the kids off, checking them off our list until every one had been accounted for as having been picked up by parent or guardian. When we had them all on their way, I took Minerva in one arm and my duffel in the other and we headed for the portal to platform nine.

This was perhaps the worst transportation challenge that I faced as a Muggle in a wizarding world. I took Minerva's hand and walked forward to the solid brick wall that I knew would squash my nose if I didn't have Minerva's help. I walked forward, never sure that I wouldn't squash my nose.

As usual, I appeared on the other side of the barrier, and I automatically looked around, searching for the person who might be out of place, who was not dressed quite right for a Muggle. It's amazing how wizards study Muggles and dress 95% right but miss in what would be a minor way to anyone but a Muggle. For example, I once saw a wizard who was wearing an impeccable grey suit, a pair of black wingtip shoes, a black homburg bowler, an off-white shirt and a neon green tie with red sprinkles.

No one who seemed to meet the profile of a wizard trying to masquerade as a Muggle was apparent. Minerva actually had her wand out (surreptitiously) and was doing the same scanning. "Looks clean."

Minerva was looking away from the direction I was, "Yes. I think it's ok." We walked to a secluded spot near the Men's loo and I took her hand again. We disappeared. We reappeared outside the alley door of a small restaurant in my neighborhood. I could smell the pungent odors of the trash bin altogether too easily.

I nudged Minerva a little further away, and she said, "I don't want to be seen with you. So why don't we kiss now, and we'll be in touch later?"

"Don't want to be seen with me, eh? I don't blame you, what self-respecting witch would want to be seen with a Muggle?"

She laughed, "You know it's for your protection. Get on your way, now."

I did. I found my way to my holiday lodgings. I used my key and went to the kitchen where I picked up the notepad that's always next to the phone. I would write a little note informing my landlord that I was back, and would be around until the first Sunday in January, the fifth. It occurred to me how close it was to the BIG year.

$$\triangle$$

I went through my normal round of Christmas shopping for friends and relatives in the States. I was rich enough to splurge a little bit, but long-established habits kept me from spending a lot. I made the annual hours-long phone call to Customer Service for JCPenney in the States. I was always amazed by how late I could order and still be assured of getting presents delivered by Christmas AND gift-wrapped.

When I'd finished all that, I had a call from Minerva. Yes! She called me. She wanted to visit the Diggory's. "Wendt, it's the first

Christmas they'll have without Cedric. I think it would be nice if we paid them a visit."

I wasn't anxious to make that visit, but I agreed. She said that she'd send them an owl to make an appointment and get back to me when she had a time set up. The next day, I got another call from her. She'd arranged to have lunch with them on the Saturday before Christmas. We were going to meet at the Cauldron at noon.

She arrived at 11 AM that day, and she disapparated us directly to the street. We entered and found that the main dining hall was crowded and more people were arriving by floo by the minute. Tom had taken on some more help, and the hostess that day took our reservation. It wouldn't be available until 12:30. We stood at the bar waiting for the Diggory's to arrive.

When they did, a little after noon, the bar area had enough seats that the women could sit as Amos and I stood close enough to talk. The conversation was strained. We hadn't seen the Diggory's since the spring. Cedric had been their only child, and now that he was no longer at Hogwarts, we didn't really have a reason to see them. We started talking about all the inconsequential, meaningless things that people who haven't seen each other in months start with. There was the weather and how was business. How was Hogwarts?

That broke the logjam. There were tears and sobs and Minerva had the good sense to just let them be. They came and seemed to overwhelm both the Diggory's, and then they were gone. Minerva talked about what it was like with the new educational czar at Hogwarts.

Amos said, "I don't see that it's so bad having someone that's impartial, from the outside, representing parents' interests at the school."

Minerva looked at me to be the heavy. I sighed and started in. "Well, Hogwarts is a school with a fine headmaster. And, if I may be permitted a bit of prejudice, an Assistant Headmistress who is very nearly as good an educator as Professor Dumbledore."

I had some fear about where I was going now, but I forged ahead anyway. "If you compare it to the other main European magical schools —Durmstrang and Beau Batons, you'll see that Hogwarts is the pre-eminent magical school in Europe. That's evidenced by the fact that the only two students to even complete all the competitions of the Tri-Wizard Tournament were both Hogwarts students."

Immediately Minerva kicked my shin, and I only barely kept from shouting out my pain. Both Amos and Reina teared up again. I went on, "Nothing has changed since then."

Amos answered me, "But there is. Dumbledore says that He-Who-Must-Not-Be-Named has returned and we all know that he hasn't. The Minister of Magic says he hasn't. He can't have."

I carried on the thought, "So Dumbledore must be wrong. The harder he insists that Riddle has returned, the more that people are sure that Dumbledore has gone round the bend?"

"Well, yes. Surely, that's true."

"And therefore, there must be someone sensible to carry on?" All this time, Minerva was kicking me under the table more fiercely.

Reina nodded and said, "Isn't' that true?"

"Well, I'll tell you what I think. It's a pretty hideous idea and I wish to goodness that it weren't true, but I really think that Dumbledore is right. Minerva agrees, don't you?"

Minerva kicked me one last vicious kick and said, "Yes. It's terribly depressing. As a member of the old Order of the Phoenix, I know as well as anyone just how terrible it is to say that, but yes."

Just then, the hostess came over and seated us. We ordered. As we waited for our food to arrive, I talked about the new class of first years and how there were some very bright students among them. Minerva was happy to change the subject to that one. She talked about the good transfiguration students that she had.

Reina brought the subject back to Cedric and asked me, "Do you have any English students like Ced?"

I smiled, "No. There really isn't anyone who is even remotely in the same class with him. I wish there were. It was a real joy teaching in the classes he was in. I was looking forward to dropping in on Cambridge every once in a while to see how he was doing."

Amos nodded vigorously, "He was one in a million, wasn't he? I only wish that I'd gone to more of his chess tournaments." He fell silent for a minute and then said, "You know there are still days that I wake up in the morning and just expect to find him at the breakfast table when I come down." He only barely finished the sentence before he had to stifle a sob.

We all nodded our agreement. Our orders had arrived by then and we could remain blessedly silent while we ate. It was a meal that we ate slowly, and we decided to share a desert. As we waited for it, we talked again. We talked about Christmas, and Minerva talked about what we usually do for Christmas.

Reina asked MInerva and me about our relationship. "You two seem to spend a lot of time together and seem very comfortable together. Do you mind if I ask why you haven't gotten married?"

We looked at each other. Then Minerva said to me, "Go ahead."

I looked around and saw that the room was emptying finally. I looked back to Amos and Reina, "I have a theory."

Reina laughed and Amos exclaimed, "You have a theory! What do you mean, you have a theory? How can you not know?"

I went on, "Well, it's not so easy as you might think. I've brought the subject up a number of times and, well, the lady seems less than anxious.

"Anyway, my theory is that. . ."

Minerva kicked me under the table. I'd been getting a lot of that lately. I tried to proceed, "Well, I'll just say that these are troubled times, and maybe it doesn't seem like such a great time to make commitments, right now."

The desert, a creme brulee, had arrived and we split it up among us. After that was over, Reina asked Minerva, "You mean to say that he's asked you to marry him, and you're not satisfied?"

Minerva harrumphed and said, "Well, you can't take anything HE says at face value. He's always joking and doing crazy things."

I turned to Reina and said, "Well, I suppose the engagement ring that I offered her was a crazy thing"

Minerva said to Reina, "You see what I mean. You can't trust a man that makes crazy gestures like that!"

Reina looked at me and asked, "You did a crazy thing like offering her a ring?"

I looked sheepish and said, "Well, I know that it's pretty unconventional and all, but it was a gesture made with the best intentions."

Reina turned to Minerva again and asked, "That's what you call crazy?"

"Well, you had to be there to understand."

Reina looked from one to the other of us, shaking her head, "You two are the craziest couple I've ever known." To Minerva she added,

"Why you aren't interested in an eager suitor like Wendt, I will never understand."

We finished the lunch and argued about who would pick up the check. I claimed that my recent business successes made me the perfect candidate, and with Minerva's support I carried the day.

After we left the Cauldron, Minerva suggested on a whim that we go visit the Weasleys. I didn't have a problem with that, so she disapparated us there. We arrived and found that we had probably passed Bill Weasley who had taken the younger Weasleys to Diagon Alley for last minute Christmas shopping. Only Mr. and Mrs. Weasley were there. That turned out to be just fine because it was really them and especially Mr. Weasley that Minerva and I wanted to see.

When I saw him, I was shocked. He looked better than he had in the hospital, but he still had bruising and a wound that still looked like it might be seeping blood. Mrs. Weasley made us some tea and brought out some biscuits as well.

I asked Arthur how he was getting on. "Oh, I'm better than I look. They stopped the bleeding, and I just have to take it easy. I think I'll be able to go back to work after the New Year comes."

Mrs. Weasley insisted that it wouldn't be soon after New Year's day, but Arthur tut-tutted and insisted that he was feeling better every day. I asked if they had special plans for Christmas. Mrs. Weasley spoke about having a few friends over on Christmas Eve and listening on the radio to the annual Celestine Warbeck concert. She was talking to us and looking at us, but I could see Arthur wince. I thought that didn't have anything to do with any physical pains.

Mrs. Weasley cited her favorite Warbeck song—"A Cauldron of Strong Hot Love." She nudged Minerva as she praised the song. "That was our favorite when we were dating, you know?"

I admitted that I didn't know it.

"Oh, you should listen to it. It's really good. I'll go get the phonograph out."

Mr. Weasley objected, 'Now, Molly, they don't want to put you to that trouble."

Being somewhat averse to being kicked in the shins again, I didn't say anything. Molly replied, "Oh, it's no trouble at all. I'll be back in a minute."

Mr. Weasley just grinned and mouthed silently, "Sorry." In a moment, Molly was back with gramophone in magical tow. She cranked the crank, placed the vinyl record on the turntable, moved the pickup over the record, and lowered it gently to the vinyl surface.

A slightly scratchy voice emerged from the trumpet, singing the song that we'd been talking about. It was a sappy, sloppy love song. Minerva and I listened respectfully—for what else could we do? When it was endured, Molly looked expectantly from one to the other of us, hoping for some sort of validation of it as one of the best songs ever written. Minerva looked at me, as one who can shovel shit with the best of them when the occasion requires it.

So, I got warmed up. "Well, Molly, you have to understand that I reputedly have a tin ear and. . ." Minerva knew me well enough to know the general direction that I was headed and what was needed to keep the wheels from coming off. So she did her part by nodding vigorously and added, "Absolutely Tin!"

I continued, "And most people just tolerate the music that I like. But having said that, I have to admit that I've never heard a song that I thought was a better example of the sort of song that it is. If you're looking for a love song dripping with plenty of feeling, you can't beat it."

She looked at me and seemed to be unsure just what sort of praise it was. However, she was fairly sure that it was what was called for. Having decided that, she offered us some more biscuits and asked if we would like to spend Christmas Eve with her family. "We always have a lot of old friends over for Christmas Eve. We listen to Celestine, play games, and have desserts and have a generally good time. What do you think?"

Minerva nodded and said, "Well, if you're looking for 'old' friends, you needn't go further than me."

Molly was overjoyed, "Great. We normally get together for supper and have a pot luck . . "

Minerva hadn't stopped speaking, though. "But my sister and I and now Wendt, here, have a tradition of our own for Christmas Eve. We get together, sometimes with another relative or two, for something a good bit like what you do, but at my sister's house."

Molly thought that over for a moment and pressed her point, "Well, we could make room for your sister and maybe another one or two. We'd really like to have you, right, Arthur?"

Arthur nodded and Molly went on, "See. He'd love to have you over."

While Molly's head was turned away, he mouthed silently, "No. No."

Minerva apologized and explained that we loved being with her sister and didn't want to disappoint her. "But, I do appreciate the offer, and we would like to get together some other time with you."

Molly said that she understood and then had another idea. "You know our Bill has been seeing that Fleur Delacour." She said the name with an obvious distaste—sort of like medicine that it was necessary to take, but which she disliked. "Anyway, he's been wanting to invite her parents over for a visit for some time. You both already know her. That would be an excellent opportunity for us all to get together."

I said, "That sounds like a really good time. Fleur seemed like a very nice young lady when we met last year." Minerva kicked me in the shin. Molly didn't seem very pleased with the comment, but Mr. Weasley gave me an encouraging smile.

We talked about our plans for the rest of the Christmas Holiday and travel plans and so on. As we got ready to leave, Molly went off to get some home-made pralines for us and Mr. Weasley leaned toward us and whispered, "Good show, not being able to come for Christmas Eve. It's deadly dull listening to Celestine all night." Then he quickly leaned back as Molly re-entered the room with a tin of candy.

We all got up and Molly said that she was sorry that the kids weren't there for our visit. I commented, 'Well, really, since they're all students at Hogwarts, they probably would be just as happy to have missed us and reminders of what we'll all be soon returning to."

We donned our coats and walked off into the light snow that was falling.

Christmas Eve arrived, and we were NOT listening to Celestine Warbeck. Instead, we were sitting around the dinner table talking about Christmases past. The sisters talked about how their family would take the floo network to a beautiful Christmas village. There was a family who moved their toy store into the far north of Scotland. They picked a spot where there was almost always snow on the ground in November and December. They decorated one of the buildings as a workshop with tools bought from sales of woodworking businesses. They would buy old nearly worn-out tools and put them in the "Elves Workshop". They "borrowed" a few house elves from friends to "man", or is it "elf", the workshop. Then there was "Santa's Barn". That was where the reindeer were stabled. That was hard to manage, but they'd bought enough land to support a small herd of reindeer. Finally, there was "Santa's Gifte Shoppe". There the staff sold toys of all sorts for all ages from babies to retired grandparents. Of course, babies don't want anything more than a piece of clean cardboard for a toy—like the box the toy came in, but that doesn't deter parents from buying them the toy as well. There was even a special room with inexpensive gifts designed for parents so that kids could go in with a few galleons and buy presents for their parents and family.

Margaret had started the discussion with one of those reminiscences about the time that they'd gone to the "North Pole" with parents when they were nine and seven years old. "Do you remember the time that you wanted to ride the reindeers, and you levitated yourself over the fence outside Santa's Barn and onto the back of a reindeer?"

Minerva frowned, "I remember that you ran and told Mum about it, and I got a spanking when we got home."

Margaret laughed, "Yes. Weren't those wonderful times! I'm afraid I was an awful sister. You had such pretty long brown hair. I remember the year that Mum made me cut my hair short because that was THE style in Witch Weekly for young ladies. You were too young for those sophisticated styles, but I wasn't."

Minerva laughed, "Yes. Daddy insisted that we not cut my hair from the day that I was born. He had Mum cut your hair when you were only two years old, and he said he wasn't going to let that happen again."

"So, your hair was always longer than mine. You had these braids that went down your back to somewhere on your legs. I was so jealous! Then when Mum made me cut my hair when I was nine, I was so mad at you that I did all sorts of things to get you in trouble that year."

"Yes, Maggie, I was kind of jealous of you. You got to do all the new hair-do's, but I always had to just let my hair grow. And you were always pulling my braids. Remember that time that you levitated that bottle of ink over my head and dropped on my head while I was brushing my hai?. It took a week to get all the ink out—even with the scourgify spell that Daddy used. That hurt."

I watched and listened to this discussion with amazement. I'd grown up in an all-boy family, so I never had any insight into the workings of families with daughters. They finally got back to the topic that had started the discussion.

Minerva went on, "What's the earliest that you remember going to the North Pole?"

Maggie thought for a while and said, "I think I was four years old. The only thing I remember was Daddy holding you in his arms while Mum and I walked into the floo and we came out at the North Pole. I was so jealous that you got to ride in Daddy's arms. Daddy made a big deal about the trip for days and days before. He told us about Santa Claus and the North Pole where house elves made gifts for good little girls."

I asked, "He didn't say anything about good little boys?"

Minerva said, "I think that Daddy thought there wasn't such a thing as a good little boy—at least none who were good enough for his girls. He used to tell us that boys got coal in their stockings."

Maggie smiled, "For the longest time, I thought that all the boys at school were lying when they claimed that they got real presents for Christmas. Of course, that was at Muggle schools where almost all the boys and girls were Muggles, and we didn't believe anything that they said anyway."

Maggie got back to the first visit to the North Pole. "Well, I was excited about going to the North Pole and, really, a little scared too. I'd never seen a house elf, and I imagined that they were some sort of huge monster, like trolls. So, I actually didn't want to go when the day came. I tried to get Mum to not take me—just you.

"But she told me that I'd like it and talked about all the wonderful things we'd see and do. I still didn't want to go, but Mum made me."

"Is that why you told me all those awful stories about the North Pole?"

Maggie just shrugged her shoulders and went on, "But you know, after the first time both of us loved going to the North Pole. And the thing that I think I loved the most about it was that it was always the same. It was like time stopped at the North Pole. The house elves never changed, the reindeer never changed. The toy shop and the workshop were always the same. It was one thing that you could always depend on."

They both sighed in that joint realization. Minerva said, "Yes. When I was eleven years old, I began to realize that the 'North Pole' wasn't really the North Pole, the elves were just ordinary house elves, and Santa Claus on whose knees we got to sit and tell our secret desires for Christmas to was just Carl Clausewitz who ran the toy store in Diagon Alley. I tried to recreate the magical wonder of the trip to the North Pole. But I never could."

"Yes, but it was always a fun trip. I guess that I have you to thank that we still got to go the North Pole when I was fourteen. Otherwise, Mum and Daddy would have stopped going when I was thirteen."

"Yes, like they stopped when I was just a second year at Hogwarts. But while we were still going, that was Christmas to me. I felt such a loss the first year we didn't go just like Christmas didn't happen that year."

Maggie nodded agreement and then said, "Do you remember the year that you ran into the kitchen at the restaurant that they had? I laughed my head off. Mum was so embarrassed. She made Daddy run after you. I don't know what you two were doing in there, but it seemed like it took forever for him to catch you and bring you back."

"I don't remember that at all. I wish I did. I'd like to know what I did too. But I do remember that I always wanted to watch the elves making toys—but, of course, they never did. They were just as much props as all the old woodworking tools were."

Maggie turned to me and asked, "What were the traditions of your family at Christmas."

I had to admit that we didn't have much in the way of traditions. "Well, I guess the big tradition was about the Christmas tree."

Maggie asked, "What happened, did it just appear by magic in the parlor?"

"Well, I guess that you'd say that. The real story that our parents told us was that Santa Claus not only brought all the presents, but also brought the Christmas tree and the decorations, set up the Christmas tree, and decorated it overnight."

Minerva laughed, "He was one busy old elf."

"Oh, yes. But, you know, if you're delivering presents to hundreds of millions of kids in one night, what is delivering trees and decorating them to boot?"

Maggie said, "Then, you didn't have a Christmas tree until Christmas Day, itself?"

"That's right."

She looked a little sad, "You lost all those days of having the Christmas tree up before Christmas. That must have been awful."

"Well, we didn't realize how we were deprived until we got older. But, we did get to have our Christmas tree up later than anyone else after Christmas. We kept it up all through the twelve days of Christmas and sometimes a little later, depending on how the tree held up."

Maggie was puzzled, "But didn't your parents use a preserving spell to keep it fresh?"

I've found that when someone presents you with an inconvenient fact for your story that the best thing to do is to admit ignorance and move on, "That's a good question. I don't know. I wonder what the deal was.

"But we enjoyed Christmas tremendously anyway. I don't ever remember visiting Santa Claus, except maybe once."

We spent almost the entire evening talking about Christmases past, both ancient and recent. We had some wassail spiced with brandy. It was a very pleasant way to spend Christmas Eve. Another tradition that the sisters had from their youth was reading A Christmas Carol on the last couple of nights before Christmas. We didn't have time to do that, but I talked them into starting it. When we wanted to, we could stop reading. We took turns and all took a shot of wassail when the next reader started. That was an interesting formula. Since readership changed whenever the current reader said so, it could have turned into quite a drinking tournament. Who would be the last man (so to speak) reading?

We each read for a half-hour apiece. After her turn, which was the last of the first round, Maggie drank down the shot glass and commented, "I really did a good job making this wassail. I think we ought to change to reading a page at a time. It's a shame to wait so long to get a taste of it." Maggie suggested one page per round. After a couple of rounds that way, Minerva stopped at the end of a paragraph and, without comment, we read a paragraph each per round.

After a couple of rounds that way, Maggie unceremoniously dropped her head on her chest and passed out. At that point, I asked, "Have you ever heard of shtrip poker?"

Minerva stared at me, having some difficulty focusing on my face and slurred, "It's shome short of game?"

"Yessh. Let's add that in. After each round, yuooo. . . UH. . . . have your shot and take off a piece of clothesh."

"Whee! Soundsss like too much funk! Er Fun!"

So we started doing that. Somehow we migrated to our room to finish A Christmas Carol. Just before we passed out, we were reading the same paragraph over and over again and the last piece of clothing that I remember being removed was Minerva's bra. I helped her with that because she was having such an awful time managing the clasps. I think that I actually succeeded in removing the bra. The last memory I have was her toppling over onto me with my face buried in her breasts.

She woke up first and her breasts scraping across my face woke me up. Her hair had somehow partially come down and was splayed across my face. My head throbbed like my jaw had when my wisdom teeth had been extracted. I said, "How can my head hurt so much."

Minerva started to laugh and then said something like "Oh, my. . ." She got up and half-staggered half-ran out the bedroom door and a moment later I heard the toilet flush. When she staggered back in, she said, "I'm glad that's off my stomach." My head was swimming too much for me to lift my head off the bed. We spent the rest of the morning sprawled on the bed wishing the world would come to an end, but it didn't.

The evening had been so blasted that Maggie couldn't remember how the night had ended. No matt, she declared it was a great Christmas Eve despite her off again/on again unhappiness about Minerva and I sharing a bed in her house (or anywhere).

The rest of the week between Christmas and New Year's Eve was pleasant. We went to a concert in London, featuring the Fort Worth Symphony orchestra, which was on tour with their new music director.

We got the tickets at the last minute. As a matter of fact, we walked up on the evening of the concert and got tickets in the second Balcony. It was a very good concert, consisting of some standard favorites that would please any crowd—except the most discriminating. The main work on the concert was Dvorak's New World Symphony. Minerva and I treated Maggie to her ticket and she admitted that it was a good concert —especially since she didn't have to buy the ticket.

As usual, New Year's Eve was spent with the three of us and Beryl. She made a show of examining Minerva's ring finger for an engagement ring. But Minerva had a good come back. "Well, Beryl, if you are so enchanted with Wendt, why don't you marry him yourself/"

I stuck my foot into it by saying, "Maybe Minerva would be your bridesmaid." We were sitting around the card-table that I'd set up to play our annual Back-Alley Bridge Tournament, so Minerva had free reign to make my shin suffer, and she did.

We drew cards at random for partners. We used the "means and extremes" technique to decide. That technique pairs the two players with the highest and lowest ranking cards and pairs the middle two ranking cards. This joined Beryl and me. Maggie commented that we getting married seemed to be "in the cards."

Minerva snickered, "In my experience, there's nothing more likely to break up a relationship than being partners at cards."

This brought up a discussion of being bridesmaid. They did a poll and couldn't decide whether Beryl or Maggie had been a bridesmaid more often. On the one hand, Beryl had been a bridesmaid three times while Maggie had been a bridesmaid four times.

But Beryl pointed out, "But Maggie, I was a bridesmaid for three different brides, while you were only a bridesmaid for two different brides."

I asked how that could be.

Maggie replied, "Well, I was bridesmaid for two classmates, a couple of years after they graduated from Hogwarts. Then after a few years, each of them got divorced and later got re-married. When they got re-married, they had me as bridesmaid again."

I said, "Really? In the first place, that seems like it might be bad karma."

"Bad what?"

Minerva explained, "You know, Karma, luck."

I went on, "And, I thought that second marriages were usually quiet affairs, maybe just a few family as guests?"

Beryl said, "Oh, that happens, sure. But lots of second and third marriages are big affairs too. I remember in my time a witch who on her third marriage hired the Atrium of the Ministry of Magic. She had the water turned to rose color, the color theme of the wedding. Bad idea. She had a dozen bridesmaids." Her eyes took on a faraway look and then she added, "Now that was bad karma. She was divorced again within a year."

Then Beryl turned to Minerva, "Were you ever a bridesmaid?"

Minerva's eyes dropped and Maggie said, "That was interesting. You were a bridesmaid for the woman who was your bridesmaid—right?"

Minerva muttered something like "Right." Then she took a deep breath and looked up, "Yes, my best friend from Hogwarts and I got married within a year of each other. We were bridesmaids for each other." Her throat seemed to be filled with emotion for a minute and went on, "Both of us lost our husbands in the war against Riddle, the first time around."

We had been playing as we talked and the play of the next several hands proceeded in silence. Then Beryl and I didn't make our bid on a big hand. The general release of tension when Beryl used a few choice expletives opened the dam on conversation again.

The rest of the evening was pleasant with no other painful remembrances. When we went to bed that morning, a little after midnight, Minerva wasn't interested in making love. She just asked me to hold her. I could feel her sobs gently convulsing her body. We slept in the next morning and took it easy for that day. I spent the next day with Minerva at Maggie's place and then returned to my flat to put things together for the return to Hogwarts.

Second Term

On our return from the Christmas Holiday, there were a few changes, including one in staff. The new professor of Divination was a Centaur, Forensee. He rarely was present for meals in the Great Hall, but the first day back, he was introduced at the beginning of term dinner.

I made a point of coming to his classroom to visit him after he'd had a week to settle in. He seemed a bit surprised that someone would come to greet him. "Profesoor Whhhennnt, is it?"

"Not quite. The name is pronounced a good bit quicker. It's simply Wendt. There's a little sound of the 'D' near the end. Welcome to Hogwarts. I wish you well. You're aware, of course, that your predecessor was fired. It was probably the first time that has happened this century, at least."

He looked at me for a long time before saying, "If I were prophesying, I'd say that you might be not that long off, yourself."

"Oh, I could make that prophecy myself. A Squibb, teaching English Literature at a school of Magic is here only at the sufferance of the headmaster, who, fortunately, is well-disposed toward me."

He shook his head convulsively, "You may make your jokes, but I would be careful if I were you."

"Oh, I agree. But, I keep my head low and stay away from politics and I've done OK so far.

"So, are you more on the theoretical side of Divination or a practitioner?"

He looked at me carefully. "If you're asking me if I have any more prophecies, it's hard to look up to the heavens and not have prophesies about young Mr. Potter."

"Really? Would you be willing to share?"

"It's been obvious for decades that the stars of the Dark Lord are opposed to the star of Mr. Potter and that they cannot co-exist for long."

"Would you care to give a number to how long there will be before one of them ends." I paused and added, "And which one it is who will survive?"

Forensee shook his head sadly, "It is always, 'when, when, when?' with you doubters."

I'd been bating him a little, and I decided to turn completely serious. "Well, I am a doubter, but, really, what good is prophecy, even if it is right, if it never provides a reasonable but flexible timeline? I could have told you years ago that the two of them weren't going to last forever."

Forensee relaxed a little and said, "That is the first sensible question that I've heard since I became a Professor here. The answer is, 'Isn't it valuable to know what will happen, even if you don't know about the timing?'"

I said, "Do you know who's going to win?" I was absolutely serious. If he provided an answer to that, I'd take it as gospel.

Forensee looked at me directly and said, "I don't know. And most centaurs don't care. We are suppressed and attacked by all wizards, regardless if they are followers of The Dark Lord or followers of the Minister of Magic."

I was so tempted to reply that there were other wizards besides the followers of those two. I bit my lip and Forensee noticed.

"Do you want to refute that truth?"

"No. I couldn't prove anything. I just wish that you would look at who Riddle is and who he has around him."

"Oh, you're preaching to the choir, Mr. Whendt. I agree with you."

I finished by saying, "I'm glad to hear that. Good luck this term. I have no idea how the students will take to a centaur teacher, but I wish you the best with your classes."

"Thank you, Professor Whendt." He succeeded in shortening his pronunciation of my name and added the "D" but he couldn't quite make the "W" sound without the "H".

January was a month of tension. The school seemed to be broken into two factions. For an outsider, as I was, when the most "wizardly" issues came up, I had a hard time understanding what was happening.

Apparently, there was a faction led by Potter who were opposed to Umbrage. She in turn had her supporters, who seemed to be mostly Slytherins. That had been going on for a couple of months, but there was a fever pitch to it now. Umbrage had deputized a group of students as a sort of band of professional snitches (pardon the pun). As well, there was a shadowy organization that was led by Potter. They called themselves the DA. I didn't even know what the letters stood for. I would occasionally overhear a comment or two at the end of a class about a meeting.

Then one day, I was teaching my 6th year class and was facing away from them, writing on the board when I noticed in the reflective surface of my framed photo of Professor Dumbledore, a student holding something in his hand that was not a quill. "Mr. Hilbert, don't put away whatever you've got in your hand and come up here immediately."

He reluctantly got up and came to the front of the class. I held out my hand and he delivered a galleon into it. But it was the most unusual galleon that I'd ever seen. It had faintly glowing letters that said "7 ROR". I told Hilbert to stay after class.

After the classroom had cleared except for us, I asked him, "What does '7ROR' mean?"

He looked at me apologetically and said, "Sorry, sir. I can't tell you."

I had to decide whether to threaten him with detention or not. There wasn't anything wrong with having a galleon. And, I couldn't accuse him of wrongdoing based on having enchanted glowing letters that faded away on the galleon. So, I gave him a stiff warning, "Hilbert, I don't see that there's anything wrong that you've done, but I warn you. If I ever find out that '7ROR' has anything malicious about it, I assure you that you'll be explaining it to Dumbledore AND will be serving the most deviously devised detention that I can determine.

"Now, last chance. Is there anything you want to tell me?"

He shook his head, "no."

"All right, you can go." He turned and I added, "Oh, one last thing, the last essay was really an improvement. Keep up the good work."

He turned his head and said, "Thank you, sir."

After dinner, I intercepted Minerva and told her about the incident and asked her what she could make of it.

"Well, amazing. I've heard rumors of that sort of thing. Fascinating."

"Yes, but what was it?"

"Oh, it's a messaging device. It's magically linked to some number of other similar coins. Whenever one of the possessors wants to send a message to all the others, she simply writes on her coin with her wand. It shows up on all the others."

"But what does it mean?"

She thought a moment and nodded her head vigorously, shaking her bun which had loosened through the day, "Yes. I think that if the message were written in full, it would read something like, 'DA meeting tonight at 7 PM in the ROR.'"

"That's not exactly in full. What's the DA?"

She laughed, "I'm almost certain that means Dumbledore's Army. As far as I can tell, it's an organization that Potter formed to teach Defense Against the Dark Arts."

"I knew that Umbrage's idea of teaching that class was pretty loony, but do you mean to say that Potter's taken it in his own hands to teach a creditable course."

"That seems to be the case."

"Then what about ROR?"

"Oh, that's the Room of Requirement."

I felt like I was just going deeper and deeper into the rabbit hole. "OOOOh.K."

Minerva answered my implied question, "What's the ROR? I'll start by telling you what we don't know about it and then add what we do know.

"First, we don't know who made it. Was it in the original construction by the four founders? We don't know. Was it made later? Don't know.

"Next, we don't really know what its intention is."

I interrupted, "You talk about it as though it had a will of its own."

"That's another thing we don't know about it. However, we do know some things that you can do with it, but we've no idea why it exists."

"So, now, what we do know? The first I heard of it was from Professor Dumbledore. The way he tells it, he discovered it one night during the original reign of terror of Slytherin's monster. He was patrolling somewhere on the third floor and needed a bathroom. He turned a corner and saw a door at the end of the corridor that he didn't recognize. He opened it on the off chance that it might be a bathroom that he didn't know about.

"What he found was a room full of chamber pots."

I couldn't help laughing and interrupted. "A little behind the times wasn't it?"

Minerva was not amused but went on, "So, he relieved himself, resumed his patrol and has never seen the room since.

"That name for the room, which seems to me to be as good as any that I've heard, came from the house elves. They call it the Room of Requirement because if you're on the third floor and have a need for something specific, the door appears and you find within the room what you require. The key is that you have to have a real requirement that can be satisfied by a room with the proper equipment. I think that Dumbledore never found it again because he didn't have any particular need of that sort when he was looking again.

A thought occurred to me, "That may explain why Umbrage can't find where the DA is practicing. She would actually have to have a need to practice defense against the dark arts for the room to become apparent to her.

Minerva agreed and I went on, "She'd almost actually have to get a member of the DA to show it to her." That sparked another idea. "You know, it's ironic. Umbrage is here because she's afraid that Dumbledore is plotting a coup against Fudge and the very attempt to prevent that from happening has actually caused it.

"I suppose, in a way, it's lucky in the long run for the fight against Riddle. If Umbrage hadn't come and we'd had an ordinary DADA professor, we'd not have Potter putting together an army of sorts to resist Riddle. The Order ought to thank Umbrage or make her an honorary member or something."

Minerva agreed, "Talk about 'heaping burning coals.'" and then added, "You know, I wonder if maybe the house elves didn't invent the Room of Requirement. After all, they have the name for it. They apparently use it more than anyone else, maybe except Potter."

I took up the idea. "Yeh. They maybe originally created it as a way to escape from oppressive masters for a few hours. Which makes me wonder. If I needed a place for a couple of people to have complete privacy for a couple of hours, could I use it?"

"I think I know what you're driving at. In the first place, you may have to be a wizard for it to work. Besides that you actually have to be up there on the third floor when the need strikes. WE already have a good place to have as much privacy as we need."

"But you never know who might just force her way in at an inconvenient moment."

"Oh, when I'm in your office, I make sure that the door is locked so that no one like Sinistra can get in 'by mistake'."

"Well, then. Back to my original question. I don't suppose that I really need to discipline my student for having that coin."

"I wouldn't."

"Oh, yes. Have you ever been in the ROR?"

"No."

"I wonder what would happen if two people tried to use the ROR at the same time."

Minerva considered that. "Well, there are two possibilities, I think. One is that the first one there got priority. The other would have to wait until the first was done. The other is that they would both get to use the room at the same time for different purposes."

"Would they see each other?"

"I'd guess—and it would be pure guess—that they wouldn't."

After that I spent a little time every week up on the third floor seeing if I could conjure up a need that would trigger the door. I never had a success.

In the mean time, I had a visit from Snape one afternoon. He appeared at my office, took the red leather chair and asked his question, "Ms. Umbrage has made a very unusual request of me."

"Why am I not surprised? What is it?"

He leaned over toward me, as though even saying the words out loud would be in some way a betrayal of somebody's trust. "She wants Veritas serum."

I was genuinely surprised, "I suppose she wants to interrogate someone."

Snape leaned back and flipped his head in disgust, "Someone! She wants enough to interrogate an army."

That was scary. "Do you think that she wants to use it on students?"

He sneered, "I'm sure she does."

"Have you talked with Dumbledore yet?"

"No. I'd rather not involve him in this. It's clear that In the long run, he couldn't keep her from forcing me to provide it. All that would happen is either: 1.) He'd have a confrontation with her that he'd ultimately lose or 2.) He'd decide not to oppose her and then he'd have it on his conscience that he'd permitted it to happen."

I reflected. "OK. I know that you've threatened to use Veritas on Potter, but isn't it true that using Veritas on a minor would amount to child abuse?"

Snape nodded.

"Then, can't you threaten to report her to the Minister or—no, get this. Even better, threaten to report her to the aurors!"

Snape shook his head, "You are naive. Do you really think that a political appointee like the head of the aurors would risk his job to oppose the Minister when the public opinion is running so much in his favor?"

I slumped back in my chair, "Well, then. I guess you've only got two options.

"First, you could resign on principle and make a big deal of it in the press.

"Or second, you could just go along with it.

"But if that's true, why did you come here and tell me about it?"

Snape smiled a wicked little smile. I answered my own question, "Oh, I get it. You're looking for cover and if I don't turn you in, you've got me as an ally when we're both brought up on charges of child abuse. Misery loves company, eh?"

Snape's smile never wavered, "Something like that."

"Well, at least, maybe you could string her along. Take your time brewing it. Send off for fresh ingredients to brew it from. Only brew small batches each time. Maybe even flub the first and blame the fact that you've not brewed it in a long while. Anything to slow the process down."

"You're right. Those are all good ideas, and you even had one or two that I'd not thought of. But, we can't prevent her getting it forever, and if I slow things down too much, she'll just go to a separate source AND probably sack me to boot."

"I think that's it. I'm sorry that I can't do something more to slow you down."

"You've done enough. Now, aren't you going to offer something to drink?"

"You're right. I haven't, and I should. This needs something to wash it down with. I think you know what I've got. What will you have?"

We agreed on some of my fine whiskey, and we shared a drink. Then, Snape used a spell to remove the odor from our breaths. Quite handy. It's something I wished that I could do.

The poisoning of students proceeded after a couple of weeks of Snape's delays, and I even felt the effect in my classroom on rare occasions. During one class session of third years, a girl had wandered in late and didn't have her assignment. I asked her where it was.

Her answer was, "I was lazy last night and gossiped with the other girls in Ravenclaw all night and didn't get around to doing it." Her eyes had a sort of faraway look, and she didn't blink. I asked her to come up to my desk.

I whispered to her, "Were you just in Professor Umbrage's office?"

"Yes."

"Did she give you a cup of tea or a glass of water?"

"Yes."

"OK. Here's what I want you to do. Go back to the back seats in the classroom. Just sit and listen. Don't volunteer and then after class, come up here and we'll see how you're feeling. Can you do that?"

"Yes, professor."

"OK. Go do it, and we'll talk after class."

She went back to the back of the class and just sat. She didn't even get out a quill and parchment to take notes. I wished that I'd told her that she'd remember everything that went on in class perfectly clearly.

After class, when she came up, she seemed more alert. She asked, "Professor, are you going to give me detention for not having my assignment done."

"No, Rachelle, I'm not. Please complete your assignments tonight and have them both ready next week."

She goggled, "Really? You're always so strict?"

"I think you're not feeling yourself today. I'll give you a pass on this one, but be sure it never happens again."

"No, sir." She said animatedly, "I'll turn in both the assignments tomorrow at your office. Thank you!"

I couldn't be sure that Umbrage had actually used Veritas serum, but I wanted to see if it was happening to other students, so I invited Minerva to my office. She showed up after dinner. I asked her if she'd had any students who had been behaving oddly lately.

She crossed her arms over her chest and harrumphed, "How many examples do you want? At least a third of my students act oddly all the time. Take the Weasleys—all of them, even that Ginny—please!"

I could see that I needed to be more specific. "OK. The reason that I asked was that a student showed up in my classroom today, seeming dazed and lethargic." I held up my hand. "Don't tell me about all the students that stay up late."

"I'm talking about being so dazed that she was perfectly honest when I asked her about the homework that she'd missed. She said that she'd stayed up late gossiping with friends. No one admits to that."

She leaned forward and spoke in a conspiratorial tone, "Yes. I know. I've had a student or two who was like that the last couple of days. I asked one of them if he'd taken any Weasley concoction, and he denied it. When I asked about what he'd been doing the last couple of hours, he said that he'd just been summoned to Umbrage's office, and they talked about the DA. He said he didn't know anything about it." She leaned a little closer and said, "I think Umbrage gave him some Veritas serum or some similar potion."

"I'm sure you're right. This is the worst kind of child abuse—drugging students. What are we going to do?"

Minerva leaned back. "I've tried going against Umbrage before when she was torturing Harry—literally torturing him—it did no good. You've always got an idea. What do you think?"

I sniffed, "I'll tell you. I just wish I had the nerve to kneecap her. But I suppose a healer would just use skelegrow or something to repair her."

Minerva brightened a little, "Kneecap her? What does that mean? I hope it's something painful."

"Oh, yes. It's painful. You shoot the kneecap off. Not only is it very painful, but Muggle doctors frequently can't repair that sort of damage well enough for the victim to walk again."

"I have to admit that you Muggles do have your occasional good idea. But what is it with you and your Glock? Does everything have a bullet as its fix?"

I laughed, "I guess I'm like the man who only owns a hammer. After a while everything begins to look like a nail."

I tried another tack, "Is there a potion that can counteract Veritas serum?"

"Oh, yes. I don't know how to make it. Maybe Snape does. I wonder if Snape is the one she's getting the serum from. But you can't just send students around with vials of anti-Veritas serum. Umbrage would find out pretty quickly and, anyway, it would be like fighting Salamanders with Fire Demons." She finished the sentence as though the case were closed. I didn't know what either Salamanders or Fire Demons were and thought I'd just as soon leave it that way.

It was so thoroughly closed that she got up and walked over to the sofa, sat down and patted the cushion beside her. I didn't need more invitation than that.

ESL

About this same time, I had a visit from Haggrid. He seemed to be recovering from being in a car crash. The knock on the door of my office was comparable to the sledgehammer of John Henry, but I invited the knocker in anyway.

"Good to see you Haggrid. It looks like you had a bad fall. How are you feeling?"

"Oh, I'm fine. I just walked into a door as someone was opening it." He wouldn't look me in the eye as he said that. I thought that the door would have looked a whole lot worse than his eye if that had happened.

"Well, what can I do for you? And please sit down."

He sat on the sofa rather than the red leather chair. I thanked God silently for that. I pulled one of the yellow chairs close to the sofa and sat near him.

"Well, professor, you teach English, right?"

"Umbrage might disagree with that, but, yes, I do teach English." I quickly corrected that to, "English Literature."

"Yeh." He paused, and I urged him on. "Well, see, the thing is that I've got a relative who wants to learn English."

I was intrigued. Haggrid never talked about his family, and this seemed like a rare chance to find something out about them. "Really. How's he doing?"

"Well, I've been trying to help him a little. But, it's going slow." He paused again—this time longer than before. "See, I was wondering if maybe you could help him?"

I thought about that for a minute. With Haggrid you never knew what you might be getting yourself in for when he got one of his projects

130

going. I hadn't been involved in it, but I knew that he had once hatched a dragon from an egg and wanted to make it a pet. This didn't seem like that at all.

"OK. I wouldn't mind helping. But you understand that teaching English to non-English speakers is not my field of study."

Haggrid was overjoyed, "Oh, thank you professor. That would be wonderful. Maybe this weekend, we could visit him and get started?"

"That seems reasonable. What is his native language?"

Haggrid seemed stuck. He looked down at his feet, and I began to get that tingle at the nape of my neck that didn't bode well. "I don't rightly know, Professor."

Then I broke one of the basic laws of the universe—Don't Ask a Question that You Don't Want to Know the Answer to, "Why don't you know what language he speaks?"

Haggrid eyes began wandering around the room looking for some place to settle on that was not me. "I don't know that it has a name."

I almost asked, "How can it NOT have a name," but I restrained myself. Haggrid added, "You'll understand a whole lot better once you meet him."

I knew that I was going to regret it, but I said, "I'm looking forward to meeting him. We can settle all that when we get acquainted."

Haggrid seemed greatly relieved and held out his hand to shake, "Thanks, Professor. Just drop by my house Saturday morning. We'll have some tea and then head off to meet .. . uh . . . my relative."

I gritted my teeth preparing for the bone-crushing handshake that was Haggrid's best attempt to be gentle. I wasn't surprised by the resulting pain that extended up my forearm to my elbow.

After Haggrid left, I composed a brief note to Flourish and Blotts asking them to order a copy of an English as A Second Language textbook. I rolled up the little scrap of parchment, stuffed it into my robes, and went to see if I could catch Minerva in her office. By good luck, I did. I asked her if she would send an owl post for me.

"Of course, dear boy. Is there anything else you'd like?"

I demonstrated, and she complied. Then she asked for the note. I handed the rolled-up scroll to her, and she promptly unrolled it and read. I was disgusted at her not even asking, "Do you mind if I check the spelling and punctuation while I'm at it?"

She detected my consternation at her reading it, "Now, now, Wendt, you don't expect me to send off something by owl sight unseen. You might be hiring a hit wizard to take Umbrage out.

"Ah, yes. You want to buy a book to help you with your English. Very wise. I'm glad you've decided to drop that execrable American that you speak."

I sniffed and said, "No, that's not it." Then I hesitated as I thought how to explain my need for the textbook. "You see, Haggrid, dropped by today."

"Oh, don't tell me about Haggrid. Haggrid isn't involved in this, is he?"

"Well, he has a relative who wants to learn English."

She gave me a sour face, but I went on. "I know that Haggrid has his little idiosyncrasies."

She interrupted me, "His little idiosyncrasies! You mean like that dragon he named Norbert?"

"It's not like he wants me to train a dragon to speak English."

Her face didn't change, "Have you met this 'relative'?"

"Well, no." I admitted sheepishly.

Minerva reached forward and held my forearm, "Please promise me that you won't let Haggrid talk you into something stupid. He's a really nice fellow, and has the best intentions. He's so innocent that it's hard to say no to him, but he has such dangerous ideas sometimes."

I agreed that I wouldn't sign up for anything that had the potential for getting me killed. On that condition, she agreed, and I decided to accompany her up to the owlery to watch her put my message on an owl leg. We climbed up the tower that had the owlery at the top.

"You know, Minerva, I'm amazed that wizards put up with the mess." The floor of the owlery was covered with guano. Someone had to clean it fairly frequently because it was never piled up like in a bat cave. But still, it was difficult to avoid the piles on the floor.

"Oh, just zip it. I don't have to send this, you know."

△

The next day, I got mail during the evening meal. It was from Flourish & Blots. They had located a list of ESL texts along with prices and brief descriptions of the books – publication date, publisher, author, and a short paragraph description. I walked up to my office, reading as I went.

When I arrived, I found a note had been pushed under my door. I discovered that it was from Umbrage. She wanted me to come to her office immediately. I stuffed the list of books in a pocket and headed up to her office.

I knocked on the door and was invited in. The room hadn't changed much. There were still the walls of kitten artwork. Somehow, having a kitten follow you with its eyes is more unnerving than having a human being in a painting do the same. She invited me to sit. I did, with foreboding.

"Professor Wendt, you received a letter from someone tonight. Would you please show it to me? Oh, by the way, would you like some tea?"

I was strongly inclined to decline the honor. The question allowed me a moment to think about my answers. I started by declining the tea with thanks. I was afraid to imagine what it might be laced with. Then I decided that she would probably threaten me with being canned if I didn't show the letter to her. So I got it out. "Certainly, professor. I happen to still have it with me."

I handed it over, and she read through it. After several minutes, she asked, "What in the world are you planning on doing? Why the list of English as a Second Language books?"

"Oh, I'm going to buy one. And the reason that I'm going to buy one. . ." Here I hesitated trying to decide how much of the truth to include in my lie.

But Umbrage almost immediately brightened, "You're looking for another job, aren't you? And you're studying up for the kind of job you want?" She was practically gleeful at the thought of my voluntarily absenting myself from Hogwarts. She was actually leaning forward slightly, and her lips were slightly parted.

That gave me time to decide how I would answer, 'I've been offered a job tutoring a student in English whose native language isn't English." I quickly added, "This isn't a full time job and I don't even think it will take much of my time. My teaching at Hogwarts will always have first priority, and I won't permit it to affect my teaching here."

She visibly deflated as I gave my answer and seemed to be on the point of dismissing me when she asked, "Who is it you're going to tutor? It couldn't be a Hogwarts student."

Of course, I didn't know whom I was going to tutor, but I didn't think that was a safe answer. It might lead to questions like, "Who offered you the job?" or "How did you find out about this job?" So, I quickly racked my brains for an answer that was possible and would not be worth the trouble to check.

Then, it popped into my head. I'd heard that Bill Weasley was seeing Fleur DeLacour. I quickly improvised, "Well, you remember the Tri-Wizard Tournament?" I quickly hurried on because I didn't want her dwelling on the reason that she was sent here. "Well, one of the French students who had come to apply to be the champion from Beaux Batons formed a, well, romantic attraction to a Hogwarts alumnus. She doesn't have very good English and wants a crash course so that she can pursue her, uh, romantic interests.

"I don't actually know any further details because I haven't met her yet. She wants to keep her intentions a secret from her intended uh boyfriend."

That seemed to disappoint her further. When Shakespeare commented that villains want to see villainy everywhere, he was certainly right. She was twirling a curl of hair idly seeming to try to find something worthy of investigation. She finally seemed to give up. "All right, but you know, it might be a good idea for you to develop outside jobs. You may need one sometime."

I got up and made to leave. She seemed to have lost all interest in me. I went to the door and turned the handle. Umbrage looked up and said, "When you find out who she is, I'll know who it is."

I opened the door and replied, "IF I find out who she is, I'll let you know. This job may not pan out. Good evening."

I went to my office and thought about the books. I picked one tentatively and decided to sleep on the decision. The next day at breakfast, I'd decide, use the list from Flourish & Blots as an impromptu order form and send it back.

That morning, I decided on the <u>Side by Side Student Book 1</u>. It was intended for youthful learners but seemed to be a good text. I found Minerva and got her to send it by owl post. It was already Thursday. The chances that they'd get it delivered by the time of my first meeting with

Haggrid's relative seemed slim to none. But it would be good to have a get-acquainted meeting anyway.

Minerva was still unhappy with me, "Oh, Wendt, this is really going too far. I have a bad feeling about this 'job'". She said the word, job, as though I were volunteering as a crash dummy for a car manufacturer. As we walked up to the owlery again, she had taken my arm in hers. I'm sure that it wasn't for support. She was quite a spry, even athletic, woman and had no need for support. I'm sure that she hoped to influence me in her argument by all means, fair and foul. Not that having her hold my arm was at all foul. As a matter of fact, I couldn't help seeing her point as she patted my arm. I was feeling very much that I belonged to her and ought to pay serious attention to her desires. At the end of the climb, she turned and smiled at me, and my heart melted. For that moment, I would have done anything she wanted.

I was about to say that she didn't have to mail the parchment when a screech owl flew down, squawking for attention. It presented its leg for attachment of the parchment. That broke the spell, and I didn't say anything even though Minerva hesitated, I suppose, hoping that I'd change my mind. The bird kept making a racket. Minerva addressed the bird, "All right. All right. Here's your mail." Then she tied the parchment on and gave the bird instructions. It flew off, and she sighed. "I almost thought I had you convinced."

I smiled back at her, "You almost did."

The next day, a return came from Flourish & Blots. It would take at least a week to get the book and have it shipped to me. So that sealed it. Tomorrow would just be a preliminary meeting.

Saturday arrived and Haggrid was positively jolly at breakfast. He was joking with Snape—which is not easy to do. After he'd finished breakfast, he came over and sat by me. "Well, Professor, are you ready to go."

I looked down at my unfinished French toast and bacon, which I'd been toying with, not being really ready to go off on this little adventure. Thinking that going to meet a student would be an adventure may seem strange to you. But having this huge, hulking person beside me rather encouraged me to think that this might be quite adventurous.

"Haggrid, give me a couple of minutes to finish breakfast, and we can go."

Haggrid smiled even wider and said, "Great!" He rubbed his hand together and said, "This will be fun." Personally, I'd just as soon that he hadn't thrown in that little bit of enthusiasm.

I finished, and told Haggrid that I would go up to my office to get a light jacket. I'd join him at his house straight-away. I went up and got my light jacket and actually trotted down to Haggrid's. Now that I was committed, I was determined to get through it as quickly as I could. I arrived, and Haggrid greeted me and set off into the forest.

We went a few minutes into the forest, and I began wondering what we were doing. "Haggrid, I figured we were going to go outside Hogwarts grounds so that we could disapparate someplace. Isn't that what we're doing?"

Haggrid laughed, "No. Nothing that hard. My uh relative lives in the forest."

I echoed, "In the forest." In the Forbidden Forest. Let's see. Who lives in the forest—giant spiders, festrals, hippogriffs, unicorns. None of them need to learn English—at least not from me. There are reputedly vampires and werewolves. I didn't think any of them really were in the forest, but Dumbledore let the rumors persist. I guessed he wanted to discourage students from wandering in the forest where there are real dangers. Then there were centaurs. If Forensee were any evidence, they were pretty darn good at English. Maybe they just needed a little help with pronunciation. I'd never heard of anyone living in the Forbidden Forest. So, who the heck was this relative of Haggrid's.

"Haggrid, just who is this we're going to see?"

Haggrid was striding ahead of me, and I huffed and puffed to keep up. The forest consisted of patches of fir trees interspersed with patches of dark deciduous trees that I couldn't identify. I thought about collecting a leaf or two to send to a friend from Ohio State who was a botanist for him to identify. I couldn't because I was having a hard time keeping up with Haggrid. It wasn't just that his stride was about twice mine, but he was tall enough that the huge roots that protruded through the ground were things that I had to jump over, while he could easily take them in his stride.

I began to notice some noise up ahead that didn't have anything to do with chirping birds or scurrying squirrels. It sounded like trees trunks were being flexed as though they were twigs. "Haggrid. That noise up ahead. That isn't by any chance giant spiders in the branches?"

Haggrid laughed, "No. No. They don't sound anything like that. You can't hear them as they travel through the trees. The only thing you might hear is the chittering of pincers."

I thought. "Great. They could be all around us and we might not know."

He went on, "No. We're far away from where they live."

"Just what lives close to where we are?"

Haggrid hmmed in thought and said, "Well, I suppose the Centaurs aren't very far off. That reminds me. If we should happen to run into some, just let me do the talking."

Oh, great. When I have to rely on Haggrid to do the talking is the day that I reach the clearing at the end of the path.

He went on, "Anyway, we're almost there. You'll soon see."

We approached a clearing, and as we approached, I saw a tall figure. It was hard to tell just how tall, because there were still lots of trees in the way, and it was a little hard to judge distance. As we came closer, it became clear that calling this figure tall would be like calling Haggrid big-boned. This person was gigantic. We reached the last of the trees before the clearing, and I realized that he wasn't just gigantic. He was. A. Giant.

"Haggrid. That person could pass for a giant without too much trouble."

Haggrid grinned, "Yeh. He's kind of puny for a giant, but he is pretty large."

I gaped at him from the edge of the clearing. "Puny, eh." He noticed us and turned toward us. As he did that, I saw a rope that reminded me of a trip to Boston where I saw the USS Constitution. It was held to the dock with a hawser that looked like the trunk of an elephant. The rope was tied to one of his legs. The other end was tied to a huge tree trunk. "Haggrid, is this going to be safe for me?"

He turned and stared at me as though I were stark raving mad. "Well, of course." But Haggrid was interrupted by the giant's sudden, explosive dash toward us. Briefly, I thought about reaching in my pocket to retrieve my purse and from it, my Gloc. In that split second of decision that we sometimes have that may affect the rest of our lives, I decided that it would be pointless. However, my bladder, working on different neural circuitry decided that I would have a better chance of surviving without its load of urine.

Haggrid noticed what was happening and turned and stood between me and the giant and said, "Now, Gorpee, you know better than to frighten new friends." He seized Gorp around the waist and pulled him to a stop. "Now, Gorpee, hold your hand out to shake, like a gentleman."

Gorpee extended his hand that was about the size of a manhole cover toward me. I was glad to see that his fist was not closed. I reached out and managed to close my hand around the two small fingers of his hand. Fortunately, he didn't shake vigorously. He just moved it rhythmically up and down. I released his fingers as quickly as I could.

Haggrid was introducing me as James Wendt, which Gorp shortened to "Jay". He went on, "Now, Gorpee, Jay is going to help us learn to speak English, aren't you, Jay?"

I nodded and managed a shaky, "Yes."

"So, can you show Jay your ball?"

Nothing happened, Haggrid shouted, "Ball. Ball. Show Jay Ball."

Gorp reached somewhere behind him and brought a #5 soccer ball out. In his hand, it looked like a large marble. Haggrid urged him to show me the ball. Finally, Gorp threw the ball to me. I felt as though I were a goalie taking a power shot from Beckham. It hit me square in the chest, and I went down backwards knocking the wind from me. Somehow, I'd managed to hold onto it.

Haggrid encouraged Gorp, "There. That's the way to play nice." I dropped the ball to the ground and kicked it soccer style toward him. He tapped it with his toe, and it shot past me. I'd failed my test as goalie. I ran after it and found it about two hundred meters away. As I brought it back, I heard a gruff sound that I identified as crying as I saw the tears in Gorp's eyes.

I shouted to him, "Gorp, Ball!" I drop kicked it gently and he had no trouble catching it. So, we played a sort of football match for maybe ten or so minutes. I was sweating pretty vigorously.

Haggrid asked me if we could start teaching.

I shook my head. "This is just a get-acquainted meeting. I've ordered a book to help us. It might be here by next weekend. I feel like we're acquainted."

Haggrid looked up to Gorp, "Gorpee, we've got to go, but we'll be back soon."

I couldn't believe my eyes. Gorp sniffed and pulled an old canvas bag up to his nose and blew it. Haggrid patted his leg and said, "I'm sure Jay and you can play some ball next time."

My jaw fell, and I vigorously signaled "NO." It was too late.

I followed Haggrid out of the forest. I had the sinking feeling that I'd soon feel like Beckham's practice goalie—only worse.

"Haggrid, you said that Gorp was a relative. Really?"

Haggrid smiled, "Sure. He's my long lost half-brother."

"Long lost? How could someone that size possibly be lost?"

"Well, he was raised by giants and they keep pretty much to themselves."

"And well they should. So, he's half giant?"

"No, he's full-blooded. I'm half-blooded."

We got back to the castle late for lunch, so I just went to my office, massaged my aching muscles, showered, and changed into a clean robe. Shortly before dinner, Minerva dropped by my office.

She stared at my bruised face and hands, "Well, how was tutoring with Haggrid?"

I gave her a frown. "Just rub it in. Actually we didn't get around to tutoring yet. I'll not have my textbook for a while."

"Well, you look like you were the goalie on the losing end of a tight Quidditch match."

"That's not a bad description."

"Seriously, who was your student?"

My face fell as I was forced to say, "I'm sorry. I can't tell you."

She shook her head sadly, "You didn't promise Haggrid not to tell?"

"No, but I can't very well tell. You see, I sort of let Umbrage think I'm tutoring a student from Beau Batons."

"And how did she get that idea?"

"Come on. You know perfectly well. I told her that to get her off my back."

"What I don't know perfectly well is why you ever agreed to this stupid idea. You're too soft-hearted by half."

The week went by. On Thursday, I was surprised to see a large owl circle over my breakfast yogurt and granola bowl and drop a heavy package. I caught it and quickly opened it. It contained to my delight, the ESL text that I'd ordered, along with an invoice for the cost—10 galleons, 5 sickles—and a return envelope for sending money. The owl landed on the table on the other side of my bowl from me. I got out my purse and pulled out ten galleons and found that I had only 4 sickles, so I threw the eleventh galleon in and wrote a brief note on a scrap of parchment that said, "Keep the change. Regards, Professor Wendt."

I sealed the envelope and attached it to the owl's leg, and it struggled off and out of the Great Hall. I'd not finished my breakfast before Umbrage walked behind me and asked, "Your book?"

"Yes." and I raised it so that she could see the cover.

She said, "Fine." and walked off and out of the Great Hall.

Saturday came altogether too quickly. This time, knowing what to expect, I dressed in jeans, a sweatshirt, and trainers. After breakfast, we made our way into the forest, and I counted every step that took us closer to Gorp.

Gorp was standing at the center of the clearing when we arrived. I didn't see it, but he was holding the soccer ball in his hand. When I appeared, he shouted, "Ball!" and flung it at me. This time, I decided to head it. That was better than taking it in the chest, but I was still knocked down. He seemed delighted to see the ball rebounding back at him. He caught it handily and threw it again. He had pretty good aim, and it was not too hard to head it—other than the fear of getting a concussion each time.

After we'd played header practice for about ten or a dozen times, Haggrid mercifully called time and declared that we were going to practice English. I pulled out my book, and Haggrid was surprised at how small it was.

"That's OK, Haggrid, can you do an engorgement charm?"

He looked a little sheepish and nodded. "OK, Haggrid. Would you double the size of this book?" He nodded, and I laid the book on the ground as he pulled out of a pocket his wand. In a moment, the book was twice its former size. I gauged the size and then asked him to engorge it again. He complied, and it was four or five times its original size. I struggled to get it up and leaned it against a tree.

I opened the book to the first page that had pictures of family members. I pointed to the drawing of a stylized brother and pointed to Haggrid and said the word, "Brother", several times. We tried to get him to say the word. Eventually he said it. Then I had Haggrid repeat the sentence, "Gorp is my brother", with as much sign language as we could.

I pulled out my purse and pulled out a small folder with my family pictures. I had Haggrid engorge it and I leaned it against a tree. I made the same signs and said, "Robert is my brother", pointing at the picture of my brother Robert.

Gorp seemed to get it. After a while we took turns saying who our brothers were. We repeated the process with "mother" and "father". By this time, we were getting tired of English exercises. We returned for a break to header practice. Haggrid wanted to take a turn taking headers. I was overjoyed, and the two of them practiced headers for a while.

Gorp asked, "Gorp practice headers."

Haggrid nodded. I told him, "Be careful. Throw them very soft. I don't want to be shagging soccer balls out of the lake." They played that for a while. Then, I said, "Gorp practice English."

He frowned, but he sat down near the book and we went on to a new lesson. There were lots of other family names, but we didn't know the name of any other relatives that Gorp might have, so we turned to body parts. That was much easier, and we quickly had Gorp saying, "This is Gorp's arm. This is Gorp's leg. This is Gorp's mouth." And so forth. Finally, I said that we were done for the day. I was bushed, and I think that Gorp was getting exhausted from so much mental exercise as well.

As we walked back through the woods, Haggrid thanked me. I replied, "Gorp's OK. I think that if we keep working with him, he could carry on a conversation with someone who doesn't know him fairly well by summer."

Over the next couple of weeks, he kept improving. I thought that he might be close to learning some concepts that are hard to capture in a painting—like time and thankfulness. Then, one day when we returned from a lesson, Haggrid had a surprise for me.

Haggrid looked down. I knew something bad was coming. I waited for it.

Haggrid eventually said, "I think I'm going to be sacked soon, and I want Gorp to keep learning."

"Look, Haggrid. Take the book with you. It's yours and Gorp's. Keep working with him. You see how. You'll have him reading clocks before long."

A tear welled up in Haggrid's left eye. "I don't think I can take him with me. He'll stay here. He can catch food for himself. He'll be OK, but he'll stop learning." The tear overflowed and was followed by more. "Do you think that you could keep coming out here to teach him? I got Hermione and Harry and Ron to come out and keep him company, but they can't teach him English."

"Oh, hell." I thought to myself, "Minerva was right."

"Look, Haggrid, let's see what happens first. You may not get sacked. But I promise I'll think about it, and we'll talk about it if you do get sacked. And anyway, even if that happens, Dumbledore will let you stay on like he did Sybill Trelawney."

But, of course, I was wrong.

Dumbledore's Army

When it happened, I was taking a walk with Minerva along the lakefront. It seemed an idyllic day. The weather had taken a warm snap, and the sky was a beautiful deep cerulean blue. As I was scanning the area to see if someone would see us if we did a little quick snogging, there was a loud bang. I couldn't identify where it came from, but Minerva immediately said, "That was the castle. Let's go."

We trotted up the hill toward the castle. When we got there, we found an unusual group coming down the hall from the general direction of Dumbledore's office. I commented to Minerva, "Well, if it isn't four of my favorite people all together here—Fudge, Percy Weasley, Umbrage and Kingsley Shacklebolt."

"What do you mean four? There are five."

"I don't know the fifth."

They stopped us, and Minister Fudge asked, "Have you seen Dumbledore in the last half-hour?"

I looked at Minerva and was happy to be able to perfectly honestly say, "No, I haven't. What about you Minerva?"

"You know perfectly well that I've been with you the last half hour and haven't seen him either." She turned to the fivesome and asked, "What in the world happened?"

Fudge stared at her intently, "Do you know where he is?"

"No."

Finally, Weasley said, 'We came here to arrest Harry Potter for treason, but it turned out that he was just following orders from Dumbledore."

Minerva asked, "How do you know?"

Fudge broke in, "He told us. He's formed this blasted Dumbledore's Army to man an uprising against the Ministry."

Umbrage was close to screaming, "You must know where he is. Tell us now."

"I think that you underestimate Dumbledore's capabilities and his intelligence." I said, 'You must realize that he doesn't need help from Minerva to escape from you and find his own hiding place. And you should realize that he is not one who would put a friend in danger by giving her information, like where he is, that she doesn't absolutely have to have."

Umbrage pulled her wand out and began swinging it around wildly. "You must tell us."

Minerva said smoothly, "I can't tell you what I don't know."

Umbrage said in a low, dangerous voice, "We could give you Veritas serum."

"You mean like you poisoned students?"

Fudge realized that things were getting out of hand and stepped in, "Now, now, Dolores. Wendt's right. Dumbledore keeps his own counsel. And anyway, we need to have Minerva do her duty and keep running Gryffindor.

After they left, I asked Minerva whether Dumbledore would need help of any sort.

"Well, I think that Dumbledore is perfectly capable of taking care of himself. As a matter of fact, it might, on the whole, be a nice little vacation from Umbrage for Dumbledore. We're the ones who have to put up with her, and she'll be more insufferable than ever."

△

And, of course, it started out that way. Without the seasoning influence of Dumbledore, Umbrage was even more odious than before. But this time, something happened that none of us anticipated.

We didn't know precisely what the cause was when things started to happen. When the disasters started happening, they came thick and fast. The castle was converted in short order to a morass of traps and bogs and who knew what all. Umbrage was utterly overwhelmed. All sorts of magical calamities started happening, and she couldn't repair most of them.

The regular staff claimed incompetence to help her.

I was thoroughly amused until one day while grading in my office. The door was flung open, and Umbrage barged in, "Why are you doing it?"

"Doing what?"

"You know perfectly well. I know you're behind this reign of terror."

"Me. How in the world could a Squibb possibly do any of the things that are going on in this castle!" I stared at her with the perfect innocence of the innocent.

"Oh, I don't mean that you actually did any of the magic. I mean that you are behind planning it. I was suspicious of you from the Halloween party. I think that you planned this, this travesty."

I leaned back in my chair as she continued to storm around the room breathing threats. It occurred to me that I'd not invited her to sit in the red leather chair. I wasn't sorry. Nor did I say anything to resist her ranting.

She seemed to run out of invective eventually, and I sent her on her way.

That evening, I visited Minerva in her office. I was submitting my final exam for review by the Headmistress or Head Inquisitor or head ache. Dumbledore was still *incommunicado* and I wanted to see what his office looked like with its new tenant. I found Minerva sitting behind her desk with a quill, grading papers. She invited me into her office.

"Aren't you going to invite yourself to come with me to the Headmistress's Office? I'm sure she'll invite me to sit in the red leather chair?"

She laughed, "But Dumbledore doesn't have a red leather chair."

"He should. But have you heard anything from him?"

"No. He's keeping his head very low."

I pulled up a chair and sat. She asked, "Don't you have any school work to do?"

"Nope. I finished it all and thought that I'd come up and pester you. By the way, do you know who's been doing all the practical jokes?"

Minerva frowned at me, "You mean that you can't figure it out for yourself?"

"Well, I know who would be doing them if there were any justice in the world—the Weasley twins."

145

Minerva smiled, "Well, there is justice in the world."

"Wow! I had no idea that they were as good as all that. You know I had to detour ten minutes on the way here to get around the swamp."

"Yes, I can't understand why they aren't graduating with honors. They certainly have the talent and the willingness to work hard."

"Yeah—when there's a practical joke in prospect. Still, it's amazing that an accomplished wizard like Umbrage couldn't undo those tricks."

Minerva harrumphed, "Oh, she's not so good. I could undo all their jokes in a couple of hours if I wanted. Umbrage is just a second rate witch who's used every rotten trick there is to get ahead. She sucks up to Fudge at every opportunity."

"Do you know that she accused me of master-minding this affair?"

"You see. She has no imagination. There are a dozen people who could have master-minded it. Why you?"

"Well, she seems to think that I had something to do with the fiasco at the Halloween party."

"Well, maybe she's not quite as dumb as I think."

"What is she going to do about the owl and newt exams?"

"Nothing. They'll go on as usual."

"Even with the . uh . problems in the castle?"

"Certainly, everyone should know how miserably-run this school is with Umbrage in charge."

"Fine by me."

We started up to Umbrage's new office. I asked Minerva how it was for her with Umbrage being Headmistress.

She sniffed, "How's it like? How's it like! Do you know how much time Umbrage spends in this office pestering me? And I'm not talking about all the odious things she does, but just sticking her nose into the business?

"Well, it's just about all the time that she isn't handling her own duties—which are pretty slight.

"For example, her idea of teaching is to have students read the approved textbook in class and that's it. And how about grading? Do you know how she grades? Do you know how much time she spends on grading?"

I admitted that I didn't.

"Well, first off, she completely depends on the Ministry-administered Owl and Newt exams for fifth and sixth years, so that's zip zero work for her. Then the seventh years she grades on pass-fail with no tests at all."

Minerva stopped and thought a minute, "Well, with seventh years, it's hard to do much more than that. They mostly have seventh-year-itis. But all the other years, she administers one mid-term exam and one final each term. And that's a twenty-question multiple choice exam."

I asked, "No practicum?"

"Not in class, not in exams, nothing, You know, YOU could walk into the final exam in fourth year Defense Against the Dark Arts and get an Outstanding. I was just looking at her final exam. Any dolt with half a brain could work the test and get at least 90%. You would do even better.

"And, of course, you'd deserve a grade of Troll. You couldn't do a single thing in a real practicum."

"Thanks." I said sarcastically.

"No problem. And so when she's not interrogating students or in classrooms boring her students, she's in here bothering me."

And just then, we arrived at Umbrage's Headmistress Office. She knocked, and there was a "HMMM!" on the other side of the door. Umbrage invited us in.

"Well, Professor Umbrage, we've come to drop off exams for review."

She looked from Minerva to me, "I suppose I should have expected to find Mr. Wendt malingering with you."

I commented, "Oh, yes. Minerva insists that if I'm going to be malingering somewhere, it has to be near her so that she can keep her thumb on top of my malingering."

Umbrage made a face. Even when she's not, most people think she is, that is, until they've seen her really make a face. In this case, her toad-like face seemed to recoil into itself.—not a process you want to see more than once. "Dear Minerva, I thought that I would volunteer to proctor exams—both mine and, well, really, all the other exams this term."

Minerva rolled her eyes and said, "Really, the teachers don't need your help. We have plenty of help. The professors proctor all of their exams and, of course, we'd expect you to proctor your exams."

"Hmmmm! I suppose I didn't make myself clear. I wasn't exactly volunteering. I was politely stating that I would be proctoring all exams. As the High Inquisitor, I have to certify that all exams were fair and were administered correctly.

"Also, I'll be reviewing all the exams that the other Professors will be submitting. Please get them to me immediately."

Minerva's face sank. "They've all submitted them to me for review, and I've not finished reviewing them all myself. I'll turn over to you all the ones that I've finished with."

"Hmmmm! Minerva, I'll have all of them now."

Minerva made another face, and I commented, "Don't be concerned with mine, Minerva. It's perfect to start with." I stood, picked it up off the desk, and handed it to Umbrage. Then I said, "Well, I've had my fill of malingering for the day, so I'm heading back to my office. You two girls probably want to do some girl talk that would be inconvenient to do with me in the office"

I thought that I heard Minerva say under her breath, "Coward."

Hagrid Sacked

Finals were just around the corner, and there was one of those events that you think that you'll never witness more than once. But it happened. A couple of months before, Umbrage had sacked Sybill Trelawney. Now, I'll admit that Sybill was no better at teaching Divination than I would have been. As a matter of fact, I might have been better. Both of us would teach from theory. I, at least, would realize that I didn't have talent and that all I was teaching was theory.

She did understand the theory. Since really competent wizards and witches like Dumbledore and Minerva didn't value the subject very highly, it didn't really matter that she wasn't very good at it.

My theory about that was that although Divination is real and the best practitioners really sometimes have true insights, the truth is that most of the time things that Diviners proclaim comes much more from clever understanding of how the world and people's motivations work. They somehow can discern their valid Divinations from the false ones that are constantly occurring to everyone—even Muggles. So the good ones would come up with Divinations based on a clever understanding of human nature.

Sybil was not among those. She once had the ultimate Divination that all Diviners pray for. I once overheard Minerva and Dumbledore discussing it. As it was top-toppity-top-top secret and above my pay grade, I could never convince her to reveal it to me. Besides that, of course, it was hopeless that Dumbledore would reveal it. Anyway, Sybil had the gift of occasionally having the true Divination but unfortunately lacked the knack of knowing the real from the false.

I think that she expected to be able to turn Divination on and off like a faucet. It just doesn't work that way. When she discovered that she couldn't control it, she tried to force it anyway. So she turned herself into a humbug.

Anyway, it happened. Trelawney was sacked, and I thought that would be it. Umbrage had taken a scalp, justified her existence at Hogwarts, and would be satisfied to rest on her laurels.

But, I was wrong. She didn't rest on her laurels. She went on the war path for more scalps, and she found one. This time, she was really stretching. Her victim wasn't the greatest professor who'd crossed the threshold of Hogwarts, but he wasn't bad. He had had a rocky start, and his intuitions were frequently wrong-headed. He loved his subject, knew it very well, and occasionally actually succeeded in interesting some of his students in it. That is an achievement that many a decent teacher might envy.

Now, realize that his subject wouldn't have interested me even if I were a wizard, but that doesn't matter. Anyway, Umbrage settled on Hagrid as her next target of opportunity. Truly, he was the next best target after Trelawney, but there just weren't any other good targets while Dumbledore ran Hogwarts. I still thought of him running Hogwarts —even though he was heaven-only-knew-where. Personally, I thought that he'd gone to Grimauld Place. Since I didn't have access to it, I might as well have suggested the South Pole.

I didn't know that it had happened until after the dust-up had settled.

Unlike Trelawney, Hagrid was not going to go quietly into that good night. He was fighting all the way. As a matter of fact, Umbrage had to import about a half-dozen thugs to do the deed, and it didn't go all that well for them either.

Minerva, who had been holding her peace most of the term, was determined not to let him go quietly either. I learned about it in the middle of the night. I'd just gone to bed when I heard a terrible racket seemingly coming from somewhere in the castle. I was up, dressed (sort of), and armed in less than five minutes. I ran out my door and started trying to find the source of the noise. I ran through half the castle before the noise quieted. By then, I'd decided that it must be outdoors. I left the main entrance and ran down the fountain courtyard. I saw a bunch of people near Hagrid's house, but I didn't see him and figured that he had probably settled their hash.

So it was that I started walking down the path in an easy-going lope. As I approached the house, I saw that there were four men, apparently carrying someone as though on a stretcher—achieved by magic, no doubt.

As we approached each other, I saw that the figure was slight, had long hair up in a bun . . . It was at that point that I broke into a run and arrived to discover that it was Minerva. As I arrived, one of the men, whom I didn't recognize said gruffly, "What do you want?"

"Where are you taking her?"

"Well, if it's anything to you, Squibb, we're taking her to the h'pital wing." Then he flung me aside with a flick of his wand. I shouted after them, "What happened?"

No one answered, and I got up and ran after them. Then, I stopped and pulled out my purse and fumbled it open. My hands were shaking and I didn't want to waste a second. I shook it out. Galleons and gloc and clips and bullets scattered around. I sat there and fumbled bullets into a clip and a clip into the Gloc. Then I stared at it, wondering whether to release the safety. No. I put it into a pocket and shoveled the galleons and other detritus into the purse. I left some behind, I knew.

I passed the toughs and went directly to the hospital wing. Thank God! Pomona was there. "Pomona, there are some men bringing Minerva up here. She's been injured!"

She stared at me, not comprehending what had happened. "Pomona! You've got to get ready for Minerva!"

She looked at me with some compassion then and said, "I am ready. What happened?"

I was forced to admit that I didn't know.

"Then, we'll just have to wait until she gets here for her to tell us."

"Oh, Pomona, I don't think she'll be able to tell us. She was unconscious when I saw her a few minutes ago."

Pomona stood then. She strode to get her medical bag and wand. She then went into a closet and pulled out something like a gurney.

"What are you doing?"

"Getting ready for any eventuality."

Just then, the four men came into the hospital room with Minerva, who appeared to be still unconscious. One, I supposed the leader, simply asked, "Where?"

151

Pomona pointed at a bed, and they quickly dumped her there. They were starting to leave, but Pomona was not about to let that happen. I'd never heard anyone, with the possible exception of Minerva, use a voice that more bespoke command. It wasn't directed at me, but I felt the influence of it. She simply said, "Stop."

All four halted in their tracks. They then turned to her. "What?"

"Tell me, immediately, what happened?"

The leader said, "We were helping sack the giant and get him off the grounds. This woman tried to interfere."

Pomona lost nothing of her voice of command, "And?"

"Well, we had our orders, so we stunned her."

"How many?"

They looked from one to the other of them and seemingly by common consent they all said, "I did."

She stared, unbelieving among them. "Do you mean to say that you all stunned her?"

For the first time, they seemed a bit sheepish. The leader answered, "Yes."

"You mean to say that one woman needed four stunning spells from four big strong brave men to subdue her."

One of the ones who wasn't the leader said in a low voice, "You didn't see her out there."

The leader said, "Shut up, Sid."

Then he went on, "We're leaving now. We've done our job and we'll be on our way."

If I thought Pomona was mad before, she was practically incandescent now, 'Yes, skulk off like the coward curs that you are. You will all sign the logbook as visitors to Professor McGonagall." Their eyes goggled, but they all went to the logbook that Pomona pointed out and signed. I never knew if they signed their real names.

When they left, Pomona ran to Minerva and took her hand in hers, feeling for a pulse. "Good. But I've got to get her to St. Mongos immediately." She went on, seeming to speak to herself, mostly, "Four stunning spells. We've got to move quickly to avoid permanent brain damage."

She looked around and seemed to notice the gurney. She used her wand and levitated Minerva gently to the gurney and onto it. With a flick of the wand she tied her onto the gurney and wheeled it toward the fireplace.

I ran to her, grabbed her free arm and said, "Wait! If you're going to St. Mongos, I want to come along."

By this time she'd reached the fireplace and the pot of floo powder, she looked back and said, "I've got enough to worry with the gurney and Minerva and myself. I can't take you with."

"You've got to!" I was near panic.

She resumed her imperial voice," You are NOT going with me. Do you want to endanger her health more/"

She had me. I fell back. She pushed the gurney into what I'd just realized was an oversize fireplace. It was big enough for her, the gurney and several more people. She threw down a handful of floo powder and said, "St. Mongo Emergency Room." They disappeared in a flare of green fire.

I ran after her, grabbed a handful of floo powder, threw it down, and repeated the words.

And nothing happened.

△

I slumped back against the wall of the fireplace, covered my eyes with a hand, and tried to hold back the tears. Then I left the hospital wing and headed for Snape's office. I arrived and burst in to discover that Snape and Umbrage were seated and talking quietly. They looked up at my appearance and Snape asked me what I was doing there.

"Do you know what just happened?"

Snape looked from Umbrage to me and asked, "The oaf, Hagrid, was just sacked, and he had to be 'helped' from the grounds."

I practically screamed, "Are you aware that Minerva was attacked and stunned several times during the 'sacking'?"

Snape looked from me to Umbrage, "Is this true?"

"Well, the silly woman got in the way of the High Inquisitor in the performance of her duty."

I was so angry at that sanctimonious voice that my right hand twitched toward my right pocket and my purse. But, I said, "Snape, can you take me to St. Mongo's. Pomona's had to take her there."

Snape's head twitched slightly and he asked her, "Is this true?"

"Oh, I suppose so, but it serves her right. You can't leave with Wendt. We're already short one Head of House. I can't allow another to leave at this critical time."

Snape seemed to think a minute and said, "No, Wendt, I can't help you now."

In that instant, I came as close to murder as I ever have in my life. I reached into my pocket and instinctively thumbed the safety off. As a matter of fact, the only thing that saved me from it was that I had the two objects of my hatred before me—Umbrage on the left and Snape on the right. In that millisecond of decision when emotion rules, and we make up rationalizations later for why we did what we did, I couldn't decide between shooting to the left or the right. And so, I did nothing.

Snape seemed to sense the instant of danger had passed, and the unperceived breath that he had been holding was released. My eyes fell from the two of them, and I stumbled around and out of Snape's office.

I wandered the halls of Hogwarts for some length of time that I know not, and then I came to myself. I looked around and realized that I was at Sinistra's office. I thought about the people who would be willing to help me to get to St. Mongos and picked her to start.

I reached her office and knocked on the door. She immediately replied, "I know that knock. Come in." The last was spoken with quite a bit of sultry sizzle. I sighed. This was the last thing I needed.

I entered, "Sinistra, I know it's late, and I suspect you've got the wrong idea of what is going on." I gave her a firm stare. She got up from her couch. She was wearing a night gown.

"This is an emergency. We don't have time for silly games. Minerva's in St. Mongo's."

In that instant when I pronounced the hospital's name, Sinistra's appearance transformed. She stood straight and asked, "What happened."

I didn't waste time with secondary issues. "She's gravely injured, and I need to get there immediately."

She stared at the floor a moment and said, "Yes. I see that. Well, we could go by either disapparation or by floo powder. The fastest would be floo powder, except I don't know the official names of different floo entrances to St. Mongo's."

I was impatient and snapped, "I don't give a shit if we end up in the kitchen of St. Mongos. I just want to get there. Now!"

She shrugged and said, "Well, when we end up in the nursery wing, don't blame me."

I just nodded curtly. She went to her bedroom and called through the half-open door, "I'm changing. I'll be out in three minutes."

I sneered to myself and muttered, "I'll believe that when I see it."

It couldn't have been longer than three minutes when she came out wearing a simple blue robe and carrying her wand, "OK. Let's go. Take my hand."

I did, and she stuffed the wand in her robe and took a handful of floo powder. We walked into the somewhat crowded fireplace, and we disappeared in a flare of green. I had my gut wrenched around as badly as I'd ever had it on one of these excursions, but I didn't feel it other than a mild tingle in my stomach.

We arrived in what I recognized as the main entrance. There was a reception witch behind the desk, and we got her to look up Minerva.

"I'm sorry, Mr. Wendt. I don't see her name on the list."

I was near frantic, "But she just arrived maybe." I looked at my watch and was shocked that it had been more than an hour before. "A little more than an hour ago."

Her face relaxed. "Oh, they'll not have assigned her a room yet." She picked up a scroll that seemed to be a floor plan for St. Mongo's. On it were a number of rooms with little balloons with names in them. As we watched, a new name appeared on it—Minerva McGonagall. She was in the MICU. She went on, "Yes, see. Ms. McGonagall is in the MICU."

She looked up from the parchment and asked, 'Are either of you relatives?"

Sinistra answered that we weren't.

"Well, then, you won't be able to see her until she's out of MICU."

I took Sinistra by the arm and pulled her aside. "Listen Sinistra. They won't let us in for a while. You can go back to school."

She nodded, "You'll stay here, right?"

"Yes. OK. Then I'll go back to Hogwarts. I'll let everyone there know what's going on."

"While you're at it, would you please post a note on my classroom?"

She nodded. I pulled a piece of parchment out of a pocket and a pen and wrote, "English Literature classes cancelled for the rest of the year. Please use the time to study for finals."

I handed it to her and said, "Umbrage has the final exams, including mine. If I'm not back by the time of finals, she can administer the test."

"What about grading them?"

I gave a single explosive laugh, "Yeh. Good question. Certainly Umbrage is NOT competent to grade them. You could bring them here, and I can grade them here, if that's OK with you?"

She smiled. "Yes, I'd be happy to do that for you."

I asked the receptionist how to get up to the MICU. She gave me directions and added, "There's a Waiting Room up there outside the MICU. You can wait there. It sounds like you may be here for a while. I'll give you a map of the hospital. There's a cafeteria in the basement. It's not bad. We have a staff of house elves who run the kitchens."

I thanked her and walked with Sinistra back to the fireplace. "Would you get in touch with Minerva's sister while you're at it?"

"Of course." She walked into the fireplace and disappeared in a flare of green.

I turned and went up to the MICU. When I got off the elevator, I found a nurse's station. I asked if they had a current status for Minerva.

The nurse said, "Who?" She looked down at her parchment. "Oh, yes. She just arrived from the ER. She hasn't been assigned a healer, but should be shortly. You could go down to the Waiting Room for the MICU. I'll let you know who the healer is, when she's assigned. "

Then she had another thought, "Oh, are you kin?"

"No. Just a good friend." Right, I thought, "just".

She nodded, and I went down the corridor until I was stopped by a door that had a window and underneath that, the letters, MICU. Beside the door was a sign that said, "Only one visitor per patient at a time, please."

I sat on a sofa in the Waiting Area. I watched the door, hoping that a healer that came out could tell me something. A white-coated healer walked out of the MICU. I jumped up and ran over to him, "Healer, healer, could I please talk with you?"

He stopped and I asked, "Do you know anything about how a patient, Minerva McGonagall is?"

He stared at me and said, "Are you a relative?"

I sighed, "No. I'm just a good friend." Just. Always, Just.

"Sorry, I can't give you any information besides that she's stable."

"Stable, what does that mean?"

His smile became hard, and he was about to say something when I heard a familiar voice behind me, "Oh, Wendt, what happened? A professor woke me up a half-hour ago to tell me that Minerva was in St. Mongos."

The Healer, whose name tag said, "Burke", asked, "Are you related to Minerva McGonagall?"

"Yes, I'm her sister."

He looked down, took a breath and asked, "Is it OK to talk before this man?"

She gasped and then said, "Go ahead. Wendt is like family."

The healer nodded, "She's in very serious condition. She's been unconscious since she arrived and we're afraid that there has been permanent nerve damage. We are keeping her comfortable and we're observing her."

"Can't you do something more?"

He shook his head.

"Can we see her?"

He was thinking. Finally, he shrugged and said, "That's OK." He added, "Just one visitor at a time. No excitement. Do you understand?"

We both nodded. I turned to Maggie, "Go ahead. You should see her first. I'll be out here if you need me."

The next twelve hours were excruciating. Most of the time I was stuck in the Waiting Room. Beryl, Minerva's aunt, showed up an hour after Minerva did, and we talked until Maggie came out. I told Beryl about politics at Hogwarts, Umbrage, and the sacking of Hagrid.

She asked me, "Why does the Ministry put up with someone like Umbrage?"

I rolled my eyes and shrugged, "Fudge is absolutely convinced that the real purpose of the 'return' of Riddle is getting him ejected from being Minister of Magic and getting Dumbledore to replace him. How he can think that a man who refused the Ministership or whatever you call it twice—or was it three times—in favor of being Headmaster of Hogwarts would want his position now is clinically insane. AND the Minister's behaving as if he were."

Maggie came out and I had to repeat most of that, except that she was more up on the current politics at Hogwarts. Then Beryl took Maggie's place in the MICU.

Maggie looked at me and observed that I was looking pretty ragged—unshaven, unwashed, and clothes almost terminally rumpled. "Why don't I take you back to Hogwarts? You can wash up, change clothes, and so on. Then we can come back here."

I thought about that for a couple of minutes and decided to go out on a small limb. "Look, Maggie, I'm a little reluctant to go back to Hogwarts. I don't want to run into Umbrage. She might make some unreasonable demand—like that I stay and teach my classes. Would you mind if I went to your house instead to freshen up?"

She agreed, and we went back down to the main entrance to the fireplace there. On the way, I asked how Minerva was. Maggie just said, "She's resting easy."

"Not conscious?"

"No. But she doesn't seem in distress."

Then, I had an idea. "Maggie, would you mind if we stopped at Diagon Alley?"

She stared me a bit suspiciously but asked why.

"Well, for one thing, I don't have any clothes at your place and I'd like to buy a few things to tide me over for a few days. And. . ."

She didn't let me finish right away. "You'd buy clothes rather than go back and take a risk of seeing Umbrage?"

I shrugged, "You don't know her."

"I guess not."

"But I'd also like to buy a book."

She was surprised. "Are you getting bored in the Waiting Room?"

"No. It's not for me, it's for Minerva."

"A sort of get well gift?"

I nodded, "Sort of. Muggles understand that people who are unconscious often can remember some of what happened around them and may even be conscious of it at the time. I thought that I'd read to her."

We had reached the main entrance, and she said, "Well, then, let's go to Diagon Alley first." We did.

We landed in the Cauldron. Tom greeted us. He did a double take when he realized that I was not with Minerva but Maggie. I noticed, gave a brief explanation to Tom, and said that we didn't have time to have a beer, but I'd stand him one right now. He was agreeable.

We first went to Madame Malkin's, and I quickly bought a couple of simple robes appropriate for most common occasions. She was unhappy that I wouldn't let her alter them for me, but I begged off, saying that I really had to have them immediately.

We then went to Flourish & Blots. Once there, I had to ask Maggie a question. "Do you have a Bible at home?"

She didn't. So, I asked the sales person to show me their Bibles. Maggie asked, "Why a Bible?"

"I'd like to read to Minerva from it. I think that it might be reassuring."

She shrugged. In the mean time, the sales witch took us to a section of the store that I'd not been in before—Personal Enrichment. She waved a hand at a shelf of Bibles. I quickly examined them and found mostly King James Versions. So, I came to the point, 'Do you have any NIV versions?"

She examined the shelf. "It looks like we don't, but we could order one. We usually have a couple. I don't know why we don't have any now."

"OK. What about Revised Standard Version?"

I needn't have asked. They were right under my nose. I quickly picked one and purchased it. Then we went back to the Cauldron. I had an idea then. "Maggie. You haven't eaten since this morning, have you?"

She shook her head. I asked, "OK. Then why don't we order several sandwiches from Tom and have a butter beer while we're waiting for them?"

She couldn't object, so we did that, sitting at the bar, having butter beers and looking around to see if we knew anyone in the Cauldron at the moment. Neither of us saw anyone. So, when Tom arrived with a sack of half a dozen sandwiches and a couple of apples, I paid him. We left by floo for Maggie's house.

She asked me why I had suddenly become so generous. My answer was, 'Generous. When haven't I been generous? All this is, is a few sandwiches and apples. Nothing expensive."

"Yes, but you usually are so scrupulous in dividing up expenses when we go out."

I had to admit that maybe I was. "Well, Maggie, I've come into some money, and this is an occasion to be generous if there ever were one."

She just hmmmed.

I quickly showered and changed clothes. Then, we were back on the way to the hospital. We got there, and we had to wait about a half hour in the Waiting Room for Beryl to leave Minerva's room. We'd already had some supper, so I handed Beryl the bag. "Have whatever you like out of there. It's my turn with Minerva. I'll see you in a couple of hours."

Beryl called after me as I opened the door to the MICU, "How much do I owe you?"

Maggie just said, "Nothing. He's being generous. Don't take a chance that he'll change his mind."

I found Minerva's room and went in. She was lying in the bed. Maggie was right. She seemed as though she were only getting a good night's sleep. Her face was unmarked by any signs of pain or worry. I found it almost impossible to resist the temptation to take her hand in mine and try to rouse her. I knew that I would regret it, considering Healer Burke's instructions. There were two chairs in the room and a table. There was a window that gave a view of the downtown London cityscape. It wasn't too cheery, but it was better than nothing.

I sat and tried to figure out what to do. It was one thing to talk about reading to the woman that you love and quite another to see the woman, apparently blissfully sleeping. and simply start reading. I decided that I'd start by talking to her.

"Well, Minerva, here's another fine mess that we've gotten ourselves into." I couldn't keep a sob from interrupting my simple statement, but once I'd gotten it out, it wasn't as, well, embarrassing as I had thought. So I went on.

"Maggie and I went down to Diagon Alley to buy some clothes so that I wouldn't embarrass you by wearing the same clothes day after day." I was stuck then for a moment but followed by, "Well, what do you

160

think of them? Oh, you'll want me to stand so you get a better view." I stood and slowly turned to show off the clothes.

"Oh, I know. Very plain. Don't remind me. I was in a hurry."

"Oh, yes. I bought a book. I thought that you might like to listen to me read from it. I'll start with the book of Psalms." I hesitated, as though she were answering, "Yes, I know. You don't have to agree with any of it. Here goes,

"**1** Blessed is the man who walks not in the counsel of the wicked, nor stands in the way of sinners, nor sits in the seat of scoffers; **2** but his delight is in the law of the LORD, and on his law he meditates day and night. **3** He is like a tree planted by streams of water, that yields its fruit in its season, and its leaf does not wither. In all that he does, he prospers. **4** The wicked are not so, but are like chaff which the wind drives away. **5** Therefore the wicked will not stand in the judgment, nor sinners in the congregation of the righteous; **6** for the LORD knows the way of the righteous, but the way of the wicked will perish."

I stopped and thought about what I'd just read. "Yes, I know, right now it seems like the sinners are in the congregation of the righteous, but they will not stand."

I gave her a couple of minutes. Then I said, 'Can I go on."

I waited a minute. "Since silence betokens consent, we'll keep going." I continued with Psalm 2. I kept reading for almost an hour and admitted that I was tired and would take a break. I resumed for a while. Then, I just sat and watched her imperturbable face.

After a couple of hours, I went out and Maggie went back in. When she came back after several more hours, we held a council of war. Beryl was very tired and announced that she was going home. Maggie agreed and suggested that we all stay the night with her and return early tomorrow.

"No, ma'am. I'm staying through the night. I can sleep in that chair next to Minerva better than I could in a bed far away."

They agreed, and I went back in and read to Minerva for a while. Then I dropped off to sleep myself.

Nurses came through during the night to check Minerva's condition. Sometimes I had to leave the room. Sometimes, I could stay.

When the first 24 hours were completed and Minerva no better, I determined to give the Healer a quizzing about her treatment and outlook. He came in about 8 AM, and I stayed as he examined her.

"What do you think, Healer?"

"She's not improving as I'd like."

I was blunt, "She's not improving at all."

The rest of the day, was much like the previous one. There was time off to have a shower, a change of clothes, and some lunch. I spent six hours in a couple of shifts in Minerva's room, reading, talking, and frankly, resting.

On the third day, the Healer came out with Beryl and asked us all to join him in the cafeteria for tea. We trudged down with much foreboding about what Burke would have to say. Our worst fears materialized.

Burke simply said, "Ladies and Mr. Wendt. I think you should probably not maintain your round-the-clock vigil."

I was afraid of the answer to my question but I asked it anyway, "Why shouldn't we?"

"Well, there's every chance that Minerva may recover eventually, but for the time being, I don't think it will happen soon. You should prepare for a long siege."

"And why would that be?" Beryl asked.

Because I think that she's sustained some damage that will be slow in healing."

The ladies objected to that, but I had been worried that he would be saying precisely that. I decided that it was time to publicize an idea that I'd had in the long hours of the last night watch. I waited for the Healer to make any further points or comments. It became clear that he was done, so I saved him the trouble of a painful withdrawal. "Well, Healer, I'd like to talk with the ladies. Do you mind if we do that in private?"

He was all too happy to let us speak in privacy. He withdrew and left the cafeteria, which was pretty quiet and empty at the moment. I leaned back and looked both of the ladies in the eye. "Maggie, Beryl, I think that it's time to speak openly."

Maggie must have had a premonition of what I would say because her face fell. She was clearly not interested in hearing what I had to say. Beryl either had no idea or was not as horrified as Maggie.

"Ladies, the Healer has as much as given up. I want to try what Muggles might call alternative medicine."

Maggie threw her hands up and said, regardless of who might have heard her, "You're talking about Muggle medicine. You want to invite one of those shamans that the Muggles call doctors to see her."

This was not a good start, but I plunged on, "In the first place. That's all that I want to do—have someone see her. There would be no treatment without your approval."

Beryl had been caught completely unawares, and she fluttered her hands, apparently a coping mechanism when the worst arrives. Maggie said, "Absolutely not. I won't take the chance that one of those quacks will do something without permission. And that's Final!"

Beryl was still frozen in place, apparently trying to take in the enormity of my suggestion, but I went on. "Look. The Healer has agreed that it's a nerve problem. There are Muggle doctors who specialize in Neurology. It wouldn't hurt to get a second opinion."

Maggie was livid and couldn't manage a sound for a few minutes, so I turned to Beryl, "What do you think? Do you think it would be awful to just get an opinion?"

She finally thawed, "Maggie, do you think it would be so terrible just to have someone take a look?"

Maggie was immovable. I allowed the idea to drop—for then. We returned to the MICU, and the afternoon went on as before. In the evening, we all went down and had dinner in the cafeteria together. While we were there, the Healer came into the cafeteria and joined us briefly.

"I'm glad that I caught you all. I wanted to tell you that we've decided that Minerva can leave the MICU. We're transferring her to room 245. It should be done by the time you're finished with dinner."

Maggie brightened, "Do you mean that she's shown improvement.'

Burke didn't say anything. But as he was composing an answer, I provided it for him, "No. He's given up on Minerva. He doesn't think there's anything that he can do, and he's transferring her out of MICU to free a valuable bed there. Right, Healer?"

Burke was clearly uncomfortable. His face turned crimson, but he made a brave front of it, "I wouldn't put it that way. Rather to say that she will get just as good care in a normal ward as in the MICU."

I threw a hand in the air and said, "See!"

Maggie's face fell as did all ours. She nodded and said, "Thanks, Healer for informing us. It'll make it easier visiting her if we can all be there at once."

This obviously relieved the healer of delivering any more bad news, and he excused himself.

I didn't say anything. They were all capable of reasoning on their own and coming to the correct conclusion. We finished dinner in silence and made our way up to room 245. When we got there, they'd finished settling Minerva in, and we found, at least, that it was a private room—in effect. There was a second bed, but no one was in it.

We all stayed until ten. I did a little reading. I discovered that it was harder reading with both awake and unconscious listeners than just the unconscious. When they left, Maggie tried to convince me to stay the night at her house, but I wouldn't have it. I found out that the staff didn't mind if I slept in the unoccupied bed.

The next morning, Maggie showed up with some hot oatmeal, muffins and orange juice in a hamper, and we had an impromptu breakfast in Minerva's room.

A little later Beryl joined us and had a little breakfast as well. She asked about any hopeful signs. There had been none.

Then something completely surprising happened. Maggie said, "Beryl, maybe we should think about bringing in a doctor. What do you think?"

Beryl shook her head sadly and said that she couldn't think of anything else. She'd been thinking most of the night. "Yes, let's go ahead."

Maggie asked me, "You can find one, right?"

I hadn't really thought through to the point of actually having to find a neurologist. However, I made a brave assurance, "Sure. I'll get going right away."

Maggie was sort of angry with me. "Well after you'd talked about it so much, I sort of thought you already had someone picked out and ready to go."

I was snappish too, "How could I do that since I've been in this hospital the whole time." I got up and suddenly realized that I didn't have a way of getting back into the hospital without help. "Uh, would one of you mind coming with me so that I can get back in?"

Beryl said, "I'll go. You hold down the fort here, Maggie." Then, we were off. After we were in the elevator she asked me, "Where are we off to?"

"A library."

She stared at me and I shrugged, "Just trust me."

We went to the London Library near Hyde Park. All I really wanted was a phone directory, but why not have a source of all sorts of information. We arrived and quickly found a Metro London phone book. In it there were hundreds of listings for Neurologists. I took one at random and phoned up his office.

It turned out that he was booked up for quite some time. So we kept trolling through the pages and finally found one who had an appointment slot open that afternoon. We disapparated to his address, and I decided that we'd camp out until our appointment time. Maybe he'd have a cancellation and could see us early.

We didn't have that kind of luck. I had a hard time getting his secretary to let us see him without providing lots of personal information, but it is sometimes useful to have a lot of money at your disposal.

So, it was that we walked into Dr. John Watson Addey's inner office. He invited us to sit and asked, "How is it that you won't give my secretary any personal information? And which one of you thinks you've a neurological problem?"

I said, "Neither. It is a dear friend and her niece who has the problem." I then introduced Beryl McGonagall.

"All right, but why isn't Ms. McGonagall the younger here?"

I could see that this was going to be a difficult interview. "Well, she's unconscious and in a hospital right now."

Addey looked to the ceiling as if to ask, "Why me, Lord?" But what he said was, "And why not use a neurologist associated with that hospital?"

"We want a second opinion."

"All right, but I can only work with her if she's in a hospital where I have privileges. What hospital is it?"

I could see that this was going to be nearly impossible but I trudged on, "It's a small hospital. You've never heard of it. I'm sure that you don't have a working arrangement there."

"Try me. I'm pretty familiar with the hospitals in the London Metro area."

"St. Mongos." I said with no hope.

He sniffed, "You're right. I've never heard of it. I'm afraid I can't help you unless you got your friend transferred to one of the hospitals I work with. I can have my secretary get you a list. If you can do that, then I'd consider helping you."

We dropped by the receptionist and picked up the short list of hospitals. Then, we left the office. Beryl was still cheerful, "What now?"

Just talking off the cuff I asked, "Can you directly disapparate from a hospital room at St. Mongo's?"

"Yes. It's considered very rude, but no one really tries to prevent it. Oh, except for places like Gringotts and the Ministry. Just what are you thinking?"

"Well, what if we could disapparate Minerva to one of these hospitals." I shook the list of hospitals that Addey worked with. "Maybe we could fool him into at least diagnosing her."

"You mean something like finding a hospital room in one of these hospitals that is empty and sort of checking her in ourselves— informally?"

I nodded.

"Hmm. Interesting. Why not?"

"Yes. We could go looking now to find a hospital that he works with and find an empty room. We'd want to find what hospitals that he does rounds at tomorrow. Then we have a chance of getting him to come in on short notice."

So, we began visiting hospitals. It turned out that the third hospital was one that he had rounds at in the next afternoon. We walked the halls until we found an empty room. This was beginning to seem like it might work. That evening we saw Maggie for dinner and told her our plan.

"Now, let me get this straight. Tomorrow morning we're going to disapparate Minerva out of this hospital directly from her room into a

Muggle hospital where we're going to steal a room to try to convince this New Row surgeon that he should see her?

I knew it sounded pretty sketchy, but I simply said, "Yes."

"And this is the best you two could do?"

"Yes." Beryl affirmed.

"Well, what do we have to lose?" I was surprised at how ready Maggie was for this chancy plan, but maybe that is what love does for you – makes you ready to try anything to heal your beloved.

So it was that the next morning after breakfast we arrived at St. Mongos and set up our base camp in Minerva's room. Maggie and I worked her up between us with her arms around us and Beryl asked if we were ready to go.

Then I said to Maggie, "Time for you to hop in the bed and make like Minerva. Should be easy."

She was a bit surprised, of course, "What! We didn't talk about that."

"Of course not. We'd have been arguing on and on. It's very easy. You just get in the bed. Cover up. Only your head will be visible. You could even take a nap. Just make sure not to move. We don't want a nurse discovering that we've gone with Minerva."

"But the nurses come in every couple of hours and check her. I'll be discovered."

"No, you won't. You're sisters. You look a lot like her. People see what they expect to see. The nurses expect to see an inert lump. You can manage that."

Maggie, grumbling indecipherably, got in the bed, then said, "We could have done polyjuice potion."

"We didn't have time. Now just stop grumbling, and maybe a nurse won't even come in while we're gone."

I was in a hurry to get going. "Let's rock & roll."

Beryl took my hand and the three of us disappeared and reappeared in a hospital room that wasn't that different from the one that we had just left. Beryl asked, "Are you sure we're not still in St. Mongo's?"

I just sniffed and we laid Minerva onto a bed and got her arranged. I went out to the nurse's station. Beryl came with me. When we got there, she raised her wand and said, "Imperio."

I said, "Page Dr. John Addey and have him come to room 384."

The nurse nodded absently and picked up a phone.

I commented to Maggie on the way back to Minerva's new room, "Well, we're in it now."

She agreed. A few minutes later, Addey came into the room and looked from one to the other of us, "No one told me that you'd transferred your niece here?"

He started to examine her. He took her pulse and listened to her heartbeat. Then he looked around the room, "Where's her chart? For the matter of that, where's her history?"

I put my hand on the Glock and said, "We took a few shortcuts here. She's not exactly been admitted into this hospital. Please exam this woman, and tell us everything you can."

He stared at me in disbelief, "Not checked in! How did you get her into the room?"

I opened my mouth to offer an explanation, but he interrupted, "It doesn't matter. I don't what to hear. I'm going to get security and get you thrown out of here."

I turned to Beryl. "Lock the door." Addey had turned to go. He didn't see Beryl pull her wand from her purse and flick it at the door. He did hear the click. He grasped the door handle, anyway. However, he couldn't turn it.

"I don't know how you did that, but it doesn't matter." He tried to depress, the locking button on the door, but it wouldn't budge. Then he banged on the door. Then he shouted for a nurse.

I commented, "That's not going to work. You'll discover that no one will notice your shouts, and anyway, all the nurses have realized that their break time has arrived or they need to go give some extra special care to some patient."

He snorted, "Ridiculous." He walked to the bedside table, and picked up the phone. I nodded at Beryl, and she flicked her wand.

Addey jiggled the switch-hook, shook the handset, punched buttons on the phone, but nothing happened.

"Well, Dr. Addey. I think you might want a little privacy while you examine Minerva. So, Beryl and I will toddle off. We'll be back in a bit. Never fear."

He turned back to us and stared. I took Beryl's hand and we disappeared.

Back in Minerva's room at St. Mongo's, Maggie greeted our arrival, "That was quick. But where the bloody hell is Minerva?"

Beryl said, "We left her in capable hands. We'll be back there shortly to see how the exam is going." She turned to me, "How much time do you suppose?"

I considered the question, "I give him ten, fifteen minutes to figure out that he's not going to get out without us. I think that he'll spend some time trying to figure out some alternative way of dealing with us. Then, he'll settle in and work. I don't know, maybe half an hour. Maybe a little longer."

Beryl shook her head, "You have way too high a regard for the intelligence of doctors. They're a lot like Healers. They're egotistical and slow-witted. And the specialists are worse than the ordinary run of Healers. I'd say at least an hour."

We heard footsteps outside our door and a knock. I said, "OK. Let's try to get her to come back later. I'll pretend that we're praying."

Maggie resumed her stunned-Minerva aspect. Beryl got on her knees as I did. Then I said, "Come in."

It was a nurse. I stood and said, "Sorry. We were just praying with Minerva. Would you mind coming back in an hour or two?"

The nurse looked from one to the other of us, and I added, "She's not flexed a muscle or changed in any way since we got here."

The nurse pursed her lips and said, "All right. But don't let anyone know that I did this."

"No, ma'am" both Beryl and I agreed.

I got back in my chair and picked up the Bible. "Maybe I should resume reading just in case someone else comes in." I opened the Bible to the bookmark that I'd left before in Luke.

Beryl asked, "I thought you were reading in Psalms. Don't tell me you've gone through half the Bible already."

"Oh, I'm doing the highlights that I like. I figured that the Great Physician would be a good read."

I read for a while. After forty-five minutes had passed, I suggested that Beryl and I go back. She shook her head but held out her hand, and we disappeared.

Back in Minerva's other room Addey had taken a chair and was banging against the window. I commented, "Well, Beryl, I have to admit that you've got the measure of doctors better than I do. I thought for sure he'd at least have turned to plotting how to deal with us when we returned."

Addey hadn't noticed that we'd returned until I spoke. At that sound he whirled around from the window and held the chair up between us like a lion tamer. All he needed was a whip to complete the image. "Don't you come close."

I sighed, "Oh, doctor, don't you realize that if we wanted to hurt you, there are a thousand ways that we could have sent you out of this room in a body bag.

"And really, you should know that hospital windows are unbreakable. At least with a chair." I reached into my pocket and into my purse and pulled out the Glock, "Now, with this, you might have a chance against the window."

Addey's knees turned wobbly and then seemed to strengthen a bit. "What do you want?"

Beryl commented, "Even someone like you should be able to remember why we consulted with you."

His mouth opened wider than I thought possible. I motioned to the bed, and he walked stiffly there. He opened his bag and took out a flashlight and opened Minerva's eyes and shined the light in them. He took her pulse. While he was doing these things, he asked questions. "How long has she been in this state? Was she showing any abnormal behavior before the attack? Was it sudden or not?"

We answered them. After about ten minutes, he said, "Look. To diagnose her, I need at least CAT scans, MRI's, and probably a couple of other tests. We can't do them this way." He turned to her and pricked her with a probe. At that her eyes fluttered.

"Has she done that before?"

"No. She's been as still as a rock."

"Maybe she's . . ."

I looked at the other two and then said to Addey, "Look. We're going to leave this room. Just before we do, we'll unlock the door. You can leave but, don't try to come back in for ten seconds.

"And when you do, I really wouldn't bring security with you or file some kind of incident report. When the investigation is over, do you really think that you'll still have privileges at this hospital—or any hospital, for that matter?"

He nodded vigorously and ran out of the room as soon as Beryl released the lock. I said, "Quick let's disapparate. Security will be here in a minute or two." We went to the bed and we all made contact and we reappeared in the St. Mongos room. Minerva hit the floor.

We got her up and into the bed and noticed that she actually tried to say something.

We all looked at each other. No one said anything. No one wanted to jinx the improvement that we'd seen.

We resumed our places. In about a half hour, the nurse returned, and examined Minerva. When the nurse took Minerva's pulse, Minerva opened her mouth and tried to say something again. At that, the nurse ran from the room, telling us not to touch her. We came close to her and she was clearly trying to say a word that started with "W".

Maggie said, "Are you trying to ask where you are?"

She shook her head feebly and tried again. Beryl nodded, "You're trying to say Wendt, aren't you/"

Minerva nodded feebly and I took Beryl's chair next to the bed and Minerva's hand. "Minerva. We've been here all the time. You're getting better."

Just then, Healer Burke entered the room. "Please get back. Let me examine her." He spent about five minutes doing various test, some were like Addey's and some were unique. Some required his wand.

Finally, he turned to us and said, 'Ms McGonagall has made a breakthrough. I think she'll continue to recover. She may have her full faculties back." We all released long-held breaths but he quickly added, "But, it's too early to tell for sure."

Then his forehead wrinkled and he asked, "Did anything happen in the last couple of hours? Was there any sign that she was recovering that you can think of?

We all shook our heads no. Then he tried a different question, "Did you do anything while you were here? Now don't think I'm going to be angry. I just want to understand how she's improved. It could be important for other patients."

We all looked at each other. No one was willing to admit the little adventure that we'd all, including Minerva, had. Then I had a mischievous thought and couldn't resist it. "Well, Healer, we were all praying together just before she started to improve."

He stared at all of us and seemed about to say something when there was a voice behind us all that spoke. It was the nurse, "Healer Burke, when I came in to check the last time, they were all gathered around her bed praying."

He asked, "And on that check she was unchanged."

I noticed that the nurse's cheeks colored a bit, and she hesitated as she said, "I can't think that I noticed anything different."

The Healer hmmed and scratched his chin.

There was another voice that spoke then that none of us had heard in quite a while. It was cracked and soft but we all recognized it, "Do you not feed patients in this hospital?"

We all swung around and found that Minerva had moved her hand and was feebly waving. The Healer said, "Of course, ma'am. We'll get something up to you shortly. I'll go see to it myself." He turned to the nurse and said, "Stay here until I've sent some food up, and she's eaten a little. We'll start with a thin broth."

He left, and we all turned to Minerva. The nurse said, "Only a few minutes of talk. I don't want you to tire her. And after she's eaten, you'll all leave and let her get some proper rest."

A house elf appeared bearing a tray with a bowl of clear broth, a small glass of orange juice and a straw. Minerva ate and made it clear that she wasn't satisfied with how little substance there was in the "meal".

After everyone left, we sat around Minerva's bed and Maggie asked, "The Healer was right. Something must have happened at the Muggle hospital. What was it?"

Beryl had an answer, "Well, it's clear. When that Muggle quack came in the room, and she realized that she might be stuck in a Muggle 'hospital', she decided it was time to get better."

I had another theory. "I think that it was NOT the shock of being in a Muggle hospital. It was the shock of disapparation. That jump-started her."

Maggie asked, "Jump-started?"

"It's a Muggle word. It has to do with automobiles."

Maggie replied, "You and your Muggle ideas."

"No. No." I found that the idea really appealed to me, "Look. There was a small improvement at the hospital after her first disapparation, and almost immediately after we came back on the second disapparation, she was much better.

"As a matter of fact, come to think of it, there's a Muggle practice in treating catatonics that uses shocks—either electric or chemical."

Maggie just said, "I rest my case."

Minerva's improvement was rapid. As a matter of fact, after the first day, the main issue was building up her energy reserves so that she could handle returning to work. Sometime during that next day, she was more than ready to return, only the Healer kept her there. At that point, she shooed me off to return to school and do my duties there. To be honest, it was not pleasant being with someone who was stuck in the hospital and clearly didn't want to be.

So, I got Beryl to drop me off at the Three Broomsticks by floo network. I insisted that she have lunch with me there. It didn't really take that much insisting. She agreed to send me a daily report on Minerva's recovery until she returned.

Back in Hogwarts, Umbrage noticed immediately when I returned, and she summoned me up to the Headmaster's Office. When I arrived, she quizzed me about Minerva. I managed to hold my temper by visualizing that she was actually the doctor, Addey.

"Tomorrow, finals start. Will she be back in time to handle the practicum part of her exams?"

"I think not. But, if you rearrange the schedule a little bit and put her test periods toward the end of finals week, I think she'll be able to handle them, especially if whoever is handling the girl's part of Gryffindor can keep that up until the end of term."

Umbrage had steepled her fingers on the desk and was staring into them as though there were an answer there. After a couple of minutes, she looked up and said, "Yes. That's possible, and we'll do it.

"I assume that you can handle your finals without help?"

I nodded.

"Well, that's all. You may go."

I didn't go.

It took her a couple of minutes to acknowledge that I hadn't left. She asked, "Is there something else?"

"Oh, I just thought that you might want to know how Minerva is."

She dismissed the thought with a wave of her hand, 'I know she's going to be back in time for finals and that she can handle them. What more do I need to know?"

I shrugged, "I don't know. But I am certain that I know all I need to know." With that I got up and left her office.

Finals

Finals arrived. Each teacher is assigned a time slot in the Great Hall for final exams. Every class has two hours. This term, my classes had slots on Tuesday and also Thursday. I was prepared for all exams and hadn't much to do. So I went down to the Hall, especially when owl exams were going. On Thursday, I was on my way down to observe just before my time slot.

Umbrage was proctoring the Transfiguration final. Suddenly, there was the most amazing thing that I'd ever seen. Two figures, on brooms, flew into the room throwing stink bombs and fireworks as they flew. Umbrage seemed to be perfectly flummoxed. I'd have been laughing if I weren't bent over double in paroxysms. The exams were absolutely destroyed. The students ran out to see what would happen next. That shot the exams for the rest of the day.

I joined Minerva at dinner. It seemed like there was so much disorder, no one would notice. As a matter of fact, Umbrage wasn't there. That was unusual. But even more unusual things were to follow. At that point, I just sat and talked with MInerva. She filled me in on details from the incident.

"Well, it seems that the Weasley twins thought that they'd reached the end of their useful academic career, and since they were adults, they utilized their privilege to resign their positions as students.

"On the way out they decided to offer a small pyrotechnics display."

I leaned in toward her so that no one else could hear, "Well, bully for them. You should have seen Umbrage's face."

"Oh, I wish I had, but I've not seen her since yesterday. Do you have any idea where she is?" Minerva asking me where someone was ranked among the great ironies of the world. How I wished that I could tell her, but I honestly had to admit that I had no idea.

After dinner she had to go re-schedule final exams. I offered to help, but somehow she thought she'd make better time on her own. So I went back to my office and continued grading papers.

The next morning, I got down to breakfast and found, well, I found that there were very few teachers present. As I ate, my *Times of London* arrived and I read it. There was nothing special there. The Friday crossword was usually beyond my ken, but I always gave it a try. I sat eating, barely looking at my plate and paying a great deal of attention to the crossword.

I had been expecting that someone in charge would show up and make an announcement about exams that hadn't been completed yet. I scanned the room and the only Head of House that I noticed was Pomona Sprout. Frankly, I didn't expert her to make such an announcement. I decided that the announcements would be in the teacher's mailboxes. I also decided that I'd go directly up to check after breakfast.

Before I could do that, or even finish breakfast, someone, I don't even remember whether it was a student or faculty, shouted out, "Look at the *Prophet*!" I scanned the teacher's table to see if anyone happened to have a *Daily Prophet* at the table. Much to my chagrin, I saw that Sinistra did. I bucked up my courage to go over and ask if I could look over her shoulder.

Actually, I didn't have to. She ran over to me and threw the *Prophet* down on the table in front of me. There were headlines—and little else—screaming on the front page. I don't remember them, but the upshot was that Minister Fudge had been at the Ministry late at night. He verified himself that the Ministry had been invaded by Deatheaters led by Tom Riddle. Of course, they didn't use the name Tom Riddle. I don't remember what the euphemism they did use was, but it didn't matter.

I scanned down the page. There was a photo of Dumbledore and Fudge side by side as lovey-dovey as you please and also a photo of Potter as well with Dumbledore. The entire paper was dedicated to different aspects of the subject.

That immediately explained much for me. Half of the staff of Hogwarts was in the Order of the Phoenix and I would be willing to bet quite a lot that most of them were there last night. Also, I'd have bet that there were precious few aurors there.

That explained why the teachers were not here. They were recovering in their own bed or in a hospital bed or . . . Then I realized that likely Minerva was one of them. I couldn't sit another minute. I jumped up, and despite Sinistra's calls after me, ran up to Minerva's office.

I found her there, grading papers. "You scared me to death! You ran off on this adventure without saying a word to me. Now, I find in the *Prophet* that you've been fighting in the ministry with Riddle. I was afraid that I was going to have to set up camp in St. Mongo's again."

She waved it away with an airy flick of her wrist, "Don't be silly, dear boy. You could have done nothing to help. Why should I worry you unnecessarily?

"I admit that I probably should have notified you after I returned, but if I had, you would probably have insisted on my staying the rest of the night. Then I wouldn't have gotten any rest. Really, you do carry on so!"

I dropped into a chair and shook my head. "Well, after all the excitement of the last couple of weeks, we both deserve a vacation. After the summer holiday starts, let's go somewhere."

She smiled, "Do you have somewhere in mind?"

Washington in the Summer

A self-evident truth if repeated often and vigorously enough will eventually be believed by even the most stubborn witch on the planet. At least that was my theory when I began my campaign to get Minerva to take a vacation with me at the end of the term. The crushing weight of so much bad news over the last term had to be relieved. That was the self-evident truth, and Minerva was the stubborn witch. Eventually my theory was not falsified in practice. Minerva gave in and agreed to take two weeks to travel somewhere. The somewhere had to be a place that did not remind us at every turn of the awful truths that we faced, that did not remind us of the death of Sirius Black, that did not remind us of the escape of so many Deatheaters from Azkaban, and that did not remind us of the return of Tom Riddle.

We argued over the place to go. She wanted to go to Brighton. My reaction was, "How in the world can you forget about things in Brighton? Every accent is Brit. Every sea breeze makes me think of Azkaban. Every time I shiver, I can't help look over my shoulder to see if we're being followed."

"And so, you want to go where? The Continent?" Her eyes were tired. They had an unspoken plea for rest.

"No. The States. There are tons of places we could go that are so different from anything here that you could think of completely different things."

"Where specifically?"

I thought a moment. Then an answer occurred to me that was staggeringly different. "Washington DC."

She stared at me for a moment, uncomprehending. Then she answered, "You mean the capital of the States?"

"Yes."

She considered and surprised me, "Yes. Let's go there. What is there to see?"

I was surprised enough that I could only think of the most obvious things, "There's the White House. Of course, it's hard to get in. You used to be able to pretty easily, but not now." I was beginning to sound to myself like a blithering idiot, but I soldiered on, "There's the Congress. There's the Smithsonian."

Minerva apparently hadn't heard of the Smithsonian. She asked, "The Smithsonian? What's that?"

"It a great museum or really a collection of museums – you might say a museum of museums. It includes the Air and Space Museum, a wonderful museum of Natural History, the National Galleries."

She shook her head, and I explained. "Like your national galleries. There's the Library of Congress."

I stopped and hit myself on the head because of the great memorials that I'd left out. "There's the Washington Memorial—a huge obelisk, there's the Jefferson Memorial." I hesitated to emphasize my personal favorite, "There's the Lincoln Memorial. They were all presidents of the United States and great men, but Lincoln was the president in the most terrible crisis that ever faced the country. The deaths that happened in that terrible Civil War dwarf even the terrible things that have happened here and are likely to happen in the future. It's worth seeing just to remind you that even in the worst times, hope survives. There's the Arlington Cemetery where many of the dead of the Civil War are buried along with the dead of other wars that the US has fought."

"I thought this was supposed to help me forget?"

"There are some terrible things that are good to remember. When you see it, you'll understand.

"And then there are all the little things like the Mall, a great grassy park in the center of all that where people throw frisbees."

She looked her confusion, and I explained. "Frisbees are disks that can be made to spin and soar on the wind. You have to see them to understand.

"And, after we've had all the history we can stand, we can go to New York City, which you never saw properly when we passed through last year."

She smiled, 'OK. OK. You've sold me. I'll start packing. I suppose I'll have to get us passage on a port key again."

I sighed. There was no escape from these gut-wrenching wizarding means of travel, "That's a good idea. Go ahead and do it."

Two days later, we found ourselves headed for the Ministry of Magic. Minerva took me to a pub where we could use the floo network to get to the Ministry. We arrived at the pub and stopped for the obligatory drink to reimburse the pub for the use of its floo connection.

I had wanted to just disapparate to the street outside the Ministry and then go through the visitor's entrance. But Minerva insisted that with the Deatheaters on the rise, it would be good to travel as much below notice as feasible, and entering through the visitor's entrance would attract too much attention.

So, it was that we arrived outside a small pub in Bowling-on-the-Green. We entered and found there were a few people at the bar, and a couple of small groups of two to four at tables. Minerva and I sat at the bar and I ordered a couple of whatever they had on tap. The taciturn barman brought a couple of dark beers. I took a swallow that convinced me that I didn't want to come to this pub again. I glanced at the barman again with his stout build and neat mustache and scowl. It seemed that he wasn't particularly pleased with strangers. After we'd each worked our way through about half the mug, he came by and said under his breath, "Go ahead, you've earned the use of the floo."

I smiled weakly, and Minerva pretended that it was the furthest thing from our minds and got up. I left three galleons on the bar, which covered the beers and included a small tip. We walked over to the fireplace. Minerva took a small handful of floo powder. We took hands, walked into the fireplace, and came out of one of the fireplaces that opened on the great Atrium of the Ministry. We went to the Welcome Desk. The young brunette at the desk barely looked up from a book that she was reading after glancing at us.

Minerva simply informed her, "We're here to rent a port key."

She simply pointed distractedly in the general direction of the Ministry of Magical Travel and we walked off to the office that we'd visited the year before.

I commented, "Security seems rather lax."

Minerva just shrugged.

The Magical Travel Ministry had a receptionist who was much more alert. She appeared to be in her fifties, with short greying hair just reaching her shoulders. She wore large glasses that seemed to surround her eyes and made them look unusually large. She asked us what she could do to help us.

"We want to rent a port key."

The receptionist nodded, pulled a form from a corner of her desk and handed it to me, "Please fill this out and note the fees for renting a port key. Please be careful to mark whether you want a round trip port key or one-way." She glanced at a couple of tables on one side of the large room, "You can use one of the tables. When you've finished, please return the completed form. I'll compute your fees and we require either total payment now or a down payment of 15% of the total. If you have any questions, don't hesitate to ask."

Then an impish smile broke across her face and she added, "Oh, you don't have to answer question 7."

I glanced at the page and smiled myself. Question 7 asked if you intended to take an illegal substance across a border. "You mean that I don't have to declare my nuclear weapons?"

The smile was replaced by a puzzled look, "Your what?"

"Oh, I was just joking." The smile returned.

But Minerva wasn't smiling, "Your what?"

"Oh, I was just joking. Nuclear weapons are Muggle devices of war. I'll never get within disapparation range of any."

We sat and worked our way through the questionnaire. There were the usual questions: Where are you going? How long do you expect to stay? Do you require return passage? Purpose of travel? Then there were the odd questions: Will there be magical creatures in the party? If so, how many? How much Muggle money will you be taking with you? Will you be carrying more than one wand? And so on.

We filled it out, and returned to the reception witch. She glanced over the form and pointed out that we'd not answered the question about controlled potions we'd be carrying. After we answered that question, she nodded and did a calculation on a chalk board, "That'll be three hundred sixty four galleons, and nine sickles. If you don't want to pay the whole amount now, I'll require a deposit of fifty-five galleons."

We hadn't been expecting the fee to be that much. Minerva started to count out the fifty-five galleons, but I had another idea. I got out my credit card and asked her, "I have an account with Gringott's bank. I can write an order to pay the Travel Ministry that amount of money from my account. Would you accept that?"

She stared at me for a moment as though I were speaking a foreign language and then said, "An account?"

I was already regretting having asked, but I explained, "Yes. Gringotts will pay anyone whom I instruct them to. If you could give me a piece of parchment, I could write the order."

Her expression seemed to be suspicious, "Just a minute. Let me check with my boss."

She got up and went through a door at the back. After about ten minutes, she returned. "That arrangement will be all right, but if the bank refuses your draft order, we'll charge you an extra 15% for the trouble."

"That's fine with me."

She pulled out a blank piece of parchment and handed it to me. I filled out a credit card transaction as well as I could remember what went on them and handed it over to her. She glanced at it, nodded, and said, "If this works out, the port key will be ready in about a week. Our port keys are normally small, Muggle objects—like tennis shoes, ball-point pens (whatever they are), old caps. Would any of those be acceptable or would you like something special. There's an additional fee to specify the object."

Minerva, who had become impatient, interrupted, "No, No. That's fine. Let's go, Wendt."

We did.

$$\triangle$$

I was surprised two days later to receive an owl from Minerva that informed me that our port key was ready. She asked me to be ready for her to pick me up the next morning. So, it was that the next morning, I was waiting on the sidewalk outside my rooming house at 8AM. It shocked her to find me waiting, 'What happened? Was there a fire in your house, and you had to evacuate."

"No such thing. You must realize that I know that you would be here to pick me up at 8 AM, so I'm here."

She looked askance at that assertion, but had nothing further to say. We went back to Bowling-on-the-Green to the pub with the floo connection. Apparently, it doesn't take much to become a regular there. The barman greeted us like long-time customers. There were two mugs of tap beer set before us before we'd rested on our stools before the bar.

A couple of true locals came up and said hello. We had to introduce ourselves. We couldn't think of anything other than our real names. One of the locals, a middle-aged woman just beginning to gray asked what we did for a living.

Minerva said, "We teach at Hogwarts."

"Oh, really, dearie. What brings you down this way?"

I decided that a dose of truth that was true but that concealed the whole truth was in order, "Well, you see, we're uh . . "

She immediately leaped in with what she wanted to be true, "You're lovers aren't you, and you don't want it known at Hogwarts. Well, you can rest assured that we'll keep your secret here, don't you see? In small towns like this, we know how to keep secrets, don't we Mabel?"

Mabel, the other local nodded and added, "You bet. Why when the local preacher was having an affair with the organist, don't you think that mum was the word, right Janet?"

Janet agreed. That ignited an exchange between the two, listing all the secrets of the town that had been successfully kept."

Minerva and I finished our beers quickly and left via the floo. We landed in the Atrium of the Ministry and stopped by the Visitor's Desk, The young witch there glanced up from her book at us and waved us on toward the Ministry of Travel. We arrived there, and the same witch as before recognized us immediately. "Your port key is ready. Just go through that door and the second to the right." Then she had an afterthought, "Oh, and Mr. Wendt, your account at Gringott's paid the bill immediately. Very fancy. I can see how that would be useful." Then she gave me a wink.

That didn't escape Minerva's notice. As we passed through the door, she asked, "Was that witch flirting with you?"

"I don't know? What do you think?"

"I think she'd better not be."

Inside the second door on the right, there was a wizard who was holding a fishing rod. "Are you Ms. McGonagal and Mr. Wendt?"

"Yes."

"Good." He handed me the fishing rod. "This is your port key. Handle it with care." He proceeded with a lengthy presentation on the care and handling of port keys. It appeared that port keys could either have preset times or no preset times for travel. This one would transport us whenever we wanted. He warned us about letting Muggles see us travel—as though wizards didn't know to disapparate out of the view of Muggles. "Finally, this port key is set to deliver you at a remote corner of Arlington Cemetery. You have to report to the local WINO within the first 24 hours of arriving?"

"WINO?" I tried to keep from laughing.

"Yes, Wizarding Immigration and Nuisance control Office."

"Last year when we went to New York, the port key took us directly there."

"Yes, that's the way they do it in New York. In Washington, they want you to arrive in one of the national monuments. This year, it's Arlington Cemetery."

He went on about the fact that it was a one-way port key, "You'll have to apply for a port key in the States to get back." He hesitated, chuckled and added, "Unless you're planning on returning by boat." He apparently thought it was quite a joke, because he broke out laughing, controlled himself, and wished us a pleasant visit in the States.

As we left, I turned to Minerva, "What a charming idea—returning by boat."

She just shook her head and said, 'You never give up, do you?"

We took the floo network to another pub that I didn't recognize. We then disapparated from there to somewhere apparently in the middle of nowhere. "Are you trying to shake a tail?"

Minerva stared and asked, "What are you talking about? Nobody has a tail."

"Oh, it's an American expression. It means that you're trying to avoid being followed. We've certainly gone to a bunch of places that I've never been before."

"It's just not a good time to be traveling openly."

She set the fishing rod down on the ground, pulled her wand and said, "Now, I'm going to set the port key to transport in 60 seconds. You'd better be holding it when it leaves."

I nodded. She pointed the wand at the port key and said, "Honorarium". I took hold of the fishing rod as did she. The 60 seconds seemed to take forever to pass, but just as I was about to adjust my grasp, I seemed to fly into the air, spinning as I went. I saw Minerva on the opposite end of the rod, spinning in synchronism with me. Then the bottom seemed to drop out of the world, and I fell and hit ground.

It had been early afternoon when we took off and was now, clearly morning where we landed. I looked around and saw that we were in a small clearing surrounded by trees. Minerva had already picked herself up and was using her wand to dust herself off. She motioned to me to come close and used the wand as a sort of vacuum cleaner to remove all the dust and leaves from my clothes. "There, that's not too bad."

"Thanks. It never occurred to you that this is a pretty messy way to travel?"

"Oh, don't whine. Let's go check in to our inn." She held out her hand toward me.

But I shook my head. "No, the guy back in the Ministry was right. This is an important historical site. We should do a little sight-seeing first."

Minerva knew a losing case, when she saw one. She just nodded and dropped her hand. I led the way—not really knowing where we'd come out of the woods. I just decided to head east and see what we found.

What we found was an open field with row upon row of modest grave-stones. Minerva asked, "How old is this cemetery?"

"It was dedicated after the Civil War—the 1860's. It's reserved for people who served in the United States military."

We walked through the seemingly endless rows of identical graves. "How many soldiers are buried here? It seems impossible that so many died fighting for their country."

We looked over the somber gently rolling hills, "Oh, most didn't die serving in war, but many did. There were hundreds of thousands who died in the Civil War. Would you like to hear an irony about this cemetery?"

She looked at me with a troubled look on her face. "I'm not sure that I want to hear an irony about this place."

"It's a good irony."

"OK." Her look was still not quite untroubled.

"The property originally belonged to the primary general who fought for the South. After the war, he gave it to the winners in the North to be used as a national cemetery."

Minerva's face relaxed, "Yours is truly a strange country."

"I'll take that as a compliment." We continued our walk through the cemetery. We reached the Memorial Drive.

Minerva offered to disapparate us to the inn, but I had a different idea. "Let's take the train to the other side of the river." She reluctantly agreed. We walked to the Arlington station, and I proceeded to buy tickets for us at a kiosk.

Minerva stopped me by taking my hand as I was about to pay using my credit card. "What are you doing with that card?"

"I'm paying for our fares. So?"

She took the card out of my hand and examined it, "I could swear this is the same card that you use back in England."

"Yes. So?"

She was clearly puzzled, and I couldn't figure out why. "But if it's the same card, how can you use it here?"

With that simple question, I had a revelation. The idea of credit cards was utterly unkown to the vast majority of the universe of magic. That Minerva understood credit cards as a substitute for what she thought of as money—small metal disks—galleons, sickles and knuts—was amazing. She had leaped over the idea of promissory notes—paper that represented the right to convert them for metal coins—and directly to credit cards, or really, to debit cards, which was what my card was really, was amazing. It was too much of a leap to encompass international credit cards. So, I started to explain the idea, "Yes. Well, money is money. The card company just converts dollars and cents to pounds and pence, and then Gringotts converts that to galleons, sickles and knuts."

"But how can that happen so quickly and across the ocean?"

I knew this might come. How could I explain all the intricacies of data processing. Networks—how many were involved? Certainly, the kiosk to the local internet node by phone line, the network of routers connected by fiber optics. The Metro mainframe that records the purchase and passes the transaction via the network again to the MasterCard processor. Then there was the link across the Atlantic by satellite or undersea cable. Then there was the Master card processor in England that billed Gringotts. Somewhere in there, there was the conversion of currency to English. Gringotts then removed funds from my account.

I decided that I'd just ask what seemed impossible to Minerva, and then attack that, "Well, what's the difference, really, between my using the card here and in England in the Tube. You've taken the Tube with me, right?"

She gave me her exasperated look of "How can you be so stupid?" "Well, of course, we've taken the Tube. But that's completely different. Your accent or account or whatever it is is there at Gringotts, not a dozen miles away. This is across the Atlantic."

"OK. Well, let me at least prove to you that my card will work here. I'll just buy us two tickets and we'll be on our way."

She seemed to be satisfied, and I swiped the card and started to select a ticket. Then I noticed that I could buy a cheap day pass if I waited until 9AM. So, I cancelled the transaction. Minerva immediately picked up on it and said triumphantly, "You see. It doesn't work. I've got some British pounds. Let's try those."

I knew it was hopeless, but I went ahead and said, "It's not that. We just have to wait a few minutes until 9AM and then. . ."

She snorted, "Oh, right! It only works at certain times. You should have said 10AM. Then you wouldn't tempt me to wait till 9."

Resignedly, I said, "Just bear with me and wait till 9."

"Well, if you insist, but you are—what is the American expression—cruising for losing."

"That's cruising for a bruising. Just wait a few minutes and you'll see."

The clock on the kiosk turned to 9 after an interminable wait in the cool morning air. Then I swiped my card, selected two day passes, and paid for them. The kiosk spit them out into a little cup. I retrieved them and started to hand one to Minerva but pulled it back at the last moment. "Now what do you think of my card?"

She reached for the card, which I thrust behind my back. She reached around my back to snatch it, but it brought her face so close that I had to take the opportunity to steal a kiss. She broke out laughing, and through the peal of laughter complained, "This was all a plot to steal that kiss."

"Well, if you want it back, I'd be happy to oblige."

"I just want the damn ticket."

I'd made my point, so I politely handed the ticket over to her. We went through the turnstile, which was much like the ones in the Tube, and Minerva navigated it without problems. We went to the platform and waited for the next train. As we waited, she groused, "Well, I suppose you were right about your card, but I just can't quite believe that it works that easily."

"I could explain the details of how it works, but I don't think you'd find it interesting. But you have to admit that it's almost like magic."

She wrinkled her nose and exclaimed, "It's not at ALL like magic. I have no problem understanding magic, but I just don't think this is 'natural'."

I just shrugged. Shortly after, a train arrived; we got on and were on our way. At that time of day, we had no trouble finding seats. I put her next to the windows. "You see, one reason that I wanted to ride the train is that you get a good view of the Potomac, the historic parts of the city, and even Reagan International Airport over there." I pointed down the river. As we approached the shore, the train descended and went below ground level.

Minerva asked "Where are we getting off."

I just smiled.

"OK. Be secretive."

We passed several stations, and when we reached the Capitol South Station, I got up and Minerva followed. We climbed the stairs to 1st Street and headed north. We walked beside one of the great institutions of the country. I turned to the right and asked, "Well, Minerva, do you know what this is?"

She gazed at it a moment and said, "This is a classic monumental piece of architecture. Besides that, I don't know."

"It's the Library of Congress. Later, we should go in and take a tour."

"But if it's Congress's Library, will we be able to go in?"

"It was founded for Congress, but every US citizen can use it. And, actually, almost anyone can use it." A thought occurred to me,

"You could use it. You just have to file an application, stating what research you want to do."

"But we're not going there now?"

"No." We turned right at East Capitol Street and walked another block.

"You still don't care to tell me where we're going?"

"We're there."

"Just where is there?"

"Come in and let's see." We walked up to the building and I opened the door for MInerva she entered and we found ourselves in The Folger Shakespeare Library and Theatre. "This is a moderately famous theatre where there are performances of Shakespearean plays. We're going to walk up to the Box Office and try to buy tickets for whatever is playing here tonight."

It turned out that *The Tempest* was playing, and there were tickets available. The only ones were in the Balcony along the stage right side of the Auditorium, but I was glad to get them. After leaving, I agreed to going to our pub and even to going by disapparation.

We walked to the east side of The Folger, crossed the street, and walked between two homes to screen ourselves from the view of the street. I took Minerva's hand. We re-appeared in what appeared to be a pleasant suburban street. There was no sign of a commercial establishment—like a pub. There was just a long street with pleasant houses. That didn't surprise me. Except when Minerva wants me to, I rarely see magical establishments. They're screened from Muggles. She took my hand and I saw what looked like a large Tudor mansion. It appeared to be made of dark stones. There was a plaque over the door with a painting of a cat in exaggerated boots. The title below it was "The Cat in Wellingtons". There was a large double door at the top of a few broad steps. We walked up, and as we approached the doors, they opened on their own. There was a Front Desk on the right of the lobby that we entered. The entire left side of the first floor was separated by a waist-high partition. Beyond it was a bar toward the back of the room and a number of tables. On the wall opposite the partition there was a large walk-in fireplace. Minerva walked up to the Front Desk and asked if there were rooms available for the next couple of nights.

The woman behind the Front Desk offered us a room with a large four-poster canopy bed or a room with a pair of smaller single beds.

She seemed to be expecting us to take the latter room, because she'd already pulled out a key as Minerva signed the register. Minerva looked up and smiled, "The four-poster please." The woman's eyes widened a bit, and she simply said, "Oh." And then she exchanged keys.

Then she fell into what must have been a well-rehearsed litany for her. The locks were "Alo Ahora" spell-proof. There was an ice-chest in the hall of the second floor. The pub was open until local closing at 2AM. The kitchen, though, closed at 11 PM except Friday/Saturday when it closed at midnight. There was room service during those hours. There was a safe in the office for valuables if we wished to use it. Any questions could be sent to the Front Desk on the Inn stationery in the rooms. It was magically enchanted to fly to the Front Desk when addressed to Front Desk.

The woman asked for two nights' rent. Minerva turned to me and asked, "Do you want to pay with your fancy crated card?"

The woman behind the desk looked up, startled, "I'm sorry, Mr. Wendt, we don't accept credit cards here."

Minerva stared at her and asked, 'You know about these credit cartons?"

"Oh, yes. Lately, there have been several guests from England who've had them. We'd never heard of them before this year. The people who've had them say that they're all the rage among the wealthy. They're apparently good for buying things from Muggle companies. We've been thinking of starting to accept them for payments."

Minerva barked a little laugh, "Who would've thought that that idea of yours would go anywhere?"

The woman looked at me incredulously, "You invented these credit cards?"

"Well, not really or at least the Gringotts goblins bear some of the blame."

She just gawked, and I turned to Minerva, "Let's go look at our room."

We turned to go, and I turned back to the Front Desk, "By the way, where is the Inn located?"

The woman gawked again but did answer. "Why Chevy Chase, of course."

The room, on the third floor, turned out to be small, but elegant. It had the promised four-poster, which was made of elaborately carved

Mahogany. There was an armoire, a dresser and a small writing table. The writing table had a stack of writing paper with the Inn's letterhead and a small pad of note paper. The floor was wood with a rug

I opened the armoire to unpack some of my clothes and found a floor-length mirror on the inside of one of the doors. I commented that we should really get a nap because the play wouldn't start until after midnight London time and would finish much later.

Then I remembered WINO. "Minerva, we've got to stop into the WINO control board or whatever it is."

She sighed, "I'd almost forgotten about that. Yes. We'll go down and use their floo connection."

We did. Minerva took some of the floo powder and said, "Wino." She threw it on the ground, and we came out of the floo in a dark pub. There were a few seedy characters sitting at the bar and nobody at the tables."

I said, "I think we have the wrong wino."

Minerva nodded, said "right", took a handful of floo powder from an old rusty pot, and we were back to the Cat. I asked Minerva why we hadn't had a drink at the pub.

"Oh, don't be irritating. We obviously went to the wrong place. I didn't want to spend a second more than I had to there."

We walked over to the Front Desk. Before Minerva had half begun her question, the clerk said, "Everyone makes that mistake. You have to use the official name of the Wizard Immigration etc. Here let me give you this card."

She picked up what looked like a business card from a stack on the desk. "This lists all the major destinations in the DC area and their official Floo Network names. It's very useful. I'd keep it with you at all times."

Minerva glanced at it and thanked the clerk. We then went back to the fireplace, but this time Minerva read the official title off the card, "Wizard Immigration and Nuisance control Board."

We arrived at a much nicer destination. The receptionist sent us to a small plain cubicle with a small desk. There was hardly room for all three of us in it. The short greying fonctionnaire seemed to be as much a part of the cubicle as any of the spare furnishings. The chairs were institutional white plastic with tubular legs. I hoped that the official's seat was a lot more comfortable than mine.

He asked to see our documents, which MInerva was keeping in her purse. She handed them over, and he scanned through them quickly and efficiently. "Very well, sight-seeing. Well, this city has as many interesting sights to see as any in the country, I think." As he went through the rest of the forms, he muttered to himself almost inaudibly.

Finally, he looked up at us and in a bored voice asked, "Wands, please." Minerva handed hers over, and I just smiled. He commented, "Oh, yes. You're a Squibb right?"

I nodded. He went on, "And an American citizen.

"Do either of you have any dangerous or forbidden or cursed objects to declare that're not listed here?"

We both shook our heads.

He handed Minerva her wand and pulled out his own. "Since the return of 'He-Who-Must-Not-Be-Named' has been verified, I'm required to put a trace on all magical visa-holders."

Minerva opened her mouth to object, but the still bored-looking official answered the question that he didn't give her time to ask. "Don't be concerned. The trace is limited until you leave the country and only tracks the Unforgivable Curses. It will be lifted when you leave the country via a WINO office."

The official pointed his wand at Minerva and spoke a rapid charm that I couldn't make out. Then he pointed it at me, and I opened my mouth to object. Again, he spoke before I could object, "I know. I know. You're a Squibb and can't do any curse, let alone an Unforgivable. But I'm required to do it. There are no exceptions for Squibbs. It's stupid. It's bureaucratic twaddle, but I'm required to do it." Then he rapidly spoke the charm.

We returned to the Cat and to our room. We took off our traveling cloaks and got as good a nap in as we could manage.

Minerva, waved her wand,.the drapes closed, and the room became quite dark. We got maybe an hour of real sleep and another hour or so of the sort of quiet rest that does refresh somewhat.

Then, we were up and dressing for the theatre, although it was still four hours away. We went down and argued over whether to go near the theatre and find a place to eat or dine at the inn. My argument was that the inn was early—it was only 4PM. Minerva's was that it was already late—9PM London time, so we should eat now, here. She won.

It wasn't a bad meal. They didn't have a very lengthy menu. The ragout that I ordered and the beef Wellington that she ordered were both excellent. There was a discussion about traveling to the theatre. I wanted to take the Metro again. We had the daily tickets, so they wouldn't cost us anything and we could go from a local station that would be a pleasant walk from here. It was Minerva's day. She won that argument as well, insisting that we didn't want to take a chance getting lost in an unfamiliar train system when we had tickets for a play that wouldn't wait for us if we were late.

She checked with the Front Desk and discovered that there was a wizarding pub a few blocks off the Mall from which we could walk to The Folger. So, we went to the fireplace, Minerva took some floo powder (courtesy of the inn for guests), and we walked into a pub in Washington—The Green Familiar. We bought butter beers (we had time to kill) and checked directions from there to The Folger. We nursed the beers and left for The Folger about 7 P.M. We arrived and had to wait for the doors to open. They had a little museum devoted to Shapespeare. We spent our time viewing the exhibits.

When they let us into the theatre we found that the Balcony along the sides had only a single row of seats. We were pleasantly surprised to find that they were not theatre seats but individual, moveable seats. Since we had a lot of time to wait and no one near yet, we turned our seats to face each other and talked. The theatre itself is made of a dark wood that gives the impression of age, which seemed appropriate to seeing *The Tempest*.

Minerva was thoroughly enjoying the evening even though the play had yet to start. We talked about the Inn, our room, the meal, the theatre. It had been a completely pleasing day, long though it had been. I found myself holding her hand, our fingers intertwined, and we were gazing into each other's eyes as we talked, "You know, I never noticed how lovely your emerald eyes are."

A frisson passed through her whole body and a shy smile crossed her face as her eyes sparkled, "Oh, you tell all your lovers that."

"Only the ones that have emerald eyes and are witches whose names start with Minerva."

She laughed and leaned toward me in a gesture that I took to be an invitation to a kiss that I immediately accepted and leaned forward to consummate. The kiss was slow and ended with a casual parting that promised much more.

Somehow the theatre had nearly filled, and we had company in the Balcony that I hadn't noticed. We rearranged our chairs so that they were both facing the stage. I was to her right and slightly behind her. After the house lights went down, I transferred my hand to her right thigh and found myself caressing her. At the intermission, we stood at our chairs and spoke desultorily about the play, and how we would pay the next morning for staying up so very late (long past midnight in London).

After the play, we were both played out. Even I could not force myself to walk the distance to The Green Familiar so that we could take the floo network to the inn. So, I actually suggested disapparating.

The next morning we were up at six. We were still basically on London time and it was quite late in the morning there. We went down and were happy to find that we could order breakfast and especially happy that they had decent hot tea.

It was way too early to go to any museums. Since we had some time to kill, I suggested that we take a walk in the neighborhood. It was a heavily wooded area with close-set houses with small yards. Although I seemed to walk at random, I was heading for the Friendship Heights Subway Station. So, at one point, I casually commented, "Well, what do you know? A Metro station. It would be easy to get downtown from here via Metro."

Minerva looked disgusted, "And I thought we were walking because you enjoyed strolling with me!"

"Oh, but I do. I also like to know my neighborhood wherever I am."

She sniffed, and we returned to the Inn. By the time we got there, it was almost time for public places to open, so we tried to use the floo network to get to a pub downtown. Nothing happened. The bartender called across the room to us, "Were you trying to go to the Familiar?"

We admitted that we were. He told us that the floo connections there only worked during normal business hours. It was still almost ten minutes until they opened. He invited us to have a cup of coffee "on the house" while we waited. We accepted but requested tea rather than coffee. That was no problem.

When we arrived at the Familiar, we found that we were the first people of the morning.

We had a cup of coffee. They didn't offer hot tea. The coffee tasted like left-overs from the previous night, but we felt that we had to drink some before heading on. As we sipped and grimaced, Minerva commented on the coffee, "Well it was refreshing." Then she turned to the WINO office of the previous night. She said that she was pleased with their efficiency.

"Even with the stupid insistence of putting the trace on me?"

"Even with that. In the Ministry, they wouldn't have apologized for the inanity of it."

"Well, I guess that's true."

After drinking a few more obligatory gulps, we asked for directions to the Mall. I was pretty sure that I would remember correctly, but I like to be sure. We reached the Mall quickly and walked to the Library of Congress. We took the tour. Minerva was amazed that the vast majority of the books weren't actually visible in the library, and as a matter of fact, weren't actually in the library at all. "When I go to a library, I expect to see books—even if I can't take them out or use them."

"Well, you can't expect them to let thousands of people just wander the stacks."

She snorted, "Madame Bins would love to run her library the way the Congressional is if she could."

I had to laugh. After that we went to the Capitol. Minerva was properly impressed by the architecture, "It's nice to be able to see a government building from the outside and for the outside to have a beautiful appearance. I have to admit it's not at all like the dump that the Ministry is hidden under."

We had lunch on the Mall at a vendor's cart. She was amazed at the variety of cuisine offered. We ended up settling for polish sausage and fries. "Not quite bangers and mash, but not bad," was Minerva's comment.

Afterwards, I suggested that we walk the Mall to get an idea of what was available to see in more detail. We could discuss the options and plan the next couple of days. She was surprised that there would be enough to justify the time, but I assured her that there was.

We walked the Mall briskly for the most part. Minerva is an amazing walker. She can usually walk me into the ground. By the end of our walking tour, she was beginning to show some signs of needing a rest. We had circumnavigated the Mall and I estimated that it had been a walk of at least five or six miles. On the way, we'd agreed to see the National Gallery, several of the Smithsonian Museums including the Air and Space and to try to take a tour of the White House.

Over the next couple of days we pretty much followed that program. That afternoon we'd toured the National Gallery. By the time we'd finished walking the galleries, we were both pretty fagged out, and we were happy to head for dinner. We asked a few people about good food somewhere near the Mall. There were a couple of recommendations for Cafe Zen. At the Gallery they suggested taking a cab but Minerva is a trooper, if nothing else. She suggested that we walk. It was near the opposite side of the Mall, and it was a good forty-five minute walk at a more leisurely pace than we normally take. However, it was worth the walk.

At the restaurant, the atmosphere was elegant, and the food was wonderful, but we paid for it handsomely. It was a special trip that we didn't mind. We were pleasantly tired, and we took our time over the meal. As we finished, and I paid, Minerva commented, "I have to admit that that invention of yours does come in handy. You've used it all the time with no problems. You do end up with lots of little bits of paper though."

After a stretch of pleasant silence, Minerva began chuckling.

I looked the question at her to which she replied, "It was just that stupid pub that we ended up in last night when we were trying to get to the W.I.N.O office."

"Yeh, you'd think they'd have some way of keeping people from getting there by mistake. There's something Muggle like that. Every now and then, someone's personal phone number is only one digit different from a commonly dialed business number. I remember knowing someone whose number was almost the same as a bail bondsman's number. He got phone calls at all hours-day and night."

"Couldn't he get a different number?"

"Oh, he eventually did, but back then ages ago, it wasn't as easy as it is now."

The next couple of days we worked our way around the Mall, visiting other Smithsonian Museums. One day we visited monuments. We visited the Vietnam Memorial. Minerva was puzzled by it. "I've never heard of all the names of soldiers killed in a war being carved on a memorial."

"I think that they wanted to impress on the viewer the hideousness and pointlessness of the war. All these people died and it never made a difference."

She was silent a moment, "Then we should do something to remember them and remind ourselves of the futility of most wars. Let's read names aloud for half an hour."

We spent a half hour reading names. We picked a random spot on the wall and took turns reading names sequentially. At the end, Minerva was crying, "This war had so many deaths—so many more than the Deatheaters have killed."

"Yes, and this is not the biggest war that America has been involved in by a long shot."

The next was the Lincoln memorial. "Lincoln was President and Commander of the Army during the worst war that America has been involved in bar none. The number of deaths is staggering, and as a fraction of the population at the time is even more hideous."

Minerva looked up at the huge statue, "He looks like he's got all of them on his mind."

"I think he did."

We finished up with the Washington Monument. I dared Minerva to walk up. She took my dare and we struggled all the way to the top. We looked out over Washington and talked about the next day when we'd see the Air and Space Museum. That would be the last day. The next day, we'd leave for New York by train. It had been a battle convincing her to go by train.

"Minerva, how about taking a train to New York?"

She didn't even look up, 'No."

"Oh, come on. You get to see the country-side, towns, cities that you'd never see otherwise."

She rejoined reasonably, 'It's time that we could use in New York."

"It's a beautiful trip, and it takes less than four hours."

She looked up from the path in front of her, "It sounds like you've done some research.'

"Yes, ma'am, and you like traveling by train. Think of the Hogwarts express. It takes a full day to get to Hogwarts."

"I do not like travel by train. I take the Hogwarts Express because it's part of my duty as a teacher. It's you who likes to travel by train."

"We could have lunch in the dining car. You don't even have that in the Express."

"It's probably miserable packaged food."

"It's great food." I tried to urge without sounding whiny. "Let's do it."

She stopped walking altogether and looked me in the eye. "You've bought the tickets haven't you?"

I've learned not to try to avoid unpleasant truths—especially with Minerva, so I simply said, "Yes."

"Well, you turn them back for a refund."

"I don't think I can."

She compressed her mouth in an unhappy line and then said, "Well, if you want to do this so much, I suppose that we have to."

"Believe me, you won't regret this."

"I'd better not!"

The next day we visited the Air and Space Museum and she admitted that there were a few things that Muggles did better than wizards, "You've been to the Moon. I have to hand that to Muggles. I don't think wizards will ever do that." We were looking at a sample from the moon when she admitted that.

It was our last night in Washington. We decided to just walk on the Mall—not the speed walking that we were used to, especially after several days of sight-seeing, but rather a pleasant walk on a pleasant evening. And the evening was indeed especially pleasant. The temperatures were in the mid-seventies. The sunset was gorgeous filtering through low clouds on the horizon. The mall was full of activity:

little impromptu baseball games, the ends of picnics, frisbee throwers, soccer games of all ages.

Minerva expressed her joy at the weather and the crowd and the company, "I understand now why you love this country so much. The heart of the capital is set aside for the people and the little pleasures of life. I'm almost sorry for you that you left it all."

I laughed, "I'll make an American of you yet, but don't feel sorry for me. I have pleasures and joys enough at Hogwarts." I squeezed her arm to illustrate it.

She laughed too and we strolled the length of the Mall arm-in-arm. Then, we disappeared to re-appear in Chevy Chase near our inn.

That night, we spent as wonderful an evening as I can remember in all the time that I've known Minerva.

We didn't have to get up early, so we didn't. We showered, packed, and checked out. We had a light breakfast and took the floo to The Green Familiar. It was a short walk to Union Station. I opened my purse to get out the tickets for New York, and we went to the platform to board. We were early enough that we were the first on board. We didn't have any trouble getting seats on the Northeast Regional. We could have taken an express, but I liked the idea of the frequent stops where we could see the towns and cities at slow speed.

I insisted that Minerva take a window seat. We left the station, and even Minerva seemed to enjoy the trip. We went through Baltimore, Newark, Wilmington, Philadelphia, and Trenton. Then I noticed that we'd stop at Princeton Junction. That gave me an idea.

"Minerva, I notice that we've got a stop at a place called Princeton Junction. It's near Princeton University."

She turned from the window and asked, "So?"

"Well, Princeton is one of the great universities of America, heck, of the world. I've never been there. I know that we can't see it, but I'd like to get out for a few minutes, buy a paper—maybe the Princeton paper if it has one, and get back on."

She shrugged and said, "Suit yourself." She started to turn back to the window and then added, "That's a good idea about getting a paper. It would be good to see some news—any kind of news—even Muggle news."

I made a face, but I was delighted, "Good. We can have lunch in the Dining Car afterward." The conductor announced the approaching

199

stop at Princeton Junction. I got up and swayed to the exit of the car we were in.

The car came to a fairly smooth stop and I exited and immediately began looking for a newspaper vending machine. I spotted a line of them, went over and tried to decide on one. There wasn't a Princeton one, but I had a choice of the *New York Times,* the *Philadelphia Inquirer*, and a Trenton paper. I decided on the *Inquirer*. I had been collecting coins in change along the trip and had a pocketful. I found the right change and bought a paper—almost the last in the machine. They were announcing final boarding, so I headed back toward our car. I could see Minerva in a window. She was turned from the window talking to someone—maybe the conductor.

I had almost reached the car when I suddenly found myself immobilized. I immediately started tipping toward the left. There was this awful feeling of helplessness as the tip slowly turned into a fall. I fell on my side, facing the train. The smack on the concrete of the platform felt like someone had slapped me on the left side of my head with a baseball bat. I started to scream, but nothing came out. I realized why. My entire body was frozen as stiff as a board. There was a terrifying instant when I thought that I had had a stroke. The fact that I couldn't make the slightest move—including batting an eye or wiggling a toe—made me realize that it was more likely that a spell like Petrificus Totalis had struck me.

I could hear perfectly well. I heard concerned voices, calling for help, wondering if I'd had a stroke or a heart attack. I could still see, barely, the window where Minerva was. She was still facing away. I tried to make myself scream for her, but it was just like being asleep and experiencing being paralyzed. The terrible feeling of lethargy, being unable to move no matter how desperately you wanted to, was full on me. Terrified, I tried strenuously to force a single syllable out of my mouth but nothing would come.

The train started to move! It was going to leave, and Minerva was not going to realize that I wasn't going to get on. Then the worst possibility occurred to me. The reason that I was petrified was that some wizard had done it. That meant more trouble coming. I could hear a siren in the distance. I hoped it was for me.

As Minerva's window was about to leave my field of view, I saw her turn back to the window. Then she started to stand just as she disappeared out of my field of view. The siren had been getting much louder but its sound was eclipsed by another sound—an explosion behind me. I felt what must have been fragments of something strike my back and legs.

There were screams around me and more explosions. Suddenly, I was being dragged away from the tracks. A voice that I guessed was directed at me said, "Can you talk?"

Later the incongruity of that question would occur to me, but I was pretty desperately trying again to talk just then. They must have been dragging me into the station because I saw a building and lots of people crouching. A face came into my field of view wearing a fireman's hat. He brought his face very close to mine and seemed to be staring into my right eye. I heard him say, "Must be in shock. I can't raise a peep out of him. Scared stiff—literally." Then he seemed to turn his conversation toward me, "Don't worry fellow. There seems to be a firefight going on out there, but the cavalry's on the way."

More sirens and then the explosions let up. I was being dragged again. We went out a different entrance to the building. I was on a stretcher in an ambulance, and we were on our way in what seemed like only a few seconds.

The EMT's were beginning to examine me more carefully. They seemed to be looking for re-flexes but weren't finding any. One of them said, "This guy seems to be catatonic. Can't really blame him. He seems to have been in the middle when that battle broke out. What do you think?"

The other EMT shined a light into one of my eyes, "Well, at least there doesn't seem to be any serious brain damage, his pupils contract with light, but, I've never seen anyone more catatonic."

Most of the rest of the ride was quiet except for the siren. Nobody mentioned where we were going. We took a couple of sharp curves and backed up. The outside light came in much brighter—must have opened the doors. Then I was being moved again. We entered a hospital Emergency Room. I was taken into a partitioned exam room and unceremoniously tossed onto a bed, facing a blank wall. Coming in, I noticed a wall clock, but I couldn't see it from my position. I had finally gotten over the maddening, claustrophobic feeling of being paralyzed—for the moment. I spent some time trying to see if the spell was wearing off. Sometimes they did.

Sometimes they didn't. Like a couple of years before when several students had been petrified by the basilisk at Hogwarts. Finally, someone came in to the exam room. It was a nurse. It was a blessing that she talked to me as she did things. They didn't always. "Alright dear, I'm going to take some vital signs—nothing to worry about. First, we'll take your temperature. She came into view with a thermometer. She tried to force it between my teeth. She tried several approaches, but she couldn't find a way in. "Sorry dear, it would really help if you could unclench your jaws." Fat chance of that happening.

Finally, she sighed, "Sorry, I've got to go in the other way, then." She didn't have a much easier time, but she finally got it forced in to her satisfaction. I was at the point of tears by the time she was done. After an eternity, she pulled it out—which was almost as bad as putting it in. "Well, you're temp is 99.2. No problem there." She had an easier time taking my blood pressure. Then she slipped a freezing stethoscope down the back of my shirt and listened to my heart. She commented as she went, "110 over 72 and 85 beats per minute. Not bad." Then she left the room.

After a while a male voice entered the room along with the nurse from before. I felt various proddings. At one point he tried to get a knee jerk reflex and, of course, failed. He did the light in the eye test. At another point, he poked me in the sole of my foot with some sharp instrument. I desperately needed to scream, but couldn't. I could feel tears dripping down my cheek. "Come around! See these tears!" I wanted to scream but couldn't. He left the room. Then there was a long wait. Eventually the doctor returned with someone else. They didn't do any tests at first, but just talked.

First Doctor, "This fellow is as still as though rigor mortis had set in, but he's got a normal pulse, blood pressure, temperature. No knee jerk reflex, but his pupils expand and contract with light."

Second Doctor, "Interesting case. Not the usual cataleptic or even catatonic presentation." I could tell they were walking around me, and they eventually came into my view. "Very interesting. Did you notice the tears?"

First Doctor, "What tears?"

Second Doctor, "Look carefully on the exposed cheek. They've dried, but there are clear tear tracks."

First Doctor, "Well, I'll be."

Second Doctor, "Do we know anything about him?"

"He was brought in from the terrorist attack at the AMTRAK station. He's the only one that we got. I gather that he was the only seriously injured one. The rest were treated for cuts and abrasions and released at the scene. He might have been as well, if he hadn't been .;. . well, this way."

"I see. But what about his identity?"

"We don't know. We couldn't find any identification. He had some coins and a few bills in one pocket. There was also an AMTRAK ticket, Washington to New York issued today. We know where he came from and where he was going—sort of." I saw him bring a tray into my field of view. I couldn't see the contents of the tray. He went on, 'A few of the coins are rather strange. I've never seen coins like these. One of them appears to be gold and is probably fairly valuable."

He bent out of view and brought something that I immediately recognized into view, "Then there was this. It was in the other pocket. As you can see, it looks rather like a small woman's purse, but the strange thing is that nobody can get it open."

The second doctor laughed, "Why, it looks perfectly easy. There's just a drawstring and the opening even looks to be partially open."

The other laughed this time, "Twenty says that you can't open it."

"You're on."

One of the few amusing things of that awful day was watching them trying to open it. The second doctor tried loosing the drawstrings casually and then with much more force. In a much more tense voice, he asked, "Get me a scalpel."

"Oh, we tried that."

"Get me one anyway."

The other reached out of my field of view and produced one, "I thought you might want one of these." He handed the scalpel to the other, who tried cutting the drawstrings, first gently and then with increasing force. Of course, nothing happened.

"Have you tried a surgical rotary saw?"

I could hear the other sneer, "No, but you don't really mean that. If a scalpel won't cut that, you might as well give up."

"Then you don't have any idea who he is?"

"No more than you do."

The second doctor looked at me and muttered something like, "I wonder how much of this you can hear?"

He went on, "Well, we've got to admit him, I suppose, as a John Doe. I don't think that he needs to be in intensive care, but we will have to keep his corneas moistened. We'll have to catheterize him until he regains motor control. I guess a feeding tube but that can wait until we're sure that he's not going to come back to the land of the living."

The other said, "A saline drip, too. That's how we'll have to administer any drugs."

I could see the other nod.

They left and there was a long wait. Eventually a couple of nurses appeared and trundled me off to an elevator. I couldn't tell how many floors up we went. I couldn't see the control panel and they didn't say anything about where we were going. They only talked about the latest episode of "Dancing with the Stars."

When we reached the room, it turned out to be semi-private. There was another patient. The nurses told him that I was comatose—not true, of course, but it at least saved me attempts at conversation from the other.

He asked one of the nurses, "Then it's OK if I watch TV?"

"Sure. Just, not too loud. You still have neighbors."

"No problem." He then said, apparently to me, "You won't mind then if we watch professional wrestling?"

Of course, I had no comment. He turned the TV up and I heard the endless inane commentary of the wrestling match. After a while another nurse came in, closed the privacy screen, and inserted the catheter. She didn't warn me, although I knew it was coming sooner or later. She just hmmed as she worked. Then she wheeled in a stand with a saline drip and worked to find a good vein. She was efficient, at least.

I was happy that the feeding tube would not be coming for a while. Before she left, she put some drops in my eye. She couldn't force my lids fully open, but she managed to get some in. In the midst of the operation, she commented, "OK. Sorry about those eyes. I'll try to be gentler the next time. See you in a bit." Then she left.

The wrestling was eventually replaced by local news. The big story was the terrorist attack at the AMTRAK station. There was a reporter, who did most of the talking.

"The attack happened shortly before noon just as the train was leaving for New York. Some law enforcement officials think the terrorists arrived on the train, and intended to kill and injure as many people as they could from the train, and make a get-away via the train.

"Luckily, there were no serious injuries except for one unidentified man who was taken from the scene by ambulance. The authorities are withholding the name and location of this man lest he might have been the main object of the attack.

"I've got an eye witness here, Ethel Mandelbrot, who was on the station platform when the attack started. Ethel, would you please describe what happened?"

"Yes. I had just arrived on the train and was waiting for my cousin to pick me up. I was sitting on a bench, reading the paper when I heard a heavy thud. I looked up and saw that a man had fallen to the ground. A small crowd gathered around him. Then, I saw a man who was standing nearby drop down to his knees as an explosion seemed to rock the station and chips of brick were flying everywhere. I was hit by one in my shoulder. Then, suddenly, there were explosions all around me. There were a couple of men who were jumping up and down and seemed to be firing at someone at the end of the platform. She was standing behind a corner of the station and seemed to be popping around the corner and firing something at the men, who kept jumping around."

"What do you mean, jumping around?"

"Just that. One instant they were here near me and then they were several feet away. It was all very confused, and when I had my wits, I ran into the station and kept my head down. I didn't see anything more."

"Thanks Ethel.

"Well, there you have it. Some sort of attack, but who was being attacked and why? Was it terrorist or an attempted gang killing? Or something else entirely? We'll keep pursuing this story and will report as we learn more."

The studio reporter thanked him and went on to weather. I went on to the boredom of staring at the ceiling and listening to network TV.

I couldn't see a clock, but the cycle of exterior light gave me hints at the time. Well after the sun had set, a nurse came and commented to me, "We don't know if you're getting any sleep, but you need to even if you can't." Without any further comment, out of the corner of my eye,

I saw her hand rise to the saline drip and then my eyes unfocussed and the comic dialog on the TV lost its meaning. It was suddenly much later.

A nurse was taking my temp rectally, a process that was never easy for me. She patted my rump, said, "I'm sorry. That was rough." Then she put me on my back again, and I was drifting away again.

The next I remembered was light—morning. A doctor came in, maybe the second doc from before. He was accompanied by someone— not a nurse, not another doctor, I think. He said, "This case is strange. I've never seen anything like it before. I would normally have him transferred directly to a psych hospital immediately if it weren't that he has physical symptoms that are very hard to trace to mental states. Before I do that, I'd like to send him through a battery of tests that I hope would give us a chance of diagnosing a physical cause for his condition. Do I have your permission to proceed?"

The other person asked, "We have no idea of his identity or relatives/significant others?"

"None."

"I've read your description, but I just can't believe what I've read. Would you mind demonstrating?"

"No. First, something simple. Try to open his mouth."

He moved in front of my face, giving me a pretty good view of his face. It was an oval with short hair, beginning to grey at the temples. He wore glasses, and his hands were protected by latex gloves. "Is he likely to bite?"

"As far as we can tell, he's not moved a muscle in the last couple of days, despite pretty substantial provocation. I think you're safe."

He stuck a couple of fingers into my mouth gingerly and I could feel pressure on my jaws, but they didn't budge in the least.

"No give at all. It doesn't even feel like his muscles are reacting to the force. It's as if they are completely locked. What do you think?"

"I think that I want to do some tests—MRI, EKG, X-rays. I'm hoping we'll find a physical cause for this."

There was silence then the second man said, "OK. Go ahead. I'll get the paper-work going. But I don't think anyone will have objections. God knows who will be billed, but fortunately that's not my department."

They apparently left the room, and I was alone with my roomy for a while. Then a couple of nurses came in and rolled my bed away.

We rode on an elevator so far down that we must have been in the basement. We went into a room with heavy doors and a big piece of equipment. The nurses lined me up beside a sort of table, all the time with a running commentary, "OK. We're going to move you onto this slide that will carry you into the MRI machine.

"It's terribly important that you not move while we're doing the scan." The other nurse tittered and she went on, "Well, I suppose that's not a problem for you. If you have any problems squeeze on this button . . ." Again, there was the titter. "OK, sweetie, sorry that you can't help out here. Just relax as much as you can and don't worry. We've not lost anyone yet." They put a pair of earphones on my head, and the rest of what I heard came through those.

They disappeared from my field of view, and I started to move into the machine. The nurse who had been speaking continued, "OK. You're going to hear some loud noises. Don't let that worry you. Even though it sounds like the machine is about to come apart, It won't"

I continued into the machine, and indeed there were loud banging noises. It's hard to believe that whatever was causing that didn't do some damage to something. I slowly entered the machine and stopped periodically. I'd been so used to claustrophobic feelings that this was no worse than anything else.

After a while, as I was moving, I felt pressure on my right knee and I started to slide on the moving slab. The voice in my ear asked, "What's going on?" And then followed shortly by, "Oh, shit. Stop the damn thing. His knee's stuck on the entrance to the machine. "

The both of them spent the next fifteen or twenty minutes trying to reposition me so that they could squeeze me in or force my knee down so that I'd fit. None of it worked. They finally took me out and transferred me back on the gurney, and we were off to other tests. The EKG and X-rays were much easier, and they eventually got all the tests finished that they wanted.

We arrived back at my room, and I faced another ordeal. There were two nurses there, including a male one. The female gave commentary. "We're going to insert a feeding tube. You must be starving. This will help. Just relax. It will help."

Of course, it didn't help. At least the tube was flexible. They managed to force it down my throat. I thought I'd gag several times and was on the verge of throwing up—which I'd do, if it went on much longer. I could feel the paste being forced into my stomach. It wasn't pleasant but it wasn't as bad as the worst of what had been happening to me.

A while after it got dark, a nurse came in and talking as much to herself as to me, said, "OK, dearie, you're going to get some sleep now. Nightie-night." The ceiling went out of focus, and the meaningless conversation on the TV became just meaningless sounds.

It was light again when I woke up. I was only half-awake. What had wakened me was the sense of drowning. The tube was forcing food into my stomach, and I was throwing up. I couldn't breathe. Once I'd been swimming, and a big wave had hit me just as I was coming up for breath. I took in a big gulp of water, and I found myself gasping for air and only getting water. That time, I'd coughed up the water and got my breath. This time, I coughed up water and only got more liquid. I was frantic. Move. Move. I'm going to die. I heard an alarm going off. I was so panicked and so drugged up that the significance of that alarm bringing help didn't occur to me.

Later, I resolved the words that I'd heard into meaning. A nurse had said, "He's in respiratory failure. Get that tube out and clear his air passage."

Getting the tube out was a synch. Getting my bent and locked air passage clear was another matter. I heard someone say, "It's not working. We've got to open the trachea." Luckily I was not aware enough at that point to understand the significance of what they were going to do, but just then another nurse had got my air passage clear and got me breathing again.

One nurse had said, "You've got to be more careful how you place him on the bed. We're damn lucky that he isn't dead now."

The other muttered something that I think only I heard, "Maybe he'd be better off."

The rest of the day was uneventful—other than the frequent application of eye drops.

That night I was scared to death of the nurse who brought the sedative. Was I going to wake up to find that I was drowning in my own juices? I pleaded with my eyes that she not give me the drug, but she chattered thoughtlessly, "Well, baby, you've had a bad day. I'll bet you'd like to get some rest in. This will help you."

I screamed in my head, "No! NO! NO! I don't want to get a good night's rest in. It'll be my last."

Of course, she might as well have been the world's best occlumen. She didn't hesitate in the slightest nor did her voice reveal the slightest hint that the message I was trying to send had the least effect. She squeezed the trigger on the syringe. Despite my most determined effort to stay alert, her face went out of focus. Then I didn't care anymore, and then the sounds were just a buzz in the background."

I slowly awoke the next day. When I was finally aware enough to realize what was going on, I knew that I was being fed again. This caused a moment of panic followed by relief when I realized that I wasn't going to throw up.

The day went on boring as it could be, and I was actually rather happy that it was boring. However, I realized that I had to face a bad consequence of the fact that it had been boring. Shouldn't Minerva have shown up by now? Had she been killed? Or captured? Or something else? With the continuing absence of Minerva from the scene, I was becoming progressively worried that something serious had happened to her.

The next couple of days had passed when something serious happened. Doc #2, who seemed to be the responsible doctor on the case, showed up with someone whose voice I didn't recognize. The conversation was troubling.

Doc #2, "We've tried a number of tests, both scans and blood tests looking for physical causes of the paralysis. So, far everything has turned up normal. The MRI of his brain and upper spinal column show absolutely nothing abnormal, likewise the X-rays.

"Blood tests have shown that his Hdl cholesterol is a bit high, but blood sugars are normal, and there are no markers of cancer or brain or other neural abnormalities.

"At the same time, there has been absolutely no change in the paralysis. The nurses have reported no signs under any circumstances of responsiveness. One nurse, who will remain nameless for obvious reasons, got so frustrated with him that she tried to stimulate his penis. There was no response whatever."

I could have told her that the experience was very stimulating. I thought that I was going to ejaculate on the spot, But it didn't happen.

The other merely "hmmed" throughout the recitation that included lots of technical details that I couldn't remember. Doc #2 finished with, "I've completely run out of physical possibilities."

The other then said, "I can see why you want to transfer him to a psychiatric unit. Frankly, I've never seen a case like this myself.

"Catatonic cases almost always are limp and easily manipulated physically. The few that aren't can be manipulated physically with difficulty. May I?"

They were behind me while they talked, and I couldn't see what sort of gesture the other was making when he asked permission, but I prepared myself for something painful. What happened was that suddenly, he grasped my left arm and tried to bend it. The pressure that he applied was painful but not excruciating. I was sure that my arm hadn't changed at all, other than showing some bruising.

"Well, that has never failed me before." He huffed, as though he had applied quite a lot of force.

Doc #2 asked, "That looks like it would be extremely painful, was that necessary?"

"Oh, you'd be surprised what levels of pain catatonic patients can consciously block."

"I suppose that I would."

"Yes, I think that he should be transferred to our unit. We have pretty good success working with catatonics. Almost 40% become communicative before we're finished with them."

With that cheerful thought, they left my room. After it had begun to get dark when I was expecting to have the nightly visit by the agent of Morphius, someone did come. It was a male nurse. He applied the syringe to the port, but this time, rather than the relatively slow onset of unconsciousness, my eyes simply went dark as did my consciousness.

Crackerbox Palace

I'm not sure whether the next thing I remember is a real memory or if it was a strange dream. My eyes didn't focus, I just heard disconnected words. They were like the ones of the night nurse but I couldn't form them into coherent meaning. I just heard a female voice say, "Dearie. . . Night . . ." Then, there was another period when I couldn't focus my eyes. I heard the same voice say something like before, and I was briefly unconscious again followed by several more similar episodes.

Then, I woke fully. My head was beating with a headache unlike any that I'd ever had before – even that crazy Christmas Eve last year. For a long time, I just suffered in the wordless pain. I sometimes heard voices that were saying nursy things like, "Take your pills, now."; "How are you feeling today?", "Are you feeling all right?"

I couldn't focus my eyes for what seemed like hours. When I finally did, I found an older nurse who I would have called a battle ax except that my experiences lately had been full of battle axes. I could tell I was in a different ward because there were many voices—certainly more than half a dozen. I never saw another patient.

The battle ax tried to talk to me, asking me questions. It had been a long time since anyone had spoken to me as someone that you could interact with, so I was puzzled. Of course, even if I hadn't been puzzled, I wouldn't have been able to interact anyway. She occasionally would ask me if I felt something just before a sharp pain struck me in the sole of my feet or my ears or even, once, in my balls. Once or twice those brought tears of pain but no one noticed them.

After a few days of this, I had a visitor who was not a nurse. I realized after he'd spoken a bit that he had the same voice as the voice in the previous room. There were also a couple of other people whom I thought must have been interns. They rarely spoke, and when they did, it was to ask a concise, pointed question. The teacher or warden or whatever he was did almost all the talking.

"Gentlemen, I've come to show you a most unique case. He is obviously a catatonic. Possible physical causes of his paralysis have been investigated thoroughly before he came here.

"As with all catatonics, he shows no reaction to any physical stimuli regardless how distressing they would be to you or me.

"What he doesn't share with any catatonic that I'm aware of is the utter completeness of the paralysis. Not only can he not move any part of his body, NEITHER can we. Quite unique. Would any of you like to test that assertion?"

There were general negatives. He then went on.

"So far our treatment has been to use a sort of mild shock therapy. He was transported here under complete sedation and has been kept under sedation for a week." I was shocked by the length of time. Had I actually been unconscious for that long?

"We hoped that this complete deprivation of sensory input would restart his brain and might allow him to communicate. Unfortunately, his case is utterly unchanged.

"So, now we come to the next stage of treatment. Fairly frequently, shock therapy is successful. Of course, in the old days, we would have used electric shock. But nowadays, we find that chemical shock is much more effective—and safer. The reaction of the body to the chemicals that we use is much more predictable and safe. You're about to observe the effects of this treatment. This is the initial treatment for this patient."

I tried to scream out that they didn't need to do that. They didn't need to take a hammer to my mind. I'd love to talk with them. But, of course, nothing happened. The last thing that I remember is being transferred to a gurney and starting to roll out of the ward, surrounded by interns.

It was the most bizarre experience that I'd ever had. My next recollection was lying in my bed in the ward. Had I actually left it? Maybe they'd decided that I didn't need to have the shock treatment after all. That night, the nurse came with my shot and this time, it was completely different. It didn't send me into unconsciousness. Instead, it was as though the room were spinning but somehow I didn't care. I eventually entered a kind of sleep where I dreamed of a train station and the walls around me exploding. I knew that something like that happened with me, but I couldn't quite remember when.

There were a couple of days of jumbled memories of that sort of half-sleep and the boredom of only seeing the ceiling. Then, the director (for I'd begun to think of him as the director of the sanitarium) entered my room with his entourage. I heard his voice approaching my bed. When he arrived, he began without preamble,

"You all remember I'm sure, this patient—which may be more than he can do. Frequently, shock therapy is accompanied with memory loss. Sometimes it only precedes the shock by hours and sometimes it is days, weeks, even more.

"Four days ago, we applied chemical shock therapy, and he's been given some time to recover. We've observed him to determine if he is more communicative. His is a fairly resistant case, so we must apply a second shock. We'll do that today."

I didn't have any memory of the shock, but I was suddenly struck by panic such as I'd never felt before. "NO! NO! NO! DON'T DO IT!" I tried again and again to scream, but nothing happened.

The next thing that I remember I was laying in the ward and my persecutor arrived with his henchmen. His voice, strangely, sounded tired, "Gentlemen, this patient is beyond my experience. We've applied shocks to him a total of four times without noticeable improvement."

FOUR TIMES! I could only remember two. Yes, two. Or actually, I couldn't remember any, but I could remember being taken away to shock therapy twice. And why was it that I was being shocked anyway? Oh, yes. I couldn't move.

"We've decided that his case is probably beyond our understanding. Consequently, we must regard him as a potential danger to himself and the rest of the people in the ward. There is no knowing when he will wake from his catatonia and what he might do. So, we're going to keep him permanently tranquilized."

One of the interns asked, "Isn't that where the padded cell usually comes in?"

The rest tittered a moment, and then the stern voice of the director cut through them, "We run a humane facility. There are no padded cells—as you all well know. And there are no straight jackets.

"Since he already has a port installed, it will be easy to give him periodic, precisely measured doses that will insure he is incapable of doing himself or others harm from now on. A sad case. Very sad."

After the director left, a nurse came by with a syringe. All that I had strength left to do was to plead silently, "No, please."

The syringe was emptied into my port, and what I feared didn't happen. I was half afraid that I would never be conscious again—that those thoughts would be my last in this world. Instead, everything became fluid. I was always exhausted. I could barely find the mental energy to wonder whether it was day or night. That was because it was so hard focusing my eyes. It was easier concentrating on hearing and finding out what the nurses were saying about me. It turned out to be nothing. As far as I could tell—which wasn't very far—they spared just enough attention to me to insure that I didn't drown in my own food, administered through the feeding tube. Oh, yes, they also made sure that I got the next day's dose of tranquilizer each day. I tried concentrating particularly hard at those times, hoping that I could somehow communicate to them not to give me the dose—that there was absolutely no chance that I'd move a muscle with or without tranquilizer. But nothing went through, invariably, the dose was injected. I swirled rapidly into a near-coma of exhaustion and couldn't understand or even perceive until much later. I tried to count the doses that I received but I rapidly lost count. I would forget to count a dose when it happened, and then hours later wonder if I'd counted it or not. Eventually, I gave up counting and cried real tears of surrender to the inevitable that weren't noticed because the nurse was dutifully applying artificial tears. When that happened, I gave up completely and was swallowed by the drug induced lethargy. I could no longer tell when I was more aware and when not. I'd stopped trying to remember the difference. I don't know how long I was in this near-death state.

◿

Then one day, I did notice that they had begun taking me outside during the day, for air I supposed. I didn't know how long they'd been doing that and didn't care. But then, one day, there was another difference. I was on my back, but traveling—not on a gurney—but in something else. I tried to think what it was that meant traveling but not gurney. I didn't try very long and soon forgot that there was something that was different. Then I was in a gurney again—for real—and I was in a bed again, but I thought vaguely that it was not the same bed that I had been in before. Strange, I was full of wonder that there was a bed that was a bed but not the same bed that I had always been in—for as long as I could remember.

There was the comforting familiarity at night of a nurse coming to put me to sleep. But it wasn't familiar. This time, when I slept it wasn't the exhausted sleep that takes away all caring but the sleep with dreams—real dreams.

I awoke and was really awake. For the first time in a very long time, I could focus my eyes on the ceiling, and I could understand people when they talked to me. Like now. And I could focus on a face—a woman's face. She was saying, "Ah, good. You're conscious. I know that because you focused and focused on my face. My name is Cuddy. Dr. Cuddy. You're here because of a very dedicated young neurosurgeon who just joined staff from the institution," she pronounced the word differently from all the other words, "you were at, thought that your case might have been uh. . " She stopped as though trying to decide if she should say what she was about to say and then went on, "Mis-handled before and he thought that we might be able to help you.

"I'm not going to be your doctor. We have one of the best diagnostic teams in the Western Hemisphere here. I know that you may not be able to understand what I'm saying, but I wanted you to hear anyway. Later today, part of the team will be visiting with you. Good luck."

Vague recollections of previous experiences in "institutions" like this came to mind, and I knew that there was reason for hope, but I couldn't think of what it might be. But the continuing hope of that possibility buoyed my spirits for the first time in who knew how long. And as a matter of fact, Dr. Cuddy's promise came true.

A woman entered the room, but I didn't think she was a nurse. Even before I saw her, her voice convinced me that she was serious. She came into my field of view and said, "I'm Dr. Cameron. I'm on your diagnostic team." The way she said, "your" made me think that she actually thought of herself and her team as, in some sense, belonging to me rather than the other way around, which was the only recollection that I had from the past.

"Now, we know a lot about you. I sooo much wish that you could tell me something about yourself. Is there any way that you can communicate? Can you blink an eye? Or can you wiggle a toe?" She touched a toe gently. "Or can you cough?" I tried. I'd tried a million times before, but I couldn't do any of them.

"All right. Well, we've got a lot of tests coming up for you. I know that you've had a lot already, so just get yourself mentally ready. It will be tiring for you. Please believe that we're putting you through all this because we have real hope for you. Some of the tests, you'll have done before, but our boss doesn't trust other people to do the tests, and we'll catch hell if we don't do them ourselves."

Then she walked out of the room, but for the first time I allowed myself a little hope—not much.

In the late afternoon, two young doctors arrived and started preparing me to move. They didn't say anything. I knew it was coming, so I wasn't afraid that I was going to end up back in hell. We went down a hall, down an elevator and into a room that looked like it had an MRI in it. They put me on the MRI conveyor and went to the control area. Just then I heard a voice that I recognized. I remember it from the afternoon. It was Dr. Cameron. She hadn't given me her first name. She said something to them that I overheard bits of, "Didn't tell him. . Introduce yourself . . ."

Then the voice, came closer and brought the two men into the field of view. She said, "These two gentlemen want to introduce themselves." Both were looking down at the floor.

Once said, "I'm Dr. Chase."

The woman said, "And what's your specialty, Dr. Chase?"

He cleared his throat and said, "It's immunology."

The other man said, "I'm Dr. Foreman. I'm a neurosurgeon."

The woman stared at them and Foreman said, "And we're going to do an MRI of your brain to see if there were any problems that were overlooked before."

Another look and Chase said, "Oh, yeah. Just in case you don't remember from the last time. You have to stay very still and . . . " He gave me the rest of the spiel from before.

I wish that I could have explained about the problem with the knee but they never got that far down. The rest of the evening, we took rounds of a number of imaging offices, some that I'd been in before and some that I hadn't. In all cases these three doctors were performing the tests. They finally took me back to my room and a nurse showed up with a syringe. Dr. Chase asked what was in it. He heard and then said, "Let's just leave that off tonight. I'd like to see if he may have been overmedicated before."

I had a hard night of it, getting very little sleep, but somehow I preferred that to what had come before. After a long time, I did get a few hours sleep and then was awake. Nothing happened almost the whole day. Then Chase came in and drew some blood. Before, it had always been nurses who had done that. That night, I got a fair amount of sleep—interrupted by nurses taking vital signs.

The next morning, I was enjoying the sight through the window to the outside world. In the morning, someone had given me a sponge bath and left me on my side looking out the window. It had been so long since I'd seen the outside while I was fully conscious that the wonder of it swept over me like a wave of joy. In the afternoon, there were four Doctors who came into my room. There were Chase, Forman and Cameron and somebody else. He was tall, thin, and seemed to be in his forties, but walked with a cane.

He sat down in front of me by the bed and he introduced himself, "Hello, Mr." here he looked down at a clipboard, "John Doe. It's amazing how many people try to kid me that it's their real name. And you know that it's because they're trying to hide something from me. You know that patients always lie. They lie about banging their mother. They lie about their age. They lie about diseases they've had before. I have to admit that your approach is almost unique. If you don't say anything, you can't be lying can you?

"Well, I'm going to tell you the truth, I'm your doctor. Don't you let these, these cleaning staff kid you. They're not doctors. I'm your doctor. My name is Gregory House.

"Now, I hear that you're catatonic. That's what they say at the state psychiatric institute, and God knows that THEY wouldn't lie. Is that true? Is that what you say?" There was silence for a while. He bent down and put his ear next to my mouth. I could actually feel a lobe of his right ear on my lips. "What was that you said? I couldn't quite hear. Oh, yes. 'I'm not catatonic, I'm just misunderstood.'"

He got up and swung his cane around at the other doctors and said, "You see, he's not catatonic, he's just misunderstood." He swung his cane around again and struck my face with it, it swung so wildly. Of course, it hurt like hell, and I wished that I could just grab that cane out of his hand and knock his bad leg out from under him with it. I felt the blood flowing down from my nose and I tasted the salty taste of the blood on my lips. He asked, "Foreman, did you see him react?"

Foreman just shook his head. He looked at Chase and asked, "You?" Chase just lowered his head and shook it. Then he turned to Cameron who just swung around. I thought that I heard a gasp escape her lips.

House swung around and looked at me. "Well, we can't let you drown in your own blood can we?" He said, "Cameron, clean up Mr. HEWHOCANNOTBENAMED." She did.

Then he picked something off a table that I'd not seen before. Or had I? It seemed familiar. What was it?

House said, "This somehow survived your trek through all the hospitals and ambulances and what not." He held it up in front of his eyes. "It must be pretty important if it came all this way. I wonder what it is." He stopped for a moment. "What was that? I didn't hear it. Did you say it was a lady friend's purse? I wonder what might be in it." He tried to open it. I was as curious as he was about it. It seemed to be important to me, but I couldn't think why.

Somehow, despite his best efforts, the fragile-looking thing just refused to open. He frowned and said, "Chase, get me a scalpel. We'll see what's in here."

A moment later, Chase returned and handed House the scalpel. He tried to cut it in the middle. It deformed, but the scalpel couldn't even nick it. His frown deepened. "Foreman, I know you keep a diamond-edged saw for opening craniums, go get it." After he left, House went on, "Unless Mr. KnownNothing here would like to tell us how to get into it." Another pause, then, "OK. Have it your way."

Foreman returned with the saw. House cautioned everyone to get out of the way. He put the purse down on a bedside table and drew the saw across it slowly, then more vigorously and faster. "Damn."

House struck his forehead with his hand and exclaimed, "Of course, you're Superman and your tights and your purse are made of thread from Kryptonite and can't be opened by earthly means."

He paced a moment and said, "OK. Well, since we can't open it, there's no reason to keep it. Cameron, take this out and throw it in the trash."

Cameron's eyes widened, and she turned and walked out without the mystery object. House turned to Chase and said, "You're not a sissy, Chase. Go throw this in the trash compactor."

Chase got down off the back of a chair that he'd been sitting on. He accepted the tossed purse, and started to walk out the door. House said, "Vite, vite. There's no time to waste."

He then turned back to me and said, "So, you won't talk will you? Even to save your precious purse." He turned from me and walked out, shouting behind him, "Don't waste any more time on him."

They all walked out, and the rest of the day was quiet.

The next morning, House and his three musketeers came in dragging a white board. Cameron asked, "So, tell me again, why we're moving your office in here?"

"Haven't you been listening? This is such a tough case, I want to be near him so that we don't waste any time if an idea occurs to any of us. And he can't hear us, so it doesn't matter if he hears our clumsy stumbling for ideas. So start. Chase, what symptoms do we have?"

Chase ticked off a list—paralysis, lack of reaction to stimulants."

"OK." He wrote those on the board down one side. "So, Cameron, what tests have we done?"

She listed a long list—MRI of brain and upper spine, the first hospital had done a whole body MRI, which they had. They were consistent and showed nothing. There were EKG and EEG. Nothing out of the ordinary—and consistent with earlier results. There were X-rays and PET scans. All negative. House was busy writing. There were all kinds of tests of nerve reactions—both normal and unusual. No responsiveness was observed. There were blood scans for drug use. There had been lots of drugs, there was thorazine—lots of it, a variety of barbituates and sedatives, but all were prescribed at previous facilities and even this one. There was no sign of marijuana or cocaine or heroin, etc. There were blood scans for markers for cancer. None observed.

House had filled the dry erase board with very small print. "OK, what's the differential diagnosis."

Chase said, "Wait one minute. We can't do a differential right in front of the patient."

House laughed, "Why not. He's catatonic. He can't hear any of this, can you buddy? Whatever your name is."

Cameron agreed with Chase, "This is unethical. Cuddy will let you get away with a lot, but this is just plain stupid."

House asked, "And who's going to tell her, hmmmmm?"

Chase snapped back, "Well, maybe Mr. Whoever here if we actually cure him."

"He doesn't seem like the sort of man who would turn around and bite his benefactor, if I cure him."

House kept it up, saying, "I don't think you would. Do you, Mr. HEWHOCANNOTBENAMED?"

Foreman said, "Well, since all tests have shown nothing out of the ordinary, I'd say that the psych ward got it right. He's catatonic. That's the only differential that makes sense."

"Oh, you think so. Well, let's think of some more tests."

House and his crew tossed possibilities back and forth. They were esoteric, and I really didn't understand the point of a lot of them. That was just as well, because he ruled most of the tests out. Then, he mentioned one that caught my interest.

House started innocently, "OK. Hands. Who here thinks this is catatonia?"

Chase and Foreman raised their hands. House went on, "Then, he's conscious and he can even react. He is just choosing not to react to spite all us dumb doctors, right buddy?

He hesitated for me to answer, "See? Silence betokens consent. So, then, if we just stimulate him enough, he'll eventually say, 'ouch', right?"

Cameron cut in, "Just a minute here. You're saying that if we torture him enough, and he's just crazy, he'll object."

"Well, not very elegantly put, but, 'Yes.'"

Chase hesitantly asked, "Well, you could do serious damage if you go too far."

"We'll monitor the pain level and not go too far."

"But everyone is different. One man's bearable pain is another man's heart failure."

"Well, then, it would behoove this guy to say ouch early, wouldn't it."

"What if it's not catatonia?"

That question went unanswered.

The rest of the day went by all too quickly for me. I got no sleep that night. I never could decide if that were a blessing or not. The next morning, the force-feeding by tube was one that I actually wished would keep going longer. They couldn't do anything until that was done. After it was over, I had to wait long enough that I ended up wishing that they would just come in and get the torture over with. I was remembering more and more of my past ordeal, and it seemed like it might not be much worse than some things that had happened to me before.

The three musketeers arrived and transferred me to a gurney, and we lumbered out of my room and down the hall and to the elevators. Down we went into hell. The elevator door opened, and we went down another hall painted in beige. We reached a double door that opened at the touch of a pad. We wheeled in, and I thought that all that it needed to make it complete was a motto over the door, "All Ye who enter here abandon all hope."

They put me in a fairly comfortable bed and started attaching electrodes. For measurements, I supposed. There was no commentary—not even from the always helpful Cameron. Then the really ominous electrode was attached—to my penis. My heart sunk, and for the first time, I wished that the Deatheaters had gotten me. That must have been who they were at the beginning. I'd been in their hands before, and I knew that if they'd gotten me, I'd not have been tortured a fraction as much as I had already been.

House was as jaunty as ever when he arrived. "Well, munchkins are we ready to start?" No one said anything, except House, "Good, all ready then. Let's do a little calibration first." There was a hesitation, "No. No. Not that. We'll start with something light so that we can see how reactive his nerves are. I brought along a pin." He pushed it against the sole of my left foot—first lightly and then with more pressure. There was definite pain. "Ah, OK. We've got a data point. Let's try something more noticeable."

He suddenly pushed the pin under my left toenail. I would have screamed for mercy if I could have. Nothing came out of my mouth. House said, "Well, that was more serious than intended. Did anyone notice any muscle twitches or other involuntary reactions."

Cameron almost screamed, "Of course, we didn't House. He's consistent. That last was way too much. He's not catatonic. No one could voluntarily endure that without reacting. Let's go back to the white board."

House was in the field of my vision now. He shook his head, "No. No. We've got to pass a pain threshold where voluntary suppression of reactions is impossible. Let's start out with a half-second jolt of 0.1 amp. That should be good enough." There was silence and no pain. "Well, go ahead, let's get this over with and then. . . "

But he never said another word in my presence. At that moment, there was a flood of light as the double doors were blasted off their hinges. There were several flashes of green light, and then thuds as something heavy hit the floor.

There was the most blessed sound that I'd ever heard in my life. The voice that I will always be able to recognize (even though at that moment I couldn't name its owner) said, "Well, I should have known that you'd be here helping these quacks with some sort of experiment or another."

Her face swam into my view, and I blessed it as fervently as I could, silently. She said, "Well, I know that you don't like disapparition, but I think that in this case, even you might think that it was worthwhile."

I only had a vague idea of what she meant, but whatever it was, if she was in favor of it, so was I. She made one last comment, "Oh, don't worry about them. I know that you're always concerned about collateral damage. The Petrificus Totalis spell will wear off in about two or three hours."

I would have laughed, if I could, but I couldn't. Then in the next instant we disappeared from the hospital and re-appeared at the gates of a large, old building that looked like it might be an Ivy League school. Somehow I was lifted up to her waist height without any sign of gurney or stretcher. The gates seemed to dissolve before her. We went through them and up the stairs to double doors that opened and led into a reception area. I couldn't see, but I could hear quite a number of people talking in hushed tones.

The woman who was with me asked where the Emergency Room was. The receptionist pointed off toward her right and said, "Go straight down that corridor, through another set of doors and you're there.

We somehow did that. When we arrived in that room, there was a nurse who looked me over efficiently and asked, "Petrificus Totalis?"

The woman with me said, "I'm not sure. He's been this way for several weeks."

The nurse gasped, "What happened!"

"It's a long story, but could we get him treated."

"Of course, yes." She motioned to the second of several partitioned areas and said, "Take him in there. The healer will be in very quickly."

I heard him before I saw him. He had a firm, determined voice that said that he would brook no funny business. "How did this happen. What do you know of the spell that was used on him?"

The woman said, "We were attacked near here several weeks ago. I didn't hear the spell and just know that he's been paralyzed ever since. I think that the attackers were Deatheaters."

The healer(?) hmmed like many a Doctor that I'd heard recently. "Well, I'll need to do some research then, to determine what the proper counter curse is. We'll take him up to a room and start tests immediately."

I heard him leave the room. Then two orderlies arrived and said to the woman, "We'll take him upstairs. You can come along if you like. We're going to room 322." I levitated and we traveled down a hall, up an elevator and on to 322.

After we arrived, they had a series of people arrive in the room. Each looked at me and took a sort of small wooden rod thingee that they passed over my body. Then they left the room without comment. The oh-so familiar woman stayed with me the whole time. I wanted so much to ask her questions, but somehow, I felt very safe when she was there. When she left the room to go to the loo or something, I was worried.

After a number of hours, the healer returned and took a chair facing her and me. He started reassuringly. "We've diagnosed the original curse, and luckily, there's nothing really dark about it. It's just a variation on the standard Petrificus Totalis that doesn't have a time limit.

"The counter curse is pretty straight-forward, but you have to be kind of careful with it. You could have used it, but I'm glad you didn't. If he's really been suffering under this curse for weeks, there could be complications when we lift it.

"We need permission to use the counter. Are you next of kin?"

I could hear the smile in her voice as she answered, "Technically, no." The smile broadened, "Goodness knows that he's asked to make me next of kin enough times, but no."

"Well, then, can we get his next of kin here quickly?"

She said something then that I didn't understand at all, "They're Muggles."

The Healer said, "Oh." There was silence for a few minutes. He'd said it as though I were some sort of freak. "I suppose that you'll have to do. Will you sign the permission form to have the counter curse applied?"

"Of course."

"I'll have a nurse bring it up in a few minutes. Once it's signed, we'll apply the counter curse. I want another healer here just in case there's a bad reaction."

She asked, "What kind of reaction could there be?"

Then he said the name, "Ms. McGonagall, there's a chance that he'll loose his voice or the use of a hand or something else permanently."

Her "Oh." said volumes. I knew that name. And I knew that it was one that meant quite a lot to me, but I wasn't sure why.

He left, and Ms. McGonagal resumed her seat next to me and took my hand in hers. I wondered if she were single. I wondered if I'd remember what she meant to me after the counter-curse, whatever that was, was applied. I wondered what a Muggle was and why I was related to one.

The healer came up with another man and a woman. The woman had some sort of paper that was rolled up in a scroll. Ms McGonagall unrolled it, read it, and took a funny looking pen and signed it. She handed it to the woman who looked it over, signed it, and showed it to the two men. They seemed satisfied and the woman, who it turned out was a witness, left.

Then the first healer turned to me and gave me instructions. "OK. I'm going to do the counter-curse. You're going to regain control of your body. You're going to be tempted to get up or shout or something. DON'T. It could lead to permanent damage. Let me examine you first before you do anything. Then, I'll ask you to perform some simple movements to let us determine if you have full use of your faculties restored. The other healer, MacAvery, will be your physical therapist. He'll help you fully recover control of your body and restore it to full strength. We're not sure how long this will take."

Mac took over the instructions here, "Ordinarily, it's only a matter of a day or two until someone who's had the Totalis curse used against them has full recovery. But I've only heard of a few cases of more than a week passing. I may want to write you up in the *American Journal of Magical Maladies* when you're done. Don't worry. I'm confident that we can restore you fully within a week or so."

The healer, who maddeningly hadn't told me his name yet, went on, "So, Ms. McGonagall, if you're ready, we'll proceed. It shouldn't take more than a minute."

McGonagall nodded and sniffed back a tear, I guessed. The healer drew the rod thingee from his robes and pointed it square at my head and said, "Reverso Petrificus." And that was it. For a moment, I thought nothing had happened. Then, I realized that I could open my mouth, and I did. I said, "Ms. McGonagall."

She had been holding my hand. Then, she squeezed it. I was able to squeeze back feebly. But then, Mac said, "That's entirely enough for now. I want you to get bed rest for the rest of the day. We'll have someone in later to help you eat, and we have a pot if you need to urinate. The nurse will help you with. . "

But McGonagall broke in, "I'll help him with that if it's necessary, thank you." Mac smiled and nodded. "I suppose you'll help feed him?"

"You'd better not try to keep me from doing."

"I thought so." He turned to me, "It's fine for Ms. McGonagall to help you, but please don't over-exert yourself. I understand how you might be tempted to if you've not seen her for weeks. Just don't give in to temptation."

McGonagall just sniffed and shooed them out. The unnamed healer said that he'd be back later to do a thorough exam.

As my strength returned, so did memory. The first night I didn't have the strength to speak much, which was good because I felt strange calling someone who was feeding me and taking care of other intimate details, "Ms. McGonagall."

The next day when I awoke, I awoke to more memories—such as Ms. McGonagall's first name, Minerva. I also remembered why she was so important to me. I remembered a little of that awful day when I was first cursed, but I didn't have the strength to ask for an account of what had happened to me that first day after recovering.

The Healers were back the next day. Mac started me on some exercises to test and strengthen my muscles. The other, whose name turned out to be Abrams examined me. He didn't use any technology but felt my body all over, gently stretching muscles and tendons and doing other things with his wand that I didn't understand. After the first serious examination, he asked Minerva if she thought I were up to talking about my ordeal.

"You might ask me." I said.

"No, for now, I think your friend is a better judge of your physical and mental health and resilience than you are. Now, Ms. McGonagall, what do YOU think?"

She looked at me closely, examining my eyes. Then she said, "I think that he's up to it. He doesn't remember lots of things. He's had a pretty awful time of it, but I think he can take it."

He nodded and then he turned to me, "Did the Deatheaters have you for long?"

I stared at him. I didn't know what Deatheaters were. I might have been tempted to call some of the people at the Psych ward Deatheaters, but I was pretty sure that they weren't. "No. I don't think that these Deathiters had me at all. I was immediately taken to a hospital and was there for a while. I don't remember how long. Then, I went to a psych ward somewhere else and was there for weeks, I think. Then I went to the hospital where Minerva found me. I don't think I was anywhere else."

Abrams nodded. "I suspected something like that. I saw clear tracks where the Muggle 'Healers' injected some drugs into you. Then there was the . . uh . . I think that the Muggles call it a port which they installed in your shoulder so that they could easily pump drugs into you."

At that, Minerva gasped. A hard look came into her face, and she muttered something.

Abrams said, "Now, ma'am, don't think too badly of them. They do the best that they know how. You can't blame them for trying to help your uh . yes."

226

Minerva spit out, "I'll blame whomever I want to. I think I might just pay that Dr. House a visit before we leave."

I was too weak to make the protest that I wanted to, but I squeezed her hand and shook my head in the negative. Minerva replied, "You two are altogether too good for your own good." However, she relented and said to me, "We'll talk about it later."

The Healer went on. "Good. You have trouble remembering things that happened to you? I think you have the most trouble remembering the things at the 'Psyche ward'?"

I nodded and said, "I remember a doctor there saying that frequently after treatment at their ward, patients had partial memory loss. I received four of what they call 'shock' treatments. I only remember two, or really, I only remember being told that I would have two. It's all very confusing, especially at the end when they gave up on treating me. They just decided to keep me quiet by giving me tranquilizers."

The healer said, "Yes, I've heard of shock treatments and tranquilizers. They are both dangerous things to take and are normally used only in the most desperate of cases. I'm sure that your strange symptoms seemed very desperate to them."

Minerva asked the key question, "How long will it take Wendt to remember everything? Will he eventually remember . . uh . . everything?"

sAbrams said, "I don't know. I do know that sometimes patients never completely recover their memories, but that happens very rarely."

Minerva was silent. Then she asked, "Is there anything that I can do to help?"

"I'd suggest talking with him as much as his strength will permit. That should help trigger memories that are buried and partly lost."

I said, "I would really like to hear what happened after we got separated in Princeton."

Minerva nodded and looked at Abrams. He looked back and then seemed to get it, "Oh, you want to be alone. Sure, I get that, but it sounds like it would be a fascinating story."

Minerva nodded. "It would be, ta-ta."

After he left, Minerva said, "Well, do you remember that we were going by train to New York?"

I reflected and knew that what she said was right, "Yes, I do. We had toured in Washington and were going to do some touring in New York."

"Good. Anyway you got off the train in Princeton to get a newspaper, and I was waiting for you in the train."

Minerva's Story

I was waiting in the train, not paying any attention to you. There were new passengers coming on the train, and the conductor was coming around checking tickets as they did. He stopped at me, and we spoke for a few minutes. He recognized me but also remembered that someone else was traveling with me. He asked if he were elsewhere on the train or had gotten off for a few minutes.

"He wanted to get a local paper. He was hoping to get a Princeton paper."

"Oh, that's a sad story. There used to be a daily Princeton paper, but no more. It's now become bi-weekly, and I doubt that it will survive much longer. That's too bad, too. I sometimes got off to buy it too, to get a different perspective on the news."

As we were talking, the train started to move, and the conductor told me that he hoped that my friend had gotten on. I looked around to see what you were doing and saw you lying on the platform. I got up and headed for an exit. By this time we were moving quickly and I couldn't get out. So, I disapparated to the edge of the platform near the train.

As I started to head for you, I saw a man near the opposite end of the platform holding a wand. I raised mine and just in time because he aimed a curse at me. I did the protego spell and deflected his curse. Just then another spell hit the shield, and I realized there was at least one other wizard attacking me. I ducked behind a corner of the station and shot an expelliamus charm in their direction. I didn't expect to hit anything, but I must have hit the station because I heard an explosion as a brick shattered. In the meantime three or four spells hit the corner of the station near me. Then, I disapparated out near the edge of the platform, took aim, shot off two spells, and disapparated back.

We traded spells for a bit. I heard sirens. That meant that "pleasmen" were coming, but I couldn't depend on them for help. I tried disapparating to the end of the platform near their end of the station and got off a spell or two at them and disapparated again. I have no idea how long the battle went on. I just know that suddenly they'd disapparated away.

By that time, the platform was empty except for us. Even you were gone. Then my heart fell. Had one of them disapparated next to you and taken you? You seemed to be the target. I had no idea where to go other than to try to find the American aurors. I disapparated back to the Inn that we stayed at in Washington. I arrived outside and walked in.

The Front Desk attendant—still on duty from the morning when we'd checked out—greeted me, "Did you forget something? Is that why you're back?"

I must have seemed a ninny. I had to take a deep breath and then I composed myself, 'No. Something terrible happened. I think that my uh friend, was attacked and might have been kidnapped. How do I get hold of the aurors?"

She gasped, "Really. Oh, I'm so sorry. But here". She took a card from behind the desk and handed it to me. "This is the floo network address to reach them. Please go use our connection right away."

I turned immediately and ran into the bar area and to the hearth. The receptionist called after me, "Good luck! I hope he's all right."

I arrived directly at the Auror Office. In front of the hearth was a desk. The wizard was older and tending a little toward fat, but he immediately stood, "What can I do for you ma'am?"

"I'd like to report." I hesitated. What did I want to report? A kidnapping? An attack? A missing person? I decided on the last, "I want to report a missing person."

"Very well. Just a moment. You'll need a visitor's badge. Please sign in here." In a few moments I had a visitor's badge and was being led back into a nondescript office space with many cubicles with low partitions that it was easy to see over. My guide called over to someone, "Lockhart, this woman wants to report a missing person. Will you help her?"

He nodded and motioned me to come over to his "office". He introduced himself as Auror Jeffrey Lockhart. I couldn't resist asking, "Are you any relation to Gilderoy Lockhart?"

"You mean the author? No. As far as I know, at least, but I need to ask you some questions."

He wanted to know your name, where you were from, what our relationship was. I was a bit wary of that question but decided that I had to be perfectly open. "Well, we're both teachers at the Hogwarts School in England."

"Really? I've heard of it. The headmaster is the real McCoy."

"I guess I'll take that as a compliment to him."

"Oh, you should. So, you both happened to be here in the States, because. . .?" His rising inflection showed that he wanted a full explanation.

"Well, I guess I have to tell you that the two of us were—that is —are very close."

"Just how close would that be?"

I didn't want to be graphic about how close we were, so I said, "Well, he's asked me to marry him several times."

"And how did you feel about that?"

"This is reaching the edge of impertinence, young man." There has to be some advantage to being a teacher and knowing how to deal with impertinent young men is one of them.

"Well, I can't start an inquiry without knowing what the nature of your relationship is. It wouldn't be appropriate to start a 'missing persons' for just anyone that walked in the door."

"OK. Let's just say that I was tempted—strongly tempted."

He looked up at the ceiling, released a long breath and said, "OK. I guess I can start an investigation on the strength of that. Then, I need for you to give me a complete description of him. Do you have a photo that we can copy?"

"I certainly do." I reached into my handbag and got out my small photo album that I always keep with me. I opened it to the first page where I keep the photo of us taken in the Azores that time we were there.

Lockhart looked at it and said, "You're both in this, but that's OK, we can edit you out of course."

My heart fell when he said that. It wasn't anything big, but the idea of editing myself out of your life just seemed so awful. He asked about all the usual things, age, height, eye color, were you M, or F and so forth. Then he asked when I'd last seen you.

"Well, it was this morning about 11:50."

He stared at me and frowned, "Well, we don't usually start a missing person's search until the person has been gone for at least a week. Was there something unusual about how he disappeared that brought you here. For example, is it possible that he just disapparated someplace and couldn't get away for a while. You know, some normal reason?"

"Well, in the first place, he couldn't disapparate." I was getting indignant. Something awful had happened to you and this oaf wasn't taking it seriously.

"Oh, he'd never passed the test?"

"No, he was a," I stopped again there. Should I tell the whole truth or the convenient lie that we'd been telling all along. I decided on the truth, "He's a Muggle."

Lockhart nodded and went on as though I'd said nothing at all abnormal, "Well, how did he disappear?"

"We were on a Muggle train going to New York from Washington. He'd got off at Princeton to get a newspaper." Then I went on and told him what I'd told you.

He nodded, "Then you're also reporting a crime." He got out another scroll and started filling in blanks. After several minutes that seemed to stretch on like centuries, he re-started, "OK. Is he a Brit like you or an American or what?"

"He's American."

He looked up at the ceiling again and seemed lost in thought, "OK." He dragged the word out as though it covered a great deal of explanation. "Here's the thing. You've reported a crime, and we'll investigate it fully. Thanks for the tip by the way. This sounds like it could be Deatheaters. We've been afraid of the chance of them moving here, but this is the first definite example I've heard of. We'll want to keep in touch with you about this. Don't leave the country right away."

"Leave the country right away! I'm not going until we find him!" I was indignant.

He sighed and opened a drawer in his desk and pulled out something that looked like a coin. "This is for you. It lets us get hold of you if we need to. It's a. . ."

"Thank you. I know perfectly well what it is. I've used them before. And I can get hold of you, using it too?"

"Yes." He stopped again, apparently trying to decide how to proceed. "This missing person angle. That's something that we really can't investigate here because your friend is a Muggle. We've got an agreement with the American Muggles. We investigate crimes involving wizards. They handle Muggles. Sometimes—maybe even this case—we both get involved. But when that happens it's a real mess. Believe me, you don't want it to go that way unless it's absolutely necessary. I'd advise talking to the Muggle police. But let me tell you something. The Muggle police won't start an investigation—unless a crime is definitely involved—until the person's been missing for a week.

"And, let me warn you that the crime you described is clearly a wizard crime, and the police won't touch that sort of thing. So don't think that you can go to them and talk about kidnapping."

I sneered, "Well, that's a fine kettle of fish. What do you suggest I do?"

He grimaced, "Well, there are a couple of things that you could do. First, on the off chance that your friend was picked up and taken to a wizarding hospital, you could go to the regional one here and ask them about it." He opened the drawer again and pulled out a card, which he handed to me. "Here's the floo address of the hospital admissions department."

"Second, if that doesn't pan out—and personally, I don't think it will, you could go to Muggle hospitals yourself. I don't have a list of them here, but you could look in what the Muggles call the *Yellow Pages* and get a list along with their street addresses. There must be dozens of them that he might have been taken to. Just go to them and ask if they admitted your friend. They're kind of touchy about giving out personal information, but they would probably at least tell you if he'd been there.

"Next, if you're in a hurry. . "

I couldn't stand it! If I were in a hurry? I was tempted to show him just how much of a hurry I was in, but I held my temper. "And what about our conversation suggests that I'm not in a hurry?"

"OK. OK. If neither of those works, you could go to a detective agency."

"What's that?"

"They are companies that sell the service of investigating things. They look for lost people among other things."

"Would you recommend one of these Defective Agencies?"

"No. We don't deal with them much, but you can find them listed in . ."

I interrupted again, "Let me guess. The *Yellow Pages*."

"Right. They're very handy for Muggles—the *Yellow Pages*."

I got up, completely disgusted, and was about to leave. Lockhart had a request, "Let me show you out." He got up, but I motioned him back. "OK. Just be sure to drop off the visitor's badge AND don't forget to stay in the country until further notice from me."

"How long would that be?"

"It's hard to tell, but I'll let you know as soon as it's OK to leave."

"Thanks." I called over my shoulder as I left.

Back at the entry, I looked at the address for the St. James Healer's Hospital and walked into the fireplace. I arrived in a large Waiting Room that was much like St. Mongo's. It was full of people, mostly with obviously magical ailments. There was a kid who looked like he'd eaten one of George's ten-ton-tongue-toffees. There were several cubicles with witches who were working their way through queues of people coming in to seek help. I got in the shortest line. I'd been in this sort of line before. I knew that it was no good trying to cut to the front claiming that my problem was more important than the rest— even though it was. It might not have been the best line. There was a person in front of me that had been hit by a stuttering curse, and it took a long time to process him.

I eventually reached the front of the line. The bored-looking nurse laconically asked, "Name?"

"I'm here looking to see if a James Wendt has been admitted today—probably in the afternoon."

"Oh. You could have gone to the main reception desk." She apparently saw the grim look that was on my face because she immediately said, "But since you're here, I'll take a quick look." She got up, picked up a clipboard that was hanging on the wall, scanned through a couple of pages, and returned to me, "No. No one by that name today."

I'm sure there was some desperation in my voice as I asked, "He might have been unconscious, and you didn't get his name."

She shook her head and frowned, "No John Does admitted or seen either."

My eyes dropped from hers, and I turned to go. She said, "Oh, miss."

I turned to her and she said, "Did you try the Auror Office? I've got a card with the address."

"I've just been there. Thanks anyway."

"Good luck. I hope you find him."

I did too. I went to the floo connection and went back to the Inn. I glanced at my watch and saw that it was 4 PM. The same Front Desk witch asked me how things had gone.

"No luck. I guess I'll need a room for tonight. No, make it for the next several nights."

"Yes, ma'am. Would you like the same room you had last night?"

God, had it really been last night when we'd been here? It was a world of difference from before! "Yes. Yes. I'll take that one if it's available."

"No problem ma'am. Anything else that I can do?"

I thought for a minute. "Do you know where I can find a . . what is it. . . something like Orange Pages or some other color?"

She smiled, "It's *Yellow Pages*. And we keep a copy—just in case a guest might want to look up a Muggle restaurant or something." She reached behind the Front Desk and pulled up a thick paperback book that looked like no book I'd ever seen before. It was a garish yellow— even the pages were yellow. No wonder they called it the *Yellow Pages*. I flipped through the pages. They were organized like a dictionary. There were alphabetical headings at the tops of pages, but I couldn't make sense of it. If you didn't know what category to look in, how did you know where to go?

She said, "I know. It's pretty daunting. But I've had some practice helping people use it. What are you looking for?"

"Hospitals in the Princeton area."

Her mouth dropped, "OH. Well, let me show you how these things work in general. Then you can go to Princeton and look at their *Yellow Pages*."

I nodded. She opened the book and showed me how to find the hospital category. I gaped at it. There must have been ten pages of tightly spaced listings. She saw my face and said, "It's not as bad as it looks. The *Princeton Yellow Pages* probably has a lot fewer. And, there are several telephone numbers for each hospital, so you probably have more like one or two pages of real listings here and much less in Princeton. What state is Princeton in?"

I thought about that and realized that I didn't know much about US geography, "I don't know. It's between here and New York on the train line."

"Oh! Then it's the big Princeton—in New Jersey."

"I guess so."

She gave me the key to our old room, and I put it in my purse.

I walked back out of the Inn, took a deep breath, and concentrated on the Princeton Train Station. I appeared there. The platform was empty, and I had the sudden realization that I didn't know anything about how to find *Yellow Pages* here. I had begun to get hungry, and I decided that a restaurant might be able to help me. So, I walked away from the train station. There was a huge car park around the station. I searched along the edge systematically and finally ran across a restaurant called the Asia Bistro. By this time it was after 5 PM. I decided that I had to get something to eat anyway, so I went in. I like Indian, and I can live with Chinese. So, I figured I couldn't entirely miss with this.

It was early for the locals, so I was seated immediately. They gave me a menu that had a lot of familiar things. So as soon as they returned with Hot Tea, I ordered and asked if they had a *Yellow Pages* that I could look at. They did, but they kept it at the bar. I went there and borrowed it and returned with it to my booth.

I got a piece of parchment out and a quill and prepared to take down information. I opened the *Yellow Pages* to Hospitals as I'd been instructed and was immediately relieved. There were fewer than a page-full of listings. I started copying them. I got the name and number, but found that some didn't have addresses. I wasn't half done when my order arrived. I began eating mechanically and continued copying. I was still copying when the waiter dropped by to ask if there were anything else that I wanted.

I was about to say no, when a thought occurred to me, "Can you help me with the *Yellow Pages* for a minute." I added, "I'll give you a very good tip, if you do."

He smiled and asked what he could do.

"Well, I'm looking for a hospital that a friend of mine might be in, but I didn't find out which one. Are all of these listings hospitals?"

He looked over my shoulder, "No. Most of them are clinics or doctors offices. I don't know why they're in the hospital listings. But you can find out easy enough. Just call them."

"I beg your pardon."

"You know. Just give them a call on the phone. If they're a hospital, they will have someone to answer the phone all the time. If they're not a hospital, you'll get an answering machine." Then he added, "But you'll have to be careful. The larger hospitals have answering machines answer their phone all the time. You just hit zero when the answering machine starts, and if it's a real hospital, you'll get a person. Then you can ask if your friend is there."

"Thanks very much, but I don't have a phone—a cell phone."

He thought a minute, "We have a pay phone, but if you end up calling several of those, you might run out of change. Just a minute. I think you could use the office phone—for a really, really nice tip. Just don't make any long distance calls."

"Done! Please get my bill."

He was back in a minute, and I decided to see how that credit card thingee really worked. You'd left it with me when you went off to get the newspaper. I'd heard you say a number of times that if you just act like you know what you're doing, most people will assume that you do. They'll even help you do what you want to, as though you knew perfectly well yourself. So, I just handed the card to the waiter. He took it as though it were second nature and went off.

A minute or two later, he returned with my card and a piece of paper with the charge printed on it. Below that was a dotted line that said "tip" and then "total" and then a place that said "signature." He looked over my shoulder and hinted, "Don't forget the really, really nice tip."

He had brought a pen, and I picked it up and hovered over the area around the word "tip". "What do you think would be a really, really nice tip?"

"Oh, considering the help with the phone book and phone calls that I'll have to reimburse the management for, say, forty dollars."

My face revealed my shock. He quickly said, "But, because you're a nice lady and all, we could just say twenty-five."

Picking up on the I-know-what-I'm-doing attitude, I nodded casually and wrote 25. He then told me that I didn't have to add it up. He'd be happy to. I decided that maybe I'd better do the adding. He reminded me about signing, and I was stuck for a minute, but he even helped me there. "Just go ahead and sign with your name. If you're authorized to sign. It'll be OK."

So, I did. Then, he led me back to the Manager's Office, and he introduced me as a friend who needed to use the phone. He assured her that I'd only make local calls and he'd reimburse her. She looked a little doubtful, but I smiled my best little-old-lady smile. She nodded and left the room.

I picked up the phone and punched the numbers the way that you had taught me. I could actually hear the phone ringing, and when a voice answered, I couldn't understand what she said. I asked her if this were the Princeton Walk-in Clinic. She answered, "Of course it is., What did you think we were? Isn't that what I just said?"

"Of course."

"Well, we're closing in about ten minutes, so if what you want is urgent, come in tomorrow or go to a real hospital."

"Thanks. I guess you're not a hospital then?"

"Do you see hospital in the name?"

"No. Thanks again."

That was the way most of the calls were. Every now and then I hit one of the answering machines, and eventually I hit a couple of hospitals. I asked them if there were a James Wendt who had been admitted recently. They all answered "no."

That left me confused. Had he been taken to some other hospital? Or had he been kidnapped and now perhaps was dead? OR was he unconscious and they hadn't had a name when he was admitted. I decided that I had to investigate that last possibility. I thanked the manager and the waiter, and I left the restaurant. In the time I'd been there, the sun had set, and it was rather dark, but I was able to read the addresses that I'd written down. I picked the first of the legitimate hospitals that I'd found and disapparated to the address on the page.

I appeared outside a modern-looking building, that is, modern by Muggle standards, which meant nondescript exterior marked by rectangles with no decoration whatever. The material was concrete and glass. Ugh.

I walked up to the entrance and found my way to reception. There was a person at a desk in the main entrance. I asked if there were any anonymous people who had been admitted that day.

"Anonymous? What do you mean?"

"Anonymous? I mean, you don't know who it is. What else could it mean?"

"Oh, you mean John Doe."

"John Doe?"

This seemed senseless to me, but she went on, "Sure, any time we don't have a name to attach to someone we admit, we name him John Doe."

"Oh. Then who are the John Doe's who you've got?"

She looked down at some sort of list and looked back a second time. "No, there aren't any John Does in the hospital."

What required a second look? I wanted to know. I needed to know. I had to know. I reached into an inner pocket and pulled my wand out. I grasped it firmly and said "Imper..." And in the middle of saying the spell, I remembered something. I remembered something so important that had I not remembered within another half second, it would have been tragic.

◁

I had almost used the Imperious spell. If I had done that, the trace that was on me, would have gone off and aurors would have arrived within minutes, perhaps within seconds to arrest me. One of them might even have been Lockhart. Then it would all have ended in a big hurry regardless what I learned from the receptionist. I nodded and walked away and sat in the lobby area. How could I find out if there really were a "John Doe" in the hospital somewhere.

I thought about other ideas. I could try walking the halls, sticking my head into rooms to see if you were here. I actually started that.

I walked around the building, starting on the main floor. I could go almost anywhere, but there were doors that were locked. I used Alohora and went past most doors. But then there were a few doors where Alohora didn't work. Those doors had some other kind of locking mechanism besides mechanical bolts.

It was a surprisingly large building. I entered almost all the rooms there were. It was almost midnight by the time I had done it and I still wasn't sure that I hadn't missed some people. I was exhausted and I was sick to my heart that maybe you were somewhere in that building and I'd missed you. It's a sign of how poorly I was thinking that I hadn't thought of disapparating past some of those doors that I couldn't pass. But maybe there'd have been someone on the other side, and then what would I have done?

I took my wand in hand, disapparated, and appeared at my Inn. I went in and trudged up to my room. After I was in, I locked the door behind me. For the first time since noon feeling safe and secure, I dropped off to sleep immediately in my clothes.

The next day, I had slept almost till 8 AM. I got up and had a quick breakfast. I disapparated to Princeton and went on to the next hospital on my list. It was a slow slog. I kept working my way through floors and wards and rooms. By lunch, there was nothing that even looked like a hopeful sign.

I ate at the Asia Bistro for lunch. Then I went on. And on. And on.

By supper, I was tired, foot-worn, and scared – scared that I would never see you again. They were probably getting tired of seeing me at the Bistro, but I had my waiter from the last night who was more than anxious to serve me. We talked a little about my hopeless search.

He asked the obvious questions: Had I tried the police? Had I tried all the hospitals on my list? Really? Sorry.

I went to the Inn and fell into bed and dissolved into sleep. The next day there were only a couple of hospitals left. Were there more that should have been on the list? I didn't know. What would I do if I didn't find you by then?

By the early afternoon, I learned the answer to some of those questions. There wasn't a Wendt or John Doe in any of the hospitals. There wasn't a room that I could reach that had a Wendt or John Doe in it. I thought about the suggestions from Lockhart—a detective agency. I went to what I was beginning to think of as my office.

My favorite waiter was working, and I got assigned to his table. He asked, "You having an early dinner?"

"I'm having an afternoon snack AND a look at the *Yellow Pages*."

"Just order a cup of coffee and I'll get you the *Yellow Pages*."

"Tea."

He had already left for the kitchen. He turned, "What?"

"Tea. I want a cup of hot tea."

"Got it."

He did "got it" and returned with the *Yellow Pages* as well. It had a very short list of detective agencies. I got up and found the waiter and said, "I need to use the phone to make a couple of phone calls."

He laughed and said, "The tea and the phone are on the house."

I sat down at the phone and picked the last name in the short list. I dialed and got an answering machine. Forget that. I then dialed the next up. That one gave me a human being. I made an appointment for 4PM that afternoon.

When I disapparated to the street, I had a hard time finding the address. Eventually I realized it was on the second floor of a building with outside stairs and halls. I knocked on the door and entered. There was a desk, a few book shelves, a sofa and a table with some magazines that were about six months old. There was a sign on the desk that said, "If no one is here, walk into the inner office." I knocked on the only door in the "suite", and someone from within said, "Come on in. Don't be shy."

I entered the inner office and found another desk, a couple of mismatched chairs, a couple of bookshelves, and a man sitting behind the desk. He was short, wiry, with thinning brown hair, combed over the balding spot in the middle of his head. He was leaning back in his chair. He asked, "You Ms. McGonagall?"

I admitted that I was.

"Tell me what you want."

I explained about the strange case of the missing traveling companion.

"So, what do you think that I can do?"

"Well, I was hoping that you could find him."

"Tell me what you've done already."

I left out the Auror Office and went through most of the rest, including trying to find out about "John Doe's" at the hospitals.

"Not bad. You've done most of what I would do. But if you want more done, you'll have to give me a lot more information about yourself."

241

I was surprised, "About me?"

"Sure. That's a start. Let's go. You're from England, and you're traveling with an American buddy. Why did you choose here?"

"Well, I didn't exactly choose here, if you mean Princeton. We're both teachers. We like visiting interesting historical spots. We went to Washington DC and toured there for several days. Then we were going to New York where we were going to sight-see for a few more days. We took the train. It goes through Princeton."

He looked at me and shook his head, seemingly sadly, "That doesn't explain why he got off the train in Princeton."

"Wendt wanted to buy a Princeton paper. He thought Princeton University was one of the best schools in the world. He wanted to walk in the station and buy a Princeton paper." I paused, trying to come up with the sense of what he'd wanted at the train station. "I think it was like a souvenir of Princeton. You know. Some people collect glasses with the name of a city on it. He wanted a newspaper that said Princeton on the front page."

"That's what he told you?"

"Not in those words, but that's what he meant."

"OK. Tell me about your relationship?"

I knew this was coming, and I'd thought about it and even thought I knew what I was going to say. But, it just wouldn't come out. So, I told him more of the truth than I'd intended to, "Well, we've been close. Very close for at least four years. We've taken a couple of trips together."

He casually said one word that I knew was coming too, "Lovers?"

He was watching my face very closely. I tried to be as casual as he was, "Yes." He nodded acknowledgment.

"OK. Do you have a recent picture?"

I nodded and reached into my handbag. I quickly got out the photo and handed it over. He looked at it and stared for quite some time. Then he said, "There's something strange about this photo, but I can't put my finger on it." He was still staring at it. Then he gasped, "I could have sworn that the background moved a little."

I nodded. "Yes, that kind of picture has become very popular where I come from."

He was still troubled, "But how do they do that?"

I remembered one of Wendt's maxims. It's always OK to claim ignorance just so long as you stick with it.

I shrugged, "I don't know."

He nodded and seemed to dismiss it from his mind. He handed the photo back to me. Then he asked, "Did he ask you to marry him?"

I was surprised. I didn't see how that was relevant. This time I had a hard time being casual, "Well, yes."

"You refused him."

"How did you know?"

"You're not married are you?"

He looked at me for at least another minute. Finally he said, "I'm going to suggest a possibility to you. It doesn't mean I believe it. It just means that it's a possibility that we have to consider.

"When a younger man falls for an older woman, it's not unusual for the man to ask and the woman to refuse. And it's not unusual for the man to later reconsider and want to deny even the possibility that he has had a relationship with her let alone asked her to marry him. In those cases, it sometimes happens that the man just disappears."

My reaction was violent. "That's not it. That's not it at all."

"I want you to search your heart. Most women at the gut level understand the truth of it—even if they don't admit it to themselves. Take a minute and think."

I stood suddenly and was ready to stride out the door, but then I didn't. I needed this man's help. It would be stupid and maybe deadly to refuse it because he was honest. I sat again and forced myself to think. "I've thought. I don't think that's true. I think James Wendt is in a lot of trouble. I want to find him before something terrible happens." I looked him straight in the eye as I said this.

He smiled, "I believe you. I think he is in trouble. But I can't help you. I could do a couple of things that you weren't able to, but they'd not be likely to find him. You need somebody better than me." He reached into a desk drawer and pulled out a standard business card. He held it in his hand and said, "This is an agency that has more resources than I do. I'm OK for husbands who wonder if their wife's cheating on them. I'm not the agency for this job. Good luck. I've got a feeling that you're going to need it." Then he handed me the card.

"Do I owe you anything?"

"No. The first half-hour consultation is always free."

I looked at the card. It had an address in Trenton, New Jersey, wherever that was. It was getting late, but I had a chance of catching someone before they left for the night. I went down to the street level and found a restaurant. I went in and asked if I could use their phone. The waitress behind the counter pointed over at the wall. I was puzzled at first but then realized that the device on the wall could be a phone of sorts. I went to it and read the instructions. I tried to follow them. The one said that I could get help by dialing "zero". I lifted the handset and punched the zero. I got some kind of machine that asked me to enter the phone number with area code. I didn't know what this area code was but I just punched in the number on the card. Then the machine asked me to put in 75 cents for three minutes. I opened my handbag and looked for some of the stupid Muggle coins. How much was a quarter worth? I had a bunch of pennies, but there was no place to put them in the damn phone!

I was saved by the machine. It got tired of waiting and somehow a person came on the phone. "Can I help you?"

"Yes, I want to make this call, and I don't know if I've got the right coins for the phone."

"That's all right. Do you have a credit card?"

"Yes."

"Tell me the credit card number, and you can complete the call that way."

"Thank God. Yes." I gave him the credit card number. It was a miracle. The phone rang. And someone answered it.

A woman's voice said, "Carter Detective Agency."

"Really!"

"Yes, really. What can I do for you?"

"I want an appointment with a detective."

"Well, the office is about to close for the night. Can I make an appointment tomorrow morning for you?"

"No. This is very urgent. Now, please."

There was silence, then the voice said, "I'll let you talk with Mr. Carter right now. Hang on a moment."

Shortly a man's voice came on, "This is Carter. What's so urgent?"

As so often, I realized how hard it is to communicate the very real urgency that one feels. In desperation I just said, "I've lost my boy friend. I'm afraid that he's in trouble."

The voice on the other end of the line sighed. I suppose he'd heard that more times than I could count, but he said, "OK. I was just going out to have dinner at a restaurant near here. You could meet me in the lobby of my office building, and we could go around the corner to my favorite restaurant for dinner and talk about it. Would that be OK?"

Relief flooded my voice, "Oh, yes. Thank you so much."

"How long will it take you to get here?"

"Two minutes."

"Are you in the lobby?"

"No. No. I suppose I was exaggerating. I can be there in ten minutes."

"Don't get in an accident. Make it fifteen minutes. I'll be in the lobby waiting for you. I am wearing a white pair of slacks and a blue serge shirt."

"Thank you, thank you, thank you."

"See you in a few. What's your name?"

"Minerva McGonagall."

I walked out of the restaurant and into an alley and disapparated to the address. Then I decided to walk around the block for fifteen minutes. After ten minutes, I couldn't stand waiting any longer, and I walked into the lobby of the office building. There were a number of people leaving the building—I suppose leaving offices for home. However, there was only one man standing by the elevators, not going anywhere wearing a blue shirt. I walked up to him.

"Ms. McGonagal?" he asked.

I nodded. We walked out of the building together and down the block. It wasn't actually around the block. It was near the corner and across the street. He asked me if I minded if we did something he called j-walking. I didn't say anything, but he just took my arm, and we crossed the street and found ourselves in front of a small Chinese restaurant. He opened the door for me, and I found a dozen or so tables and a counter where you could order.

"It's the best Chinese at the best prices in the city."

I asked, "What do you recommend?"

"Pick the kind of meat you like best, and then choose a dish. Doesn't matter. You'll like it."

With that vague recommendation, I chose a favorite of mine—moo-shu pork. I insisted on paying because we were on his time. He shrugged and accepted.

We found a table. They were all alike—linoleum tops, tubular steel legs, ditto the four chairs. We sat, and he started, "You've bought my time. Go."

I had become fairly good at telling my story in a compact way. I told him about traveling by train. Stopping in Princeton. The attack—I didn't specify what kind of attack. The disappearance. Searching the hospitals.

He nodded and said, 'Rather inconvenient losing your boy friend."

I actually jumped up indignantly, "I did not *lose* him. He was kidnapped, and I've tried everything I could to find him."

He was completely unaffected by my temper, "Good. I just wanted to find out how much you care about this–really. Now, let me guess.

"You've seen another detective, maybe the police."

I couldn't help being surprised, "How did you know?"

"Your vehemence, the way you told your story. You're obviously smart and independent. You've done as much as you know or could guess to do. I've heard a lot of people report. You've told this a lot of times, had to answer questions about it. You've got all the important details. I could tell where you'd answered questions before, like what you'd done on your own to find you 'friend'."

"So do you think you can help me?"

"First I've got to ask you a few questions that you didn't cover. When you talked to the other detective," He paused and asked, 'By the way, who was it who recommended you to me?"

I told him. He smiled. "Yes, he's plodding and unimaginative, but he's like a bull dog. He won't give up. He solves a lot of cases by pure determination and dumb luck. He's also honest. Most other detectives around here wouldn't recommend someone whom they thought was better than them. He would–and has."

"Did he talk about fees?"

"No."

He leaned back and began talking in a relaxed manner. This was standard boiler-plate that he had to tell every client, "OK. First off, just level-set, you're not going to find a detective who'll work for less than one hundred dollars per hour. You won't find a decent one for much less than the two hundred that I charge. You still interested?"

I gulped and thought a second. "Yes, I am."

"OK. You were either just unlucky and your friend and you were caught in a terrorist incident or he was involved with some kind of illegal activity. It makes a difference. Which was it?"

That posed a problem for me. It was almost certainly Deatheaters, definitely illegal, but he wasn't involved with them, exactly. I thought a minute. "First of all, I know him really well. I know he wasn't himself doing anything illegal, but I know that the 'terrorist' attack wasn't really a 'terrorist' attack. It was a British criminal gang. James had been kidnapped once before because he spoke out against them."

Carter asked, "How did he get away before? Did someone pay a ransom?"

I chuckled. When was the last time I'd felt like doing that? "Well, he sort of escaped on his own."

Carter seemed to think about that for a minute. "It happens sometimes, but they wouldn't let that happen a second time.

"OK. What was the name of the gang?"

Being perfectly honestly, I answered, "The Deatheaters."

He actually laughed. "These youth gangs have no imaginations. Do you know that there are youth gangs here called the 'Cryps' and the 'Bloods'?"

"No."

"Well, what were they doing here?"

That was a good question. "I really don't know. I suppose that they must hate him a lot more than I guessed."

"If he were kidnapped, he's either dead or being held for ransom. Who would they contact with a ransom note?"

I had very much wanted to keep Wendt's parents out of this, and I still would try to until there was no choice. "His parents are really nice people. I don't want them to know that he's in danger until we're sure. I don't want them contacted unless we have to."

He shook his head. "We've got to find out if they've gotten a ransom note. But we don't have to let them know that he might be in trouble. I'll give them a call right now, if you've got the phone number, and we can find out without alerting them to trouble."

I was incredulous, "Really!"

"Yes. I promise you that they'll not know any different if they've not received a note."

I let him go ahead. I rummaged around in my handbag to find my notebook. I kept their phone number there. He took a cell phone out of his pocket and dialed the number. Apparently, they answered.

"Hello, am I speaking to Mrs. Wendt?" There was a pause.

"Thanks. I'm trying to reach a James Wendt. Can you let me talk with him?"

"Surely. I'm a private investigator, Robert Carter, in Trenton, New Jersey. I've been hired by a client who would like to discuss a confidential matter with him. I'm afraid I'm not at liberty to discuss with you what that matter is. Can you help me get in touch with him?"

There was a pause that stretched on a few minutes.

"Thanks very much. Let me give you my cell phone number." He gave the number, "When he shows up, please have him call this number as soon as possible—day or night. Thank you." He hung up.

"What did she say?"

"He's expected home from England in a few days, but she doesn't know how to reach him before then."

He went on, "Now that's either good news or bad news. If they got him, he's almost certainly dead now. If they didn't, he's probably alive in a hospital someplace, maybe in a coma."

I didn't know how to react to that other than the disappointment that I still was really in the dark, "Can you help me?"

He leaned back as a waiter brought our food out. He excused himself for being hungry and had several mouthfuls of food before he went on. I suspect he was using it as a cover to have time to think.

"Well, I think you've got a couple of choices here.

"First, you could go to the police. They have lots of resources and can trace people through hospitals a lot easier than we can. The disadvantage is that to file a missing persons report, you'd have to wait at least several more days. Now, you could tell them your international gang theory, and that might get them started sooner, but they'll treat finding your friend as just a part of the investigation that they're already doing of that incident a few days ago. You could just as well sit around and wait for results. Also, if you volunteer information, you might get arrested as a material witness. That's a damn inconvenience at best."

I was definite about that. I wanted action. "No. There's got to be a better way."

"The next thing you could do would be to hire me. Missing persons isn't exactly my expertise, but I could work the job. It could take a good bit of time. I'm fairly busy right now, and I'd not be the best person for the job anyway. If this were something simple like watching a wayward husband, I could farm most of the work out to a free-lancer that I'd direct and you'd get off fairly cheaply. But this is more complicated and it would take a lot of my time. I might have to slow down one of my other jobs."

I interrupted. "Is this an invitation to outbid your other work to get priority?"

"No, ma'am it isn't. I wouldn't offer you that. I have another option."

Infuriatingly, he didn't immediately offer his other option. He continued eating in a leisurely way. Then, he sat back and looked at me for what seemed like ten minutes, but it must have been much less. I finally decided that he was evaluating me. Then he went on.

"Ma'am, I hope that you don't take what I'm about to suggest the wrong way." He paused again. This was infuriating. If I didn't absolutely need his help, I'd have been sorely tempted to tell him what I thought about his interview technique. He eventually shook his head and muttered something like, "There's no other way for it.

"Ma'am, you're not going to like what I have to suggest, but it's all that I can offer you at the moment." Again, he paused.

"I will put aside some of my other work tomorrow and do the first step of investigation that I would do, if I were going to commit myself completely to your case. That's all I can offer now."

I couldn't restrain myself. "Stop beating around the bush and just offer it. I'll take it or I won't."

He shrugged, "Here's what I'll do. I hate to say it, but it's the mostly likely thing to work. I'll do inquiries at all the morgues in New Jersey. I might be able to finish by noon, but I will be definitely finished by the end of day."

For a moment, the import of what he'd said didn't strike me. I started to say, "Well, what was all the fuss about. I don't . . ." Then what he'd said struck me. "Morgues. Then you think Jim is dead." I looked off into the distance remembering what he looked like the last time I saw him, maybe the last time that I'd ever see him.

He shook is head vigorously, "No. I only think that it's fairly likely. And it's definitely the most useful thing that I can do in under a day. And that's as much time as I can give you now."

I looked down at my plate, and for a moment, I'd forgotten that the plate in front of me was mine. I shook my head and felt my bun shift around. That returned me to the necessities of the present. "Yes, do that. BUT what happens after you fail to find him?"

He brightened somewhat and nodded, "Yes, after we eliminate that he's in a morgue somewhere in Jersey, you'll have to go elsewhere. I'll think about recommendations for you, but for now, let's stay focused on tomorrow. I'll start first thing in the morning. If I learn something, how do I get in touch with you?"

I hadn't thought about that. I struggled for a minute thinking about how to handle that, but he broke in on my thoughts. "I suppose you don't have a cell phone that works locally."

I shook my head and said, "I left my English one back there."

"If I were going to be working for you for a while, I'd suggest that you get a local pay-as-you-go cell phone. But if I find something, it won't be very urgent to get hold of you. You'll probably need to get one if you stay here for any length of time, but you can worry about that later. Are you staying somewhere local?"

I was still a bit stunned by what he was proposing to do, so it took a few seconds to register what he wanted to know. "Oh, I'm staying at an inn, but not near here."

For the first time he showed a little exasperation, "Well? What's their phone number?"

Of course, I didn't even know if the Cat in Wellingtons had a phone, let alone the phone number. I said, "I'm sorry. I don't know, but couldn't I call you to check on your progress?"

He became more exasperated still. I could see from his compressed lips that he was trying to hold back a comment. He seemed to control himself and seemed to be exercising some amount of restraint as he calmly said, "Madame, neither I nor any other investigators give out their cell phones to clients for the purpose of allowing checks of their progress. It is not very conducive to progress in an investigation. Let's do this. Call my office at noon tomorrow. I might have results by then. Whether or not I do, we should meet tomorrow at the end of the day."

I smiled, "We could have dinner again here. The Chinese is pretty good."

He agreed to that. Then I had another thought, "Do you want a down payment or something?"

He shook his head, "No, I'll not be putting in a lot of time and I won't give you results until you've paid. Come to my office at 5 tomorrow. You'll pay there, and then we'll come here to discuss next steps."

I began to think about how I'd pay. "Would you accept a credit card payment?"

"Yes. It shouldn't be much more than a thousand dollars. If it were much more than that, you could still pay by credit card, but I'd have to check your credit limit first."

I mentally released a sigh of relief, which he seemed to pick up on. "If you don't have much local money, you might want to go to a bank and get a cash advance on that credit card. There are some places that don't accept them."

After our dinner, we parted company, and I returned to the inn. It wasn't really late, and I didn't want to go to my room for a couple of hours. So I sat in the bar and slowly had a butter beer in the corner. Somehow the time flew by, and the barman interrupted my wandering thoughts to tell me that the bar was closing. I thanked him and went up to my room.

I had a very troubled night with very little true sleep until the early morning. Then, I really did sleep until almost 10 AM. I dressed and went down to see if there might be something like breakfast available. The kitchen did fix me a couple of scrambled eggs, which I picked at desultorily.

The rest of the day was the worst that I had spent since – well, since the time my husband had disappeared.

The clock went its wearing way round a couple of times. At the stroke of noon, I suddenly realized that I didn't know where there was a phone to call the detective agency. I went to the Front Desk. The usual clerk was there. I asked if she knew where there was a telephone.

"Oh, ma'am, we have one here at the Front Desk for the convenience of our guests who need to phone a Muggle establishment." With that, she reached under the desk and pulled up a telephone with a cord. "Would you like some help with it?"

I immediately answered, 'I've made many phone calls. I shouldn't need any help." But then she turned it around to face me, and I discovered that it was a type that I'd never seen before. It had some sort of ring of numbers.

My puzzlement was evident. She said, "Well, maybe it's been a while. First, do you have the phone #?"

I just felt like screaming, "Of course, I have the phone #" but I just said it softly.

"Good, now do you mind if I dial it to remind you how it works?"

I just glumly said, "Go ahead." I handed her the business card with the phone #. The clerk put her index finger in a little hole over the number that she wanted and then sort of rotated the dial as far as it would go. Then she pulled her finger out, and the dial spun around and came to rest. She did that for each of the seven digits. Then she handed the receiver to me.

I put it to my ear and listened for the ringing sound, once, twice. Then someone spoke, but it wasn't the secretary from yesterday. It was a strange sounding voice – as though it weren't a person at all. "Sorry, this number has been disconnected. If you're sure you have the right number, please dial again." What the bloody hell was that? I'd called the number once before, yesterday. Maybe the phone was defective.

The clerk asked, "Not at home?"

"No, the phone said that the number was disconnected, but I called it yesterday. I don't understand?"

The clerk puzzled and then said, "Maybe I made a mistake, let me dial again." She took the phone back and dialed again, but this time she kept the receiver and listened, "No. It definitely says that the number is disconnected."

By this time I was getting worried. It was already well past noon and getting later with every misstep. It must have shown in my voice because the desk clerk quickly suggested something, "We can call the operator and ask for help."

My dumbfounded look caused her to amplify. "We dial zero, the operator will answer, and we can ask for help."

I pulled the telephone to me, and sure enough the number zero said Operator. I dialed it and a female voice asked, "How can I help you?"

I just blurted out, "I'm trying to call a number that I called yesterday, and today there's a message that says the line's disconnected. What's going on?"

"Can you give me the number, and I'll dial it for you."

I read the number off the card, the operator dialed it, and the message came up again. She somehow hung up the disconnected line and was silent for a minute. Then she said, "I thought so. That number isn't a valid phone # in the Washington area code. That's from a different area code."

I spluttered, "What's that about?"

"Area codes?"

"Yes."

She seemed to take a deep breath – as though about to explain about the floo network to a four-year old. "Well, the country is divided up into hundreds of regions. They all have their own sets of 7 digit phone #'s. To call inside your own area, you just dial the seven digit phone number. For you, that would be Washington DC. But if you want to call someplace outside your area, you have to dial the number one and then the three digit area code number and then the seven digit phone number. I think your phone number is in a different area code. Where is it located?"

I turned to the desk clerk and signaled for her to hand me the business card. She didn't understand, so I just pulled it out of her hand. "It's in Trenton, New Jersey."

"Oh, that's 609. I can dial it for you, but if I do, it'll be more expensive than if you dial it yourself."

My exasperation was reaching the explosion point, I just said, "Dial it!"

She said thanks, and in a minute the phone was ringing. I glanced at my watch. It was already almost 12:30. The secretary from yesterday answered. I asked, "This is Ms. McGonagall. Do you have any news for me?"

The nasally voice replied, "Yes, there is a message from Mr. Carter. He says that he'll meet you tonight as arranged."

I managed to thank her and slammed the phone down harder than I wanted. The desk clerk asked, "Not good news."

"I don't know. I guess maybe it is good news. It was no news and I guess no news really is good news."

She brightened a little while I stood there thinking. I had to do something rather than just stay here in the inn, but what? I finally decided that exercise would be good. I asked the clerk if there were a park around here that would be good to take a long walk in.

"Oh, ma'am. There are all sorts of places in Washington that are good to walk in. You could step outside and walk the neighborhood. It's very pleasant. You could go to the Capitol Mall. You could go to Arlington Cemetery. I always like it when I'm troubled."

I nodded. "Yes, maybe the Mall. I walked outside and disapparated to the place near the Library of Congress that we'd disapparated the first time that we were here. There was plenty of opportunity to walk, and I walked most of the afternoon.

The afternoon stretched on interminably, but it did get to be 4 PM. I decided that I could disapparate to Trenton. I arrived, took the lift to the right floor, and found the office. It was very different from the Princeton detective's office. For one thing there was a receptionist present. There were also several pieces of comfortable furniture–a couple of chairs, a couch, and a couple of Impressionist prints. The receptionist asked my business, and I gave my name.

"Ms. McGonagall. Mr. Carter is in and is waiting for you. Please walk on through to his office." I opened the door, and there was a short corridor and three doors. The one immediately opposite the door that I'd come through had a name plate with Carter's name on it. I opened that door and found Carter on the phone. He motioned me to sit and finished his phone call. I sat in one of the chairs on the other side of the desk from him. The desk was a modern wood veneer desk. I could tell because one corner was chipped, and the underlying material was revealed. The rest of the office was furnished in a sort of institutional/functional style. As I sat, he finished his phone call, and he turned to me.

"I didn't find anything. It's actually better than I hoped for." He must have seen my face fall. "No, really. It is good news. It's certainly still possible that your friend is dead, but it's much better news than if I'd found him.

"Now, I want to assure you that I tried hard. Not only did I contact all the morgues in New Jersey, I also contacted ones in Philadelphia."

I suppose that I should have been happy, but no news was still disappointing in a strange way. "Well, what's my next step?"

That question seemed to cause Carter some discomfort. He avoided my eyes but pressed a button on his phone and spoke at it, "Ms. Wainwright, would you please bring the credit card thing in?"

It spoke back to him in the receptionist's voice, "Yes, sir."

"Well, the next thing is for you to pay for my services." He picked up a piece of typed paper from his desk and handed it to me. It was some sort of itemized bill. It listed six hours of time at $200 per hour and something called "phone charges" at $50.

"Mr. Carter, what are the phone charges?"

"Oh, I had to make a number of long distance phone calls. They weren't cheap."

I could only say, "I see." I had no idea if that were reasonable or not, but I wasn't going to argue. By this time, the receptionist had come in with some sort of small machine. She held out her hand toward me, as though she expected me to give her something.

She asked, "Could I have your credit card?"

It made sense after she asked for it. I rummaged in my purse for the card and handed it to her. She put a piece of paper in the machine and the credit card and slid a handle. For a minute, I was afraid she'd break the credit card, and then where would I be? She didn't. I knew that I'd have to sign the piece of paper that spent $1250 that belonged to you. Then she left the room.

Carter perked up after that had been completed. He went on, "To get back to your question, I think that you will have to look elsewhere than New Jersey to find a detective who can help you. I could make suggestions for you. There are detectives who live in New York City who can solve your case if anyone can. It's dinner time. Let's go to my favorite Chinese restaurant and discuss it. This time the dinner will be on my nickel."

So, we did. After we had placed orders and were seated, I asked, "But it would be more expensive to use this detective that you're thinking of?" I asked.

He drank some coffee that the waiter had just brought. "Well, it's complicated. He's eccentric. He's the best if you can get him. We also need to discuss his uh eccentricities." He stared at me for a while, evaluating me again.

"Ok. Ms. McGonagall. Before I give you contact information for this detective, we're going to have a little interview. I've never sent him a client before, and I don't want to look like an idiot by sending him someone that he wouldn't work with."

I smiled, "Well, we certainly wouldn't want that."

"No. So, here we go. First off, fee. He may not be the most expensive detective in the world, but he tries. I've never heard of a client of his paying less than eight or ten thousand dollars. That's just the price of getting in the door and hiring him. Most detectives charge by the hour. He charges mostly by how much brain power it takes to solve the case. He values his genius very highly, and make no mistake, he is a genius. I've never heard of him charging more than forty or fifty thousand dollars, although grateful clients do sometimes pay him more."

He chuckled as though at reminiscence, "I've even heard of a fee in the six figure range. Now, this is purely rumor, and I don't know if I'd credit it, but the story that I've heard is that he once tangled with the FBI."

I interrupted, "The what?"

"You've not heard of the FBI?"

"No."

"Well, even for a foreigner, it's strange not to at least have heard of it. Well, to be brief, it's a US government police organization. They are famous now for both investigation AND for being ethical, but thirty years ago when this story happened, they had a tough director who was famous for breaking the law in the pursuit of upholding the law. His power both legal and political was amazing. Even Presidents were afraid to cross him at his prime."

As he said that, I couldn't help thinking of Minister Fudge.

"Anyway, he was hired to prevent the FBI from harassing someone. AND he succeeded."

I was appropriately impressed. He went on. "So, long story, short, this will surely cost you at least $10,000, probably much more. Possibly, $25,000 or conceivably even more.

"Knowing that, are you still interested?"

I hesitated, wondering just how many "dollars" you had in your account. After a minute, he said, "Do you know how you know if a boat is too expensive to buy?"

The seeming incongruity startled me, and I blurted out, "No, how do you know?"

"If you have to think about whether it's too expensive."

I made a snap decision. I'd trust to your account and cross the bridge if there weren't enough there. "I don't have to think about it. I'll afford it."

"OK. You've got some disadvantages in trying to get him to take you as a client. One is that you're a woman."

"What?" I was genuinely startled, "Isn't $25,000 good enough inducement!"

Carter went on undeterred, "Oh, he isn't a misogynist. He just doesn't like the way women try to manipulate men with tears, sob stories, and so on. A word of advice: Don't cry in his presence. Don't show excessive emotion of any kind. Now, you strike me as the kind of woman he'd like—if he were ever to actually like any woman. I think you can probably control the tear ducts."

I shook my head in disbelief at this attitude, "I think I can."

"Good. Another thing. He has an assistant who is sort of a combination, personal secretary, assistant detective, gad-fly, and all-around gofer. It's good to get him on your side early.

"The office hours are a little unusual. They start at 11 AM. He has a late lunch, and, unlike me, he won't discuss business over meals. He takes some time off in the late afternoon and will work in the evening.

"I'll give you his phone number, but I'd recommend that you go to his office, which is also his home, about 10:30 in the morning. His assistant will be in the office working then, and you'd be lucky to get him on your side before you see the boss. His assistant is something of a ladies' man but thoroughly a gentleman. He's also got an impertinent sense of humor. Don't let him put you off, though. He's a good man and would be very good to have on your side even without the boss.

"Now, maybe the most important point: be completely honest with them. There are several good reasons for that. First, it's just all-round good policy when you're doing business.

"Second, in the investigation business, holding things back just causes problems and slows down getting your needs met.

"Thirdly, eventually that pair will get to the bottom of everything anyway and find all the dirty secrets. It's better to have them out up front.

"So, the oath you take on the witness stand—the truth, the whole truth and nothing but the truth—is absolutely the way to deal with them.

"Now, I know that you haven't been up-front with me."

I started to say something, but he interrupted, "That's natural and that's OK. You aren't my client, now. But, if you become their client, you'd better be up front with everything. Let it all out of the bag, as they say."

I was ticking off the points, mentally, "That's quite a lot."

"Well, that's not quite all. I want to warn you. No, let's just say that I want to be up front with you about him. There are a couple of things.

"He's quite old—and fat."

"What do you mean, 'old'?"

"Well, he's in his early nineties, I guess. Now, don't jump to conclusions. When you see him, you'll wonder that he can do anything, but you must understand that he never leaves the office. He just sits behind his desk and thinks. And that's exactly what you want him to do. That's what he does best. He's never left his house—or even his office when he's working on a problem. And don't be contemptuous of his abilities at 90+. I know a couple of lawyers who are in their nineties. They're smart and capable. They even occasionally show up in the courtroom, which is more than he's ever done—voluntarily, at least.

"He doesn't have to travel around because he has his assistant to do that. The assistant is in his seventies, but he looks like he might just be in his upper fifties. He's fit, slim, hard. I know a guy who owns a ranch in West Texas. He rides the range every day—herding cattle, repairing fences, running things in general. He's in his eighties. When he talks to people about the future, he says things like 'IF I die'. That's the kind of guy this assistant is. Now, he's probably not up to punching a tough guy's lights out, but don't underestimate him."

I interrupted. "Don't think that I underestimate people who are above ninety. I don't know my boss's exact age, but he's certainly above one hundred, and he's just as fit as that West Texas rancher of yours."

He didn't take the interruption badly. He just nodded as I told him about Professor Dumbledore. Then he went on, "Finally, there's one kind of case that he absolutely won't touch."

I had a bad feeling about this but I asked, "What kind?"

"He will not take a case that involves divorce or marital infidelity or jealousy. You've got to make it clear that even though the missing person is your love interest, this isn't that kind of case."

I was surprised of course. It made me think of djins with all these rules for dealing with this genius. There are well-known rules for dealing with them. They're very powerful and can be used effectively, but only if you follow the rules carefully. Otherwise, disaster can follow. One of the most important rules is stating your request extremely carefully. You can't give a djin any leeway to interpret your request in a malicious way. I've only been involved with a djin once in my life. That time, I was only involved indirectly. Perhaps sometime, I'll tell you about it.

The thing that I was most surprised about was that this guy needed to work at the age of ninety. If he were so smart, surely he'd have saved up enough for a comfortable retirement.

Carter talked about that, "Well, he's what most people would call 'independently wealthy', but he has expensive tastes. He lives in a brownstone in New York, and he's converted the top floor into an orchid garden. That's expensive. He has a professional gardener who helps him take care of the orchids. He's also a gourmet. He has a professional Swiss chef, who could be the head chef at any New York restaurant– probably any Paris restaurant too—prepare meals and live-in. His assistant lives in. He's got quite a payroll. And, despite the fact that he claims to hate working, he always takes cases on.

"He's the very best person that you could have working on the case. Your real problem is getting him to take it. Do you still want the contact information?"

I agreed and we finished dinner, mostly in silence, but he asked if I were here sightseeing. I agreed and mentioned where we'd gone. He approved your choices.

We went back to his offices. He unlocked the door and turned on the light. I noticed the name on one of the other inner doors—June Carter. I asked if she were his wife. He shook his head, "No, a sister-in-law. She's pretty efficient, though. She understands these computers besides being a decent investigator. She usually gets the cases where the client is on the distaff side." She apparently also understood decorating.

The second look at Carter's inner office was different. I noticed that the decoration was more eccentric than the outer office, but also modern. There were a couple of photos framed on the wall. They all had Carter along with someone. He was in a military uniform in one of them. The desk didn't have a computer. There was a credenza, several chairs, and a sofa. He apparently had conferences there at times with a number of people. Carter started rummaging in his drawers for the business card.

"I thought I had his card here someplace. Well, that's all right. I have him in the rolodex."

He pulled a strange cylindrical device that seemed to have 3 by 5 cards in clear envelopes attached to a wheel. He spun the wheel around, looked, spun it back a bit, and found what he was looking for. Referring to the card that he'd found, he wrote on a yellow legal pad. When he'd finished, he tore the sheet off, and handed it to me. "This is his address and phone number. It's got his name, his assistant's name, and the office hours as I remember them. Do you have any questions?"

"How much do I owe you for the reference?"

"You bought me supper the first night, didn't you. If Wendt or his parents call, I'll get in touch with you right away. How can I reach you?"

I thought a moment. I didn't know the phone number of the Washington Inn where I was staying. I temporized. "I was staying in Washington, but I'll be moving to New York tomorrow. I don't know where yet. I'll call you when I have a place."

He nodded and then had an idea, "Well, if you can afford this guy, you can afford to stay in a decent hotel in New York. I'd suggest the Churchill. When you're located give me a call."

He stood and held out his hand, "Good luck, Ms. McGonagall. I've got a feeling you'll need it. Oh, and leave a good word for me with your next detective."

I took his hand, which was dry and firm without crushing, "I will. Thanks for your help. I hope that your other jobs turn out well."

He nodded and thanked me. I turned and left the office. I never saw him again. When I was on the street, I found an alley and disapparated back to Washington. The night was a long one, waiting for tomorrow to interview my third detective in only three days.

The night finally ended with my getting a few hours sleep. I packed and checked out for the second time. The clerk at the Front Desk wished me luck looking for my friend. I told her, "For once, I think I'm starting to have some good luck."

She asked, "How can we get in touch if we need to?"

"Just use owl post. I'll be in New York."

The Muggle Hunt

I might as well start off by telling you what we were looking for, because I had never heard the term before. We were looking for a Muggle. It turns out that a Muggle is an everyday garden variety human being. Why have a special name for people like you and me? Because our client was magical, and a lot of the people we ended up dealing with were magical. Muggle was their name for us.

I was at my desk working on the damn computer. I had almost begun to regret talking Wolfe into buying it for me. It seemed like such a good idea. His voluminous germination records seemed the ideal application to keep on a computer. I'd expended a lot of time and effort convincing him that the MacIntosch would be just the thing to make it easy to trace the hybridization that he and Muhlman did. I was not going to admit defeat or let him think that things weren't going better than with the paper records, but I was beginning to wonder how long I could keep up the tedious conversion of paper records to spreadsheets.

It was in the middle of this that the doorbell rang. I got up and went to the door, noting the time—just after 10:30. Why was it that so many people came about this time with Wolfe up with the orchids? You'd think that everyone in America by now would know what his office hours were.

I looked through the one-way glass. Wolfe had absolutely forbidden installing a remote camera system so that we could tell who was at the door without leaving our desks. He had long been opposed to any automation. I was actually really surprised that he had agreed to the computer for the orchids.

When I looked through the one-way glass, I saw a woman who was middle-aged but who had maintained her figure more than well enough. It was shown off fairly well in a dark green dress that was calf length and left enough to the imagination of the viewer to be intriguing. She was of average height and wore a strange sort of hat that reminded me vaguely of the dunce cap from grade school days in Ohio. This chapeau seemed to be scattered with sequins that rather made me think of constellations of stars. They seemed to be in patterns and were rather sparse. Her face was nicely flushed, and she wore her reddish brown hair pulled up underneath her cap. Her eyes were shadowed by the cap, and I couldn't tell much about them.

I immediately opened the door and introduced myself, "I'm Archie Goodwin, and this is the residence of Nero Wolfe. Would you like to come in and discuss something—anything?"

She thanked me and crossed the threshold. Once inside, I got a good look at her eyes that were also green. They went well with the dress, but then, they'd go well with anything. "I've come to hire Mr. Wolfe to do an investigation for me."

The more that I saw of her, the more I liked what I saw. She wasn't Lilly Rowan, but she was a decent stand-in. "Well, Mr. Wolfe has another appointment at the moment, but if you accompany me to the office, I can help you almost as well." I led her to the office and put her in one of the yellow chairs that was close to my desk.

"Now, I'm Mr. Wolfe's personal assistant, and we collaborate on all investigations. He's a bit choosy in the jobs he takes on, so it's rather lucky that you came before he is free. Why don't you tell me what you'd like us to do for you, and I'll see if I can get Mr. Wolfe to take your case."

She folded her hands in her lap and looked me directly in the eye as she spoke. She had apparently rehearsed this speech a good bit, because she delivered it flawlessly. The gist of it was that she had been traveling with a friend on the Amtrak line between Washington and New York. Her friend (male) had left the train to get a paper. Just before the train left the station, there was a commotion on the platform, and she saw her friend collapse to the platform. She went out to assist, and some sort of battle ensued. In the confusion he had disappeared. She had heard nothing since and wanted help finding him.

I asked, "Isn't this the incident at the Princeton station last Monday?"

"Yes, it is."

"Well, Ms. McGonagall, this sort of case is usually handled by the police fairly well. Why not let them do their investigation? The word is that some sort of terrorists are involved."

"I think that my friend was the target of that attack."

This was a twist that I'd not expected. "Why do you think that?"

"Well, for one thing I think that I know what terrorist group it was, and I know that my friend had acted against them."

This was definitely going differently than I expected. I decided to temporize while I considered whether we wanted to get involved, "You don't happen to have a picture of your friend?"

She reached into her bag and pulled out a small leather frame with a photo inside. There was something wrong with it. As a matter of fact there were several things wrong with it. She asked for it back almost immediately, "That's my only picture I have here in America. If you don't mind, I don't like its being out of my possession."

I handed it back and reflected on the several things wrong with it. For one, it showed Ms. McGonagall with a much younger man. He didn't have my rugged good looks, but I could understand that women of any age might find him attractive—not just women of a certain age. The other, more disturbing thing was that through some trick of lighting or shadow or whatever, the photo seemed to be in motion or shifting in some subtle way.

I decided that this would have to be one for Wolfe to decide on, so I asked her the critical question. "Ms. McGonagall, there are certain cases that Mr. Wolfe won't touch with a ten foot pole. The strictest rule is against divorce cases or ones that might involve marital infidelity. Is this one of those cases?"

"Not at all. I had a husband once, a number of years ago. He died long before I met Mr. Wendt. He's not married and never has been. I'm not involved with any married man and, as far as I know—and that's pretty far—he isn't involved with anyone else either.

I nodded, "Very well. Then, this is a case that might interest Wolfe. I'm going to try to get him to take it, but you see, he has this thing with women. . "

I was about to expound, but she interrupted, "I know. He doesn't like emotional or clingy women, right?"

"Not precisely, but that's close enough. Just don't get emotional and there's a good chance that I can talk him into it.

"By the way, just for my curiosity, do you dance well?"

"I do. But you'll never learn about that by experience."

"OK. Just curious. You look like you have good legs for dancing."

"Thanks."

"One other important thing. Mr. Wolfe is not cheap. As a matter of fact."

Again I was interrupted, "Don't worry, I've heard about his typical fees. I'm prepared to pay them."

"Good. He'll be down from the plant room in a few minutes. Is there anything that I can get for you to drink?"

"No thanks."

"Do you have any questions?"

"Not until Wolfe arrives."

I got to the last touchy point. "Uh, one last thing. I trust you perfectly, but as Mr. Wolfe's secretary, I have to be sure about the credit-worthiness of clients. How do you intend to pay?"

She opened her purse and pulled out a credit card.

"Do you mind if I borrow that for a minute to check your credit? Few credit cards allow the size of transactions that we do."

She nodded and handed me the card. I called Experian and checked Wendt's credit. It was top notch. I then called MasterCard to see if there would be a problem with a $25,000 charge. They reported that there would be no difficulty, although they'd want to verify the identity of the person making the charge.

Then we spent the next five minutes in silence, finally broken by the sound of the elevator coming down from the plant room. Wolfe entered the office carrying a sprig of a blue Vanda. He put it in the vase at his desk. He turned to Ms. McGonagall and nodded slightly before sitting.

I introduced her and explained her case briefly, "Ms. McGonagall is from England on a sightseeing trip with a friend. He disappeared in the attack at the Princeton Amtrak station on Monday. She wants us to help her find her missing friend."

Wolfe's eyes narrowed to barely more than slits, "Ms. McGonagall. Please tell me your story in your own words. Leave nothing out that you think relevant. If I want more detail, I'll interrupt you. Please proceed."

She repeated what she had told me with details added. She explained that she and Wendt were both teachers at an exclusive finishing school in England. Wolfe interrupted to ask, "Please don't think that I'm being needlessly intrusive, but were the two of you intimate?"

She didn't blink an eye. She'd apparently been prepared for that question, "Yes."

"Frequently?"

"That's a relative term. We were intimate when our duties as teachers of impressionable youth permitted. That is to say, when school was on Holiday and when our duties took us away from school at the same time."

"I see. Then the school is a residential school?"

"Yes."

He turned to me and asked, "This isn't a divorce case?" His voice dripped with displeasure.

I looked a question at him, "You know that I wouldn't let her talk to you if it were."

"Good. Go ahead Madame."

She went on filling in details about their time in Washington DC, their train trip to New York, and the stop at Princeton Station. When she started to explain about the attack, she took a totally unexpected tack, "When I saw Wendt fall, I immediately suspected something other than an accident. I got up and ran to the exit of the rail car, but the train had started moving and I couldn't get out, so I disapparated to the station platform."

Both Wolfe's eyes and mine stared. This was different from the story she'd told me. He asked the question, "What do you mean 'disapparated'? I don't think that I've heard that term before." When Wolfe says that he's not heard a term, he usually means that the word is not a valid English word because he has an encyclopedic knowledge of the English language.

She was untroubled, "I would be surprised if you had. It's not a term from common English. It's a term that wizards have invented."

He leaned back in his chair, "Madame, do you mean wizards as in those practicing 'slight of hand'?"

She shook her head and sighed as though dealing with a slow student, "No." She said emphatically, "I mean wizards as those who can use real magic."

Wolfe shot me a glance that I knew meant that he wanted to know why I'd not screened her out. At the same time he started to get up.

She interrupted him saying, "Is this the sort of hospitality that clients normally receive in your home?"

That stung him into sitting, "It's the sort of hospitality that we reserve for those who should be constrained in an asylum."

She shot back, "Give me one minute for a demonstration and if you still think that I'm the one who belongs in an asylum, then leave. Otherwise, let me finish."

He compressed his lips together and squeezed out, "Go ahead."

She opened her handbag and started to pull something out. Wolfe shouted, "Archie!"

I leaped up and saw what she had in her hand. It was a carved piece of wood that some might have called a wand. I decided to give her a chance to hang herself, but I wished that my Smith & Wesson weren't locked in my desk drawer. I decided to surreptitiously unlock it.

She casually pointed it at the paperweight on his desk, a chunk of jade that a woman had used to crush her husband's skull. It rose into the air about a foot, apparently completely unsupported. Wolfe instinctively leaned back in his chair as far as it would allow his one-sixth of a ton to go. When it became apparent that nothing terrible was going to happen, he leaned forward and brought his nose within six inches of it. He got up and walked around the desk, observing the paperweight from all directions. He passed his hand under it and then passed it over it. Then he sat down again.

"Archie, try to move that paperweight."

I finished getting up. I found that I'd been half-standing for the last minute or two. I came to his desk and reached out. I gingerly touched it, as though it were electrically charged, but I felt nothing unusual. I closed my hand around it and then gently tugged at it. It didn't budge. I put a little more force into it. Nothing happened. I gave it a really hard pull. Still nothing. I gripped it with both hands and yanked with all the force that I could. As far as I could tell nothing happened. I asked Wolfe, "Did it move at all? I couldn't tell while I was doing that last tug."

He shook his head. Then he asked me, "Did you ever leave this woman after she entered the house?"

"No, sir."

"Has she ever had access to the house—as far as you know?"

"No, sir."

He started to ask, "Are you susceptible to hypnosis?" He only got about halfway through the question and stopped, thinking better of it, I suppose.

He leaned back into his chair, closed his eyes and started the lip routine. I spoke to her. "There are very few outsiders who have ever seen the lip routine. He's rarely ever done it when clients were in the room. It's his way of thinking when he's got something really difficult to mull over."

She asked, "Won't you disturb him, talking, when he's doing that?"

"Not a chance. You could set off a bomb in here, and I'm not sure he'd notice."

We watched a moment, and she asked, "How long does this go on?"

"Anywhere from a minute or two to half an hour. Usually when he's finished, he's resolved the key problem of a case."

We continued to wait. I asked her if she wanted something to drink. She shook her head. After a half hour had elapsed I announced, "Well, this sets the record for the lip action. I've never seen him go longer than this."

She just said, "Gratifying, but will he come up with something by the end?"

"He always does. It's the most hopeful sign when you're working with him."

After forty-three minutes, he stopped the lip routine. He looked at Ms. McGonagall and asked, "This attack was made by a 'magical' gang. It was intended to result in the capture of your friend. I'm sorry. If he were captured, he would almost certainly be dead now."

"How do you know that he isn't being held for ransom?"

"If he were being held for ransom, you would surely know by now, wouldn't you?"

"Yes, I suppose so."

"Then, we must proceed with the assumption that he was injured, is in a hospital right now, probably unconscious or unable to communicate for the moment."

"I hope you're right, but I've already searched all the hospitals that I could find."

Wolfe said a single word, "Flummery." Then he said to me, "Archie, wasn't the name of a victim of the attack being withheld and his location being held secret to protect him from further attacks?"

I nodded, "Yes, sir. I think you're right."

Wolfe turned his head toward McGonagall, "Madame, can you prove that you and he were traveling together?"

McGonagall looked down briefly and then back at Wolfe, "I'm afraid not. We didn't enter the country through—uh—Muggle channels."

Wolfe looked the question at her, but before she could answer he said, "Oh, yes. Muggle means non-magical, right?"

She nodded.

I gave an answer for her, "She showed me a photo of herself and a man that she claims is Wendt. The photo proves a certain level of intimacy if we can verify that the man is Wendt."

He went on, "Then you've entered the country illegally."

"Not exactly. You see there's a treaty between Muggle authorities and magical. There are separate legal systems. You either belong to the one or the other."

"But now, this magical friend of yours is in the Muggle system. I suppose only the highest level of authorities are aware of this dichotomy of the legal system?"

She nodded again, but said, "Actually, he's a Muggle."

"I see your dilemma now. We must work outside the purview of the normal authorities – both Magical and Muggle. Not outlaws, but not exactly legitimate either. I suppose that you've been to the magical authorities?"

She smiled, "I'm afraid they haven't been very helpful either."

"They don't want to interfere with the Muggle authorities?"

"Something like that."

"Archie, what time is it?"

Wolfe could have turned his head and seen the wall clock behind him and to his left, but that would be too much effort for a genius. So he always asked me. "It's five minutes to one o'clock."

"Madame, we've arrived at our lunch hour. Would you join us?"

McGonagall looked a question at me, but Wolfe answered aloud, "Yes, I would be aggrieved to send someone away from the house hungry. We always have adequate provender for guests. Please join us.

"Archie, inform Fritz that there will be a guest for lunch."

One of the rules of the house is that business is never discussed over meals. It interferes with the digestive process. After we were seated, Wolfe asked Ms. McGonagall about her visits to the United States and where she had been. After hearing about the itinerary for this trip, he remarked on the fact that Philadelphia was excluded.

"Philadelphia was the base of operations for the American revolutionaries for many years. The Continental Congress met there. Benjamin Franklin worked much of his life in Philadelphia."

He went on to talk about Franklin as the Renaissance man of America and discussed his many discoveries and inventions.

Fritz had tried making a dish that Wolfe had long admired, but which Fritz had never attempted—chicken and dumplings. Wolfe claimed it was one of the few truly American dishes and probably his favorite. We all enjoyed it.

Fritz came in with coffee. Wolfe invited us to move back to the office. Once we were there, we could talk business, which we couldn't do in the dining room. Wolfe turned to me, "I believe that we can undertake this."

He then rotated his head an inch and said to Minerva, "Now, Madame, we need some information about your friend. First, do you have a recent photo?"

She handed over the photo that she had showed me. Wolfe looked at it for two full minutes. "I see. This is not a Muggle photo is it?"

She shook her head.

He asked me, "Do you think that we can make a decent photocopy from this?"

I took it and swiveled my chair to the Xerox machine, "We can try and find out." I lifted the cover of the glass and placed it face down. I adjusted the controls so that it would create a double-size copy. The machine whirred and out came a copy. It was a bit fuzzy. I guess it was because the image was constantly in motion. The picture was a conventional sitting portrait with Ms. McGonagall seated in front of Wendt. But after a while, you began to notice that something in the photo was changing subtly. After a while, I identified it as the light and shadow in the background.

"Madame, this man is a young man. Are you quite sure that this 'attack' at the station was not an elaborate charade arranged by Wendt because he was not anxious to have a row 'breaking up' with you but did want to separate himself from you?"

Her face set in a grim determination, and I leaned back to enjoy the show when she exploded. "If you think that I am so unfamiliar with my lover or that he is so cowardly that he can't be open and honest with me, you should think about what the rest of your life would be like as a toad."

I could barely restrain my laughter. I decided that the copy was good enough and set the machine to make several from it. I handed back to Ms. McGonagall the original. Wolfe went on, "This seems like it should be either a straightforward investigation or one that will fail because your friend is dead. If you are willing to go forward on that basis, we will begin."

She looked him directly in the eye and said, "Yes. Spare no effort. I will find him alive or dead."

"Good, Madame. We will begin. How can we reach you? Where are you staying?"

She looked a bit flustered for the first time since she entered the office, "Well, I've not decided. Someone recommended the Churchill, but I've not decided."

Wolfe nodded, "The Churchill is a good choice. We recommend it to people who need a decent hotel to stay in."

She began to get up—I suppose to leave. Wolfe said, "One more thing. We require a retainer. How much do you suggest, Archie?"

I considered that we'd probably need to get Saul and maybe one or two others involved. There'd also be expenses for bribes. Say, two thousand for a couple of days of the help and four thousand for us. "I'd suggest eight thousand."

Wolfe asked her, "Madame, how will you pay?"

She opened her handbag again and pulled out a small purse, "Would a credit card be acceptable."

Wolfe smiled, "Perfectly, if Archie has . . ." I immediately nodded assurance back at Wolfe.

"Archie, please take the card number and security code and charge her account for that amount."

He turned back to her and said, "We won't charge your account again without your permission. We'll provide itemized statements of the work before the next charge if you wish, but we normally wait until we're finished for a total itemized statement. Is that acceptable?"

"Certainly. Will you provide progress reports? Who will provide them?"

"If it's acceptable, Mr. Goodwin will give you personal reports only when necessary to advance the investigation. He will do that at the Churchill."

She smiled at that and said, "I would just want reports when significant results happen."

Wolfe agreed and got up to go. Wolfe, of course, didn't turn to say farewell. I showed her out to the door and asked her if I could give her a ride to the Churchill. She declined with thanks.

"Then, at least, let me call a cab for you."

"No thank you," but she favored me with a smile, "You're quite courteous, but I really will have no trouble getting there."

Then it occurred to me that she might really have ways of getting around that would be easier and faster than a cab. I watched her walk down the steps and turn off to the right and walk down the street. For a moment I thought of trying to follow her to see how she would get to the Churchill. When she approached the corner, she turned and looked back with a smile. Then she turned the corner and disappeared.

$$\triangle$$

I went back into the office and decided that it was probably just as well that I didn't know. I sat at my desk. Wolfe had his eyes shut and after a few minutes opened them, "Well, this is a job more suited to Cramer's army but we should be able to find where he's located. We'll need Saul, Orrie, and Fred and we may need a few more if we have to look more widely than the hospitals immediately around Princeton.

"Let's decide on our approach to this. What do you suggest?"

I didn't see any complications except one, "Well, I agree that we should start by canvassing hospitals in the area. It might be a little tricky with the new HIPAA rules that all healthcare providers have to follow for patient privacy. We'll see what the hospitals let us get away with. If we don't get a straight answer, we can try a couple of other things."

Wolfe agreed, "Yes. Let's get Saul, Orrie, and Fred on that. I'd suggest that you try ambulance companies. They may be as difficult about HIPAA as the hospitals, but it's a start.

"Also, get hold of Lon right now. Let's find out what he knows."

Lon had been retired for a number of years at the *Gazette*— shortly before it folded. You can take the man out of the newspaper but you can't take the reporter out of the man. He moved to *The Times* where he was an editor on the crime beat and had lots of contacts at the *Post* and the *Daily News*. I got his house on the phone, and he picked up almost immediately. He answered himself, "Hi Archie. What's up?"

"How did you know it was me?"

"Come on, Archie, get with the times, I had caller ID installed a month ago. You shouldn't be surprised when people know that you're calling."

"OK. So, are we in your debt or are you in ours?"

"Oh, Archie, I'm eternally in your debt. BUT the real point is am I in my working buddies' debt, or are they in mine? The answer to that is that I owe a couple of them something. So, if you want something off the record, you have to agree to give me something."

I covered the mouthpiece and said to Wolfe, "We're in his debt."

"Then we'll have to take the crumbs that he'll drop under the table and figure out something to give him. But I can't see how there will be something out of this for him."

I uncovered the mouthpiece and said, "OK. Lon. Give us what you can now, and we'll try to sweeten the pot for you later."

I could hear the silent wheels turning in Lon's brain as he calculated, "What is it that you want?"

"Well, you remember the terrorist attack at Princeton last Monday?"

"Sure. Have you got something going with that?"

"In a way. Really, a side issue, we think. We'd like to know what you know about it."

"Only what I read in the newspapers."

"Come on Lon, you must know something."

"Just kidding. Here's the deal. The Feds are in it, of course. They've brought in a response team from Washington, but it's being directed here in the New York office. It's got them puzzled. No one was seriously hurt—except for one man, whom they've got under wraps. I can't even get his name. It would be a real coup if we had a name and location where we could send a reporter to get an interview. You don't happen to have anything like that?"

"You don't know how much I wish that we could give you those, but we're as much in the dark as you."

He laughed, "So, you're looking for him—eh? Can't you give me something?"

"Nothing now. And I have to admit that there might be nothing ever. What else do you have?"

"There were lots of witnesses, but their accounts are really confused. There were lots of explosions but no one was much hurt. No one could agree on how many people were involved. Was it three or four or more? Some people claim that there were people all over the place.

"The Feds haven't been able to identify the weapons used. No bullets recovered. No spent rounds. No traces of explosives. That's got them stymied. There's nothing for the scientists to go to work on."

I was stymied too. Wolfe had lifted his receiver while the conversation was going on. He told Lon, "Thanks, as always. I don't know how much we'll be able to tell you, but we're certainly indebted to you and we'll give you exclusives on whatever it's possible to share."

Lon said, "Gee thanks. You at least owe me one of Fritz's dinners for this and something out of your liquor cabinet."

"Consider that a commitment." Then Lon hung up.

"Well, Archie, not exactly surprising considering whom we're dealing with. Get the boys working on it. Give them copies of the photo. Damn those witches and their moving pictures. It may be hard to identify Wendt from that photo."

"Yes, sir."

I called Saul and the rest of the crew. They were all retired, but they enjoyed an occasional gig on the side. They came into the office to get the photo and instructions that evening along with a request to call in every two hours to the Brownstone. Wolfe didn't believe in cell phones. So I didn't have one, and no one except Saul had one. I opened the safe and pulled out a thousand dollars each for expenses and went to bed wondering what I'd find when I started looking for a wizard.

The next morning, I had a quick breakfast. Fritz always complained about how fast I ate when I was on a job. I scanned *The Times*, looking for any last minute revelations about the "terrorists", but there was nothing. I took the Jag sedan out of parking and headed toward Princeton on I-95.

When I arrived, I went into a cafe and had a cup of coffee as I planned my assault on the ambulance companies. Orrie had the Fire departments. I got the *YP* from the waitress who pulled it from behind the calendar. It turned out that there were quite a number in the phone book. I made notes of addresses and phone #'s in my notebook.

I started with the A's. AA Ambulance. It turned out to be an old filling station that had a couple of bays for car repairs. Now the bays had ambulances. The office was run by a middle-aged man who was turning toward fat.

I walked in and introduced myself. "I'm Archie Goodwin. I'm a detective, and I'm looking for someone for a client. We think that he took a ride in an ambulance last Monday. I wonder if you'd mind checking whom you gave rides to then?"

He looked me up and down trying to size me up. "You know that I can't give you that information. It's that new HIPPApotamus law." He laughed at his joke. "So, beat it."

"Are you sure that you might not just accidentally leave your trip log open to that day on the desk. I wouldn't look at it, but my friend, Ben, might get a glance at it." I'd pulled a folded up 100 out of my inner jacket pocket. It was folded so that the only thing you could see was Benjamin Franklin's portrait.

The manager looked left and right and said, "You sure Ben doesn't have a friend?"

"No chance. Take it or leave it."

He nodded, pulled a ledger out of a desk drawer, and put it on the desk and said, "I've got to go take a piss. It usually takes about five minutes." He got up and walked to the back of the room and walked into a hall.

I flipped the ledger open, quickly found the page for Monday and went down the columns of names, hospitals delivered to, etc. There was no Wendt. There were no Does, John or otherwise. There wasn't even a James. I closed the ledger, leaving the Franklin in it as a bookmark. I had to wait another two minutes before the guy came back. I went to the door and said, "Sorry you couldn't be more cooperative."

He stared and said, "What the?" Then he noticed the bookmark and nodded. "Just being a law-abiding citizen, right?"

"Right."

The rest of the morning and early afternoon were much the same. I stopped in at a diner that happened to be near the latest of the ambulance companies that I'd visited. It made me long for Fritz's cooking or any of a dozen diners that I've eaten at over the years. After lunch, I started with the next spot on the list. I'd done two more when I decided it was time to call in. I didn't have anything to report but Wolfe would have finished with lunch and not be up to the plant room yet.

I dialed the number I know best and got Fritz on the line. He said that Wolfe wanted to talk. Fritz put him on. He never says anything to introduce himself other than grunt. I've been trying to get him to at least speak his name, but decades of needling him have not had any results.

"OK. So, don't tell me who's on the line. You know, one of these days it will be Cramer. I'll open the bag when you don't want it opened, and you'll wish you'd been polite on the phone.

"I've not found anything yet. I've visited about eight ambulance companies and I'll not finish until tomorrow morning unless there's a breakthrough."

"Archie, you recognize my grunt perfectly well. Why should I waste time and effort? The others have reported in from the hospitals and they haven't had any results either. They all have run into problems with HIPAA. Saul has an idea for attacking that problem. But we can't use it before tomorrow. I'll see you for supper won't I?"

"Of course—unless something comes up."

That was it, and I started for the next place on my list.

Nothing new showed up. I left for the city so that I would arrive in time for dinner unless I ran into bad traffic coming into town on I-95. The traffic was a little slow in town, and I arrived just after Wolfe started dinner. Wolfe greeted me as though I'd been gone for a week. He regards driving or any other form of conveyance as being extremely hazardous. Fritz's meal was up to its usual excellence.

After dinner, the trio reported in. They all dropped by so that we could confer on Saul's idea. Saul, of course, is worth more than all the other operatives that we've employed rolled into one. We were all in the office, and Saul had the red leather chair. He explained his idea. "The hospitals wouldn't co-operate, of course. So, I started walking around in them and talked with various staff. They were all pretty quiet whenever I mentioned a name. I noticed that there were people whom no one paid attention to and who seemed to get around everywhere."

Wolfe's eyes narrowed on Saul's hook nose. "You mean the cleaning staff, I suppose."

"Right. I found the company that employs the ones that work in my hospitals. I called their employer and asked if I could leave an advertising brochure for them tomorrow before they left for work."

Wolfe nodded appreciatively. "Yes. That's good. Archie, a letter."

I got my notebook out and nodded to him that I was ready.

"I'll dictate. Please type this on both sides of a standard 8 ½ by 11 sheet. One side in English. The other side should be in Spanish."

"I may have a hard time getting this typed before tomorrow morning if I have to have it translated into decent Spanish."

"Archie, you know that I have quite passable Spanish."

"No, sir, I didn't."

"All should be 28 point text except the first word that should be 48 point. 'Greetings.' Paragraph. 'We will pay a reward of one hundred dollars to anyone who can prove that they have seen the man pictured below within the last week. Paragraph. Call.' Insert our number here.

"Have a copy of Wendt's photograph on both sides of the page."

I had to ask, "If we get a Spanish speaker, you'll do the talking?"

"Of course."

We had the trio remain until we'd gotten the page arranged with photos and text on both side. Then, I ran six hundred copies through our office machine. It was not intended for quite that heavy a duty cycle, but it held up nicely. They were to come back in the morning to pick up their fliers before heading for Princeton.

The next morning the boys showed up early. Fritz fixed them all buttermilk hotcakes served with honey and rashers of bacon. Thus fortified, we went off on our appointed rounds.

I hit the jackpot with the next to the last ambulance service on my list. Not only was there a John Doe on their ledger, but the driver happened to be in the office and recognized the photo. He gave me an important freebie. Wendt had been paralyzed when he'd dropped him off at the Robert Wood Johnson University Hospital. I guess they had figured that his ailment required more expertise than they had in Princeton.

I called that in to Wolfe. He said that he'd have Saul get on it right away. I objected that I was here, too, and I could do the investigating. Wolfe is selfish. He wants me where he can be sure that I'm not getting into dangerous situations—like driving on the Jersey turnpike. Anyway, he'd pulled my ticket and required that I come in.

I arrived about a half-hour before Wolfe left for his afternoon stint with the orchids. I asked him if he'd heard from Saul. "Yes. I just hung up with him. He's on his way there and we should hear something by the time that we're done with dinner. Possibly sooner."

"So. Does that end the case for us?"

Wolfe frowned, "We'll see. Somehow this seems too easy for that."

Wolfe went to the plant room; I worked on catching up with germination records. He returned from the plant room. We had dinner and no word yet from Saul. We returned to the office for coffee. It was after nine before the phone rang. I picked up the phone and heard Saul's voice.

I said to Wolfe, "Saul's on the line." He picked up, and I said, "Go ahead Saul. In case you didn't recognize Wolfe's grunt, he's on the line."

"Good to hear your voice Archie. Well, Wendt may have been here, but he's not here now."

Wolfe grunted. "Can you find out if he were there, and if so, when he left?"

Saul was ahead of us as usual, "I'm going to the cleaning staff company tomorrow first thing to distribute our fliers. I'll let you know immediately when I learn something."

"Saul, why don't you spend the night there? Do you need more funds for tomorrow?"

"I've hardly spent any so far. No problem."

"Satisfactory."

The next day we released Fred and Orrie and paid them with thanks. Saul called and said that he'd distributed the fliers with no immediate response. Wolfe asked him to remain there another night in case we needed him to check out anyone.

The afternoon passed and the evening with no news. The next morning nothing happened until 10 AM. Shortly after, there was a call. The first words convinced me that this was a call that Wolfe had to take.

I called up all my Spanish to say, "*Uno Momento!*" I wrung Wolfe on the house phone. Of course, he was peeved but I told him. "*Un caballero* on the *telephono* for you."

Grumbling, he took the phone and I stayed on, although I might as well not have. There was not anything that I understood for sure of what was said. They hung up, and Wolfe didn't come down until eleven.

He sat in his chair and closed his eyes. After a few minutes he said, "Get Saul, Orrie, and Fred on the phone. We'll have a phone conference as soon as they're all available."

I made the calls. I had to leave a message for Orrie, so I decided that we'd all try after lunch. Wolfe wouldn't tell me what the *caballero* had said, so I was stuck until they all called at 2PM.

We were all on the line by 2:05. Wolfe started, "Saul, one of the cleaning staff whom you contacted called us this morning. He saw Wendt in the hospital, but he said that yesterday, early, someone came for him and took him away. He doesn't know where. I want you, Fred and Orrie to work the ambulance companies as quickly as you can. Meet tomorrow at your motel, Saul, and let me know as soon as you can. Archie will give you his list over the phone, and you can divvy them up.

"Saul, tonight the cleaning person, Juan Sanchez, will come to your room for his reward. Double it. Give him $200."

Saul acknowledged that and said, "I can start as soon as I get off the phone."

"Good. I don't care if you only have a half-dozen left when you start tomorrow morning. I want you all on it. When we find out where he is, we may want to take action that will require more manpower."

I spoke up, "I'll drive down right now and share your room, Saul."

Wolfe snarled, "You will not, Archie. I need you to help me think when we're ready for action."

I finished the call by reading off the list that I'd developed of area ambulances. The afternoon went very slowly for me, hoping that we'd have a call from Saul at any minute. Of course, Wolfe had his time with the plants and didn't seem to be bothered by the delay in events.

After dinner, Wolfe asked me to see Ms. McGonagall and bring her up to date. I asked if we needed more money from her.

"Maybe we should get another ten thousand. You never know what we may have to do."

So, I put in a call to the Churchill. The phone rang at her room a number of times before she finally answered. I'd almost given up when I heard her hesitant, "Hello?"

"Minerva, Wolfe wants me to drop by and report to you."

"Can't you do that over the phone?"

"Wolfe doesn't trust the phone for confidential conversations. I can be there in ten minutes."

She laughed, "I can be to your house quicker than that."

"Oh, I think that Wolfe would prefer to keep women at a distance whenever possible. I'll be there quickly."

"OK. There's a coffee shop in the hotel. I'll meet you there."

I took a cab there as quickly as I could. The Churchill is just far enough that I normally don't walk, but certainly being in a hurry made me want to take the Jag. That would have been almost as slow–especially in the early evening.

She was in a booth in the far corner of the coffee shop. There wasn't anyone there except a cop nursing a cup and a donut. How they can eat donuts at this hour of the night, I'll never understand.

She smiled a warm smile as I took a seat. The waitress came over and asked what I wanted. "A glass of milk, please."

"Do you usually drink milk? I thought that you'd have something stronger than that."

"Oh, this job has lots of stimulation without resorting to drugs."

She laughed, and I realized that it was the first time that I'd heard her laugh. I could begin to see why Wendt was interested in her.

I asked if she'd eaten supper yet. She shook her head no, and I suggested that we have dinner. The Churchill coffee shop has a pretty mean pastrami on rye. She asked, "Will that go on the bill?"

I gave my best shocked look, "Of course not. It's on my nickel."

She laughed at that. She asked where that expression came from, "I've heard several people use that expression and I understand what it means, but where did it come from?"

I couldn't help laughing, "Oh, it's not a dark secret. Telephone calls in a pay phone used to cost a nickel, so people started to say that they were doing something–like a phone call–"on their nickel" meaning that they were paying."

I started off with the results. "We think we know where Wendt WAS. Notice the past tense. He's not there now. We're getting up a little party to see where he went after the Robert Wood Johnson University Hospital."

She sighed. "That wasn't one of the ones that I checked." Then she brightened, "But that's wonderful news. He's alive and probably well."

"It wouldn't have mattered if you had. They were being very mum about him and all patients."

"How did you find out that he'd been there?"

"Oh, we have our little ways. When you work for and with geniuses, it usually makes a difference."

"So, it was someone else besides you who found him."

Somehow, I didn't want to share Saul's name and I especially wanted to claim some of the credit. But I squelched that impulse. Instead, I said, "Only the best operative this side of the North Pole."

She laughed, and I began to wish that I either wouldn't hear it again or would hear it every day. "Do you need help then if you don't know where he went next?"

"No, we're still plodding on. But that does bring up the subject of money. We want to drawn another ten thousand."

"Oh, of course. Do you need a signature or something from me?"

"No. That's not necessary."

My milk arrived, and I took a long sip. She was resting her chin on her arms and looking at me as though I must have some more good news to relate. I really wished that I did. Finally, I just blurted out, "Are you sure that you wouldn't like to do a little dancing?"

She smiled, "No. Isn't it bad to mix business and pleasure?"

"Ordinarily, but you are a very unordinary woman."

She chuckled deep in her throat again, and I decided that I had to leave before I started trying to think up more clever things. "Well, I have to get back to Wolfe. He worries if I'm out after ten."

She laughed again, and I said good night. I found our waitress and paid for our meal. I left as quickly as I could.

The next morning was another lengthy bout with the germination records. I thought every half-hour that surely Saul and the others must be done by now. Wolfe came down from the plant room and scowled at me, "Well?"

"Well, nothing. No word yet."

"That's bad."

"Yeh, that had occurred to me."

Lunch came and went. Wolfe said, "Saul must be waiting for us to return to the office."

We returned to the office and waited. I was beginning to worry that Wolfe would be leaving for the plant room without hearing from Saul. Then the phone rang. Wolfe surprised me by answering it. Then he surprised me again by actually saying, "Wolfe here."

I'd picked up my extension and heard, ". . .Saul. We canvassed every ambulance between Wilmington Delaware and Princeton. Nothing. He's dropped off the face of the earth."

Wolfe made a face and then said, "All right. Can Fred and Orrie stay there tonight?"

After a moment, "Yes. That's fine. They'll stay in the same motel with me."

"Good. We'll think and call you back before the night is over."

We hung up, and Wolfe asked me, "What do we do next?"

I said, "You're the genius. You're asking me?" Then I added, "Expand the search."

"Yes, but where?" Then he closed his eyes and started the lip routine. It was a sign of the difficulty of this case that he'd done it twice. I couldn't think of another case that had required that. This was much quicker than before. He was only a little over three minutes.

"Archie. Why would they move Wendt from a fine hospital?"

I considered that. "Because they required a specialty hospital?"

"Right. And what specialty would that be?"

"How could I know? Maybe he has a weak heart and he had a heart attack or something."

"No. Not after several days."

"I see. You think that they sent him to a Funny Farm or maybe the hospital for terminal stubbed toes?"

"More colorful than I would have used, but 'yes.' Get Saul on the line."

I did and joined the conversation. Wolfe told him, "Saul, find all the psychiatric hospitals in the state of New Jersey, both public and private, and the three of you start checking them out."

Saul had an objection, "That will be harder than ordinary hospitals. They normally protect their patients' identities extremely well."

Wolfe nodded and said, "Do your best. You're ingenious. The cleaning staff approach might work, but I wouldn't bet on it. Keep us informed twice a day on progress."

"Yes, sir."

We hung up, and I asked Wolfe, "Do we tell the client?"

"Not yet. We may have luck tomorrow. Not until tomorrow night at earliest."

The next day there were two reports that were completely negative. They had found that there were a couple of dozen hospitals scattered around the state and going in person would be time consuming. Saul had found that the cleaning staff for the first hospital he saw worked for the hospital itself. He couldn't even get past the reception desk without the name of someone that he wanted to visit. And John Doe was not a name that was accepted. Fred had found a hospital that employed an outside firm for cleaning and was working on the staff.

After dinner, Wolfe tried to read off and on, but he kept getting up and spinning the globe. That was a sure sign that he was stuck. I had completely given up trying to read and went to my room to try watching the Mets on the TV. That didn't work out so well either. They were losing to the Padres.

Then the doorbell rang. I ran down the stairs and looked through the one-way glass to see the last person in the world that I expected. Actually, the first person in the world that I hoped to see was Minerva, but I was so desperate that even Inspector Cramer was welcome. I was tempted to just fling open the door and invite Cramer in, but I kept the urge back and went to the office. "You'll never guess who's on the porch?"

"I won't even try. Who is it?"

"Our favorite homicide inspector."

"Cramer? What does he want?"

"There's only one way to find out."

"Oh, yes. Let him in." Wolfe said resignedly.

I returned to the door and opened it. Cramer was positively polite. He called me Archie, which he only does when he wants something and doesn't have a crowbar to get it with. I took his hat and led him to the office.

He was being polite to Wolfe too, "I'm sorry to bother you at this hour, but I need a favor."

"Really. I can't imagine what you might want from us. We're not working on any homicides."

Cramer leaned forward in the Red Leather Chair, "Well, maybe you are and don't know it."

Wolfe is rarely surprised, but that did surprise him, "Enlighten us. What case are you working on? I've not seen any important homicides in the paper lately."

"And you won't if the US attorney's office has its way. But there was a homicide in my district, and they can't keep me out of it."

"Someone in the Attorney General's office?"

"An FBI man who came here from Washington for the. . . ."

Wolfe interrupted him, "For the investigation of the terrorist attack in Princeton."

"Well, yes. How did you know? And more important, what do you know?"

Wolfe made a tent of his fingers under his chin and narrowed his eyes. "But why did you come here, and why do you think that we're investigating it?"

"Well, it's kind of hard not to figure that when Panzer, Durkin and Cather are down in Jersey beating the pavement to rubble trying to find someone. Hell, even Goodwin here put in some time there."

"How do you know that?"

"Well, the Feds are being more cooperative than usual. I think that they're almost." He hesitated a minute as though reluctant to go on because he was afraid of being overheard. He glanced to his right, "Well, almost scared and want help."

Wolfe asked, "What would scare the FBI?"

"Well, for one thing this special liaison died in the FBI office."

Wolfe was impressed, "Then surely they have security cameras that show the murderer."

"You'd think that wouldn't you?"

"But there aren't any tapes, right?" Wolfe said slowly reflecting as he spoke.

"Right, the cameras on the floor failed just before the time of his death."

Cramer went on, "And that's not all. They did an autopsy. No cause of death."

"Surely, there was a proximate cause of death. You just mean that the root cause of the death wasn't known. For example, there was a crushed skull but no object and no blood."

Cramer smiled, "No. I mean that the scientists couldn't figure out what you would call the proximate cause."

"Oh." Wolfe closed his eyes for a moment. When he opened them, he went on, "All right, what is it that you want?"

Cramer said, "What do I want? A murder happens, I start to investigate, and what do I find? Your man Goodwin here is poking around in the territory. I want you to open the bag and give me any material evidence that you've got."

Wolfe raised an eyebrow a millimeter, "Mr. Cramer, until you walked into the office this evening, I had no idea that a murder had been committed. I have no material evidence. All I know about this crime, you just told me.

"I do have a client but the job that we're doing for this client is looking for a missing person."

Cramer leaned back and said, "Nuts!" He pulled out a cigar and began rolling it between his hands. Cramer never smokes the things, but they seem to give him comfort in some way. Then he said, "Well, do you have any suggestions?"

The corner of Wolfe's mouth raised an eighth of an inch. "Let me suggest something to you. I think that there is some remote relation between our case and yours. I could complete my job without ever learning the identity of the killer, but you could make my job easier. We could help you with your case. We could work a *quid pro quo*."

Cramer eyed Wolfe suspiciously, "Just how could I make your life easier—as though I cared to?"

"We believe that the missing person is actually in a psychiatric hospital, possibly in New Jersey. With the passage of the HIPAA act by Congress, it's become much harder to obtain information about patients."

"Is this client of yours related to the patient? That should make it easier."

"Unfortunately, no. In addition, we think that the authorities are keeping him under wraps for his own protection. You can easily understand why."

A shrewd smile came over Cramer's face, "And you think that I can loosen the Feds up on your behalf?"

"Something like that."

"Well, I certainly wouldn't mind your help on this one. But if. Notice I say, 'IF', I agree to try to help you, I can't guarantee that I'll get results."

Wolfe's grin widened a bit, "Of course, as Homicide Chief—East—you have much influence in New York City. You have less in the state of New York and even less in New Jersey.

"With that understanding, I agree to help you." Then he added with a further smile, "Once you've given me the killer."

Wolfe nodded but added, "Or established to your satisfaction who the killer is."

Cramer's smile deflated a bit, "OK. OK. Have it your way. But I've got a bad feeling about this."

Wolfe asked, "Can we have access to your files on the case?"

What was left of Cramer's smile turned into a grimace, "I suppose, but he. . ." At this point, Cramer was looking straight at me, "has to view them in my office, accompanied at all times by me or someone from my staff, and NO note-taking. Goodwin here has a photographic memory, so he doesn't need notes."

Wolfe's smile grew as Cramer's waned, "And you don't want written evidence that you granted us that privilege. I understand perfectly."

Cramer got up and headed for the hall. I went with him and handed him his hat from the coat rack. "Thanks Goodwin."

"Oh, it's Goodwin now. What happened to Archie?"

Cramer just stuck his cigar in his mouth, growled, and slammed the door behind him on the way out. I went back to the office, sat at my desk, and asked, "Well, how are we going to find one or more wizards, who can pop in and out of places at will?"

Wolfe was unflappable, "By getting them to want to come and visit us."

"Good idea. What do we have for leverage?"

Wolfe only smiled and said, "Get me Saul on the phone."

I turned to the instrument and dialed the number of Saul's motel. After a couple of minutes I had him on the line. I nodded to Wolfe. He picked up his instrument and spoke, "Hello, Saul. This is Wolfe. I have your program for tomorrow."

I could imagine Saul's smile at that, and he said, "Yes, sir."

"Can you get Orrie and Fred to dial in, and we'll do a conference call?"

"Sure."

A few minutes after that we were all on the line. Wolfe began, "We have a change in program. Tomorrow I want you to start inquiring with detective agencies. We're looking for ones that have been hired to search for our quarry—any that are looking for Wendt or John Doe.

Orrie asked, "OK. We can do that, but what's your idea? Do you think they might have succeeded where we haven't?"

Wolfe entered his pedantic mode, "No, Orrie, we're looking for other people who are looking for Wendt. We've got something to pry the psychiatric hospitals open, but we have to have the other people who are looking for Wendt to use that pry bar. If they're looking for Wendt, the natural thing for them to do is to hire detectives."

Fred said, "Yeh! That actually makes sense. And maybe they've found him already."

Wolfe said glumly, "I certainly hope not. And because we have three of the best operatives looking, I doubt that they've made more progress than we."

Saul asked, "What approach do we use? And what do we do when we find the agency?"

Wolfe said, "Be open. We have a client who wants to find him too. We don't want to poach their client. By combining our efforts, we have a better chance of succeeding."

Saul said, "Sure. We'll get on it first thing tomorrow."

"Thanks. Get a good night's rest."

After hanging up, I said, "And you don't want me helping them?"

"No, Archie, I've got a more important task for you."

"You wouldn't want to share that with me?"

"Tomorrow."

Get a good night's rest indeed! How did he expect me to get a good night's rest with that hanging over me? But I can usually do that, and get my required eight in.

The next morning, when Wolfe came down from the plant room, I was half expecting a call, but of course, one hadn't come. However, he told me what the important job was that I was supposed to do.

"Archie, I want you to talk to the client. We're entering a difficult phase of the investigation. I have an idea about how to run these wizards to the ground, but it will require her cooperation in a rather dangerous stratagem. I haven't got it fully worked out, but I want you to find out if she would be willing to take that sort of risk, and if she can play her part in a difficult deception."

Wolfe has this idea that I have a mystic insight into the motivations of women and have powers of persuasion over them that ordinary men don't. I usually don't object too much to that opinion, but I was a little concerned here, "Wolfe, I know you think that I can work wonders with impressionable women, but this one is not impressionable."

"I trust you. Just take her dancing. That usually helps."

I laughed, "This one has already refused dancing with me."

"Then take her out to lunch. Rusterman's. I know that it's not the same as when Marko ran it, or when I had stewardship over it, but it's still a fine restaurant."

"I'll see what I can do."

Rusterman's was originally owned by Marko Vuckchek. When he was murdered, Wolfe solved the crime. He was executor of the will, and Wolfe oversaw the operation of Rusterman's for years until it was eventually sold.

I called the Churchill and was connected to Minerva's room. She answered, and when she heard my voice, hers brightened, "Do you have any news?"

"Well, there have been some developments—big developments, but I need to discuss them with you. Could I take you out to lunch?"

She seemed uncertain. I assured her, "Don't worry, it doesn't go on your tab."

"I almost wish it did."

"Come on. We'll go to Rusterman's. It's not as good as eating at Wolfe's table, but you'll enjoy it, and it may take a while to discuss what we've found. It would be good to do it over a meal."

"You don't mean that you've found Wendt?"

"No. Not that good, but it's worth hearing."

"OK."

"I'll pick you up about one. We'll stay away from the noon rush —if that's OK."

"Yes. That's fine."

I hung up and turned to Wolfe, "Done."

"Good."

When we arrived at Rusterman's I requested the private room upstairs. They hadn't had a legal arrangement with Wolfe for decades, but they were still happy to cooperate with us on little things like this.

We were seated, I ordered milk, and Minerva wanted tea. So the waiter left us to ourselves and the menus. Minerva asked me to order for her. "What do you like? Steak? Chicken? Something else?"

"Oh, I suppose chicken."

"Filet Mignon Steak at Rusterman's is beyond compare."

"Fine. I trust you."

When the waiter was back I ordered "Filet Mignon medium rare for her and a rare Porterhouse for me."

Salad came quickly, and then we had time to talk. I told her about Cramer's visit and our change in strategy.

She was not happy. "You don't know what you're getting into trying to track down Deatheaters. They're . . "

I interrupted her. "What did you call them?"

"Deatheaters. I don't know where the term came from exactly. That's what they call themselves, and it communicates the idea pretty well. They are extremely dangerous for fully capable wizards to face, but Muggles? It would be a massacre."

Wolfe was right about convincing her. "Well, you shouldn't underestimate Wolfe. Or, me, come to think about it." Just then the main course arrived, and we took a pause as we started.

Minerva commented on the bread, "This is wonderful bread and the Steak is marvelous! I think it might actually be better than at Hogwarts. The house elves there are amazing."

"You should try some of this steak."

She surprised me by cutting a small part off and putting it on her plate. She tried it and agreed.

I asked about the house elves. She thought for several minutes and finally said, "They have to be seen to be believed. Let's just say that they take extreme justified pride in their cuisine."

Then we got back to the subject. "You're right–that Wolfe is playing a very dangerous game, but I can assure you that he will involve you in planning when we have a lead on the Deathbeaters."

She laughed, "Uh, that's Deatheaters. Not Deathbeaters."

"Never mind. But seriously, we understand the dangers. Before we go much further, we want to be sure that you are prepared for playing a dangerous role in the charade that Wolfe is working up."

Minerva sat back and looked at me directly in the eye. "How likely is it that this would result in finding Wendt?"

I held her eye contact, which was a little hard as I thought that question through. "There isn't any guarantee in life. Look, I don't know what Wolfe's got in mind. When he's planning one of these shows, most of the time I'm not in on it, but I can tell you that he almost never fails when he sets his mind to it."

She kept holding my eyes, "What would you do if you were I?"

This was getting very personal. I was in danger of letting my feelings intervene here, "Well, I guess it depends on how much you want to find Wendt. If you're will to risk it all on one throw of the dice, Wolfe is your man. Now, we could keep working it the conventional way, but Wolfe won't keep that up forever, and you couldn't afford it. "

She still held my eyes as she answered, "Yes. I want to get him back. I've taken risks with these people a number of times before, and they don't scare me. I just don't want you to go into this blind and take risks YOU don't understand."

Still she held my eyes, but this time answering was easier, "We take risks too. One time, someone sent us a box filled with dynamite. I'd be dead now if Wolfe hadn't had a last minute thought. We're with our clients to the end. I'm with you to the end."

I hadn't quite meant for that to come out that way at the end, but she didn't seem to notice and said, "Good." Then she broke eye contact, and we finished our lunch in comparative silence. I dropped her off at the Churchill and returned home.

Wolfe was reading a book when I came in–*Angela's Ashes*. He looked up and asked, "Well?"

"She's in to the bitter end. Not exactly her words, but they're close enough."

"Good. Now, all we have to do is wait for results from Princeton."

"You're sure that the Deatheaters don't have another way of finding Wendt?"

"No, but if they did, they'd have him by now. And they wouldn't be tempted to kill a federal official."

Sometimes Wolfe's confidence in his hunches drives me crazy. I asked, "Do you want to keep trying Psych hospitals while we wait? I could drive down there in an hour and . . ."

Wolfe looked up from his book, "Archie, no. We may be driven to that later, but we'll have lost if it comes to that."

My pessimism seemed justified. The day ended and the next without hopeful word from New Jersey. They called twice a day and the only thing they had to report was that the search was getting wider and wider. I was forced to comment, "If this goes much further, they'll be checking New York agencies. Hey, maybe they hired Doll Bonner's agency."

"Stop, Archie. You will not goad me into changing course."

In the end, I was right. It was a New York agency. Actually they hired one on Staten Island. We learned about it after dinner one evening. Saul had called in, but it was Orrie who'd found them.

Wolfe asked him, "We need to talk with him. Can you get him to come here tomorrow at 11 AM?"

"Get him to take the Staten Island Ferry? I don't know. Maybe Archie had better go and work on him."

"All right. Archie, go early tomorrow and get him here at 11 tomorrow. And Orrie, Fred, Saul, thanks very much for your patience with this miserable case. Most satisfactory. Please stay available. We may need you in the next few days."

They all agreed to and hung up. "Well, it looks like we've got a breakthrough."

"Yes. A breakthrough, yes, but to what?" He went back to his book.

The next morning I waited for the rush hour to be over and drove to the Frederick Milton Detective Agency. I'd heard of them but knew very little about them. It must have been a bit larger than most. It had a decent secretary in the front office. I'd called earlier for an appointment. When I arrived, I found a dumpy middle-aged woman who it was hard to believe lived in the same universe with Minerva. She showed me in to Milton. The office had standard office furniture—nothing special. He greeted me, "Goodwin, what can I do for you?"

"Well, you could come to see Nero Wolfe at 11 AM. He has a proposition for you that I think you will find attractive."

"Why'd he send you rather than coming himself?"

It was always hard for me to believe that there are people—especially in the business—who don't know that Wolfe never leaves his office. I explained that, and Milton was still reluctant.

"Well, suit yourself. Wolfe won't offer you this opportunity more than once."

It appeared that he might have known something about Wolfe because he said, "Wolfe deals with high-end clients. Is he offering me a cut of his fee?"

"I don't negotiate the money end of things. Only Wolfe does that. The only way to know would be to come and talk to him."

"OK. I'll come. But why doesn't he just call?"

"He doesn't trust phones for negotiations. I'll drive you. We've got a garage. It's pretty hard to find parking this time of day."

He left instructions with his secretary, and we drove to The Brownstone. I left him at the entrance and told him to tell Fritz to seat him in the office, and I'd be there in a couple of minutes. I parked the car and got back to the office with about ten minutes to spare.

292

"Where's your boss?"

"He'll be along shortly. He's in the plant room tending to the orchids—his hobby."

"Sheese."

Wolfe came down and greeted Milton. "I have a proposal for you. You are looking for Mr. Wendt for your clients. We are looking for Mr. Wendt for our clients. I propose that we work together. Together, we are more likely to find him, and any finding bonus that they will pay you will be yours. Our finding bonus, we'll keep, and we'll both be better off. What do you say?"

"Are you asking me to break detective-client privilege?" Milton didn't seem to be complaining—just asking for information.

"Not at all. We ask no information that they've given you, and likewise, we won't offer any from our clients."

His eyes narrowed, "How do I know that you won't work a deal with my clients and undercut me?"

"If we were going to do that, we wouldn't have brought you here at all. Why would we? To give you warning? No, we'd have approached them ourselves. But we're not that kind of operation, and you should know that. You work here in the New York area."

"Then what do you get out of it?"

"Easy. This is a hard case. Surely you've discovered that yourself. Since there are other clients willing to pay, we can improve our search by coordinating efforts, and we'll get the bonuses the sooner—if they're to be had. Frankly, we think that we'll find him, but you might have luck. Your chances of getting the bonus improve, and our chances improve as well. It's a—what do they call this situation these days, Archie?"

"Win-win."

"Oh, yes. Both sides win. Nobody loses."

It was clear that Milton was not easy about the deal but he couldn't find any other reason to object. "OK. It sounds like a good deal. But I have to admit that I don't entirely trust you, good reputation or not. I want something on paper."

Wolfe looked askance at him, "Lawyers?"

"No crummy lawyers. Just a simple document. Signed and notarized."

"Do you want to dictate it or shall I?"

Milton looked down and thought for a moment. "You dictate it and I'll make corrections."

"Very well. Archie, your notebook."

"Title. An agreement covering cooperation between The Milton Detective Agency and Nero Wolfe LLC. concerning the investigation of the disappearance of James Wendt on or about the fifth of July, 1997.

"Paragragh. Both the undersigned, having authority to enter into binding agreements for their respective agencies, undertake that they will co-operate in the investigation mentioned above.

"Paragraph. If either discovers the whereabouts of James Wendt, they will immediately share that information with the other and arrange for a meeting with all the principles including all clients of each agency. In this meeting the location will be revealed with proofs.

"Paragraph. Each agency undertakes that they will accept reimbursement solely from their own clients for the completion of the investigation.

"Signed this day, etc. etc. Include a notary block."

Wolfe turned his head from me to the red leather chair, "Is that satisfactory, Mr. Milton?"

"I want to see it on paper."

"Of course. Archie. Type it up immediately in quadruplicate and call the notary across the street to see if she could come to notarize it."

I did that. While I was working on it, Wolfe asked Milton about meeting with their clients. "Mr. Milton. Would it be possible to meet with your clients in the next day or two?"

Milton was immediately suspicious. "Why?"

"I just want to be sure that they're aware of the fact that we've entered into this agreement."

"I'll keep them informed. What about your clients. Can I meet them?"

"Certainly. But it would have to be here. I don't travel, you know."

"Couldn't Goodwin come to my office to meet my clients?"

"I suppose so."

"Then I come here to meet your clients."

"OK."

Shortly after that, I'd finished typing the agreement. The notary from the residence across the street arrived. I let her in. In the mean time

Milton had been reading the agreement. "I suppose it's OK. It seems to cover everything. Let's sign and get this notarized and I'll be out of here."

They signed, and Ms. Ginger Spooner notarized the documents. I kept the original and another copy. Milton took two copies, and we left. I drove him to a restaurant near his office because it was the noon hour. He commented on the Jag. "I guess your boss does have a healthy business."

I agreed and asked about visits with clients. He said that he'd talk with his clients on the phone tonight, and he'd arrange something for the next day, if possible. He'd call with details. I accepted that and said that he could come to the office this evening if he wanted to.

He thought a minute and asked what time.

"At nine o'clock. I think I can answer for our clients. I'll call you later this afternoon if that won't work." He thought a minute about it and agreed.

The meeting in the evening went off as planned. He arrived a little early. I'd picked up Minerva immediately after dinner, and we'd talked in the front room until Milton arrived.

The brief meeting that held no surprises. Wolfe introduced Milton and Minerva. Milton asked where the other clients were.

Wolfe waggled a finger at Milton, "Oh, I was just being general. I will not reveal any information about my client or clients that I don't absolutely have to. Until you agreed to our working arrangement, you had no need to know the number of my clients or anything else about them."

Milton wasn't happy, but he had nothing that he could do about it. He left almost immediately without talking to Minerva at all.

Then, Wolfe laid out more of his plans, "I want you to know the broad outlines of what the program is for the next several days. If you have any objections, now is the time to voice them.

"First, tomorrow you will be accompanied by Saul Panzer who is. . ."

She interrupted to say, "The best operative this side of the North Pole."

Wolfe grimaced, "You've been spending too much time around Mr. Goodwin. I wouldn't have said it that way, but yes, he is very good. In any case, he'll drive you to Mr. Milton's office or at least the block it's on. The clients of Mr. Milton will show up and you'll observe them from a distance. He'll have binoculars and you'll be able to get a good look at them. I want you to verify—if possible—that they are the Deatheaters who attacked you at Princeton station. If they are or if you can't invalidate them, we'll go on to the next stage.

"A day or two or maybe three later, we'll announce that we've found Mr. Wendt and arrange a meeting with Mr. Milton and his clients at this office."

Minerva interrupted again, "Do you have any idea how dangerous that is?"

"I'm aware that there are significant dangers. However, there will be factors mitigating that danger. First, we will in advance notify wizard law enforcement authorities of our intention of having them appear at our offices. They will be present and will greatly mitigate the danger.

Minerva thought a moment about that and said, "If we know who they are, why even have them show up here? Why not just have the aurors pick them up?"

"A good question. We want more than just to have them arrested. They have no idea where Wendt is. That is manifest in that they have hired investigators to find him. No. There is a way that we can get significant help in finding Mr. Wendt, but only by convincing a certain police inspector that we are being 'straight' with him. Trust me, I've tried a number of other stratagems in my mind and am confident this is the best."

"But can't you tell me more of your plan?"

Wolfe growled and then said, "Part of the plan requires ignorance on your part so that you and others have realistic reactions at critical points. I'm sorry that I can't tell you more."

Sorry, indeed. I'd asked that very question a thousand times and this was the most complete answer that I'd ever heard him give.

"Then you want me to help you get in touch with the aurors?"

"Yes, please. That is essential to the plan. When can you get them here?"

She looked puzzled. "Get them here? Why, because you never leave your home? Surely you make exceptions in cases like this?"

"Archie, please give Ms. McGonagall any assistance she needs in convincing the aurors to come here."

"Thanks." I said sarcastically. "Yes," I turned to Minerva, "he REALLY never leaves his home, and I'll do my best to help you convince them. Believe me; I've had lots of practice at it."

That was the end of the evening, and I took her to the Churchill. When we arrived and the doorman opened the car door for her, she turned toward me, reached out her hand, briefly touched my arm, and said, "I don't know how to thank you." In that moment, I was really glad that I'd not been able to convince her to go dancing with me.

"Oh, don't think about it. We're a long way from home yet. Saul will give you a call, but I don't know when, so be ready at any time."

The doorman closed the door, and I watched her into the lobby. She turned briefly as she entered the door to wave. Yes, please don't think about it.

The next day we got a call at 8:30 PM. I was in the kitchen having an extra portion of Mousse Flambé de Brenner when the call came through. We were to meet at 10 AM the next morning. I called Saul and Minerva and set them in motion.

The next morning at 9, I got the Jag out and started down to Staten Island. I wanted to be sure that Minerva and Saul got there before me. So, I crossed by the Goethals Bridge and took my time getting to Milton's office. When I arrived, I saw that Saul was parked across and down the street from the office. He winked at me as we drove by. I have to cure him of that some time.

I parked and entered the store-front office at about ten to ten. The secretary waved me into the office. I hoped that the clients hadn't arrived yet. They hadn't. He had me sit on a chair near the corner of the desk. That was fine by me. I wasn't here to see them. They arrived about five minutes past ten. The secretary opened the door for them, the three entered, glanced at me, and sat. They were all wearing cloaks that seemed like they might be warm for summer, But they didn't appear to be sweating. Maybe some new miracle fabric. The tallest was blonde and must have been 6' 8" if he were a foot. The other two were average height. One had a scar on his right cheek. The other was a red-head. It wasn't flaming red – more of an orange. Milton introduced them as Sven Haggarstoed, Arnold Hofstedter, and Bruce Palmer.

Milton introduced me and told them about the deal that he'd struck with Wolfe. He was pretty accurate. There was some discomfort among his clients. Sven asked if he could meet our client.

I answered that they would get to meet the client when Wendt was found. I added that I thought that that would not be too long. At that Sven asked about his hiring us.

"I'm sorry. My employer already has a client. We don't change horses in the middle of the stream as we say here in America. But be patient, and you'll meet. I personally think before long."

I definitely had a spooky feeling with them, and I was happy to excuse myself to other duties and left the office. I got in the car and drove away, the opposite direction from Saul. He can take care of himself. I didn't want there to be any chance of Minerva and his being spotted.

I got home and Wolfe was just sitting down to lunch. I joined him and could tell that he was anxious for me to report, but it was lunch. He finished it in record time and we adjourned to the office.

"Well, report." He asked gruffly.

I reported what little there was to report.

"What about the clients. Do you think they are wizards?"

"You've got me. I know that I felt that they were spooky from the first moment that I saw them. It probably didn't help that one of them looked like a blonde Frankenstein's monster, and another had a scar on his cheek to match."

"What is keeping Saul and Ms McGonagall!"

We didn't have to wait long. They arrived before we'd finished coffee. I opened the door for them. Saul winked at me again as I took Minerva's hat. I have definitely got to cure him of that. Saul took her into the office on his arm. There are times that I wish he weren't the best operative this side of the North Pole.

Wolfe was all business. Saul had just deposited her in the red leather chair. Neither Saul nor I had sat before Wolfe barked at Saul, "Report." It's a sign of how this case was wearing on Wolfe that he could snap at Saul.

Saul just looked over at Minerva as he said, "We established surveillance at 9:47. The subjects arrived a minute or two after 10. They left about thirty minutes later—ten minutes after Archie left. I'll let Ms. McGonagall tell you what she saw."

She drilled him with her eyes. "There's no doubt about it. I recognized two of them for sure. You could hardly mistake the blonde and the one with the scar was there at the train station too. I'm not sure about the third, but I can't say that he wasn't there. And they were all wizards."

Wolfe sighed, "Satisfactory.

"Then we'll start the next part of the plan. Ms. McGonagall, get in touch with your auror friends and get them to come here as soon as feasible – today if possible."

She looked over at me, "I think that I'll need Archie's help for that."

Wolfe turned his face toward me and smirked. I knew that I would never live down my reputation at this rate. Minerva went on, "You see, I'm pretty sure that they'll want you to come to the Auror Office and I don't think I can convince them to come here to see you."

Wolfe, still with a corner of his mouth raised, said, "Of course, you have Mr. Goodwin's assistance. Archie, accompany her now and get the aurors to come here."

"Yes, sir."

I got up, and as I passed Saul, I winked at him. Two can play at that game. I drove her to the Churchill where she said, "We'd better stay here in the lobby. I've got a medallion." She rummaged in her handbag and finally pulled out a small metal disk. Then she pulled out a wooden wand and tapped it. It glowed yellow for a moment and then went back to dull metal. "I don't know how long it will take the auror, Lockhart, to get here. I suppose it depends how busy he is."

So, we sat on a couch in the lobby and mostly were silent. But it was only a couple of minutes before a man in a long cape entered the lobby, walked directly to us, and said hello to Minerva. She introduced us and told him that I was a Muggle who could help him in his investigation. He asked how.

I looked him up and down. He was athletic, had a steady eye, and wanted only a black suit to be a lieutenant of police. "We understand that you're looking for some wizards who were involved with an attack on Muggles at a train station. I think that my boss could help you find them."

The somewhat sour expression that he'd had on his face from the moment that I was introduced as a Muggle turned a bit happier. "Fine, can you come to my office right now?"

It didn't seem much like a question, but I demurred, 'I don't think that would work so well. In the first place, it's not me but my boss who can help you. And in the second place, if you were to take me to your office involuntarily, I'd just clam up, and you'd probably never get anything useful out of me."

The scowl was back, "Come on. We'll see how you feel after cooling your heels for a day or two."

Minerva said, "Lockhart, I don't think that he's kidding. I've seen enough of him to know that he can be pretty stubborn when he wants to."

Lockhardt looked back and forth between Minerva and me. Then he sighed and said, "OK. Let's go. When can I meet your boss?"

"Right now would be fine if we move quickly. He has a date with his orchids in a couple of hours, and he never misses that."

"Fine. Let's go outside and find someplace to disapparate."

I had another objection, "Look. I drove my car over here, and I really don't want to leave it parked unattended for hours on end. Let's take my car."

"You go ahead and drive. Ms. McGonagall and I will disapparate."

"That won't do you a lot of good. You won't get admitted to see Wolfe without me."

The scowl got deeper. "OK. Drive."

We made good time, and I led them into the office about 2:30. Wolfe looked up and motioned Minerva to the red leather chair. Lockhart seemed to want that seat, but Minerva was the client, and the client always gets that chair except when Inspector Cramer is there to collect someone.

Wolfe smiled at me and simply said, "Satisfactory."

He turned his head to Lockhart and introduced himself. I introduced Lockhart. Wolfe began, "I suppose that Mr. Goodwin has told you that I have some information that we might be able to leverage so that you could find your Deatheaters."

Lockhart was surprised, "You know about Deatheaters?"

"I know enough for practical purposes. Now, we need some assistance from you to allow that to happen."

Lockhart said, "I require you to tell me what you know immediately. I'm engaged in an official investigation, and you must turn material evidence over to me immediately."

Wolfe shook his head, "You've gotten started on the wrong foot, Mr. Lockhart. You should ask what I know. It will go much more quickly that way."

He smirked, "I could arrest you for withholding material evidence."

Wolfe let a corner of his mouth rise. "I doubt that. In the first place, we're Muggles, and you would have to prove something serious before you could arrest us, right?"

Lockhart said nothing.

"In the second place, you don't even know whether we have material evidence."

"In the third place, if you did arrest us, Archie and I would simply refuse to talk. He can be very stubborn, and I'm even more stubborn than he is."

I added, "You don't begin to know how stubborn he is. You would not believe how long it took me to convince him to buy that copying machine over there."

He turned to me and then back to Wolfe. "I can arrest your client."

Lockhart couldn't tell, but I knew that Wolfe was at the verge of an outburst. Wolfe said, "I thought that you might respect the rule of law. But apparently not."

"What do you mean? We respect the rule of law." Lockhart appeared to be at the verge of an outburst himself.

"Is blackmail sanctioned under the rule of law of wizards? Do you arrest people as material witnesses who don't have any material information?"

Lockhart had pulled a pipe out of his cape and had been absently cleaning it. At that word, he threw it down to the floor, "Damn you. This isn't blackmail."

"What is it?"

Lockhart said nothing but fumed.

Wolfe said, "Even if you arrest her, we will do nothing to assist you."

She looked at me with iron in her eyes, and I nodded slightly. Thank goodness for clients like Minerva.

I commented to Wolfe, "Remind you of someone?"

Wolfe just grunted.

Lockhart mulled on that a moment. He looked up and said, "OK. I suppose that I don't have any real choice. I'll go along with your idea. Just what is it?"

Wolfe carefully phrased it, "We'll get those men here in a couple of days."

Lockhart interrupted, "Why wait so long."

Wolfe was more than exasperated, "Do you think that I am a dunce. We are trying to lure these dangerous and wary criminals in. We do not want to seem to be too anxious to have them come."

"All right. Go ahead."

"When we have set our baited trap, you would be present in the front room. It is sound-proofed, so you can be there without being heard. For my purposes, I have to interview them to learn certain key facts. Then, you will be able to come through those doors," he indicated the doors behind them that connected with the front room, "and capture them.

"We will notify you at least eight hours in advance, so that you can make preparations."

"I still don't like it. There are too many opportunities for them to escape."

"Be that as it may, those are the terms under which I will agree to work with you. You may accept them or let us work on our own."

"OK. OK. But there are more details that must be worked out. We should do them now."

Wolfe agreed, "We've spoken too long, without offering you beverages. Is there something that we can get you to drink? We have good beer and various liquors." He turned to me and pushed the button that signaled for Fritz to bring beer for him.

Wolfe went on, "No one is interested? Very well. Archie, would you please accompany Ms. McGonagall into the front room and demonstrate how well sound-proofed it is."

I got up and smiled at Minerva. "Let me show you our comfortable waiting room."

She addressed Wolfe, "I want to be present for these discussions."

"Of course you do, Ms. McGonagall, but there are certain things that you must be ignorant of for the moment. I assure you this secrecy is necessary, and you will learn all of them eventually."

I held the door for Minerva, and she reluctantly came. When we were in the front room, she turned on me, "Is he always this high-handed. I am his client after all, or is he mine?"

"I'm afraid that he is. I may not even learn what he's talking about before you do. You know that when you work with Wolfe, you have the best, but the way he becomes the best is by allowing him to let his genius lead him as it will."

Minerva cracked a smile, "I suppose so, but it doesn't make me feel any better about it."

We were there for almost an hour while Wolfe palavered with the Auror. They finally finished, and I let him out. I made sure that he didn't get confused and end up on the wrong side of the door. Then, we went into the office. Wolfe seemed pleased. Minerva sat in the Red Leather chair, and I at my desk. She asked, "What were you two discussing at such length?"

"Madame. We were discussing details of the plan for the capture of the Deatheaters. As I said before, all details that are relevant to you will be discussed with you before we proceed. For now, you have a respite of a couple of days. Take it with gratitude.

"Archie, would you give Ms. McGonagall a ride home."

I got up rapidly and reached the door first, which was not easy to do with Minerva having a head start, but I did. She allowed me to drop her off at the Churchill.

When I arrived back home, Wolfe told me, "I had a call from Cramer while you were gone. The scientists want a DNA sample of Mr. Wendt prior to his disappearance so that they can verify that the person that we find is really Mr. Wendt."

"But why would they doubt it if Ms. McGonagall assures us that it is he."

"They tell me that there are magical means of counterfeiting people. The scientists think that they can overcome that."

"How much do they need? And where can it come from? Do they need a finger?"

"Just a small amount of any part of his body—finger nail clippings, hair, even a tear-stained handkerchief would be enough."

I thought it a little suspicious that this call had come while I was gone, but I couldn't find any reason to doubt it. "Do you want me to see if Ms. McGonagall has anything that would do right now?"

"No. No. It can wait for tomorrow."

It was another evening lost. This was the night that I usually went to Saul's to play poker with Fred, Orrie, and Lon, but it was too late to start.

The next morning, I was up early, had breakfast, and called the Churchill. They connected me to her room, and she sounded content—unlike I'd heard her sound ever, "Good. It's you, Archie, what can I do for you?"

"Well, I have a big favor. It might even turn out to be impossible, but I'm hopeful."

"Don't be mysterious. What is it?"

"Well, like Wolfe, I don't like talking about these things on the phone. Can I come over?"

She thought a minute, "Yes. That would be good, but I'm not ready to receive visitors yet. Why don't you come around 11:30, and we can have lunch?"

"That sounds peachy. I'll be there then."

I left the house around 11 and arrived in about 20 minutes. I wasted some time in the lobby and was about to call her room when the elevator doors opened, and she walked out. She saw me, smiled, walked over, and beamed as she said, "I thought we could have a picnic lunch. I've seen very little of New York. I thought we could do some walking and stop somewhere to picnic."

That was a pleasant surprise, "Sure. Now, I like walking more than most, but if you want to see some of New York, I suggest that we take a little ride."

"In your car?"

"No, on the subway."

"Sure. Where are we going?"

"Oh, I'll keep that a secret. It'll be a little surprise."

"One good surprise deserves another."

We went into the coffee shop to pick up the picnic lunch, which was in a large fancy paper sack with the Churchill logo on it. Then we were off.

We walked out and descended to the subway a couple of blocks away. Minerva had been in subways before. She had no trouble with them. As a matter of fact, she bought the subway tickets for us, using her credit card.

I asked her which subways she'd ridden. "Oh, Archie, I don't want to give all my little secrets away, but you can probably guess two."

I thought a moment, "Well, surely you've been on the London Tube."

"Right."

"And I suppose that you've been on the Washington DC metro since you were touring Washington recently."

"Right again."

We got off at the 81st station. Minerva noticed that it was the Museum of Natural History stop and said, "I think I know where we're going."

"I think you don't."

She shrugged and said, "Well, I'll find out really soon now."

We got to the street level, she looked around and smiled, "We're going to picnic in that park. What one is it?"

"It's Central Park. But if you want to visit the museum after lunch, we certainly can."

We crossed the street and walked in the park. It was a warm, almost a hot day, but there were lots of shade trees, so we had no trouble finding a nice, cool spot to sit and lunch. The picnic lunch turned out to be an assortment of deli sandwiches—four altogether, an apple, an orange, and some potato salad (French). There were several utterly delicious cookies. There was a disposable box of coffee, which was fairly good.

After eating, Minerva mentally flipped a coin, and we walked further into the park. She said that Central Park reminded her of Hyde Park in London. We walked to the reservoir and began circumnavigating it. Minerva was surprised at how fast we got around it. She commented, "I almost wished it would take us forever."

"Why?"

"Because I promised myself that I'd ask what you wanted when we finished."

We eventually finished, and I couldn't avoid answering the question, "The scientists want a sample of DNA from Wendt."

"Well, they'll just have to wait till we find him."

"No, they want it from before. Before he disappeared."

"What is DNA?"

"I don't know that I understand it myself, but they tell me that it's in every cell of your body, and they don't need many cells. It could be a fingernail clipping, a tear on a handkerchief, or a bit of hair."

She thought about it. "Funny that you put it that way."

"Why funny?"

"Oh, nothing. Let's go on back and I'll look to see if there's anything like that in my room."

We walked back to the Museum, and I suggested catching a cab, so that we wouldn't lose more time. We rode the elevator up, and I thought that it would be a hopeless task. In her room, she went directly to her luggage and opened it. I stood in the open door, reluctant to come in. She was pulling things out at random and spreading them on the bed. She noticed that I was still standing at the door. "Come in, close the door, come over here, and help me sort through these things."

I closed the door and walked deliberately to the bed. Without looking up she said, "Come on, help me with this. Do you think that you'll get cooties if you put your hand in my bag?"

"No, I was afraid that I'd give you cooties."

She laughed and kept pulling things out. I couldn't believe how many things had been stuffed into that bag. "I just don't know. Even if I found some nail trimmings in my personal kit, how would I know they weren't mine?"

She pulled out what looked like a Dopp kit. She opened it. I asked, "Is that his?"

"Oh, yes. He was always so forgetful. I was always finding things in hotel rooms that he'd left. This was one of them."

She started taking things out. One was an electric razor. I exclaimed, "That's it!"

She gasped, "Of course, he shaved with it. It might have his hair in it, right?"

I nodded and held out my hand for it. She extended her hand that was still holding it. I closed my hand over it and her fingers. We stood there for a moment, both holding it, and then she loosened her grip while I squeezed to take a firm grip on it. I took it, never taking my eyes from her face. "I should get going. The scientists will want it."

She nodded, still keeping her eyes on mine. "It was a pleasant lunch."

I could only nod, and then I turned to leave.

When I got home, Wolfe hadn't left for the plant room yet. He took the razor and said, "Satisfactory. Most satisfactory."

I didn't know what was so satisfactory about it. It was lucky getting it, but why he cared about the scientists I couldn't imagine. I called Lily Rowan and asked her to go dancing. She agreed. We danced, but she noticed that I wasn't on my best form. Finally, she just pulled me off the floor and asked what was going on.

"Oh, it's this crazy case. There are so many screwy things happening. He's got a party coming up that is going to be the wildest thing I've seen him pull in a long, long time.'

Lily looked me in the eye. "Are you sure that's all that's going on?"

I didn't have an answer. We made it an early night, and Wolfe was not in a talkative mood. I tried to pry a hint about the one critical thing on his party, "I've been thinking, I think we could get Rich Little to impersonate Wendt. What do you think?"

Wolfe just turned the page on his book and kept reading. I went to bed early.

The next day, nothing happened. Wolfe went to the plant room. I worked on germination records.

The day after, Minerva called and asked if anything was going on. When I told her that there wasn't anything on the program for today, she sighed and then brightened, "Then let's take that tour of the Natural History Museum."

I couldn't think of any reason not to, so I agreed. It turned out to be a better time than I expected. She was impressed by the Hayden Planetarium. Sitting in the dark and seeing the night sky that neither of us had seen in weeks, she was charmed, and we forgot for an hour all the things that were coming up.

I got home, and Wolfe put his book aside. "Call Mr. Milton. We've found Wendt. Set up a meeting for some time tomorrow. Nine if possible."

"Wow! I'm glad to hear it. Should I call in Lon to get a story on the front page of *The Times*?"

"Don't be facetious. After you've set it up, get hold of Minerva and have her get hold of Mr. Lockhart. Get hold of Cramer."

"OK. I'm very happy that we've found him. Should I prepare the bill?"

Wolfe snarled, "Archie."

I turned and picked up the handset of my phone and started dialing. Milton was easy. He'd made no progress, and he was more than happy to close things out and collect his bonus.

When I called Minerva, she was relieved that we were finally going to move. She agreed to get hold of Lockhart.

I called Cramer's office and eventually I got him. I signaled Wolfe to get on the line. He said, "We're ready for the meeting here. It's going to be at nine PM tomorrow."

The eagerness in Cramer's voice was clear. "Finally. It was a tough one."

"Yes, but we've got some special rules for this one."

If he'd been in the office, you could have seen Cramer's face redden, "Sure, when did you ever not have special rules? What is it now?"

"We want you to observe from the peep hole. Get here at 8:30. You can stay in the kitchen while we set up."

"OK. I guess we can do that."

"We?"

"Purly and I."

Purly Stebbins was a reasonable cop, who sometimes did me the credit to admit that I might have turned out all right if I'd been a cop. "Sure. It'll be a little crowded in there, but that's fine.

"Here's the real catch, though."

"I just knew it was coming."

"No matter what happens in the office, you have to stay at the peep hole until I call for you."

There was silence on the other end of the line. Finally, "You know that I can't do that. What if a crime is happening on the other side of the painting?" The peep hole into Wolfe's office was behind a painting. People in the alcove where the peep hole is can see AND hear what goes on in the office.

"If you don't swear to that, you're off the invitee list."

He thought for a minute. He knew that we desperately needed him there to complete the deal with him, but he also knew that Wolfe was serious when he gave an ultimatum like that. He agreed.

I also got hold of the supporting cast as well—Saul Panzer, Fred, Cather, etc. They were to come at 8 PM to help set things up. And they were to come armed.

That was it for the day. Tomorrow would be it for better or worse. The day dawned bright and beautiful. It was working out to be the biggest show that Wolfe had put on, and the one with the most moving parts. In the front room were to be the aurors. They had a party of four, including Lockhart. They set up something they called an extendible ear so that they could hear what was going on in the office without being heard.

The office was to initially have Milton, his three clients, Wolfe and his client Minerva, and Saul and I who would ostensibly be there to keep the beverages flowing.

The alcove and earlier the kitchen were to have Cramer and Stebbins.

Fred was in charge of the ersatz Wendt and was to be located, appropriately, in the guest room on the third floor.

Altogether there were to be fifteen, not counting Wolfe and Fritz. Wolfe was staying mum about the identity of the faux Wendt. That bothered me, of course, but there was nothing I could do about it. No matter how much I plugged away at Wolfe, he was mum on the subject.

Saul and Fred arrived very early of course. Saul helped set up the drinks in the office. Minerva arrived for dinner. It was Saul, Fred, Minerva, and the rest of the household at dinner. Wolfe discussed the future of space travel. He thought that there would be a habitation on Mars by the middle of the next century. He commented on the bet that a

London bookie had made that men would not land on the moon during the '60's and how they had made their next bet much more conservative.

After dinner the rest started arriving. I answered the door and directed people to their respective rooms. When Cramer and Stebbins arrived, we stopped by the alcove to make sure they would both fit. It was probably not necessary. More than once both Wolfe and I had stood there and watched at the same time. I took them back to the kitchen then, and Stebbins had some left-overs. Purly and Cramer refused any drinks in the kitchen.

The aurors came. They were wearing robes of sorts that had "AUROR" printed on the back and front. They set up in the front room. Nobody in the auror party wanted anything to drink other than water. They had this strange thing that looked like an ear on a string. They slipped it under the door between the front room and the office. It was barely visible—and then only if you knew what you were looking for. They also did some sort of incantation with their wands. I couldn't get the gist of what they were doing, but they seemed very intense.

I checked on Fred in the guest bedroom. "When's the fake Wendt supposed to arrive?"

He seemed a little nervous and said, "Sometime after the Deatheaters. We don't want them getting a look at him early."

"Right. I just wish that I could get a look at him early."

"You and me both."

Fritz brought the cart with potables. It was located near Saul's yellow chair in the back of the room. At ten minutes to the hour, I took a quick tour of the positions, especially making sure that Cramer and Stebbins were in place.

At five minutes to, Milton arrived. I took his hat and ushered him into the office. Minerva and Saul were already there. I had told Minerva to sit in the Red Leather chair, as the guest of honor. But she took one of the yellow chairs near my desk. I took that as an honor for me. I asked her if she'd move. She insisted on staying there, so I put Milton in the Red Leather chair.

Eight o'clock arrived, and none of the real guests of honor had arrived. Wolfe was in his room waiting for all the guests to be present so that he could make his triumphal entrance. It got to be five after. I had begun to wonder if the whole party was going to be a dud, but just then the doorbell rang. I answered the door and found the three stooges on the doorstep. I invited them in. None were wearing hats, so I didn't have to take them. We went to the office, and I seated them next to their detective.

I said that Wolfe would be down in a minute, and he didn't make me a liar. It couldn't have been 60 seconds when he entered, detoured around all the guests, and sat at his desk. He nodded at Minerva and asked me for introductions.

I began at his left and introduced the two Deatheaters to Milton's left, Milton, the DeathEater to the right of Milton, Minerva, and in the back, Saul. I then went on, "Saul is in charge of refreshments. If anyone would like something to drink, he'll be happy to help you."

No one said anything. Wolfe asked, "Surely someone wants something to drink. You Mr. Milton. What can we get you?"

Milton looked around and changed his mind, "I'll have a beer."

Wolfe agreed, "Excellent choice. I'll have one too. Anyone else?"

Sven muttered, "I'll bet you don't have butter beer."

Wolfe turned to Minerva, "Ms. McGonagall, anything to drink?" She shook her head no, and Wolfe nodded.

Wolfe heard the comment and said, "I'm not familiar with the beverage. I'm afraid we can't provide it, but we have a number of alternatives."

No one was taking.

Saul delivered the beers, and Wolfe started the show, "This doesn't have to take much time. If you'll please not interrupt, we can have you all on your way shortly.

"First, I want to be sure that everyone is aware of and understands the agreement that Mr. Milton and I have made. We've committed to each other that we would not attempt to 'poach' the other's clients. The agreement states that after Mr. Wendt has been found that neither investigator will attempt to bill the other's clients and that the clients should not attempt to pay the other investigator for additional services related to this case. Are there any questions about this agreement?"

No one said anything, so he proceeded, "Hearing none, we can proceed to the real business of this meeting. In a few minutes, I'm going to send Mr. Goodwin out to place a phone call so that another associate whom most of you haven't met, Fred Durkin, will bring Mr. Wendt. He's not in this house, but he's nearby, so it shouldn't take more than ten or fifteen minutes for him to arrive.

"Now, once he's here, and everyone has had an opportunity to satisfy themselves that it really is Mr. Wendt, I'm going to ask you all to sign an affidavit stating that Mr. Wendt has been found and that both of the cases are complete. We're going to ask everyone—clients and investigators to sign this affidavit. It will be notarized by Mr. Panzer. Are there any objections to doing that?"

No one said anything. It was a sign of Wolfe's confidence in what he expected that Saul wasn't a notary and couldn't have performed as specified.

Wolfe said, "Very well. Silence betokens consent." He turned to me and said, "Mr. Goodwin, go get Mr. Wendt."

I played my part, got up, left the room and headed for the guest room. Wolfe had never held a charade with less behind it than this one. I sure hoped somebody besides Fred would be up there when I arrived.

I went in, found Fred sitting on a chair and a suit of clothes lying on the bed and that was all. I asked, "Well Fred, where's Wendt?"

Fred smiled and said, "He's here."

Wolfe's Narrative

Sometimes Goodwin asks me to report on something that has happened. That was the case in this incident. He wanted a second perspective for the narratives that he sometimes writes.

In the office, I asked Saul to distribute copies of the affidavit and read it aloud. After about twelve minutes, the door was opened by Fred, who went in followed by Wendt.

Minerva shrieked, leapt up, ran to Wendt, threw her arms around him, and kissed him violently. Everyone else, except me, was momentarily stunned into inaction.

They broke the kiss simultaneously, which was one of Goodwin's measures of compatibility, but he had lots more to worry about. She had run her left arm through his right arm and was grasping him like a vice grip. That was a problem. If he had to get at his S & M quickly, he'd have to fight her off him first. That would cost the time that might be the difference between life and death.

I was talking, "Well, we can see that Ms. McGonagall has cast her vote. Are the clients of Mr. Milton satisfied?"

One of the shorter clients, the one with the scar, stood up and answered, "I think that is good enough for us. Now, Mr. Wendt, if you'll just accompany us, no one has to get hurt."

I, still sitting, interjected, "Don't be preposterous. You still have to sign the affidavit."

The other two Deatheaters rose and drew what I now recognized as wands. Out of the corner of my eye, I saw Saul put his hand in his suit jacket near his holster. The Deatheaters looked around and apparently didn't notice what I had about Saul. The tall blonde one said, "We're leaving, and nobody had better interfere if they want to live another few minutes."

I stood and said, "Don't be silly. None of you are going to hurt anyone."

The leader of the Deatheaters said, "Shut up."

But the blonde went on, "Oh, you don't think so? We killed that stupid Muggle FBI man for not co-operating, why not you, fatso?"

The leader shouted, "Enough."

"Why? We'll be out of the country in less than an hour, and we might just as well 'off' them all anyway."

I said, "I don't believe it. Why would you kill an FBI man? That would be stupid."

The blonde was completely out of control, "You idiot. We have been trying to find Wendt for weeks. We've wasted too much time. He knew where Wendt was and wouldn't tell us!"

With that, he started to raise his wand. I shouted, "Archie" and started dropping. Cramer's muffled cry came from behind the painting, "This is the police. Drop your weapons." Wendt threw my left arm around Minerva and pulled them both to the floor with his body between her and the Deatheaters. A green bolt like a laser beam went over Wendt and struck the wall of books behind them. Books flew everywhere. There were other green bolts and Minerva broke loose which was fine with Wendt because then he could get at his weapon. Saul's PPK went off.

There was a giant explosion that sounded like the crack of Doom. It had to be a high caliber hand gun firing. Wendt rolled to get his gun into the fray. I saw the doors to the front room fly open and more bolts of light come from the front room. Wendt got his gun free and took aim on the blonde whom he was determined to get. I was pretty sure that he'd fired that green bolt at Minerva. But the Deatheater was struck by a bolt of light, and he collapsed.

Just then Cramer came in through the door followed closely by Stebbins. Cramer had this giant 45 Magnum revolver raised. That made me think of Clint Eastwood, and Stebbins had some gun or other out as well. All three of the Deatheaters were on the floor. The aurors, who were now in the room, seemed to have them in hand. Wendt looked to see if Minerva were hurt. She was standing next to him with her wand raised, moving back and forth. Her hair was partly down, and Wendt smiled at her. He advised, "I think it's all over, Minerva."

I got up from behind his desk, which had a deep gouge cut in its top, but he seemed to be all right.

The leader of the Deatheaters was bleeding on the Kashan rug. It must have been Saul's shot because the Deatheater didn't seem to have the giant wound that you'd expect from Cramer's cannon.

The first person to speak was Cramer. He was standing over the three Deatheaters and said, "I'm Inspector Albert Fergus Cramer. I arrest you on behalf of the City and County of New York for the Murder of Matthew Crane."

He turned to Purly and said, "Cuff them."

Lockhart looked at him and said, "Sorry. We've got priority. They're wanted for multiple murders and torture in England."

Cramer smiled, "But you're in my jurisdiction, and I take precedence."

Then one of the aurors threw off his cloak and revealed underneath a flak jacket that had printed on it US Marshall. He said, "Sorry, Cramer. Take a look at this." He had a sheath of papers in his hand. Cramer reluctantly took it.

The Marshall went on, "I'm Thomas Corbet. I'm a US Marshall." He displayed his badge, and Purly came close to examine it. "That is an extradition warrant for the three men lying there. I'm afraid Lockhart has priority over you."

Cramer looked around for a moment, pulled a cigar out of an inside pocket of his coat, and threw it to the floor, "Wolfe, I should have known that a deal with you would go sour."

The three Deatheaters had been paralyzed. The aurors dragged them out of the room and disappeared—literally.

Corbet said, "My work is finished here. I'll be on my way too."

Cramer said, "Hold it. I need a statement from you."

"Why? Has any crime been committed here?"

Cramer sputtered and pointed around, "Look at the office. It's a shambles. Destruction of property."

I said, "It's a crime only if I prefer charges. I don't. Thank you very much Mr. Corbett."

He walked off. Wendt went to get his hat and make sure that when he closed the door, he was on the porch. Milton said, "I suppose that I won't be paid by those three."

I agreed, and Milton turned to leave. Then he turned back and started to speak, "But you owe me . . ."

I said, "You signed an agreement, and besides that you were never going to find Wendt. As a matter of fact, we haven't either. This is just an actor."

Wendt came back to the office and Cramer was starting to leave, but I said, "Wait a minute Mr. Cramer. We've got business that hasn't been completed."

Cramer said, "Nuts." But he walked to the Red Leather chair.

I interrupted him, "Sorry, inspector, my client is present. I'll have to ask you to take one of the yellows."

Cramer looked ready to have apoplexy, but Minerva spoke up. She had pulled the loose hair back over one shoulder and released the hair that made up what was left of her bun. It fell over her other shoulder. She crossed her legs and sat on the edge of Goodwin's desk. "I like the view from here. Cramer can have the Red Leather chair." Purly took one of the chairs next to Cramer, and Wendt went to Goodwin's chair. As he passed Minerva she told him, "We'll have to talk about this later."

I addressed Cramer from behind steepled fingers, "I've fulfilled the terms of our agreement. How are you going to fulfill yours?"

Cramer pointed over at me, "Look here, you've got Wendt. What more do you want."

But Wendt started to have a change in his skin. We don't have a mirror in the office, so Wendt don't know what he looked like but he could tell from Cramer's expression. Cramer asked, "Who is that anyway?"

He responded, "I'm truly shocked that you don't recognize your old buddy. How long have we known each other?"

"Is that you Goodwin? You sure don't look like you."

"I'm afraid it is. I admit that I'm not my usual handsome self, but it is me. Or is that I?"

"Quit clowning. OK. Wolfe, you mean to tell me that you don't know where Wendt is?"

"No, sir."

"You haven't exactly delivered the murderers to me."

"On the contrary. I delivered them, which was more than I undertook to do. Remember that I only agreed to prove to your

316

satisfaction who the murderers were – not more. If you weren't able to keep them, once delivered, that is not my fault or concern."

Cramer had another cigar out and was chewing it. He growled and said, "I suppose that you've fulfilled your part of the bargain. I'll see what I can do about finding what hospital Wendt was in."

"Thank you. Would you have a beer with me?"

Cramer looked around and said, "You've always got good beer. Why not?"

Saul delivered another pair of bottles. Minerva asked Goodwin, "The front room is sound-proofed, right?"

"Sure."

"Why don't we go there and talk a little."

Goodwin nodded and they went through the still-open doors to the front room.

Goodwin Resumes

Wolfe rarely reports to me, but his report provided a good perspective on events that I was far too close to emotionally to report on as dispassionately as Wolfe always can.

Once in the sitting room, Minerva sat on a sofa and patted the spot beside her. She wanted to know how I became a stand-in for Wendt. I explained.

"When I'd asked Fred where Wendt was, he'd pointed to me. He went to the dresser and picked up a hip flask. He told me, "OK. Here's the deal. You drink this down. Don't spill it for God's sake. And be prepared; the Auror told me that it tastes like goblin piss, whatever that is."

I started to object, but he interrupted me and went on. "What's going to happen, so help me, is that you're going to turn into Wendt—or at least, look just like him. So, scoot, scoot and gulp down that goblin piss—I'd hold my nose if I were you."

I was tempted to tell Fred what he could do with the goblin piss, but I realized that I didn't have time to debate taking it and other options. Wolfe hadn't left me any. So I did hold my nose and it was good that I had because it was so bad that I almost gagged and threw up despite the warning. Fred immediately urged me to change because my body size would be changing shortly.

I slipped off my hand tailored jacket, shirt, slacks, my Smith & Wesson, and the armpit holster that it was in. While I was doing that, I felt as if my skin were turning to putty, and every bone in my body ached like the dickens. I tossed the clothes away and glanced into the mirror. I now looked like a pretty good imitation of the photo that we'd been carrying around. I quickly put on the clothes on the bed. There was a pair of jeans, a short-sleeve black shirt, a jacket, and a pair of Adidas Stan Smith tennis shoes. They all fit adequately—nothing like my hand tailored clothes. I wondered if they were actually his clothes from Minerva's spacious luggage. I put on my holster, having to adjust it hurriedly for the different body size.

I finished dressing, took a good look in the mirror, and glanced at our photo of Wendt. It would be pretty good. Fred urged me to get going. He led the way. I felt a little uncomfortable in the body but thought it would do.

Fred opened the door to the office and preceded me in. Then I entered. I heard a scream, and suddenly you were wrapped around me and kissing me as though I'd returned from the Moon. I hadn't been prepared for that but tried to make it seem like the feeling was mutual, which, come to think of it, might not have been that far off the mark."

"I have a question for you: did you volunteer for impersonating Wendt?"

"No, ma'am. Wolfe usually doesn't keep me any better informed than his clients about his little charades. I didn't know until I went into the guest room that I'd be playing Wendt. But I've got a question for you. When did you know that I wasn't Wendt?"

She smiled coyly. "When do you think?"

"The moment that you kissed me, you knew." I said. "Was it better? Worse?"

"Neither. Just different."

"Another thing. You were a real pain holding onto me. I wanted to be able to reach my gun. I wasn't able to get free when I needed to. Why did you hold onto me so tightly?"

She held off answering for a minute, took a deep breath and said, "I saw the gun."

"You knew it was a gun?"

"Sure. Wendt carries one when he's traveling."

"But then."

"I didn't want you to get hurt. I thought you might do something crazy and get yourself hurt."

We were silent for a while. I offered to take her home. She answered, "No. I can get myself to the Churchill faster than you can. And it might be just a little too dangerous if you were to take me." She hesitated again and added, "Especially if you escorted me to my room."

I had to admit to myself that she was probably right. "OK. Let's see if Wolfe wants you for anything before you leave."

We went back into the office and I interrupted Wolfe. "Do you need Ms. McGonagall for anything more tonight?"

"No, Ms. McGonagall. You were very courageous tonight. I apologize that I had to involve you in a deception that included your being deceived at substantial peril for you."

Minerva said that she'd do it again to get the Deatheaters and keep the search for Wendt moving forward.

Wolfe offered my services, "Ms. McGonagall, why don't you let Archie take you home. It's been a difficult night."

I said, "I offered, but she's not having any of it."

He waved her away. I walked her to the door, which I opened for her. She turned quickly and planted a swift kiss on my cheek. Then, she walked down the steps and at the sidewalk, turned, waved and disappeared. Well, at least, I knew what her means of transportation looked like.

◿

The next day, we heard nothing from Cramer. That didn't surprise me, but after the next day passed without news, I was beginning to get worried. When Wolfe got down from the plant room, I asked him what was going on with missing persons.

"I think that we need to let Cramer have a couple of days before we begin pestering him."

The next day, shortly after we were back in the office from lunch, the phone rang. I answered. It was Cramer. He said, "I've got the hospital."

I said, "Hold a second." Then I covered the handset and said to Wolfe, "Cramer with the hospital. Do you want on?" Wolfe nodded.

I uncovered the mouthpiece and said, "Go ahead." He gave me an address that I wrote down.

Wolfe came on the phone. 'Mr. Cramer, I appreciate your diligence in this matter. On behalf of my client and myself, I thank you deeply."

Cramer said, "Sure."

We hung up, and Wolfe said, "Get hold of Ms. McGonagall. Get her over here immediately if possible."

I called the Churchill and told her the news. She said she'd be here immediately. I didn't waste my time by asking her if she wanted a ride, but I didn't quite expect to hear the doorbell ring before I had hung up the phone. Wolfe asked if it could be her already.

"Five will get you twenty that it is."

So, I wasn't really surprised to see her through the one-way glass. I let her in, and she beat me easily to the door to the office. I tried to open it for her, but it was hopeless.

She ran around Wolfe's desk and looked like she was going to do something like hug him, but he shouted, "Madame!" And then, "Archie."

She had stopped, and I took her arm and pulled her around the desk. "Minerva, why don't you take the Red Leather chair?"

She smiled up at me, "Oh, I think I like the view from your desk."

"I think Wolfe and I would be more comfortable if you took the chair."

She pouted at me and took the proffered chair. Turning to Wolfe, "Where is Wendt?"

Wolfe began, "Madame. We'll tell you shortly, but first, I want to cover a couple of points with you.

"First, the hospital that Cramer named is a psychiatric hospital. There is no guarantee that he's still there.

"Second, even if he is, there's a real chance that he's been damaged by the sort of treatment that patients who are not able to communicate get at such institutions. I want you to be prepared for all possibilities before you and Archie visit it."

She was surprised, "Archie and I? Let me assure you that I can take care of myself."

Wolfe grimaced, "Please, Madame, I have a great deal of evidence of your courage and intelligence, but you probably don't have the resourcefulness that Archie has. All may go well, but I really wish that the two of you would go together."

She clearly wasn't entirely happy but agreed to have me tag along.

"Well, then, can we at least leave immediately?"

Wolfe agreed to that. I got up and said, "Any time you want."

She came close and looked at me. "Don't you want to get your gun?"

"Well, these institutions have metal detectors. I wouldn't want them to find my gun. They might object to me entering with it, but I doubt that they'd detect your wand."

She smiled, "I think you're right. Let's go."

We left through the front door, and I made sure the door was locked behind us. I got out a piece of paper with the name and address of the institution on it. She glanced at it, closed her eyes and then opened them and said, "Take my hand and prepare for a shock. Wendt always complains about this means of travel, but it's so much more convenient and faster than your Jag."

I remembered the goblin piss and prepared myself for the worst. It was, if anything, at least as bad. I staggered as one foot set on the concrete of the pavement in front of the Brownstone, and the next foot squished on the springy grass on the lawn outside a utilitarian looking building that certainly could have been a hospital. The sign labeling it thus was small and almost not legible from the road in front of it.

We walked up to the entrance and found that we could enter a reception area that didn't have a metal detector. It must have been beyond the reception area. We walked up to the reception desk, and I introduced us to the woman behind the desk. She smiled up and asked what she could do for us.

Minerva let me explain, which I was happy for, "We're friends of a man whom we believe has been admitted here. We think he was admitted as a 'John Doe'. We have a photo."

Minerva started to reach for her handbag to withdraw that disturbing moving photo of them. I took her hand and said, "Let me show her the photo that we've been using to search for him."

I pulled that photo from my pocket. I unfolded it and showed it to the receptionist. She studied it a minute and said, "I can certainly see that Ms. McGonagall is in it. The man might be one that was admitted here a couple of weeks ago. Let me call our director, Dr. Balzac. Please take a seat. I'm sure he'll see you shortly."

We did. She got on the phone and had a lengthy conversation. Then she got up and came around to us. "Dr. Balzac was in a conference. But he should be out in fifteen or twenty minutes. He'd like you to wait in a conference room that we use for family conferences." She led us to a room off the Waiting Room. It was a corner room and had windows that looked onto the lawn.

"Archie, why don't they just let us see him?"

"I don't know, but let's give them the benefit of the doubt. We are pretty sure that he was here at some point, anyway. Let's see what this Balzac has to say."

It was more like a half hour, but the door did open and a tall, thin man in a neat tailored business suit entered. He introduced himself, and we introduced ourselves. We all sat around the conference table. "It is unfortunate that you didn't come a few days ago. He was admitted here, but he's been transferred to another hospital. Under the new HIPAA rules, I can't tell you where unless you can prove that he's next of kin."

Minerva's mouth turned hard. I tried to finesse him. "Really, Doctor. You haven't seen the photo that we showed your receptionist. They are clearly very close." I got out the photocopy and showed it to him. She was looking up into his face, which was clear in the photo.

"It appears that you are close, but are you his mother or perhaps an aunt?"

She hesitated, and I knew that we were lost. If she had answered directly and confidently we might have been able to pull off a deception, but she was too slow. To keep Minerva from blundering, I squeezed her hand and said, "No. They're close. They are both teachers in the same school and were traveling as part of a school tour when he suffered his stroke or whatever it was."

He looked carefully at the both of us. Finally, he said, "No. I'm sorry. I can't do anything without documentation from some bona fide relative."

I was about to threaten him with lawyers when Minerva squeezed back and said, "Oh, Archie, don't you think there is some way that we might persuade him?" I saw her reach inside her handbag and grasp her wand.

I nodded, "Yes, Minerva, you're right."

I turned to Balzac and said, "I really think that you should reconsider. There are various sorts of pressure that we can bring to bear of which you have no conception. Will you not reconsider? We would certainly not reveal where we got the information. It would be such a blessing to Minerva."

He sighed and shook his head and in mid-sigh he froze in place. I said, "Wow! Is he really incapacitated?"

She nodded. Then she said, "I really have to urge you to give us the information. It would be unfortunate—for you—if you didn't cooperate. Is there anything you'd like to add, Archie?"

I moved so that my face was directly in front of his, "Minerva, can he feel it if I tweak his nose?"

"He most certainly can."

"Good." I gave his nose a good tweak. "I've always wanted to do that ever since I got my first shot at the doctor's. Now, understand that we are not cruel. We have no intention of harming you further. That tweak is the last physical harm that you'll get from us, but you stand in jeopardy of being paralyzed completely for the rest of your life?" I made it a question by rising inflection and looked at Minerva.

She nodded and then realizing that he couldn't see her nod from his position she said aloud, "Yes. That's true."

"OK. So, I'm going to give you a few minutes to re-consider. Also, when we do release you from paralysis, we'd appreciate it if you'd not make a sound. If you were to, we'd have to paralyze you again, and I just don't know what would happen to you next."

I walked out of his field of view and motioned Minerva to do so, as well. I watched the clock. I thought that five minutes would be jarring enough for a start. I whispered to her, "Can you lock the door so that it can't be opened from the outside?"

She nodded and did it.

After the five minutes were up, we walked around into his field of view, and she released him. He gasped and his eyes goggled out but he managed to keep himself from screaming. I congratulated him. "Good going. You saved yourself. Now, let's have that hospital."

He was still gasping, "I can't do that. It's as good as my job if I do. It might even be prison time."

I nodded. "And you can't bend the rules even a little bit. You never bend the rules with patients? You always respect patients' rights thoroughly?"

He thought about that a minute. Then he just said, "I can't do it."

I smiled, 'Prison time. How apt! This is precisely prison time—for life." I looked over at Minerva and signaled with my eyes.

She said, "Not even if the alternative were to be frozen permanently."

He gasped, and she froze that expression on his face.

I pulled her over in front of him so that he could see us and hear us. I looked at her and said, "Here's the thing about making threats. You have to be absolutely prepared to carry through with them if you're going to make them. It doesn't work otherwise. So, I want you to be absolutely sure that you're ready to do this and stick by it if you do."

She drilled me with those eyes that could be so hard, "You know it."

"Then we've got to do two things—one is to give him some real time to experience this and let him get used to the idea of what it would be like forever. Let's say a half hour. I think that they won't try to interrupt us in less time than that.

"Then, the second thing that we have to do is not drag it out. We release him and give him ten seconds to decide. If he makes a peep other than answer our question, you freeze him for good. Do you agree? If you've got any doubt, we can't go ahead with this."

She said, "How do we find where Wendt is if we freeze him permanently?"

"Oh, there are other people here who know. We just start with them one at a time until we find someone who is willing to talk. Who knows? The next one might talk or there might be eight or ten before they talk. If there are several, the survivors might think it was a communicable disease. Maybe they'd name it after our buddy here—Balzac's disease."

There didn't seem to be anything else to say, so I took Minerva's hand and took her out of the line of sight of the good Doctor. Then we waited. The thirty minutes was hard time, but it was harder for him.

When it finally expired, Minerva led me over. She did the talking this time, "OK. I'm going to unfreeze him shortly. When he is, you start counting to ten slowly. If he doesn't tell us where Wendt is by the time you reach ten, I freeze him forever. If he shouts, I freeze him forever. Are you ready?"

I looked over at him, and I said, "Go ahead any time. I've got eidetic memory. Whatever he says, I've got it."

She nodded, "Then count down from ten. When you reach zero, I unfreeze him. Then start counting up to ten. If you reach ten without him telling, he's frozen forever."

I started the count. When I reached zero, I could see him relax and then do his best not to scream. I started the count, "One. Two. Three."

He begged, "Please don't do it, It's inhuman."

"Four. Five. Six."

"What have I ever done to you?"

"Seven. Eight. Ni..."

He almost shouted, "The Princeton Lying-in Hospital. I don't know the address, but you can look it up in the phone book."

I looked at Minerva and said, "OK. We need to do a little further talking. Here's what's going to happen. We're going to disappear out of this room in a moment. You'll be free, but if we find that you've lied to us, we'll be back for you.

"Now, just in case you're thinking that once we're gone, you could protect yourself from us, we're going to give you a demonstration of what we can do. First, we're going to disappear from the room. Second, we're not going to unlock the door. You may have a key, but it won't work. The receptionist will have to get someone to demolish the door or break one of the windows to get you out. Oh, yeah, I bet the windows are unbreakable. Well, it doesn't matter. They'll get you out eventually.

"So, if you were thinking that you could get away with lying to us, just remember that you're stuck here for a while. We can find out if you've lied before they could break you out. We'll come back, and it's back into the deep freeze you'll go. "

I then said brightly, "Now, last chance. Take sixty seconds and think hard. Are you sure that you've given us the right place? If you decide that you might have made a mistake, there will be no retribution. But once we disappear from this room, it will be too late forever to fix things."

I glanced at my watch, and he just shook his head no. I announced the time left in ten second intervals. When I got to six, I took Minerva's lead and started counting down. He just kept shaking his head no. I said, "Zero," and we disappeared.

We landed in Minerva's room at the Churchill. She asked if I could find out where the Princeton Lying-in was. I picked up the phone and punched nine to get an outside line and then 411 for information. A person came on, and I asked for the hospital. There was a minute's hesitation, and they came back with a phone number with a Princeton area code. I asked for its address. The operator gave it to me. I wrote it on the pad of notepaper they have in every room. "Well, the hospital exists and has a phone number. Here's the address. Can you take us there?"

Minerva looked at the address and nodded. She held out her hand.

"You know that Wendt was right about these wizard means of travel," I said.

"Oh, don't be a sissy. Take my hand."

I squeezed the cool strong hand, and we disappeared. We landed in the parking lot near a shade tree. We walked up to the main entrance. There was a receptionist. She was polite, "Can I help you find someone?"

"Sure, he's a John Doe, but I have a photo if that will help."

She smiled. "The photo won't help me, but I can tell you if there are any John Doe's here." She checked a computer, started to look up, looked down again and then looked up. She drawled out, "Nooope. No John Doe's."

I turned to Minerva saying, "Well, I guess we'll have to look elsewhere." I mouthed, "Stun her." Minerva reached into her purse but didn't pull the wand out. However, much to my surprise, when I looked around, I saw that the receptionist was frozen.

I ran around behind the desk, pulled her back into her chair, and swiveled it around to face me. "Are you all right?" I looked up at Minerva to signal her to look at the computer screen, but she was already around the other side of the desk and was glancing down at the screen– brilliant girl that she is.

In the mean time, I said, "I'm going to call the Emergency Room for you." Behind her, Minerva nodded. I picked up the phone and dialed zero. Meanwhile Minerva pulled the wand out and did something.

The receptionist unfroze and gasped, "What happened?"

I answered her, "You looked like you had a stroke. How do you feel?"

As she tried to come up with an answer, the operator had answered, and I said, "Please get someone to the reception area from the Emergency Room. The receptionist just fainted or had a stroke or something."

I hung up after the operator said that she would. Minerva was signaling me that she wanted to go, but I shook my head. I said, "We've got to wait until they get here. It won't be more than a couple of minutes."

As a matter of fact, it was closer to five than two, but a pair of nurses with a gurney showed up, and we pointed to the receptionist. They put her onto it and rushed out of the room. Minerva had been grasping my arm in a vice-like grip and pulled me off as soon as they were on the way. She whispered insistently in my ear, "Why did we have to wait for them?"

"We don't want anyone remembering us as running away as soon as the receptionist had her fit. We might be getting a visit from city employees otherwise."

She sniffed and reported, "There's just one. He's on the third floor in a private room—332."

We headed for the elevator. Hospital elevators are as slow as molasses, and I could see behind Minerva's eyes that she was thinking of disapparating us up. However, she didn't. We arrived on the floor and quickly found 332. It was empty.

Minerva sat down on a chair and started to cry. I took her hand and lifted her up. "Come on. Maybe they've taken him to physical therapy. We'll go to the nurse's station and find out."

The nurse's station had one nurse who was in a deep conversation with a doctor. I cleared my throat, and she spoke louder and said, "All right, Dr. Wilson, we can talk when I have a break. I'll see you later."

She came over to us and asked what she could do. I asked if she knew where the John Doe in 332 was. She looked at a clipboard and said, "I don't know. . . No, wait, he's down in the basement having some tests done in room B37. I can call down and see. . ." She'd stopped talking because Minerva had mysteriously disappeared.

I apologized, "She's been trying to find him for a while. She just couldn't wait. I'm sure she's on the way down now."

The nurse just kept staring at the place where she had been, and I found stairs and ran down, hoping to arrive before anything drastic happened. Three floors down, I came out and had a hard time finding B37, but eventually did.

Even before I entered, I saw that the door was sprung from its hinges. I took a deep breath and walked in. Everyone that I could see was on the floor. I went to a young woman, felt for a pulse and for rigor, but she was not rigid and was starting to come around—as though she had fallen and was stunned. I helped her get up, and then we found the other three.

When they were up and moving, they went to the Emergency Room to check for concussions—except for Dr. House, who self-examined and assured everyone that he was OK. He insisted on me accompanying him to his office.

$$\triangle\triangle$$

He asked me to sit, and he started swinging the cane around. "Interesting that you arrived just after we were attacked."

"Don't you mean lucky. No one might have happened along for quite some time."

"What were you doing down there anyway? Pretty far off the beaten track."

"I was looking for your patient." I pulled out the well-worn leaflet and handed it to him.

"Yeh, that's him OK. Good old John Doe. But you call him Wendt."

"Yeh. That's his name."

"Looks like you just missed him. Who are you, an uncle or something?"

"I'm a private investigator. I work for Nero Wolfe."

"So what does this Wolfe want with him?"

"You're a little confused. Wolfe's not my client, he's my boss. Maybe you'd better go get yourself checked for a concussion."

"OK. Who's your client?"

"Now, now, doctor. Have you forgotten about the principle of confidentiality?"

"Why, have you got a mafia boss for a client?"

"Now, now, doctor. You won't trick me into telling you which mafia boss we're working for."

House whipped his cane around so that it was at the tip of my nose. "Somebody roughed up my team and me. I want to know who it was."

"Just a word of advice. As I was telling my client today, don't stick that in anyone's nose unless you intend to use it."

Just then, an attractive young woman entered the office without knocking. We turned to look at her. Her face fell, "Are you applying for a new lawsuit, House?"

"I was just trying to find out who roughed up my team."

She said in a strained voice, "House!"

He went on, "And stole my patient."

"House, did someone take your patient?" and flung her hands in the air.

I said, "I think he just mislaid him. Maybe if you look in the broom cupboard or the men's room."

House stood up and said, "He stole him."

I smiled, "Feel free to search my pockets–really."

House smiled wickedly, "I'll be happy to."

Wiggling a finger at him, I said, "No S & M."

The woman introduced herself, "I'm Dr. Cuddy. I run this hospital except for House's department."

"It's a pleasure to meet you. I'm Archie Goodwin. I work for."

She smiled and said, "I know you. You work for Nero Wolfe."

She turned to House and said, "He's done here. 1 would like to talk with him." She turned to me," Would you mind coming up to my office. I want to apologize for Dr. House."

As we walked out the door House shouted after us, "No she doesn't. She wants you to tell her what your client did with my patient. In exchange, you can work your will on her willing body."

I called back over my shoulder, "Maybe he checked himself out."

I heard a crash which I deduced was the impact of a cane against a wall.

We reached her office and she invited me to take a chair. She sat behind her desk, "Seriously, I want to be sure that you don't sue us.

House is a temperamental genius. He is a wonder at diagnosis, but he doesn't have the best people skills."

"I know about working with genius. Don't worry. We were just having a little fun. I wouldn't think of suing you or the hospital."

She looked relieved but asked, "Are you sure?"

"Certainly. As a detective, I have to deal with police lieutenants who are a lot more irritating than House. I usually can find a way with them." I chuckled, "There's one by the name of Roecliff. He has a tendency to stutter. When he's irritating, I can usually work him up into stuttering. If I had to deal with House a lot, I'd find something similar."

"I wish I had you as a personal assistant. I wouldn't have to deal with House then. I'd just send you." She started laughing, "And. . . ho ho. . . And you'd start. . . oh no . .You'd start him stuttering." After a moment she controlled herself, "I would do almost anything for someone who could induce stuttering in House. Ah, well. I suppose we all can dream."

I smiled, "It would be a real pleasure working under you. It would have the added bonus of getting to drive House around the bend a few times a week."

She smiled dreamily for a moment, "You know. That's why you couldn't work for me. There are laws."

I stood, 'Thank goodness for laws. I don't think I'll see House again. Good luck with him."

She stood, held out her hand, and said, "Thanks for being a good sport about House. But one last thing before you leave."

"Sure."

"Do you know what happened to the patient?"

"I was trying to solve a missing person's case. Oh, here's a flier we had made up," I got the flier out of my pocket. "You can keep this as a souvenir. We have more. We'd traced him here, and I apparently just missed his departure when I arrived. Believe me, I know how hard it is to get information from medical people about patients without their authorization. We'll have to continue our search elsewhere. We may ask people in the area if they saw him leave, but considering what I know about his condition, I doubt that he walked out. Maybe someone came with an ambulance for him. We can pursue that angle. It was nice meeting you."

She patted her hair absently, and then the spot just below her throat and said, "Well, if you have any non-medical questions, please call."

I nodded and turned and left her office and her hospital.

The Last Chapter

I got back to the Brownstone. Wolfe was in his office reading. I reported fully. When I reported about House, he said, "Satisfactory. Very satisfactory."

"So, you think that Ms. McGonagall, kidnapped him."

Wolfe shrugged, "It's the only thing that makes sense."

"Then we've completed our job. I'll make out a bill for her and get her approval to collect. I'll probably have to see her in person to go over it. Who knows, I may ask her to marry me."

"Archie!"

"Of course, we'd eventually want to move out of my room, but I think you'd want us to honeymoon there."

With more force he said, "Archie. Just bill her and let us get back to normal life."

"Yes. sir."

I completed the bill and handed it to the genius. He glanced over it. He looked up and said, "What kind of flummery is this?"

I shrugged, "I didn't know there was more than one kind."

He ignored the jab and said, "You've omitted a couple of items haven't you?"

I smiled, "I don't know what you could be talking about."

He actually moved his one sixth of a ton enough to nod his head toward the floor where the Kashan rug used to be. "What about cleaning the Kashan? That will surely cost nearly a thousand dollars."

"They estimated 850."

"And then there's the book that was rendered unreadable by that blast from the Deatheater's wand-*A Brief History of Time*."

I scratched my head, "I'm not sure about that, let me look it up on Amazon."

The genius asked, "More flummery? What would the river know about book prices?"

I chuckled, "No, not the river, the website. It's a new business that sells books online." I turned to my computer and brought up the Amazon website. It was currently selling there for $19.99 plus shipping. "I'll order one right away."

"Do that, but keep our original copy. It's autographed by the author."

My jaw dropped. "How does a quadriplegic autograph a book?"

Wolfe chuckled, "He actually used a kind of mouse pad to write it."

I was still amazed. "How did you convince him to do it?"

"Oh, I made a generous contribution to the ALS Association in his name."

I was still doubtful. "I don't remember any big donations from the checking account."

Wolfe frowned, "I didn't want to be badgered by you for spending money on what you would consider a frivolity. I took it out of my emergency account that you don't have access to."

Wolfe also owned a home in Egypt that was sort of an emergency retreat. I knew there was an emergency account as well but I didn't even know how much money was in it.

I asked Wolfe, "Aren't you forgetting repair of the desk?" It seemed amazing to me that he'd not mentioned it.

"Oh, I don't intend to have it repaired. The bolt that did that didn't penetrate to the interior of the desk. It's perfectly usable. I'm going to keep that jagged scar on the desk as a memento of this case."

He had placed the jade paperweight beside it.

I said, "Well, I agree that someone should have to pay for the rug and *A Brief History* but I don't see why it should be our client."

"Archie, when have we not charged clients for damages done to our property in working on their case?"

I had to admit to myself that I couldn't think of a case, but I wouldn't admit that to the fat slob, "The real people who are responsible are those Deatheaters, so the aurors should reimburse us. Or if not them, then the FBI." I paused for a moment and went on, "Or for goodness sakes, Cramer! We solved his case for him."

Wolfe wagged his finger at me, "Archie, you're ensorcelled."

I objected vociferously, "I am not – whatever that is."

"You've let that witch enchant you."

"I just want us to be fair to her."

Wolfe responded with a command, "The rug and the book go on the bill."

I was tempted to resign as I'd done before when Wolfe was being totally unreasonable, but I didn't want Minerva to be embroiled in our differences. I gave in. I re-typed the bill and handed it to Wolfe. I mentally dared him to declare, "Satisfactory."

He didn't.

There were lots of items on the invoice—all of which I intended to review with her in person. She called wanting a final bill and to pay. We made an appointment to meet over lunch the next day at Rusterman's.

△

We had the private room again. She ordered for herself, and we had lunch without talking business. That idea of Wolfe's about not talking business over meals I thoroughly agreed with in this case. Afterwards over tea and coffee, I showed her the itemized bill. She didn't ask any questions except for one line."What is this line for medication–Imodium D."

"Well, my reaction to disapparating was so violent that I had to buy something for nausea."

She squinted at me, "You're being facetious."

"No, I'm not. But I'll remove it from the bill if you insist."

"No. Don't change the bill. You have my authorization to charge the account for that amount."

She didn't ask about the rug or the book, so I brought it up, "I'm surprised that you didn't object to the charge for the rug and the book."

She smiled, "Not at all. It was a beautiful rug. I hope it cleans well. The book is one of Wendt's favorites."

I asked her how Wendt was doing.

"The Healers say that he will recover well, but it will take time—perhaps weeks."

"I'd be happy to help you occupy your time. It's a free perk when you hire Wolfe."

She laughed, "You'd joke on your deathbed."

"I hope so. But I wasn't joking."

"I appreciate the offer, but I'll be at Wendt's bedside."

"Well, you have my phone number if you ever change your mind."

She assured me that she'd remember.

We never heard if Wendt fully recovered or not. I hoped he did. He had a really good reason to recover. When Wolfe and I discussed the case later, he took to calling Minerva, The Woman. He had been impressed by how reasonable, resilient, and self-possessed she'd been. I doubt that Wolfe could ever have married, but if he ever considered who might have been suitable, I think it would have been The Woman.

Back to Work

I had recovered enough to listen to Minerva's story and understand it. I sometimes dropped off—exhausted, trying to fit what I remembered into the story that I was hearing. The first couple of days, I heard only bits and pieces, but by the end, it was beginning to make real sense. I was fitting it into my recollection of days. When I'd reached that point, I asked Minerva if she minded repeating the story from the beginning. I also asked her to go back a bit and cover the last couple of days in Washington.

She objected, "Of course, I didn't think I was good enough at storytelling to make that enjoyable."

"You are very good at everything you do."

She smiled and nodded agreement, "I'll start again. Interrupt any time that you like. Tell me to stop for a break any time you like."

So, she told me the story again, starting from the last couple of days in Washington. I still tired pretty quickly, but we slowly worked our way across the days and weeks. By the time that we reached the point where she showed up, I was telling my part of the story. It had gaps and was told in fits and starts and occasionally re-told in part when I remembered that things went a bit differently than she said.

When we reached the end, I was going without breaks for rests, and I had almost all the details settled as well as I could. She brought my healer in, and we discussed whether I was ready to return to work or not. He looked over my physical rehab reports and nodded. "I don't ever like letting someone go before they're 100% but you are at least 75 or 80. I really can't justify your staying here unless you want to, and if you did, I'd not hesitate a second to keep you here another week or so."

"No. I'm ready to go, right Minerva?"

She just shrugged and nodded.

"OK. I'd suggest that you go back to England and . . " He was glancing through his file on me. "You're a teacher, right? At a residential school?"

"That's right," Both Minerva and I said in unison.

"Well, if it's feasible, I'd suggest that you return and take up residence at the school, getting re-acclimated to the surroundings a couple of weeks before school starts."

Minerva said, "That would be the normal thing to do in any case."

"Good. Then, I'm ready to sign you out and wish you good luck —the both of you."

Minerva helped me pack, and I carried my duffel down to the office where we paid and cleared the last hurdle to leaving. I commented that in a Muggle hospital a patient would never be allowed to walk to the exit. He could walk to physical therapy, but he'd have to ride a wheel chair to the exit.

"That shows the inferiority of Muggle medicine." Minerva said.

"Or maybe the superiority of Muggle lawyers."

She laughed at that.

When we cleared the entrance, Minerva disapparated us to her hotel room in the Churchill. I noted that it was about the same size as the one we had at the Inn that we stayed at in Washington, but the room was much more "modern"—in other words, not nearly so comfortable. It was nice by "modern" standards, though.

Minerva asked me, out of the blue without any preamble, "Do you want revenge against any of these idiot 'doctors' who treated you?" Her tone of voice left no doubt that she was serious and perhaps even that she was hoping that I did.

I had had a lot of time to consider that subject while I was lying inert, frozen, paralyzed, but strangely now, I found it hard to have real revenge in my heart for most of the misguided doctors who'd treated me–certainly not for the Emergency Room doctors. The psych ward was a little different matter, but the people there were treating me the only way they knew how to—the way that had succeeded in at least some other cases. However, there was one doctor who should have known better. There was one doctor who was arrogant and treated me as if I were responsible for my illness. There was one doctor whose cane I would have knocked out from under him had I had the chance.

"Well, there is one guy who really deserves a hard time of it."

Minerva smiled, "Let me just guess. He's tall, thin, uses a cane and his name rhymes with mouse."

"Yes."

She said, "I don't have the slightest idea."

"What do you have in mind for him?"

Minerva smiled and brought her mouth close to my ear to whisper.

When she finished, I approved except for one thing. "Do you really want to disapparate directly into his office? I thought that was a 'no-no' in polite society."

"We're not in polite society any more."

"But what if he's there with others?"

In answer, she just frowned and held out her hand. I took it. We appeared in a dim office, lit only by the parking lot sodium vapor lamps.

"Do you want the doctor's chair?" I asked her.

"No, you deserve it. I'll take one of these."

We had no idea how long it would be before he came back to his office, but we waited. In time, a key turned in the lock, the door opened, and someone was silhouetted in the light from the hall. He closed the door behind him and seemed about to walk to the window, but then he noticed us.

He flipped on a light, and we were all there.

"What the hell are you doing in here? And who are you?"

Minerva said, "Don't you recognize us?"

He glanced at Minerva and shook his head. Then he took a more careful look at me, "Nooo, I don't think that I recognize. . . Wait, you're the paralyzed patient, aren't you. It's not easy to recognize you without the rictus." He stopped and then looked at Minerva again, "Then that means that you must be the one who attacked me!"

"I think of it as defending my man."

He raised his cane and pointed it at her like a rifle. She pulled her wand out of her robes and pointed it at him. That seemed to disturb him more than you would have expected. He demanded, "Are you threatening me?"

Minerva smiled a cruel smile, "I don't know. Are you threatening me? Haven't you ever heard that it's impolite to point?"

He suddenly seemed to realize that he was pointing his cane. He dropped the tip to the ground and said, "Well, what is it that you've come for?"

I told him the truth, "The only last bit of business is finding my purse. I wonder where it is." I was watching House's face. When I said the word, purse, his eye's turned toward a cabinet. "Thank you Dr. House."

I walked over to the cabinet and tried to open it. It was locked. I glanced at Minerva, she raised her wand, and the door unlocked. I opened it and almost immediately saw my purse. I reached in and took it out.

House immediately protested, "You can't do that. That's my property."

I smiled, "Oh, really? Can you open it?" His face turned a darker shade of red. "I know that you can't, but I can." I pulled the drawstrings easily, and the purse opened. I re-closed it and put it in my pocket.

But, Minerva drew her sleeves back from her wrists and rubbed her hands together. "I've got one more thing that I want to do. We've come in the hopes that you will learn some humility by the experience."

He laughed, "And who's going to teach me humility? A great git like you?"

He froze in the middle of the word, "you". Then he fell, starting ever so slowly and accelerating as he fell. He landed on his face. I got up and walked over to him, finding there was blood dribbling from his nose. "Why don't you pick him up? We'll lean him against the wall and he'll look natural." I hesitated, "Well, at least as natural as he ever does."

She levitated him, and I leaned him against the wall with his back toward the door. He did look almost natural. Minerva began, "Now, you're in the same state as Wendt was." She turned to me and asked, "What do you think they'll do when they find him?"

I shrugged, "I don't know. Probably put him in a room and see if they can cure him." Then I turned to him, walked up beside him, leaned on his shoulder, and said, "What do you think? I think that you might just get a disease named after you. Yeh, House's syndrome. You're going to be famous.

"Now, you may wonder why we don't allow you to talk. It's simple, really. Some people think that having a bastard beg for forgiveness is satisfying. Personally, I don't. I think that assholes should just suffer in silence."

Minerva said, "Well, it's time we were on our way." She stood up and joined me. We took hands and I gave House a pat on his back. We saw him start to fall again as we disapparated.

△

Our next destination was to check out of the Churchill. I paid for Minerva's stay, and we disapparated to the Port-Key Authority of New York. We found that there was a long line of people who were applying for a port key for vacation travel as well as the normal business travelers. They were queued up at a reception desk. When we arrived at the end of the line, we received a disk. I'd seen ones like it several times now. The receptionist told us that when an agent was available, the cubicle number would flash on the disk.

We found a seat and talked about the summer. By this time we were more than a week into August, and it was past time for us to get back to Hogwarts to prepare for the next year.

"I suppose that this was not one of your better vacations, Wendt?"

"No. It started off looking like the best. I guess that I should be happy at this point to be alive and on my way back to England. I know that my parents will be disappointed that we can't spend more than a couple of days with them. They must have been frightened out of their wits."

Minerva frowned at me, "You could have given them a call sometime in the last couple of days."

"I know. I should have, but I just couldn't face telling them what happened over the phone. I hope they can forgive my hesitating so long. I'll call them as soon as we get the port-key setup, and we can visit them for a day or two before we return."

She agreed to that. After we got our port key set to return, which allowed us to travel anytime for a week, provided that we arrived at the Ministry of Magic during normal working hours, we went looking for a phone booth. With the rising popularity of cell phones, it was getting harder and harder to find one, but it was still possible. As we walked about trying to find one, Minerva kidded me about the Port-Key Authority functionaries who had taken our application. He asked if we'd had a pleasant visit.

She laughed, "I thought you were going to have apoplexy. You could have really given him a pranging, but I think you showed admirable restraint."

"Admirable restraint my foot. I didn't give him a pranging because I couldn't get my breath, I was trying to keep from laughing so hard. I mean, I could either have laughed or cried. It wouldn't have made much difference."

We found a phone booth in Grand Central station. I called home. It was a difficult conversation. My dad was contained fury about not hearing from us, but he wanted us to come. We had to admit that it could only be for a couple of days.

When we arrived, there was a restrained day when we only talked about non-threatening things—like when school started, when we had to be back to Hogwarts, how my relatives were doing in Ohio.

Then, over breakfast, Minerva opened the topic of what happened in New Jersey. It was a tough morning. I won't torture you with the details. After my mom had gone through a box of Kleenex, and my dad had done his best to talk me out of returning to England, we were all exhausted and went to see a movie—*Titanic*. It maybe wasn't the best choice, but we could sit for a couple of hours in the dark and have our minds on someone else's troubles that weren't anything like ours.

The next day, my dad took me aside and went into the back yard —supposedly to see how the tomatoes were doing in the vegetable garden. He said, "I'll not try to convince you any more not to go back. As a matter of fact, I want you to know that I think that you've got more courage than I would. I can't imagine facing the sort of things that you have and still go back for more." He was struggling to hold back the tears, so I turned so that we could both pretend that he wasn't.

I laughed for the first time in a long time, "You better never believe that I'm going back in order to have more. I'm going back to share whatever it is that Minerva can't hide from." We were both silent for a while.

"Well Dad, I think I've pretty well seen all the tomatoes that I can stand. You know, I never really liked tomatoes."

He laughed this time, "I know, I could never get you to even try one when you were a kid."

"Do you remember the time that you sneaked a small slice into my hamburger?"

"And on the first bite you gagged and spit it across the table hitting your mother?"

"I had to do all the dishes for a month after that. Yeh, I kind of remember it."

There was a moment of shared memory as we walked back to the house. On the threshold he said, "You know that the only thing that I want is for you to do your best, and if it comes to it, give those asshole Deathreapers or whatever they are an introduction to Hell."

I looked at him, hair thinning but still as brown as the day that he turned twenty-one. I was happy that he gave me the best blessing he had.

He turned from looking directly at me as he opened the door and said, "But don't you dare tell your mom what I said."

"Yes, sir."

That was the last day before we returned. On the day we left, Mom asked how we were traveling. Minerva used the word, disapparating. Mom asked if she minded if we did it where she could see us.

Minerva leaned forward toward her conspiratorially and whispered, "Strictly speaking, we're not supposed to let Muggles see us do it, but for you we could bend the rules a bit. However, we'd have to do it inside your house. Otherwise, we'd have to walk to a deserted alley."

My dad was pleased. I know that he wouldn't admit it, but he was fascinated by the idea of disapparation. He would have liked to have seen it when he first heard of it. So we all stood in the kitchen. Each of us had a piece of luggage in hand and we took each other's hand. Mom wanted a final hug from each of us, so we broke our grasp, and we had hugs all around.

Minerva and I took hands again, I nodded to mom and dad, and we were standing in the main Atrium of the Port-Key Authority of New York. Or Minerva was. I was bent over trying to keep myself from retching. She just rolled her eyes and said, "Don't be such a wuss. Let me know when you're ready to take the port key."

I nodded because I couldn't speak yet for the gorge in my mouth. I led her away from where we'd landed by a few feet and nodded, "OK. I guess I'm as ready as I ever will be."

She looked at me assessing. "I don't think you're quite ready. Would you like a nice cup of tea?"

I had to agree, and we went into a little alcove where there was, of all things, a Starbucks. I had an Earl Grey, and Minerva had some other variety. As I paid, I asked how it was that there was a Starbucks in a magic facility.

The clerk said, "Oh, it's easy. You find Starbucks in all sorts of unlikely places—grocery stores, car showrooms."

"But, how do deliveries get made?"

"Oh, that's no problem. We have a 'partner' program. Our partner is a Starbucks in a service plaza on the Jersey turnpike. They order supplies, etc. for both us and them. We pay them a small handling fee."

"Thanks." I guessed it was inevitable. Starbucks for wizards.

Minerva and I had our tea and talked about what the travel plans were to get back to Hoggwarts. The port-key would take us directly to the Ministry of Magic. We'd take the floo network from there to the fireplace in Minerva's office and once there, well, who knew what would happen?

I was feeling a lot better, and with that little added incentive, I felt sure that I could make it just fine. We walked back into the Atrium, we both grasped our bags, and we both took hold of the port-key. Minerva's hand covered mine, and we were suddenly in a deserted corner of the great Atrium of the Ministry of Magic.

The Blasted Hand

From there we went to the Port-Key Authority and went through what passed for customs in the Ministry. We filled out a form asking if we had any dangerous magical creatures or class three restricted magical objects and so on. We filled out the forms as quickly as possible, and I was amazed that we did go through a fairly thorough magical exam checking that we were honest on the forms. As usually happened, they found my cell phone, and there was some discussion about what it was.

The customs official asked, "What is that thing?"

"It's a Muggle good luck charm."

"Really?" He turned to Minerva and asked, "Is that really true?"

She could hardly keep a straight face and said, "Yes, we were visiting Wendt's parents, who are Muggles. They gave it to him for good luck."

When she said that, I grimaced, trying to keep back the laughter. The customs wizard mistook that, and asked if there were something wrong.

"No, sir. It's just that I'm a little ashamed to be carrying an object of superstition around with me. But it is from my parents."

He nodded, "I have a brother-in-law whose wife's parents are Muggles. They have all sorts of funny superstitious ideas about magic. Well, that's all." He handed each of us a slip of parchment that had a stamp on it. It would have been an entry VISA, if wizards had passports.

We went to the Atrium and found an unused hearth. We stepped into it, Minerva took a handful of floo powder from the urn next to it, and she took my hand—the other one was holding both our bags. She threw down the powder and clearly said, "Hogwarts, Minerva McGonagall's office." Green flames leapt up around us but something was very wrong. For one thing, I didn't feel like I'd been through a mixmaster. For another, we weren't looking out on Minerva's office. It looked suspiciously like the Atrium of the Ministry of Magic.

There was a good reason for that. It was the Atrium. I observed, "Minerva, you're losing your touch."

We went to another hearth, stepped in, and repeated the performance—perfectly, complete with still being in the Ministry. We walked halfway down the corridor of hearths and picked one at random. There was still no joy.

She growled under her breath and didn't say anything. Instead, she, still holding my hand, dragged me off in the direction of Reception. When she reached Reception, the pleasant Ministry witch who was there asked if she could do something for us.

I had seen Minerva like that on only a couple of occasions before. I think they all involved Sinistra. Her eyes were focused like laser beams on the unfortunate witch's face. Her voice was tightly controlled. I was silently hoping that it wouldn't be as obvious to the receptionist as it was to me.

Minerva started off, 'My dear, you could help me by getting a service person to work on the floo connection in hearth number three. It isn't working."

The receptionist thanked her for letting her know and suggested that we try another, and then turned, hoping that we would go.

Instead Minerva said, "We did. Number four and then uh. . Wendt, what was the next one we tried?"

I was a little surprised by the question but said, "Uh. I think it was number fifteen or seventeen."

"Oh." The receptionist seemed genuinely surprised. I think that she had begun to grasp the significance of how angry Minerva was becoming. She looked around as if hoping to find someone that she could turn us over to. Not finding anyone, she seemed to be lost in thought for a moment and then asked, "Just where were you trying to get to?"

That had gone past Minerva's limit, "Well, if you must know, it was Hogwarts school, but how that could. . . "

The receptionist shyly was trying to interrupt—and succeeded! She said, "Well, that explains it. All the floo connections to Hogwarts have been blocked.

Minerva's anger which had been subsiding rose a bit, "What's going on? Why?"

"The Headmaster, you know, Mr. Dumbledore decided that with the problems with You-Know-Who, security there had to be increased. He's sorry for the inconvenience.

"You'll have to go to someplace in Hogsmeade."

She turned to me and said, "I'd personally recommend Ms. Paddyfoot's. It's so intimate." With that she blushed slightly.

Minerva wanted to know whom the receptionist thought we were. Her flustered reply was, "Well, Mother and older brother of someone at Hogwarts."

She turned and huffed away. I had to dog-trot to catch up with her. "You know Minerva, you didn't have to be quite so short with her."

Minerva only muttered, "Mother and older brother."

We took the floo network to the Three Broomsticks. Since it was about supper time here and roughly lunch time where we had just been, we had supper. We probably could have made the evening meal at the Great Hall, but we weren't in a rush to get back.

$\triangle$

The next couple of days we worked our way back into the routine of school: lesson planning, submitting text book lists to Flourish and Blots, and sending them to our students. For some reason that nobody knew— even the Assistant Headmistress—Dumbledore hadn't been seen at school since the end of the previous term. It didn't mean that he'd not been there—just not seen. And it wasn't really unusual for him to go on a junket, especially before school or just after. After all, there was the very capable Assistant Headmistress to cope if he weren't around.

But one evening meal, he showed up at the Great Hall. No one was especially surprised—except. Except that he favored one hand—a hand that looked like he'd been badly burned.

He gave one of his welcome speeches to teachers. He introduced the one new teacher, Harold Slughorn who was taking the post of Professor of Potions. Snape was, in turn, taking the post of Professor of Defense Against the Dark Arts. I commented to Minerva under my breath, "A marriage made in heaven." She schussed me.

Otherwise it was unexceptional until his closing remarks, "I know that you cannot have failed to notice my hand and are probably burning with curiosity about it, if you will pardon the pun.

"I will only tell you what you have to know. It will not affect my performance as Headmaster. It is not the result of an infectious disease. It represents no threat to either faculty or students."

"Are there questions?" He quickly added, "Good. Hearing no questions, the subject is closed."

I looked at Minerva quizzically, "You're Assistant. What do you know?"

She just shrugged and said nothing.

"In that case, I'm going to find out what's going on."

My first visit, of course, was to Madame Pomfrey, the School Nurse or Healer. She saw me coming and got up to meet me at the entrance to the hospital wing. "I know why you're here. You're not the first, and I don't know anything. God's Body, I wish I did. He won't tell me a thing."

"Come on. You're the healer here. Surely, he's being treated for that."

"If he is, I don't know who's doing it, or what treatment is going on."

The next day, I paid Snape a visit in his lair. "OK. What do you know about Dumbledore's hand?"

He looked up at me and invited me to sit. I did. He looked me directly in the eye with that steely gaze of his and said, "Nothing." It was a flat simple declaration. You might as well try to pry ten-penny nails out of a mahogany board with your fingernails as try to get information out of Snape that he doesn't want to give.

I tried anyway, "Snape, I know that you know something."

One corner of his mouth raised a millimeter and he said, "No."

I knew when I was beaten, so I moved on. I told Minerva about my failures. She laughed and suggested that Dumbledore had me foxed. That bothered me—a lot. I kept thinking about it, and an idea occurred to me.

One night, just before dinner, I told Minerva to hang around after the meal and watch what happened. She tried to worm it out of me, but I was having none of it. When the meal finished and Dumbledore started to rise, I came over to him. Minerva's usual spot is beside him, so there was no problem with her hearing what happened.

"Professor Dumbledore, how about telling us something more about your hand?"

He smiled and said, "I think I already covered that topic."

"Maybe, but I think you should give me a little more detail."

Now, a little wary, he asked, "And why would that be?"

"Oh, if you don't, I'll start speculating publicly about what's going on with your hand. You know that I've got a reputation for accurate guesses."

He looked at me doubtfully, "You wouldn't."

I just stared at him. He looked over at Minerva and asked, "How do you put up with him?"

She shook her head sorrowfully and said, "He is a trial."

Dumbledore sighed and nodded assent, "Let's go to my office, then." We walked off. We reached the stone gargoyle, but Dumbledore didn't have to give the password. It just rotated for him, and we went up the revolving staircase. As we entered his office, he absently asked if we'd like something to drink. Minerva asked for a chablis, and I a Johnny Walker. I was surprised that he provided it. We took seats around his desk.

Fawkes the phoenix was perched behind his chair. Dumbledore leaned back and proposed, "Why don't you tell me what your speculations are before I tell you anything?"

I was wary but agreed, "OK. First of all, whatever happened to your hand wasn't an ordinary burn, and it wasn't a simple curse. If it had been, Madame Pomfrey would have cured it, and if not her, then you have access to the best healers at Saint Mongo's. It would be cured or well on the way to cured by now.

"So, it's an extraordinary curse that caused it. Heck, you just fought Riddle himself a couple of months ago and came away whole. That's got to have been some really nasty magic. I don't think that the average Deatheater could have come up with it.

"You're not going to improve, are you? If you were going to, it would have started happening."

Dumbledore chuckled, "You answer all your own questions, why do you need me?"

"I thought so. Then, how long do you have? Surely, more than a few months. You wouldn't have told us that the year wouldn't be affected if you would be dead by then. So, it's at least a year. How much more?"

Dumbledore shook his head silently.

I said, "You don't have much longer." It was a statement.

He looked at us and said, "I'll tell you, but you have to make the unbreakable vow not to tell anyone anything of what we've been discussing."

Minerva grimaced, "Why ever?"

I realized why. "I know. You don't want the Deatheaters to know how little time you've got left. They'll waste time and effort trying to kill you and maybe give the rest of the Order of the Phoenix a pass."

He pulled his wand out and said, "The vow?"

Minerva held her hand out and said, "Take it. And hold on tight." I grasped her hand, and we overlapped.

Dumbledore brought his wand down and touched them. He recited the oath, and we repeated it. "I swear that I will not reveal to anyone the nature of the wound that Professor Dumbledore has sustained to his right hand until he's died."

As we repeated it, tendrils of light encircled our hands and tightened. And then, we finished, and the tendrils disappeared.

Only then, Dumbledore said, "It's worse than you guess. I'll be lucky to survive to the end of the year, but, Minerva, I should make it most of the way. I'm sorry. You'll have to take over at the end of the year. Forgive me for not telling you before now, but . . ."

There was a pall cast over the room and the conversation. No one had anything to say. I finally said, "Well, I suppose we're done." I got up and held out my hand to Minerva. A few tears spilt over her eyelids, and we walked down past the stone gargoyle. The world seemed a few sizes smaller that evening.

We had the problem that we couldn't say anything to anyone. Every time we saw Dumbledore we were reminded that we had one fewer day left with him as the Headmaster, to hear him practice his strange idea of a "word of grace", to know that the world was safer due to his presence.

The first day of school eventually arrived. The first feast of the term came. There were all the usual things—the sorting and the sorting hat, Dumbledore's speech, the fabulous food. And no one except Minerva and I had any idea that this was the last year with Dumbledore as our Headmaster.

The term seemed to proceed as happily as any had in years. The students went through the ritual of the year with real pleasure. Even the kid who seemed to have the most trouble being normal—Ron Weasley—seemed to have everything going his way. He and Potter got into Slughorn's Potions class. Weasley won the keeper's position on the Quidditch team. He seemed to actually have a young lady who was interested in him—although he seemed too dense to realize it.

Potter—always marginal in Potions under Snape—had seemingly become a potions genius. That was the most mysterious thing of all. All the teachers who had any intelligence realized that Potter's mediocrity in Potions was more due to Snape's prejudice than Potter's laziness or lack of intelligence. But this sudden outburst of brilliance was mysterious because Potter hadn't just shown his intelligence. It was something beyond that. His potions' life seemed as charmed as though he were taking Liquid Luck potion every day.

Potter was the heartthrob of every girl who was old enough to have a heartthrob. This was because he was rumored to be the "chosen one". If it were a confirmed fact, he probably wouldn't have been as popular, but that uncertainty seemed to be more of a motivation for young women of a romantic inclination than certainty would have been.

There was only one student who seemed beyond the reach of all the good spirit that seemed to be spread around as thick as molasses. That was Draco Malfoy. He seemed to be driven in a way that neither I nor anyone else had seen him. He had never been a great student, but he had a certain talent for magic that made up for his lack of studiousness. Now that had all changed. He spent more time in the library than anyone other than Hermione Grainger, but none of it seemed to have anything to do with his studies. When he wasn't in the library or classes, he seemed to disappear from the face of the earth. His grades had always been decent if not good. Now they seemed to plummet to barely passing.

I didn't have him in a class, but the Teacher's Lounge is always a hotbed of gossip—especially about students. His teachers were all amazed at the turnaround he was having—for the worse. Minerva confided in me that she was beginning to be worried that she'd have to call in his mother for a conference.

She was probably the only teacher who would dare do that. His parents had great influence with the Board of Directors of the school. Very few teachers wanted to give them bad news about Draco—even with Malfoy senior in Azkaban. Minerva didn't have to speak to his parents because he was doing OK in her class—not anywhere up to his potential, but not bad.

Astronomy

It was the middle of October, and things had been going too smoothly at Hogwarts for comfort. In the world outside the hallowed halls of Hogwarts a lot of families were having people go missing or dead. I heard things from the Order of the Phoenix via Minerva. Lots more people were going missing or dead than we saw in the *Prophet,* and there were far more Muggles dying than we heard about in either Wizard or Muggle publications. But in Hogwarts, everything was calm. The security around Hogwarts was serious and effective. I commented to Minerva on more than one occasion that it was bad Karma.

Anyway, it was possible to forget the sea of troubles about us a lot of the time. This was one of those times. I was doing lesson planning when there was a knock at my door. I asked the knocker to come in, and she did.

I was trying to finish a paragraph on a lesson plan for studying *The Rhyme of the Ancient Mariner* and didn't look up. I just asked her to sit.

"Well, this is unflattering." a very familiar voice said, "Don't you have anything more to say than that?"

I instantly looked up, and my frown grew, "Sinistra, just leave. I know why you're here, and I'm not buying any. The futures market on bad practical jokes and worse dates for the Halloween party has hit rock bottom."

"Oh, just listen for a minute. I'm not selling any produce in the future, and I have something important to talk to you about—something school related."

My frown deepened. "Just get up and go. Whatever it is, the answer is no. Fool me once, shame on you. Fool me twice, and shame on me. Fool me a half dozen times, and it doesn't even rise to the level of a bad joke."

"But I'm serious. This is about Malfoy."

That was a new angle. "Pretty good, bringing students in on it. That's a new low for you. I really have to give you high marks for creativity."

"Look you imbecile. Draco Malfoy is going to get booted from this school if you don't listen to me for a few minutes."

Well, I couldn't prove that she was making it all up, so I decided that I had to at least hear her out before bouncing her on her keester. "Go ahead, you've got two minutes to convince me that you're on the level about this."

"Wow, that's generous. OK. Malfoy has been having problems in lots of people's class, right."

"I've heard as much. Go on."

"Well, in my class, he's on the verge of complete failure. I've tried everything—lectures, tutoring, threatening to talk to his mom. I just can't get past his defenses. He seems not to care about anything. I need your help." This seemed to be a true plea for help.

I sat back to regard her more carefully, "Go ahead. Why do you think that I can help when all these other things don't?"

She released a sigh of relief, "Well, first, you're a male teacher. That makes a big difference for teen boys.

"Secondly, I know that you've already worked with him before —a few years ago. You seemed to have some success helping him with your class.

"Finally, you know the subject matter better than any other teacher here—male, female—heck, maybe even than I do." This modesty was most unusual for her. I was beginning to think that she just might be completely on the up and up. So I closed my eyes and thought for a couple of minutes. All her arguments were true. I supposed that she was being honest with me. Did I have the right to let him drop out because I was having a hard time with his teacher?

She cleared her throat, "Well, what do you think?"

I opened my eyes and saw that she was on the edge of her chair, looking down at her feet. I asked, "Just how would this work?"

'Oh, thank you!"

"I've not quite agreed completely to it, but just tell me what you think that I can do."

"Well, maybe, you two could start out with a couple of hours a week in two sessions. You could help him review and drill on the facts."

I nodded. At this level the Astronomy course was likely to be a straight memorize and regurgitate. "Is there any sort of lab work involved?"

"Yes, just using a telescope to find major stars and planets, but he seems to be OK at that. It's facts that he has problems with. His study skills seem to be shot to hell."

I nodded and began to wonder what could have happened to Malfoy that had shot his study skills to hell. "Look, Sinistra, do you have any idea why he's not studying?"

"You've got me. He shuts up like a clam whenever I try to find out what's going on with him. I figure that a man's got a better shot at finding that out. Do you suppose it could be girl trouble?"

"That's certainly possible. How long's it been going on?"

"All the term. He came to school in a twit and seems to not be able to get himself out of it."

"OK. How do you suggest that we go about it?"

She brightened and smiled for the first time since entering the room. "OK. I was thinking that we could have a three-way discussion with him and get him to agree to work with you. Then you'd start working with him one-on-one. Maybe you'd do it twice a week. Say, Monday and Thursday or Tuesday and Friday."

"OK. Can you get me a copy of your text and your lesson plans? And set up the first appointment for all three of us to meet. I'll handle the scheduling after that."

She jumped up and said, "Sure." She ran around the desk and kissed me before I could defend myself.

I just scowled at her, "Get out of here before I change my mind."

The next day, an owl showed up after dinner. It had a message from Sinistra. We were to meet the following Thursday after supper.

The day arrived, and after supper, Sinistra and Malfoy joined me before we left the Great Hall. We walked to my office, and I made sure that Sinistra had the Red Leather chair. She was about to speak when I interrupted, "Please, I'd like to conduct this meeting. And the first thing that I want to know must come from Mr. Malfoy." I turned to him and asked, "Why are you here?"

He seemed surprised, but he answered, "Well, because Professor Sinistra asked me to come."

"Fair enough. But do you know why she asked you to come?"

I expected a sneer and a sharp answer, but he seemed to be almost contrite, "Because she says that I might be expelled. Is that true?"

I could have given a dozen equivocal answers: in theory, who knows, it's a long shot, etc. Instead, I decided to be definite, "Yes."

His face fell. But he didn't say anything. He was looking down into his lap and had pulled out his wand but was rotating it between the palms of his hands.

I went on, "Do you want to avoid that?"

Some of his spirit returned, "Of course, I do. Do you think I'd be here if I didn't?"

I thought of reprimanding him, but I didn't want to push him right now. He seemed as forlorn as I've seen any student. Sinistra exclaimed, "Draco." but didn't say anything more.

I decided that some encouragement was in order, "Draco, you're a good student when you put your mind to it. I'll work with you as long as you work with me. What do you think?"

He looked up at me. There seemed to be a plea in his silent eyes. I pretended not to hear it. He agreed to work with me. We set Mondays and Thursdays to get together for tutoring. He left, and Sinistra thanked me for agreeing to work with Malfoy.

The first couple of sessions were difficult. Malfoy was unable to concentrate. We established that the class was studying stars. After several false starts, trying to do drills, I got him to start talking about what he knew about the subject.

He sat down, closed his eyes, sighed in resignation and spoke without looking up, "Well, stars are huge balls of glowing gas."

"Keep going."

He rubbed his eyes, "They are thousands of miles across."

I prompted him. "How large is our star?"

"You mean the sun?"

I nodded. He thought and then said, "one hundred thousand miles?"

"Good enough."

"It is?" Malfoy was genuinely surprised.

"Sure. The important thing is to know order of magnitudes."

He looked up, surprised, "What do you mean order of magnitude?"

"I mean that all numbers have a given number of digits. The size of the sun is six digits. It doesn't matter if the measurement is miles or kilometers. The size of a person is one digit – five feet, four feet, six feet – it doesn't much matter. Just so long as you know the order of magnitude."

"Oh, come on. Suppose you're in a fight with someone who's six feet tall, and you're only five feet tall. That doesn't matter!"

"Oh, it matters to you in a fight, but if you want to understand how things work, it's not so important. How long does it take to walk a continent? You're going to find that approximations are good."

Malfoy shook his head, but said, "OK."

"Go ahead."

He looked puzzled so I said, "Yes. Go ahead and tell me what else you know."

He shrugged, but then he had an idea, "They shine because they're very hot."

"Good. Keep going."

"They're hot because of . . of . . nu nu nu oh, some kind of fusion."

"You're right. It's nuclear fusion."

"Really? I was right about that?"

"You sure were. Keep going. You're doing well."

Malfoy still looked puzzled. "But what is nukear fusion?"

I was getting into territory that wasn't on the class syllabus, but I thought that it might be worth running down this path. "Well, tell me what you know about what things are made of."

Malfoy looked dumbfounded. "What do you mean, made of?"

Now, I was dumbfounded. I started slowly. "Have you heard of atoms?"

Malfoy shook his head.

"OK. Then, I've got to start with atoms. Everything is made of atoms. Sometimes, there's only one kind of atom, like iron, in something. Sometimes there are several kinds of atoms."

"But what are atoms?"

"Atoms. Hmmmm. There are about ten million billion billon atoms in a glass of water. They are made of three kinds of sub parts – electrons, protons and neutrons."

Malfoy laughed – the first that I'd heard that happen all year. "Don't tell me there are a million billion trillion electrons in an atom."

I chuckled, "No. just a handful. The number of protons determines the vast majority of the properties of the atom. There are only about one hundred different types of atoms but in combinations, they form the myriads of types of materials."

"OK. So, what has that got to do with nuclear fusion?"

"Well, the atoms have protons in a very small core, and the electrons spin around the core and take up most of the space of the atom. Atoms can join together and form a new type of atom – if you can force the atoms close enough together. To do that requires tremendous pressures, but if you can do it, there can be a lot of energy released – enough to heat stars to millions of degrees in the center and tens of thousands of degrees on the outsides."

Malfoy's eyes were the size of pie plates. "You're kidding. How is that possible?"

"I don't know. I just know that that is the way the world works."

Malfoy seemed to be trying to take it in. He was dumbfounded and seemed not to know what to say next. I decided that it was a good time to break and let him have some time off.

At our next meeting, I was afraid to open up the flood-gates of questions, but I did anyway by asking him if he had questions. Malfoy seemed perturbed and couldn't even sit down. He kept pacing about the room, seeming to want to say something, but he didn't say anything.

"Look Mr. Malfoy, are you able to work today? Should we call it a day and try again the next time?"

He stared at me and said, "No." And then more emphatically, "No. I've got to pass this course. Please help me."

The plea seemed to me to be not so much a plea to help with his studies but something else. But what? I wanted to find out. Resolving that problem might let him get back to his normal self, and then he could pass astronomy on his own. So, I asked, "Something's troubling you. What is it?"

He turned toward me and almost shouted, "Who told you that something's wrong with me?"

"No one. But you seemed to be troubled about something. It might be worth talking to someone about. What do you think?"

He blew a sort of quick laugh out of his mouth, "As if talking could solve m. . . uh any problem."

"I don't think that talking can solve your problem, but it might let you think about it in a different way. Sometimes that helps. What do you think?"

"I think that there's nothing that can help."

It was very tempting to try to force him to admit that he had a problem, but I dropped back. "Well, if you ever do have a problem, you can come to me and talk about it. I promise that I will keep it confidential and won't tell you how to solve it. That's your responsibility.

"For now, do you think that you could do some study?"

He seemed to think about it, but the question that he asked was, "Would you really not tell anyone if I told you a secret?"

It seemed to be a really serious question. I tried to be careful in answering. "Of course, I wouldn't, but I'd have to be sure that someone wouldn't be seriously hurt by my keeping the secret."

He had been staring at me, and quickly turned after I said that. He stayed facing away from me, and I eventually asked, "Are we done?"

He surprised me by turning back to me and saying, "No. Let's do some study."

I was seriously worried about Malfoy's secret. Was it just adolescent hyperbole or was he keeping a secret that was seriously dangerous? I'd have to work on that, but there wasn't anything more that I could do now. I went on with our lessons. "What do you need help with?"

"I've got to learn the different types of stars. You know: N, O, B. What do they mean? How do they expect me to know all these stupid types?"

"Well, the different star types are just different weights. The more that a star weighs, the brighter and hotter it is."

Malfoy nodded and added, "And the longer it lasts."

"Well, no. Actually, the larger it is the shorter its life is."

"Malfoy stared again, "How can that be? The larger a star is, the more fuel it has to burn. The larger ones must last longer than the smaller ones."

"You'd think so, wouldn't you? But the deal is that the larger stars burn much hotter and faster than the small stars. They burn so much faster than the small ones that the largest ones only last for a few million years while the smallest might last longer than the universe has existed – tens of billions of years."

"No. shit!"

"No shit."

'But how does that help me learn those stupid letters?"

I looked around as though I were afraid someone might hear. I leaned toward him. "Don't tell anyone but there's this little jingle that the pro's use to remember the order of star types from largest to smallest."

Malfoy looked around and said, "What is it?"

"Oh, Be A Fine Girl, Kiss Me Now."

"What!" He jumped up out of his chair and took a step back.

"You heard me, 'Oh, be a fine girl, kiss me now.'"

He stared and then smiled, "I get it. The initials of each word are the star types – O, B, A, F, G, K, M, N."

"Right."

He mused on that a minute and cracked a smile. We went on and reviewed some other facts and figures – masses and temperatures and life spans of stars. He got a lot of the basic facts memorized, and we agreed we'd continue where we left off the next time. He left with a smile on his face.

△

The next day, I visited Minerva in her office. "We need to talk."

She smiled and invited me to close the door behind me. Our discussion began with a quick refresher on snogging. Then, we reluctantly got to my business. "I've got a problem that I need your help on."

Minerva nodded, and we sat at her desk. "Here's the deal. I've been tutoring Malfoy in astronomy. He's doing awful in that course."

"Are you sure you're not helping her tutor him? Or maybe you're just tutoring Sinistra?"

"No. She thought he'd do better with a male tutor, and I agree."

"But he's scared. I think he's in some sort of genuine trouble. He almost admitted that to me in the last tutoring session. I think it's serious enough that if we don't get him to open up, somebody might be hurt – badly."

She stood and paced. After a while she asked me, "Just how sure are you of that?"

"It just makes sense. He's no genius, but he's done OK, maybe better than OK all through his years at Hogwarts. Now he falls apart? It's got to be something serious involving him in some kind of dangerous stuff.

"Do you have any ideas about how to get him to open up?"

She shook her head, "No. I never had much influence with him. Even Snape appears to be at odds with him. You're probably the last person whom he hasn't completely rejected- at least among the staff. He still seems to hang around Crabb and Goyle.

"I think that you should just not pressure him, do your tutoring and hope that an opportunity arises to get him to talk."

I was hoping for some new idea, "I guess that was kind of my plan. Nothing better to offer?"

"Nope."

"Well, I see him at least twice a week, so maybe something will come up."

She smiled, "You mean besides a certain part of your anatomy when you report back to the Astronomy Professor?"

"That comment doesn't rise to the level of conversation."

"But it does rise to the level of—oh, let us say—conjugation."

△△

The next day, there was a note in my mailbox from Sinistra. "Wendt, can I see you tomorrow? I want to check on Malfoy's progress. S."

I answered on the same parchment, "Yes. Any time after 3. W."

It was Friday. I didn't exactly fancy an academic conference late on Friday, but I couldn't very well refuse her. The day had been long. I was grading papers when she arrived. "Come on in." I waved her to the red leather chair. She sat.

"Well, Wendt. How is he doing?"

"I thought you'd be telling me that."

She seemed to consider a minute and said, 'Well, his average is still pretty abysmal, but I suppose you can't expect to raise an average in a couple of weeks. He's been getting pretty good marks since you started tutoring him. The last two quizzes were in the upper eighties. I have hopes that the test that we've got coming up the week after next will be as good.

"He seems to be more attentive in class, although he's still distracted at times."

I nodded my agreement, "I think that he's been doing well in tutoring, too. He doesn't seem to put in any time on study outside of our sessions, but he picks things up quickly when he's here." I decided to broach THE topic.

"Do you have any idea what's distracting him?"

She just shook her head. Then she added, "But you know, he still seems to be close to his buddies—Crabb and Goyle. They are thick as thieves when they leave class. When students start having academic problems, there are usually personal problems that cause them, but I can't see that he's at odds with anyone—except teachers.

"You know, Snape and he used to be pretty close, but I've seen him snub Snape as though he were the head of Gryffindor."

"Yeh, I've heard that." That gave me an idea for later.

We discussed details of what Malfoy was still weak at and her lesson plans for the next couple of weeks. After we'd been working for more than a half hour, I asked her if she wanted a drink.

"I thought you'd never ask. I ordinarily wouldn't, but it's the weekend now. I don't have any more classes before next week. I think I could use a stiff belt."

I reached into my lower left desk drawer and got out a bottle and a couple of glasses. I poured and handed one over to her. She asked, "Do you mind if I add some ice?"

"No. As a matter of fact, if you're conjuring ice, you might just throw a cube into my drink."

She waved her wand, and an ice bucket flew out of nowhere and landed on the desk between us. She got up before I could and used tongs to drop a couple of cubes in her drink and one into mine.

I raised my glass and proposed a toast, "To better luck with Malfoy."

She agreed and we each took a drink. It was bitter. I begged forgiveness and tossed the bottle into the trash. I reached into the drawer and pulled out a fresh one. As I did, I felt the beginnings of a change that was all too familiar to me. As I began to shrink, I snarled, "What have you done?"

She was unperturbed, "Oh, you know perfectly well what I've done."

I did. But I didn't know whom I was going to end up being. "Who?"

"Oh, go into your room, watch, and see in the mirror."

I did. It's hard to see anything while the transformation is going on, but once my body stabilized, the mirror told the story. I was Sinistra! "Shit. I'm you."

She called through the open door. "You should wear this. Otherwise, you'll be swimming in your robes." She handed in a set of dress robes that were obviously designed for a smaller and curvier figure. "You needn't make it sound so awful."

I was afraid to see whom she had become. I slithered into the dress robes, which fit pretty well—no surprise—and stepped into my office. There I was shocked to see myself—in a set of dress robes that she must have had from the last time she'd impersonated me. She whistled and said, "You look good.

"But I could help you with your lipstick or maybe your hair."

I just grimaced.

"Oh, just get out of here. You've played your little trick. How long will it take for this to wear off?"

She smiled, "But surely you're going to the Halloween party tonight?"

I gasped. I'd forgotten all about it. But no matter. I wasn't budging from this room, and I said so.

Sinistra didn't stop smiling, "Well, you can do what you choose to, but I'm going to the party. And I wonder whom I'll run into there?"

I knew perfectly well whom she'd run into. "You wouldn't try to, to spend the night with Minerva?"

"No, but she might just get the better of me."

I wasn't about to let that happen. "All right. You've got me between Scylla and Charybdis. I'll go with you, but I won't enjoy it."

"Whatever you say." He—or she—walked over and took my arm. When she did, an electric shock went through it. I'd forgotten that I had her hormones coursing through my system. She continued to hold my arm and gently pulled me toward the door. "You see. This won't be so bad."

I tried to grit my teeth, but somehow my mouth just wanted to smile instead. I tried to say, "Let's get going." with a snarl in my tone, but somehow it came out, "Let's get going." with an almost girlish lilt. I still couldn't seem to disentangle her arm from mine. It seemed to just pull her closer. My head was swimming a little as we walked into the Great Hall. I let myself be pulled onto the area that had been cleared of benches to form a dance floor, and the band played a slow dance.

I pulled me close and my arms encircled my waist. We started dancing, and I soon found my head on my/his/her shoulder. At the end of the dance, Snape approached us and asked the ersatz me if I'd decided to have a new girl friend. She started to answer, and I said, "No. This is just for tonight." And a freak twist of humor caused me to add, "One enchanted evening."

Snape laughed and started to leave. The band struck up another tune, and we were dancing again. I somehow just couldn't keep my head off his/her shoulder. She whispered in my ear, "How do you like the party?"

I couldn't stop myself from answering, "It's wonderful! Just WONDERFUL!"

After a few more dances, the band took a break. We found a table. I was terribly afraid that I was about to start playing footsie under the table.

Then Dumbledore came up and addressed me. "Well, Professor Wendt. I see that you've been foxed again. You might as well just enjoy what's left of the evening and pick up the pieces tomorrow."

He was right. There were likely to be plenty of pieces, and most of them would be parts of me once Minerva found out what had happened. To top it all off, Malfoy dropped by. He saw me or really Sinistra and asked her er me, "I've been doing pretty well, haven't I?" He turned to me and said, "See, Professor, I've been working. I really have. Would you consider not sending an owl to my mother?"

I gaped, realizing the situation that I was in. "Well, you have been doing better—significantly better on tests, but you know that you're still having problems in class. I. . . don't . . .know."

He frowned, "But I've really been trying."

"You can do better." Sinistra/me gaped at what I was saying, but that was just too bad. "I know that you can do better. And you might think about being honest about what your real problems are. You're not having problems in school all of a sudden because you're a bad student."

Sinistra/me was silently mouthing, "No. No." Malfoy didn't notice her signaling me.

I went on, "Until you start being serious with Professor Wendt, you'd better start counting the days until your mom has to be involved. And I don't just mean about your school—I mean, if you have problems outside school, you should talk with someone."

He stood up and glanced over at me/her and said, "I will work harder, professor." Then he walked away. I followed him with my eyes. A young lady—I think Pansie Parkinson—came over to him and tried to take his arm, but he shrugged her off. At that point, someone took my hand and lifted me up. The band had returned and started up again. I found myself pulled tight against her/me. My head was resting on his/her shoulder again, and I was gazing up into those haunting eyes. He/she whispered into my ear, "How would you like to do this again at the Yule ball?"

I found myself saying, "I would LOVE to." And I put so much emphasis on "love" that I was afraid everyone around heard. My knees turned sort of wobbly, and she/he had to hold me up for a moment.

"Are you feeling faint?"

"Only when I'm in your arms." I fluttered my eyelashes at him/her, hoping she'd notice. I sort of lost track of time then, but the band took another break, and we went to get something to drink.

As we were there, Minerva approached us. She looked directly at me and said, "I suppose you're proud of yourself. How did you get Wendt to go along with this . . . this charade?"

I opened my mouth to say something, but what was there to say? If I told her the truth, would she believe me? It was all so complicated that I decided to say nothing.

"Smart. Don't gloat. You may have won this round, but we're not through." Then she turned to Wendt/Sinistra and said, "I know that you were probably trapped into this some way. We'll talk later." Thank goodness, she/he didn't say anything either.

I wondered idly how long it would be before I started to transform back and start getting these blasted hormones out of my system. It wasn't that I couldn't resist the effects. It was just so tiring to constantly be fighting them off. I just saved my energy for fights that made a difference. It didn't matter if I sort of leaned on her or gazed up into Sinistra's beautiful eyes. However, when Malfoy was talking with us, and I could make a difference and maybe nudge him toward opening up, I had to be sharp.

Just when I began to think that I might have to spend the rest of the night as Sinistra, I began to feel the weird skin-crawling sensations that accompany the change in form with Polyjuice Potion. It was just in time, too. The band had finished, and there were precious few students or teachers still around. If it lasted another hour, who knew what I might do in her body. As soon as I felt it, I turned to Sinistra. "We've got to call it a night. I'm starting to transition back to my right self, and you will too very soon if you haven't already."

I could see that her robes were beginning to loosen. She must be starting to shrink to her normal height. She smiled, "Now this wasn't so bad, was it? You wouldn't mind doing it again sometime soon?"

"You mistake me for someone else. I'm amused by a practical joke as much as the next fellow—maybe more so, but I'm not excited to be target of one more than once a term or so. I'll send you your robes tomorrow. But for now, I'm headed for my office. See you tomorrow."

She took my arm, "Are you sure that you wouldn't like me to help you change out of that old robe?"

My heart strings twanged a bit as she said that, but the hormones were definitely dissipating. I didn't have too much trouble keeping a straight face as I shook my head, no. She laughed and said that we'd definitely do it again soon. I just kept shaking my head, no, and watched her walk off, a definite wiggle in her rear end, showing that she was well along on her transformation as well.

I jogged to my office, locked the door behind me, and slipped off the robes before I would have to cut them off. I tossed the robes on the back of a chair in my bedroom where I wouldn't forget them the next day.

Potions

The next day, I felt like I'd thrown a bender the previous night, although I'd only had the one drink and not a full shot at that. I decided that it must be the effect of having a pretty big dose of Polyjuice Potion. I'd never been transformed for such a long time before. Thank goodness it was Saturday, I'd have had a hard time performing in class. I walked down to breakfast. Each step brought some dizziness. Even standing still, my head felt like it was trying to expand out of its skull-case. In short, I had a hangover. I managed to reach the Great Hall without having to lean on the wall more than once or twice.

Luckily, Saturday and Sunday breakfasts are sparsely attended both by teachers and students. Of course, Minerva was there. She sidled up and joined me. I marshaled my resources for a defense of myself, but Minerva surprised me. As I opened my mouth, she just said, "Oh, don't bother. You know this thing with Sinistra has really been between her and me for a long time, now. You've just been an innocent bystander." And she added, "Mostly."

I decided that I was lucky to have gotten off this easily and didn't say anything. I just ate my poached egg and toast, succeeding in keeping it all in my stomach. Minerva could see that I was in some distress, and she did something a bit unusual. She patted my hand and said, "We'll talk later."

She was not the only one. The new professor, Slughorn, walked by and sat in the chair vacated by Minerva and asked, "You look like you were drinking more than pumpkin juice last night."

I managed to nod my head without setting off a wave of nausea.

"I thought so. Well, m'boy, I've got just the thing for you. It's Professor Slughorn's patented hangover elixir. There's no point in being a Potions Professor if you can't brew up something really useful, is there?"

I managed another nod.

"Why don't you come down to my office, and I'll give you the treatment?"

Of course, it wasn't an alcohol induced hangover. I figured that if it didn't cure me, it'd kill me, and it would all be to the good. So, I rose a little unsteadily and followed Slughorn to his office. He didn't waste words on me on the walk down to his office. He showed me to a chair. He got out his potion ingredients and set up a small burner to heat a small cauldron. He threw in water and several ingredients that I couldn't identify. After a few minutes it was boiling merrily and giving off an odor that I couldn't identify but which, at least, didn't send my stomach tumbling.

He turned off the heat, took out his wand, and said, "Frigio." The boiling stopped immediately, and he used a ladle to remove some and put it into a small tumbler. He brought it to me and said, "Bottom's up."

I held it in front of my lips for a moment until he said, "Oh, come on, it's not that bad. As a matter of fact it's not bad at all."

I closed my eyes and took a sip, expecting something that would empty my stomach with its disgusting taste, but I was surprised by the pleasant taste. It had a slight flavor of peppermint and was actually a bit sweet. I took the rest down and asked if I could have a bit more.

"Oh, you've had quite enough. That should do you."

And as a matter of fact, it did. It was near miraculous that my stomach was not at all queasy, and my head was not throbbing, though there was still a low order headache going on. I got up and said, "I think I'll have a little real breakfast if the meal's not been cleared."

Slughorn chuckled and said, "I'd hold on that if I were you. Best to wait for lunch. And, really, why don't you stay for a bit to make sure that you don't have an adverse reaction."

I shrugged and sat down again. Then Slughorn sat on a chair nearby and asked, "We've really not talked since I came back here. Why don't you tell me a little about yourself?"

I smiled at the thought and gave him the standard cover story that I'd developed and embellished over the years—my being a Squib orphan of a magical father. About being raised by Muggle relatives, going to school in Muggle schools through college and graduate school, coming to England, and applying for the post at Hogwarts. He nodded throughout and then asked, "Has it occurred to you that your story is not that different from Harry Potter's?"

I thought a moment and said, "Well. I suppose. If you can imagine a Squib Harry Potter whose parents were killed in a car crash rather than by the most powerful dark wizard in history."

"A car crash? Why weren't you all traveling by floo?":

"Oh, my mom was Muggle and she had some rather violent reactions to traveling magically. She sometimes threw up. I'm afraid that I've inherited some of that—not as bad, but I still find it very distressing traveling magically. So, my father agreed that we'd have a car and whenever we traveled with my mom along, we'd go by car if it was feasible.

"We were driving on a freeway and an eighteen-wheeler. . ."

Here Slughorn interrupted and asked what in the world would have eighty wheels.

"It's eighteen—not eighty and it is a slang word for what you call in England a 'lorry.'

"Anyway, the truck slammed into us, and the front half of the car was crushed. My parents must have died almost instantly. I was in the back, and the only thing that I remember—I was quite young—was the car rolling over and over again.

"I was out of the hospital and into my cousin's home in a few weeks."

I paused letting him take it in. While he was considering, I asked him, "You've come back from retirement. Why in the world did you do that?"

He sighed and said, "Well, you've shared some very personal things with me, I suppose I should reciprocate.

"Frankly, I wouldn't have come out of retirement if it hadn't been for the Deatheaters."

I stared disbelieving at him, "The Deatheaters wanted you to go back to work?"

He smiled at that, "Oh, not exactly. What they really wanted was for me to go to work for them.

"It was not too bad at first. They sent owls, once a week, pretty soon it was daily, and they had not very well-disguised threats. I had been trying to figure out a way to hide so that they couldn't find me. I went to Gringotts and pulled out most of my gold and converted a lot of it to pounds." He looked up at me. I guessed that he was expecting me to be shocked.

I just nodded, and he went on, "I have lots of influential friends. I bought them. They were students whom I thought were promising—bright or had influential parents or close relatives. I systematically courted them—rewarded them with friendship with an influential teacher. Gradually, I could reward them with more than being insiders at school. My students from before had become influential themselves, and I could promise—without ever saying anything—preferential treatment when they graduated–jobs, both in the Ministry and out, tickets to big Quidditch matches, their names in the paper, that sort of thing."

He pointed over to a table that seemed like a sort of shrine. It was covered with photos—individual and small groups of students. He seemed to have them labeled—the class of '75, the class of '81, which seemed to be quite large, and so on.

"But when I approached them for asylum or help in my need, no one was interested in angering Deatheaters. They were happy to give me advice and transport out of the country, but no one would risk their homes or families with my presence.

"Then I had an idea. I found out that there are things called teleophone directories. They have lists of Muggle travel agencies. Muggles go to travel agencies when they want to take long vacations. When Muggles go on long vacations, they usually leave their homes unattended.

"It occurred to me that I could hide in Muggle homes when the Muggles were away. So, I started haunting travel agencies. Literally. I made myself an invisibility cloak—disillusionment charm. I listened in when Muggles made plans for their vacations. I listed their names, addresses—out of the teleophone book, and the dates they would be away. The next day, I moved into the Zielewski apartment when they left for a trip to Malaga for a week.

"I bought Muggle food and kept it in their Rerigidairia. I stayed indoors almost all the time, and I cleaned up after myself at the end of the week. I even ran the vacuity-cleaner. The place was better than when I arrived.

"The next time, I added a little refinement. I decided that I ought to pay them some rent for using their home—but not a lot. For one thing, I'd been there the whole time they were gone. I was the perfect house-sitter. Their house was safer than when they were in it. Some people get paid to do that.

"As a matter of fact, one time, a Muggle robber tried to burglarize a home I was staying in. It was the middle of the night, and I heard a noise coming from the kitchen. I used the disillusionment charm and went to investigate. He'd found the jewelry box of the woman who lived there and had started emptying it. I used the petrificus totalis charm on him and levitated him out the window. Luckily for him we were on the ground floor. Oh, yes, I didn't open the window before I did that. I then used the repairo charm to fix the window. So, he lay outside the house for several hours frozen until the charm wore off."

I gaped at him. "You weren't afraid that he'd come back for revenge once he un-froze?"

"No. I used a locking charm to make sure that he couldn't break into the bedroom where I was sleeping. If he tried, I'd have done something more serious to him."

He then returned to his main story. "But I thought I should leave some little token of gratitude, so I hid a bunch of five-pound notes around the house. Some I left in plain sight—on a dresser near a photo. Some I hid pretty well, so they wouldn't be found for a while. You know, in the back of the sock drawer. I didn't want them finding them all at once and getting worried about what had happened in their house while they were gone.

"That went on for a long time. By the end, I got pretty good at it."

I stared him in the eyes, "Then something happened."

He nodded, "Yes. Something happened. But even before it happened, I was getting tired of that life. I was cut off from nearly everyone—both magical and Muggle. I was close to trying to find a way out, but before I did that, something happened.

"I was staying in a single family house in the submarines. That's what the Muggles call them, right?"

I supplied, "Suburbs."

"Oh, yes. Anyway, I was there, and I felt someone disapparate outside the house. I didn't have much time. I tried to make it look like some disaster had happened, and I'd escape by the skin of my teeth. I broke all the furniture in the living room, and I blasted a hole in the ceiling. I had some dragon's blood with. I spread it around. I was really inventive. I transfigured myself to look like an overstuffed armchair. I didn't have much time, but I thought that it would deceive your average everyday Deatheater."

Here he leaned over close to me and said *sub rosa*, "Most of them are none too bright, you know. Except when it comes to torture and murder."

I was on the edge of my seat, "So what happened, was it Deatheaters? Did you fool them and that near miss was what convinced you to come to Hogwarts?"

He sat back in his chair and shook his head almost wistfully. "No, it was Dumbledore. It didn't take him very long to uncover my deception. He detected that the blood was dragon's blood. That was the end of the trick."

"So, how did he convince you to come back to Hogwarts?"

"He had Potter along. He dangled Potter in front of me like a carrot before a mule. He knew that I'd love to have Potter's picture on that table over there, and he reminded me that the only really safe place in England was this school.

"So, I was then an official enemy of You-Know-Who."

I laughed for the first time since I'd arrived, "Oh, I think they thought of you as an official enemy long before that. 'He who is not with me is against me'. That's the gospel of Matthew."

He just frowned and said, "But when it's over, if He-Who-Must-Not-Be-Named is still around, well, I'll be in deep trouble."

I frowned then, "But, surely, just being a teacher at Hogwarts can't be any worse than just hiding out. After all, if you've not lifted a wand against the Deatheaters, what could they have against you? I mean, did you even know Riddle when he was a student?"

His head jerked up, and he stared at me. He slowly spoke, "Well, actually I did know him."

I smelled something funny, and I pressed a little, "If I walked over to that table and looked carefully, would I find a photo with Riddle as a student in it?"

He turned a shade of pink, 'Well, uh, yes. He was one of my students and a very good one. He was a favorite of several teachers. Yes, he was a member of the Slug Club."

I couldn't keep from laughing and could hardly talk for a minute, "Really. Riddle, the most terrible dark wizard of all times, was a member of an organization called, the Slug Club?"

Slughorn seemed to be on his pride, 'Well, yes. Remember, no one thought he was evil when he was in school or later. And, Slug Club was just what we called it. I thought it was a very logical name."

"I'm sorry. That was rude of me, and I didn't mean to offend you."

"Oh, no. no. That's all right. I have to admit that I sometimes laughed at that name, myself."

"But you didn't know he was going to be a dark wizard. You don't know anything that would be useful against him. You really shouldn't have anything to worry about."

Slughorn seemed to be squirming a bit. I wondered if there were something hidden that I didn't know about. I wondered if I could push him a little more and decided to try, "Do you think that there's something that you could dredge up from those early years that might be useful. Against him, I mean."

He hesitated and said, "Uh. I . . . don't . . . know."

I decided to take a chance and pushed a little further, "Let me tell you a story from my misspent youth."

He was a bit wary but asked, "You had a misspent youth?"

"Oh, yes. At least, I think so. Anyway, I was eighteen years old and had just entered a Muggle institution of higher education in the States called The Ohio State University.

"Like most entering freshmen—uh—First Years, I didn't know what I wanted to study. Unlike most entering freshmen, I had been good at school. I'd gotten good grades in all my subjects. I just didn't have a favorite.

Slughorn said, "We know what you chose."

"Well, it was a pretty close thing. I almost ended up in astronomy."

Slughorn took a little gasp. "Is that why you and Sinistra go out together sometimes?"

"That's another story altogether. Let's stick with the one I'm telling now.

"My high school math teacher wanted me to major in math or at least in one of the sciences if I didn't choose math. My English teacher wanted me to major in one of the humanities. I enrolled in math, a science—physics, French, and English. I wanted to sample them all at the college level before choosing. My first quarter, the English was composition. My second quarter, I took English Literature.

"It was a wonderful class. I had enjoyed the composition course, but I fell in love with English Lit. I got so excited by it that I would stay after class when I could ask further questions of my Instructor."

◁

Ms. Rumfield had just given us our assignment. As usual, I walked up to the front of the class to ask her a question. I almost always let any other students who had questions go before me. I had two reasons. First, I was shy, and I didn't want people thinking that I was pushing to the front of the line. Second, I usually had more involved questions or more than one question, so I thought that it was only fair that I go last and let the students with quicker questions have priority.

Today, I was the only student with questions for her. She was brunette with long shoulder length hair. She usually wore it so that it framed her face, and her bangs went from left to right and almost covered her eyes. She had deep-set dark eyes and full lips. "Well, Mr. Wendt, what can I do for you today?"

I had a hard time looking her in the eye. I sort of stared down at her desk and asked, "I had a question that's not really about our course. I just read a novel by a new author—Stephen King. I was just wondering what you thought about him. Have you read him?"

She leaned back against her desk. That was something that she usually did when she thought that she'd have a long discussion. "Hmmm. Interesting that you ask about him. I just read one of his books, *Christine*. I thought it was very well written, but I'm curious about you. I assume that you've read one or more of his books?"

I felt my cheeks reddening a bit and replied, "Well, I'd seen a lot of novels of his in the campus bookstore in the fantasy section. Frankly, I'd kind of gotten sick and tired of seeing that name. I'd kind of decided that he couldn't be that good. So, I picked one of the books at random and bought it. I intended to prove to myself that he wasn't very good. It was the *Shining*. I almost couldn't put it down. I finished it in a weekend. It was wonderful. He has such a descriptive talent that I could picture every single scene and room and person in the book as though I were seeing it in a movie.

"As a matter of fact, I think it would be really easy to make a movie of it because his writing is so clear, and his dialog so great that you wouldn't need a screen writer. You'd just have to have someone decide which paragraphs to leave out." I had somehow found that I was looking directly at Ms. Rumfield. As a matter of fact I was looking into her eyes, which I wouldn't have believed possible. That realization kind of halted me in my tracks.

Ms. Rumfeld was actually smiling. When I stopped, she twisted her head to one side in a quizzical expression, "Mr. Wendt, did I just do something funny? You suddenly stopped in your tracks. What you were saying was fascinating."

It took me a minute to realize that she'd asked me a question, "Oh, no. You're fine Professor. As a matter of fact, you're perfect." That was not exactly what I wanted to say either. "No. I just reached the end of my idea, and I suddenly realized that I didn't have anything else to say."

She nodded, "By the way, we're both adults. Why don't we drop the 'Professor'? I'm only an Associate Professor and just barely that."

"Uh. OK. Prof. . . er. . . Ms. Rumfield."

"We could drop the Ms as well. Your first name is James, isn't it?"

"Uh. Yes."

She stared at me a minute and asked, "Well, do you go by James or Jimmie or Jim or Slim?"

"Oh. James would be just fine. My mom insisted that Jimmie was just too puerile a nickname. She insisted on James. But then, what do I call you?"

She smiled a broader smile, and the world lit up, "You could call me Valerie, but my real friends call me Val."

All that I could say was, "OK."

She went on, "Now, it's interesting that you ask about Stephen King, because I just finished, *Christine*. I liked it very much as well and for a lot of the same reasons that you like the *Shining*. But, you know that he'll never win any major awards for his writing."

I gawked at her, "Why not? He's great! How come he hasn't won a Pulitzer or something? I don't expect a Nobel, but. . ."

"Oh, James, you are so naive. The great prizes aren't awarded just for great writing, which King has in abundance. They're awarded for 'meaningful' writing in certain genres. No one will say it out loud, but awards aren't for Fantasy or Science Fiction and especially not for Horror—no matter how well it's written."

"Oh." I was deflated by that. Somehow, I'd thought that writing prizes were for writing, and there wasn't prejudice about what the writing was about.

It obviously showed in my face because she punched me in the shoulder, "Cheer up. If you're thinking of winning one of those prizes yourself, you just have to choose a serious subject and write a realistic story about it."

That perked me up tremendously, "Do you mean, you think that I could uh. . ."

"That you could write a prize-winning story?"

"Well, yes."

Her smile seemed to brighten even more, and she even chuckled, "Have you been paying attention to the grades I've been giving you on your writing assignments?"

"Well, yes. Mostly A's, but I got A's all the time in high school."

She nodded and said, "A's in high school—even really good high schools is one thing. A's in college are completely different."

I was thunderstruck and could think of absolutely nothing to say. I think my mouth was kind of hanging open. She just asked, "Do you have another question?"

"I guess not."

"Then, I'll look forward to seeing you at the next class."

I left and decided that I'd write a really brilliant essay for the next assignment.

Ohio State is a really large school. It was amazing that I knew any of the students in my English Lit class, but one of the guys Ken Price had been a year ahead of me in high school. He sometimes asked me to let him borrow my notes from a class that he'd missed. He was in my dorm, and I saw him sometimes in the cafeteria.

Near the end of the quarter, I found him having breakfast. I asked him about an idea that I had. "Look, Ken. Ms. Rumfield has been a great teacher. Don't you think that the class should—well—take her out to lunch or something to show our appreciation for all that she's done?"

"You mean like giving me two D's on papers."

"No. She's a good, conscientious teacher, and we ought to do something."

"Oh, come on. She's ancient. She'd never be seen with a bunch of Freshmen and Sophomores."

"Oh, yeh." It seemed like anyone who had a Ph.D. and was a professor must be ancient, but she didn't seem stuffy. When I'd talked to her, she had a sense of humor and took all questions seriously.

Ken had been scratching his ear and then said, "Well, maybe that isn't such a bad idea. If we take her to a really nice place and spend a lot of money, maybe she'd give us a little better grade on the final. Yeh! I think it's a great idea."

I gaped and just stared. It wasn't actually what I had in mind, but I would take any help that I could get.

As the last week of classes arrived, I asked Ken again about helping me organize something, but he'd lost his excitement.

I was a basketball fan, and I went to most of the home games of the Buckeyes. I didn't have season tickets, but I could usually get a decent seat. That final week of the quarter, Ohio State was trying to get into the NCAA playoffs. I decided to go to the next to the last game on Thursday night. I had a decent seat on the upper deck close to the mid-court line. I took my seat early and was enjoying the warm-ups of both teams. We were playing Illinois. About ten minutes before game time, I had to get up to let someone through to their seat in the crowded arena.

I couldn't believe my eyes when I saw who it was. It was Ms. Rumfield. As she reached me, I could see that she recognized me as well. I said, "Profes . . I mean Val, what a surprise to run into you here."

She smiled that sunny smile and said, "Do you mean that you're surprised that I'm a Buckeye fan?"

"No." I was a bit flustered. "I just meant that I thought that professors would get better seats than this."

"What do you mean? These are great seats. We're close to mid-court and we're on the OSU side. What more do you want?"

Someone else was trying to get to his seat. She had to move on down and sat about a dozen seats away. I hardly paid attention to the game. I managed to get up and shout when everyone around me did, but that was all. I hardly even realized whether we had won or not. At half-time, Val had gone out to the concession area, and I just sat immobilized. After the game, I thought that I'd have to try to catch up with her and try to say something, but she disappeared in the crowd.

The next day was our last class before finals. After the class, a lot of people hung around and asked last minute desperation questions or tried to weasel out of her some hint about the final exam. Finally, the rest left, and I was left alone. I'd had the idea of asking her to lunch—even if it were only I. I had a silly made-up question to ask her before I asked the real question so that I could see how she might react to the real question.

She pulled her bangs back off her eye, "Well, James. You're not going to ask me one of these silly questions, trying to worm some ideas about the test out of me?"

"Oh, no." Somehow using her nickname now seemed awfully bold but I forced myself to do it, "Val. I would never do that."

We stared at each other for a minute, "But you do have a question?"

My eyes shot down to the floor, "Yes, I do."

There was another pause. I was trying to rehearse what I'd say. Maybe, "The class thought that we'd like to take you to lunch as a thank you for a great class." No. No. That wasn't true at all. Maybe, "I enjoyed this class so much that I'd like to treat you to lunch as a thank you." That was almost as bad.

Meanwhile the smile faded a bit, and she asked, "Your question?"

My heart stuck in my throat, and I realized that what I really wanted to say was, "Val, I've really enjoyed talking to you all these after-class sessions, and I'd really like you to let me take you to lunch."

But, I couldn't force myself to say that. What I said instead was, "Oh, I just realized that the question was stupid, and I shouldn't waste your time with it. Sorry."

She looked puzzled and said, "No. That's not a problem. I've always enjoyed your questions. They sometimes made me think hard. Frankly, sometimes, I spend the rest of the day thinking about the answer and wondering how I could have said it better. Really, go ahead."

My eyes were stuck on the floor then, and I just said, "No. I don't want to waste your time. I'll see you at the final."

She said, "OK. But if you think of a question that you want to ask, you've got my office number, right?"

I mumbled, "Yes." and turned rapidly and left. I never picked up the phone and called that number. I never said a word to her at the final exam.

"That class and those conversations with Val had decided my future major. I declared for English Literature the next quarter.

"Well, Horace, for years and years—through college and then graduate school and then over here for a while, there wasn't a day that I didn't regret that I hadn't asked her my final question. And even now, once in a while—like now—I think about that most deadly of phrases —'What IF?'

"I realize now that I was in love with her, and I wish to God that I'd told her that too. There are just times when you have to take a risk and speak."

I said no more. I was afraid to say anything more. A very silent couple of minutes passed. I got up and walked to the door, opened it, and walked out without turning around.

That evening, Minerva and I had gone over to Hogsmeade and had hot rum in the Three Broomsticks. I told her about the conversation that I'd had with Slughorn.

"Oh, don't tell me that you've got someone else who's keeping a secret. You don't have any idea what it is?"

"I think it has to be something about Tom Riddle, but I don't have the slightest hint as to whether it's serious or just some little nit that has Slughorn scared to death because he's afraid that the Deatheaters are going to come after him because of it."

She took a long sip from her hot rum and said, "Do you think that little story of yours will make a difference to him?"

"He seemed to be awfully downcast when I left him. I don't know. Did he take it to heart? Will it make a difference even if he did? You've got me."

After we returned from the Broomstick, we were in pretty high spirits and went back to my office. I locked the door, and we settled into some pretty serious snogging. I managed to get her bra off without removing her robes after quite a lot effort. She thought that that feat deserved a reward, which she could best bestow in my bedroom. We snogged our way in, and I was just starting to remove her robes when she happened to glance at a chair.

Of course, it had to be the chair over which Sinestra's dress robe was still lying. She suddenly turned totally sober. She walked over to the chair and said, 'I've seen this before, haven't I." She picked it up and held it up in her hands "Yes!! I saw it last night. This is Sinestra's."

I slumped down onto the bed. She threw the dress to the floor and turned to me. All she said was, "You and SHE last night."

I started to open my mouth in protest, but before I could put my foot in my mouth, she stormed out of the room. She slammed that door and the door to my office as she left.

Hogsmeade Weekend

The next weekend was the first of the weekends that Hogwarts students (third year and older) could make a visit to Hogsmeade. We'd had a rather heavy snow early in the year, and the world was painted white. The temperatures were close to freezing, so it wasn't really uncomfortable walking to Hogsmeade. Minerva had realized that Sinestra's dress robes were the ones that I had been wearing. She made the correct deduction that I'd simply taken them off and dropped them Halloween night. So she was willing to go together and have lunch at the Broomsticks before doing some shopping.

She wanted to get back early to do some grading, so I took the opportunity to stay to see if I could find a Christmas present for her early. I always have trouble finding Christmas gifts for her. I started at Gladrags. It was a trial. In the first place, there were two types of clientele that they seemed to cater to. First there were the haute couture people. After all, they had branches in London and Paris. Then there were the well-heeled student crowd. Neither were really the thing for Minerva and me. Better to stick with Madame Malkins.

Then I tried Scrivenshaft's which specializes in writing implements of all sorts. They have quills, various kinds of parchment, note-paper, etc. I arrived with high hopes. I actually found a couple of good products that would be fine as backups if I didn't find better or maybe as "surprise" gifts.

My mom had told me the facts of life with women when I started trying dating. The facts were: One, all women have things they want. Period. You'd better figure out what those are for your woman or it will be a long and tedious relationship you have with her. Two, all women like to be surprised occasionally by some little gift that she never realized that she wanted or needed but which somehow a true lover would figure out and find for her. These were "surprise" gifts. You could miss out on an occasional gift-giving opportunity and not come up with a true "surprise" gift, but it had better not become a habit. So, I made note of a couple of things that could be "surprise" gifts in a pinch. The really nice thing was that since Scrivenshaft's was in Hogsmeade, it would be easy to pick these up at the last minute in a pinch.

When you got beyond those shops, the picking became pretty thin. There was Zonko's gag shop, but that was really asking for trouble. There was Honeydukes, which was a really good source of candy that could be used–again–in a pinch, but was a dangerous shop for men whose "sweetie" had sworn off sweets. There was an antique shop, Artemus Ward's House of Antiquities. It was a long shot possibility if your young woman were a collector and had someplace to keep, or better, display the antique. That was not Minerva.

Then there were the various restaurants, pubs, etc. The possibility of gift cards or certificates had not occurred to any of them, so they were pretty much out. Although, you could take your woman out to those at any time, especially when celebrating a gift-giving opportunity. That was it. I'd gotten some information and started to head back to the castle. The day was overcast and close to sunset, but with the snow everywhere, there was still a good bit of light in the sky. It was a strange combination—almost a whiteout—with overcast grey clouds and dim white snow blending at the horizon (if there had been a real horizon in this mountainous area). I decided to stop in at the Three Broomsticks for a quick warm drink—maybe some hot chocolate.

I arrived and found that a lot of people had the same idea. I was watching the crowd—something that I like doing. There was a nice fire going in the fireplace. As I watched it, I noticed a strange commotion. A couple of girls were arguing about something. They ran out the door, and I wondered what had caused that. Of course, hurt feelings among teenagers–especially girls–is not strange. I finished my hot chocolate and headed back for the castle.

When I arrived, I found that they seemed to have brought their commotion in with them. I headed for Minerva's office rather than stop to ask someone what had happened. She was more likely to have real information. As I arrived, Snape had just left her office. He waved silently, and I went into the door he'd just vacated. "Minerva, what happened?"

She shook her head and said, "It was a cursed necklace. Katie Bell seems to have been imperioused to take it and deliver it to Professor Dumbledore."

I choked and asked, "What!?"

"Her friend suspected something was wrong with Katie and tried to get a look inside the package with the necklace. Believe it or not, they fought over it, and the necklace came out of the torn package. Katie tried to pick it up, and she was stricken."

"Wow. Do we have any idea who imperioused her?"

"Not really. We're pretty sure that it happened in the girl's loo but no one so far can identify anyone who went into the loo before her. Snape is interviewing people who were present, but it's a long shot that anyone will have noticed."

"Hmmm. Do we have a list of people who were seen in the Broomsticks when Ms. Bell and her friend ran out?"

Minerva stared at me, "Well, no. Snape is working on getting the list. But were you there?"

"I certainly was. I've been trying to remember who had been there. I'll get together with him." I got up and ran after Snape. I tried to find him at his office, but he wasn't there. I went down to his classroom and found him there.

"Ah, Professor Wendt, it's good to see you. I need to interview everyone who was in Hogsmeade within an hour of the event. You were there I believe during that period."

"Sure. I'd like to take part in the interviews. When are you going to do them?"

"I'm not sure that I want to have a suspect doing interrogation."

"What makes you think that you aren't a suspect?"

"Touche." He smiled for the first time since I found him, "Actually, I wanted you to help with interrogation."

"You bet your wand."

"At dinner I'm going to announce the beginning of interviews immediately after the meal."

He continued, "Oh, yes. Curious. Potter accused Malfoy of being responsible."

"Any evidence?"

"What do you think?"

"Nothing, eh?"

"As usual, Mr. Potter prefers his intuition to evidence and logic."

"He has a rather good track record, all the same. Maybe he has evidence that it's difficult for him to articulate."

Dumbledore was not in the castle, so Minerva did announcements at the dinner. Everyone who was at the Broomsticks when Katie Bell was attacked were to report to Professor Snape's classroom in the dungeon immediately after dinner.

There were about twenty-five people who showed up. We interviewed them. Snape asked questions, and I was recording secretary. I didn't hesitate to add questions when I thought it necessary.

I built up a matrix of names. Along one edge were the people we were interviewing. Along the other were the people that anyone had seen there. Each matrix cell contained the location where they were. There was not perfect agreement among the witnesses, but that wasn't surprising. There were a few people whom the students, I, and the couple of professors who were there couldn't identify. After we'd finished, Snape asked for suggestions.

"Well, let's talk to Filch." I suggested.

"Why in the world Filch?"

"Easy. He can tell us who from the castle had left the castle, but wasn't reported by anyone as being in the Broomsticks when the excitement happened."

"And you figure one of them is responsible?"

"Well, if I were going to curse Ms. Bell, I sure wouldn't let someone see me in the area just before or after."

"Sensible. Go interview him. I don't get along that well with him."

"Sure."

We had had it for the night and I'd start with Filch the next day.

I found Filch at breakfast and invited him to my office.

"Sure. I've not seen you much this year, Wendt. I hope you've still got some of your good whiskey."

I nodded, "Yeh. Let's go see what I've got for you. Oh, yes. Please bring up your list of people who went out Saturday."

We reached my office. When he was seated, I poured a couple of glasses, and we sat. "Let's see the list."

Filch pulled a roll of parchment out and handed it over. "I hope that's all the business that we need to do."

I nodded. Yes, let's just enjoy our drinks."

I was dying to get a look at the parchment, but I thought that I should just let us finish our drink and whatever conversation came up. Filch wanted to know what I thought would happen with Riddle.

"I don't know. You've got me. The last time around, there was Potter. This time around, Potter is still here. I guess we just have to hope that something good happens again. What do you think?"

"It'll be different. I don't know how, but it feels like something final is going to happen this time. Forget about that. Let's talk really important stuff. Where do you get this wonderful whiskey?"

"Well, that is really important stuff. You should really get out into the world a bit more. You know that there's a good spirits shop in Diagon Alley, but to get the really good stuff, you have to visit a Muggle establishment.

"Now, you take this."

"Amen." He enthused.

I raised my bottle of Dewars Whiskey. "This comes from the States—the state of Tennessee to be precise. You can get this at Muggle stores all over England."

He was all smiles.

Over the next couple of days, I interviewed every person who had been out of Hogwarts at the critical time BUT hadn't shown up on the list from my matrix who was at the Broomsticks at the proper time. After that, I corralled both Snape and Minerva, 'I got the list from Filch. Let's go review it."

We met at Minerva's office

"Anyway, I've got the list, and I did some more interviews, crosschecking it with the list from the people whom someone says was in the Broomsticks." I opened up my parchment with the matrix of people.

I'd added in the people who weren't in anyone's row on the matrix. "Let me summarize.

"There are about four hundred students at Hogwarts.

"Of those four hundred , there are about two hundred eighty who are old enough to go to Hogsmeade.

"On that day, about two hundred forty were at Hogsmeade sometime during the day.

"Of those, about one hundred forty were checked out at the critical time.

"Of those, about thirty were seen at the Broomsticks. Twenty-six were at Madame Padifoots. Thirty-two were at Zonkos. There were another twenty or so at the various other businesses at Hogsmeade. By the way, what I mean by those numbers is that at least three people agree that they saw someone for them to be in the count. There probably were more who were in one of those businesses who just weren't noticed.

"Of the remaining thirty-two, seven were occupied in a snowball fight near the shrieking shack. That leaves twenty-five. Twelve of them were fourth years or younger. I figure that it's preposterous that any of them could do a curse like the Imperious. Of the remaining thirteen, five were fifth years." I showed them the list of fifth years. "Do you think that any of them could perform the Imperious."

Minerva and Snape looked at the list and then at each other. Snape spoke first, "Most of them couldn't curse their way out of a paper bag, but I wouldn't totally rule Sanger out."

Minerva sniffed, "Sanger is a Gryffindor. He perhaps could perform the spell if he practiced it, but I can't believe that he'd do it. His parents are staunch supporters of the Order and Dumbledore."

I then pulled another piece of parchment out that had eight names in it. Three were Slytherins, two were Ravenclaws, two were Huffelpuffs, and one was Gryffindor. Minerva spoke first. "Not the Huffelpuffs for sure. Not the Ravenclaws either. I guess I can't rule out any of the others, but, really, I find it hard to believe that a Gryffindor would do it."

Snape didn't say anything. I did my analysis. "I see that Malfoy is still in the filtered list. But Crab and Goyle aren't. Interesting. Maybe Potter isn't that far off."

Snape spoke then. "Well, there are lots of possibilities besides these. It could have been anyone who lives in Hogsmeade. It could have been someone from outside."

I agreed. "Yes, that's true. But someone from the outside would have to have a confederate in Hogwarts who could suggest a target and supply information about their whereabouts. Of course, the outsider might have been using a disillusionment charm to protect themselves from view. Kind of risky though, skulking under an invisibility cloak in a crowded bar."

Snape was apparently unhappy. He paced and asked, "What do you suggest we do next?"

"Well, first, I suggest that we all pay close attention to the five names here for suspicious behavior. Second, come to think of it, I already . . ."

Minerva interrupted with her own comment, "I know whom you're thinking about. Malfoy, right?"

Snape whirled around rapidly, "What do you say?"

"Well, in case you've not noticed, Malfoy has been having problems academically—as though he were distracted most of the time."

Snape thought a moment, 'No, I hadn't noticed. He's been doing fine in Defense Against the Dark Arts. What classes is he having problems in?"

Minerva answered, "We're not at liberty to tell."

Snape went on, "So, you think academic problems are indicative that he wants to kill someone?"

It was like I was seeing Snape for the first time. I stared at him trying to penetrate his dark eyes and psyche. "Snape, you used to have a reputation for having a sharp and incisive mind.

"Of course, it isn't proof of anything by itself. Combined with other things that are going on in his life—this incident, his father being a convicted Deatheater, well, frankly, his being a Slytherin student—all add up to a pretty serious amount of circumstantial evidence."

Snape was quick to pounce on that, "I would have thought you would be the first one to eschew circumstantial evidence, considering how you regard Potter."

Minerva had been regarding the two of us and then turned her gaze on me, as if to say, "He's got you there."

I was stuck. "Well, all I'm saying is that he needs close watching, probably more so than anyone else on our short list. After all, even if the culprit doesn't kill Dumbledore, he very well could kill someone else. Actually, he came damn close to doing that already. Do you think that you're up to it?"

Snape looked away and said, "I'll do what's necessary."

Minerva said, "I'll watch the Gryffindor. What about the rest of the Slytherins?"

I quickly volunteered, "I've got Avery and Fischer in my class. I haven't seen anything unusual out of them, but I'll keep a special eye peeled for them."

Snape volunteered for the one remaining Slytherin. I suggested that we meet weekly at the same time and place. Of course, if something arose, we should get together ad hoc. I finished, "I just wish that Dumbledore were around more. You're great Minerva, but he would have things to suggest. Will you keep him apprised of this matter, Minerva?"

She agreed.

Snape just said, "I think that Dumbledore is dealing with very important matters."

Diagon Alley

Minerva and I had developed a habit of going Christmas shopping in November to get it out of the way so that we could enjoy the Holiday when it arrived. We left, as usual after breakfast and arrived at the Cauldron. It might as well have been occupied by ghosts. I didn't see a single person besides the ever-present Tom. Saturday mornings are usually pretty slow, but there's almost always someone there. I don't think I'd ever been there when Tom wasn't presiding from behind the bar. He just waved a hand at us. As we passed him, he didn't even look up.

I walked closer and asked, "You are still serving lunch, right?"

He looked up dolefully, "Sometimes I might as well not. Business has been pretty slow lately."

"Well, we'll see you then."

We went on through to Diagon Alley. As we walked through the magical portal in the brick wall behind Tom's place, I was now convinced that ghosts would be the only custom that Tom would be getting.

The last time I'd been to Diagon Alley, it had been bustling— even at this hour. Was that four months ago? No, it was more like nine or ten months ago. I remembered that five months ago, I'd not come to Diagon Alley for galleons for our trip. I'd picked some up at the branch of Gringott's in the Ministry.

Now, it was spookier than a ghost town. I knew a little about real ghosts, and they would have been an improvement on the sights that greeted my eyes. It seemed like at least half of the business were either shuttered or not open. There wasn't another soul on the street. I turned to Minerva.

She said, "I know, it's pretty gruesome isn't it? I've been here several times since you have—unless you've been traveling with a witch that I don't know anything about. The big change happened shortly after the announcement in the *Prophet* by the Ministry that You know. . ."

I interrupted her, 'Riddle."

"Oh, yes, dear. Tom Riddle. After the announcement of his return, some of the shop keepers simply closed up. Others started disappearing." She drew me down the street to what used to be Olivander's shop. "I think that Olivander was first. He was kidnapped right out of his shop in broad daylight on a busy day." The remains of the shop had been boarded up hurriedly. There were big gaps that let you see in through the broken glass. The shop was empty. Perhaps the wands had been looted.

"Minerva, was his body ever found?"

She shook her head and didn't say anything. She was holding back tears, but she eventually spoke. "When I was eleven years old my mum brought me here to buy my first wand. It was willow with a core of. . ." But she broke down again and never finished the sentence. After a while, she just said, "Let's go to Gringotts."

We arrived. My original intention was just to get some galleons out of my virtual vault. We entered. Minerva went to get someone to take her to her vault, and I started to get in line to make a withdrawal. Then an idea occurred to me. I ran over to her and caught her just before she was to start down, "Minerva, wait a sec."

"OK. What is it?"

"I thought of some additional business that I need to do here. You'll probably be gone well before I've finished. Why don't you leave when you've finished, and we can meet for lunch."

She shrugged, "Sure. When?"

I thought a second. Better to leave more time than less, "How about 12:30 at the Cauldron."

She nodded and was off. I returned to the concierge and asked to speak to a bank officer. The concierge asked who wanted the appointment. When I told him, his eyes widened and said, "Yes, sir."

I told him that I had a little virtual vault transaction to do. So, if he wanted to wait until I was finished before making the appointment, it would be OK.

His answer was a little strange. "No, sir. No problem. Do your transaction. I'm sure someone will see you as soon as you're finished. And if you'd like, I can handle the transaction for you myself."

"That's OK. I'll be back in a mo."

I found a line with only one person in front of me and was back in a couple of minutes. When I returned, the concierge said, "Good. Just follow me." We went back to an office. I'd been in the back offices several times before. This time it was Slubagg who was waiting for me.

He actually stood up and shook my hand when I entered. I was a bit dazed by that. He invited me to sit. The office was, as they all seemed to be, small. It barely had room for a desk, a few chairs, and a credenza.

When we sat, he opened a drawer and pulled out a sheet of parchment. He set it on the desk and pushed it over to me. I picked it up and looked at it. It was a simple statement of current balance for an account—my account. It stated that there were 10,000 pounds and 19, 250 galleons in the account. I stared at it incredulously.

The goblin noticed my surprise immediately, "Is there a problem, Mr. Wendt?"

"Well, I just don't understand the numbers that I see."

He released a sigh and nodded. "Yes, I'm sure you were expecting larger numbers, but you see, we haven't sent out the most recent quarterly statements yet. They explain everything. I'll give you the dragon's eye view.

"You see, you had so many galleons in the account that we thought that it would be bad to leave so many there. We transferred a good number to your vault. I don't know precisely how many offhand, but I think it was the majority."

My eyes must have bulged as much as I felt like they had because Slublagg looked alarmed again. I quickly clarified, "It's not that I'm surprised at how few galleons there are. It's that I'm surprised that there are galleons at all."

It was his turn to be surprised, "But Mr. Wendt. If you remember from your last quarterly statement, there were quite a lot of galleons added due to the implementation of your brilliant idea. It was quite a success. We've had to increase the number of galleons that we store at the branch in the Ministry several times to keep up with the volume of transactions there."

"I'm afraid I was out of the country and quite busy when your last quarterly statement came out. I haven't really caught up with all my correspondence from that time." Then I had a realization, "Did you just say that you removed more galleons than are currently in this account?"

"Why yes, sir. We had to make an assumption about how much you wanted to keep in the account. We thought that you would want the majority of the galleons to remain in your vault rather than be available in the virtual vault account. I hope that we didn't overstep our authority?"

I was trying to take in the enormity of it. I'd thought that I would get some income from my latest idea, but I'd no idea just how much it would be. While I was adjusting my thinking to this reality, Slubagg went on, "That actually brings up another point that we'd like to talk with you about if you have a little time."

"Sure. All I have is time."

Slubagg and most goblins don't have much sense of humor. He went on, "Now, this won't be a problem for a while, but I thought that we should give you a heads-up about a situation that's developing."

I shrugged. How bad could it be? "Go ahead."

"Well, sir. Your current vault—your real vault—is one of our smallest. Now that's rarely a problem, but you must realize that it's beginning to fill up." I was staring incredulously again. He sought to alleviate my worries, "Now, that won't happen for a while yet, but you must understand that it will happen. So, we were thinking that you might want to get ahead of the problem and sometime—maybe not right away —but sometime move your assets to a larger vault."

Well, this was an unusual problem to have. However, that wasn't why I wanted to talk with a bank officer, so I assured him that I would sometime—maybe during the summer. He assured me that would be fine. My vault ought to be large enough at least until then. So, I brought up my main reason for talking with him, "I have a question for you."

"Go ahead. Anything. I'll answer if I can."

"OK. I was wondering if you vault occupancy rates have been dropping lately."

He stared at me apparently dumbfounded for a moment and then said, "Mr. Wendt. Would you mind waiting a minute? I have to get someone to answer your question. This should not be long. Is that all right?"

"Certainly. We've got all the time in the world, right?" He stared at me again and then left his office. I wondered what was going on. It seemed like a simple question. After enough moments had passed that I began to wonder if he'd gotten lost or eaten by a dragon, he opened the door and stuck his head in. "Please come with me."

I got up and left with him. We walked further back into the depths of Gringotts. We reached a small waiting area that was tastefully decorated—by goblin standards. There were various heraldic shields on the walls. There was a jeweled sword displayed on one wall over the mantle of a fireplace. It seemed to be part of a display that was intended to have two crossed swords, but there was only one present. I idly wondered while I waited if this fireplace were connected to the floo network. After a moment, the female goblin who sat behind the desk noticed a light flashing on some sort of device on her desk. She got up and walked to the door into another room. She grasped the handle and said, "Mr. Glazblatt will see you now." She turned the handle and opened the door for Slublagg and me. He motioned me in before him. I had a bad feeling about it, but what else could I do.

Inside the room was impressive. It had dark wood paneling, an ornate fireplace, a long desk that must have been something like mahogany. Then I looked around the room from those main features and noticed that the walls were lined with a number of paintings. One drew my attention immediately. It was probably rude, but I couldn't help walking to it for a closer look. It was a painting of a ship at sea in a storm. "Is this a Turner?"

Glazblatt seemed amused, "Yes, it is. The 19th century pre-Impressionist. Do you like it?"

"Yes. Turner has always been one of my favorites."

Glazblatt smiled a smile that I would have called cruel had a human been wearing it, "Yes. You won't find that in any catalog of his works. We—uh—acquired it shortly after the painter executed it. The condition we required was that he never reveal that he'd painted it. All of the Muggle art here was acquired with that stipulation."

Slublagg had been hanging back, but now he introduced us. "Mr. Glazblatt, this is the wizard that we told you about—Mr. Wendt. He is the mastermind behind. . ."

Glazblatt interrupted him, "Yes, yes. I'm well aware of his services to Gringott's."

Slublagg went on, "This is the president of Gingrott's, Mr. Glazblatt."

I asked, "You're the president of this branch, right?"

Glazblatt answered, "No, I'm the president of the entire organization."

"Then, I'm honored indeed. Just what do I owe this honor to?"

Slublagg invited me to sit at the table. It was a conference room table, and I wondered why we had met here rather than in an office. Glazblatt sat at one end of the table. I sat next to him, and Slublagg sat next to me. No one was opposite me, but I soon discovered why. At that moment, the door opened, and two people were ushered in. I didn't recognize one. The other, amazingly, I did.

Slubagg got up, as did I. He said, "Let me introduce Mr. Ruugrat, the confidential secretary to Mr. Glazblatt and Mr. Weasley."

I smiled and interrupted, "No necessity to introduce Mr. William Weasley. I know him already from school.

"Mr. Weasley, I think that I never had you in a class, but I do remember your red hair if nothing else."

He stared at me and then smiled, "Of course, Mr. Wendt. You came to Hogwarts in my 7th year, I believe."

"Right. It's good to see you." And it really was. I felt like the goblins would be restrained from trying to take advantage of me in his presence.

Ruugrat requested that we all sit. He took the seat opposite me and Weasley the seat next to him. He explained why Weasley was there. "Mr. Wendt, you asked a question, and it touches on the most closely guarded secrets at Gringotts. We really would like to have a discussion with you about it. But before we do so, we need to make sure that Gringott's secrets are secure. So, we've asked Mr. Weasley in to administer the Unbreakable Vow to you."

He turned to Weasley and said, "Go ahead."

I stood and said, "Wait one minute. I'm not taking an Unbreakable Vow before understanding what I'm committing to. And maybe I won't take the vow even then."

Ruugrat looked at Glazblatt who nodded almost imperceptibly. Then he said to Weasley, "Please simply read the non-disclosure oath to Mr. Wendt." Weasley pulled a roll of parchment out of his robes, unrolled it, and began reading.

The gist of it was that I agreed to never reveal anything of Gringotts that I learned either in confidence or otherwise on pain of—well, you know what the pain is. When he'd finished I raised objections. "Well, first, I'm not going to swear to that without some alterations."

Weasley directed a quick smile toward me and then got out his quill to take notes. Ruugrat cautiously asked, "Just what alterations?"

I leaned back and thought a moment and then started ticking off points. First, this didn't apply to any information that might indicate or to a reasonable person might indicate that laws might be broken. What laws? The magical laws of England and all other countries where Gringotts conducted business. Glazblatt rolled his eyes. But I added more —or the Muggle laws of England and any other countries where Gringotts conducted business. More eye rolling. Then I added more. This didn't apply to any publicly known information about Gringotts—like from newspaper reporting, Gringotts advertising, etc.–or any information that could reasonably be deduced from publicly known information. Glazblatt's countenance fell. Weasley couldn't prevent the corners of his lips from rising.

But then I added my *piece de resistance*. "It only applies while I have any sort of commercial arrangement with Gringotts." With that Glazblatt got up, pounded his fist on the table, but didn't say anything. Weasley flashed a rapid blazing smile and then reverted to dour.

I simply said, "Those are my terms. Take them or leave them. It's getting late, and I have pressing business elsewhere."

Glazblatt looked at Slubagg and said, "I see what you mean." Then he turned to me, "Mr. Wendt, I'll agree to those terms. Mr. Weasley, please incorporate those terms in the oath."

I inserted, "And read them to me first."

"Yes, yes. We all need to hear them first."

Weasley worked furiously for a couple of minutes and then read through the revised oath slowly and at points haltingly as he discerned his own rapid hand-writing. He had done a good job because none of us had any corrections.

"Well, Mr. Wendt, are you finally going to take the oath?"

"Yes."

Then Glazblatt took my forearm with his hand, and I took his. Weasley read the oath slowly while applying his wand to my hand. Cords of cold fire encircled Glazblatt and my arms and hands. They tightened slowly with each word. By the time the final words were approaching, my arm was pulsing in agony. A strange thing happened then. The coils of fire dissipated.

Ruugrat exclaimed, "What happened, you hadn't finished!"

Weasley scratched his head. "I've never seen that happen before. It was a very complex oath. I think it must have been too complex for the spell."

Ruugrat looked to Glazblatt who looked to Weasley. Weasley just said, "No, I'm sure the oath isn't effective. Sorry."

At last it was over, and I had tried to swear the oath. With that, Ruugrat dismissed Weasley. He walked around the table, past me. He patted me on the shoulder and whispered. "See you when you leave." I nodded as imperceptibly as I could.

Then I said, "I'll swear by my honor to that oath."

Glazblatt watched Weasley leave the room and after Weasley was gone, and the door shut said, "I guess we've got to accept your personal oath. Now, Mr. Wendt. You want to know about vault occupancy rates?"

"Yes, I want to know if they've dropped recently."

Slublagg looked at Glazblatt and said simply, "See." I couldn't read his expression, but it was one that I'd not seen on a goblin before.

"Just why do you think that they'd dropped?"

I was rather amazed at the question, "Isn't it obvious. Do you ever come into Gringotts from the street?"

He nodded cautiously as though it were a trick question, "Occasionally."

"Well, then it should be obvious that commerce is falling apart. My original guess was that half of the businesses on the street are closed. It's probably not that bad, but I don't see how some of those businesses are keeping their commercial vaults.

"But I would think that that would just be the tip of the iceberg. There are personal vaults. You must be aware that it's widely accepted now that Tom Riddle. . ."

Glazblatt interrupted me, "Who?"

"Oh, I guess you know him as He-Who-Must-Not-Be-Named or maybe the Dark Lord or some such tripe."

Everyone in the room stared at me incredulously, but I went on. "Those businesses are closed because everyone is afraid of Riddle.

Everyone who has resources is hunkering down and preparing to run for the most distant spot they can find. They don't want their gold locked away in a place where they have to come out in public to get it."

Another idea occurred to me. "I'll bet that a lot of them are going to try to pretend to be Muggles and lose themselves in the hordes of them. I'll bet that you've had an awful lot of galleons converted to Muggle money lately." There were uncomfortable glances exchanged between faces in the room.

Glazblatt asked, "How do you know this?"

"Oh, come on. It just makes sense. Aren't you Goblins making preparations in case Riddle takes over the government?"

There were more uncomfortable stares around, but no one said anything.

I went on, "Well, for people whose livelihoods depend on commerce, you guys seem to be awfully complacent about the end of your business."

Glazblatt was scratching his nose on its bridge. He interrupted that to say, "Business will go on."

"Sure it will. It's just that the only vault holders will be Deatheaters. You'll get LOTS of vault rent that way." I was practically sneering.

Glazblatt asked, "Well, let's suppose you're right. What can we do about it?"

This was a question that I'd not been surprised about, but I didn't have a great answer for. "Well, to start with—and this is a pretty small start—you could support the Order of the Phoenix in any way you can."

"You mean with gold?"

"Of course, with gold, but that's only a beginning and a small beginning. You have brains. You can think of ways to oppose Riddle and the Deatheaters."

Glazblatt's face cleared some of the ruddy tint that it had taken on. "That brings up a point that I've thought that we needed to talk with you about for a while. Now that you've taken the oath, it's a good time to bring it up."

What could he be referring to—"You're not talking about my getting a bigger vault?"

For the first time Glazblatt laughed, "No. No. Let me explain. I have to provide you some history of Gringotts first.

"About seventy years ago, we instituted a change in the management of Gringotts. We brought in a Muggle consultant. We instituted a new sort of management structure. At the top was. . ."

I interrupted, deciding to make a guess based on a hunch, "A Board of Directors. That's it, isn't it? You instituted a Board of Directors."

Glazblatt's face turned ashen. Slubagg shrugged and Ruugrat's face showed anger. Glazblatt exclaimed to the room in general, "Is there nothing about Gringott's that's a secret from this, this Squib!"

Then he turned to me, "Yes. We have a Board of Directors. The idea is to get a diversity of good opinions to help run the company. All of them are from outside Gringotts. None has more than a very small stake in Gringotts."

I asked the next reasonable question, "Who are they, and what are their backgrounds?"

Glazblatt's answer was knee-jerk reflex, "That's a secret."

"In the first place, you've got my personal oath that I won't reveal this information. In the second place, one of the virtues of Boards of Directors is that they are openly known "

Glazblatt shrugged resignedly and said, "I won't tell you their names. They probably wouldn't mean anything to you anyway. One is a skilled artist. He makes the finest swords that exist. Another is the head of a security company. Another runs a liaison group between Goblins and the Ministry. Another runs a newspaper that caters mostly to Goblins, *The Goblin Gabbler*." I resisted the urge to laugh. He mentioned another whose occupation defied my understanding.

I commented on what I'd just heard. "Well, one of the real virtues of a good Board of Directors is diversity. You seem to have a modest diversity in occupations, but you've missed a major aspect of diversity—cultural and ethnic diversity. You know, Wizards, witches, maybe even Centaurs and Muggles."

Glazblatt smiled that avaricious smile again for a second, and I suspected that something was coming that I needed to be careful of. "Mr. Wendt, you've given us some very good advice over the last couple of years. I've been thinking of nominating you to join our Board of Directors at the next annual meeting. What do you think of that?"

I thought carefully. I was sure there was some sort of catch in it. "Well, I'm very flattered. I have a question or two."

Glazblatt was wary, "Go ahead."

"Well, first, I think I've heard that some Boards have different classes of members. Some have full rights—can vote, make motions, and so forth. But other classes have fewer rights—maybe can only be present, speak, etc. Would I have full rights as a member?"

Glazblatt didn't look me in the eye and mumbled. "You'd have full rights to attend and speak and even make motions, but you couldn't vote."

"NO thank you. I'm not interested."

"But no one but goblins has ever been on the Board. This is historic. You can't turn it down like that. I'm going to nominate you anyway, and you will probably be elected. Why, you would be a three-for"

"A three-for?" I asked with some amusement.

Ruugrat answered for Glazblatt, "Of course, one you are in education—a first for us. Second, you are a wizard—another first. And finally, you're a Squib—that is almost a Muggle and therefore the third. A three-for."

I clarified my position. "A Muggle general of the United States Army by the name of William Tecumseh Sherman once said it very well, 'If nominated I will not run. If elected, I will not serve.'"

Glazblatt gnashed his teeth, "The salary is really good. Directors are paid 1000 galleons per meeting."

"I'm sure it is really good, especially if calculated on a per hour basis. But I'm not going to be there just to stand in for you to make the motion that measures be taken against Riddle. If it fails, you don't get blamed for it. If it succeeds, then all the better for you.

"No. I'll make that motion if I'm elected, but I'll only make it if I'm a full Director—not some assistant suggester director."

He didn't say anything more but sat looking up at the ceiling to his right and finally said, "I'll nominate you to be a full Director at the annual board meeting, which will be February 13, 1998. If you're elected, you'll be able to attend the next regular quarterly board meeting, which should be sometime in May."

"Will I be able to attend the February meeting?"

"No. Non-Board Members are never allowed to attend Board meetings."

I shook my head, "I'd think about calling a special meeting for earlier if I were you. You may not have until May."

Glazblatt looked at me in surprise. "You don't think that Lord. . . er. . . Riddle will have won by then?"

"I don't know when or if he'll win, but I wouldn't waste time getting myself on the right side of this fight."

Glazblatt squinted, "You mean the winning side?"

"No, I mean the right side."

We seemed to have run out of topics, but I decided to fire one last parting shot. "This is a nice Boardroom. I look forward to meeting here in a few months."

Glazblatt shot a glance at Slublagg as if to say, "See what you've brought down on us." But he didn't say anything.

We departed by common silent consent.

△

Minerva had left Gringott's and proceeded to her favorite shop in Diagon Alley. Madame Malkin's always had the latest fashions and—more importantly—had fashions that a woman of a certain age could wear and feel that she had a certain fashion of her own—a classic fashion that remained admired through all the whims of the moment.

When Minerva entered the shop, Madame Malkin welcomed her with triple joy. Most importantly, they were friends. They were both women of a certain age because the sorority of such women has great mutual loyalty and friendship. Second, she was a good customer—something not to be valued lightly. Third, when she came her particular friend was likely not to be far behind—Mr. Wendt. Wendt was a good customer too—both in his own right and as someone who could be depended on to purchase nice gifts for Minerva. Also, Wendt was proof of a fact that all women of a certain age wanted occasional proofs, that is, that there was still hope of romance for that sorority. Why, Minerva had even intimated on more than one occasion that Wendt had proposed to her and proposed to her passionately. Madame Malkin could not understand completely why Minerva hadn't accepted any of those proposals.

Of course, it was true that such a marriage would be regarded with suspicion on all sides—suspicion that he had an ulterior motive and that she had "encouraged" that proposal in some unfair manner. There would be suspicion that a woman of a certain age was making a fool of herself. However, there would also be suspicion in certain quarters that such things were possible—for any woman.

In any case, Madame Malkin greeted Minerva with all the warmth that was possible. They gossiped a few minutes about Hogwarts and the suspected romances that flared up and cooled. Then they got down to serious talk.

"Minerva, what about you? Do you have any news of a, well, a matrimonial nature?" Madame Malkin wished the greatest happiness for her friend and was sure that it lay in the arms of her lover.

"Now, now, Maude, you mustn't talk that way. The world we live in is far too dangerous for everyone and especially for people who openly oppose Tom Riddle. Both James and I are known enemies of him. I would not start a life together under such unfavorable conditions."

Maude tsched, "Minerva, what better time to start an alliance than when allies are dear and loves are dearer still?"

The discussion continued, interrupted by other customers. In the breaks in the conversation, Minerva browsed and tried on a set of robes and looked at other things. When Maude had finished with the last customer, Minerva announced, "I've made some decisions. I'm going to buy this." She indicated an item.

Madame Malkin smiled, "A black negligee. I hope that someone will see you in that."

"Now, now. That's my lookout. I also really like this set of robes."

"Yes. Green is usually your color. But, along with your green eyes, this red robe should be quite Christmassy, don't you think."

"I think that it would be a good suggestion for someone who was looking for a present, don't you think."

They both laughed, and Madame Malkin wrapped up the one item and set aside the other for later. Minerva noticed the time and announced that she was already a little late for an appointment and that she should go immediately. "Don't worry, I'll ship the item to Hogwarts."

Minerva hurried to the Cauldron. She couldn't see how she could be less than fifteen minutes late. She arrived and searched the great room for Wendt, but couldn't find him. She asked Tom whether he'd shown up and gotten a table.

"I haven't seen him since the two of you arrived. And, if he doesn't hurry up, I'll close the kitchen. We're almost to the end of the lunch hour."

"Oh, Tom, when have you ever closed the kitchen so early?"

"Ever since the trade has fallen off so much at the beginning of summer. It almost doesn't pay to open the kitchen at all."

"But you'd fix something for old regular customers, wouldn't you?"

His frown broke into a smile. "Well, for very old customers, I suppose I could stretch a point, but only so far. If he's not here by 1:30, he'll be out of luck."

"I can't imagine that he'd be that late!"

But one o'clock came and went and then 1:15 and then 1:30 and still no Wendt. Minerva decided that she must go looking for him. She went directly to Gringotts. She couldn't get anyone to admit that Wendt had been there at all, let alone that he was still in his vault or in the offices. After a lengthy argument with the concierge in which she tried to convince him to send for Wendt, she decided to camp out until he showed up or they tossed her out.

Fortunately, his business finished shortly after 2 PM. As he left the back rooms, she immediately spotted him and strode purposefully to meet him. "What have you been doing? I was afraid I was going to have to get an auror because you'd been kidnapped."

He was overwhelmed by the hug she gave him as she made this declaration. He laughed, "You'd think that I'd just come back from a polar expedition."

She hustled him out of Gringotts and led him to the Cauldron. He expressed joy, "Good. I'm famished. It's hard and hungry work dealing with Goblins."

I was looking forward to some of the Cauldron's famous pea soup, but after we took a table, Minerva broke some bad news, "Tom closes the kitchen these days at one. I was lucky to talk him into keeping it open to 1:30. Sorry."

"Oh, don't be. I was exaggerating, but I wouldn't mind having something to drink." Just then Tom showed up with a couple of roast beef sandwiches.

"I'm sorry. The kitchen is closed, but I made a couple of sandwiches just in case. What would you have to drink?"

We both agreed on ale. We both needed some substance in addition to the sandwiches. After he'd delivered the ale, Minerva started the inquisition, "What in the world were you doing so long in Gringotts. Had they lost your gold?"

"No. I have to admit that I can't tell you a lot. You see, I had to take a Personal Oath not to reveal what I learned."

She shook her head mournfully. "Will you never learn about goblins?"

"Oh, it's not all that bad. I gave myself lots of escape hatches. You can deduce what you will from that fact."

"Well, what can you tell me?"

I thought carefully a minute. "Well, I've got a lot more gold in my vault than I expected. I think that good things will come out of the business arrangements that I have with the goblins. I guess that's it."

We both ate and drank as she chewed on that information. "Well, Wendt have you had your fill of Diagon Alley yet?"

"No. I came here to do some shopping, and I'll not be denied by the goblins of Gringotts."

Minerva laughed at that. "I'd suppose they would be the last ones to deny commerce, but I might be wrong. I'll tell you what. Let's take another two hours and then return to Hogwarts. No later!"

I agreed, and we separated to do our separate shopping. The first place that I went was Madame Malkins to look for something for Minerva. Her shop was empty, and she immediately came up to help me.

"I'm looking for a Christmas gift for. . ."

She interrupted me, "Minerva?"

I couldn't help smiling, "Yes."

She said, "Well, feel free to browse, and when you need help, ask."

I did. Witches' robes fall into three broad categories—casual, work, and dress. Minerva mostly had professional robes with a couple of dress robes for special occasions. So, I decided that I'd extend her wardrobe to include something for casual wear. Knowing that her favorite color was green, I had to find something in green that was casual. After some searching I thought that I'd found something good, so I found Madame Malkin and showed it to her.

She looked at it, nodded, and asked what size. I immediately replied what I knew to be true (from perusing Minerva's wardrobe)—size eight. She nodded sagely and said, "You've got the size right."

"Uh oh. That means that the robes are wrong."

"Right. I have this feeling in my bones that she'd like something more like this." She went behind the checkout counter where there were several sets of robes hanging—some in garment bags and some not. She pulled one of the robes off the rack and displayed it to me.

"But that's red."

Madame Malkin nodded sagely and said, "Very observant."

I began to catch on, "You have inside information, don't you?"

She nodded again, and I said, "Well, it sort of defeats the purpose of having Christmas be a surprise."

She leaned toward me and said, "There's still a way to have a surprise Christmas for her."

"So."

"You could accessorize."

"You mean like shoes or jewelry or . . . "

"Perhaps a smart handbag—in red."

"Yes. That sounds good. I'm sure you've got something nice."

She motioned me to follow her, and we wound our way to a display of handbags. I started to reach for a red one, but she shook her head. I tried another. She nodded at that. We went back to the checkout to complete the purchase. She offered gift wrapping and home delivery. I elected to have it delivered to Minerva's sister.

Having had such good luck with Minerva, I decided to try her sister. Madame Malkin shook her head, "She doesn't do business here. I don't know what to suggest for her."

"How about their aunt Beryl?"

"AH! Now there's a different story. She likes fancy hats. She admired that one that you bought for Minerva a couple of years ago."

"Do you still have it or something like it?"

"I think I do." She went into the back room and brought out a box which, when opened, revealed the mate to Minerva's.

"I'll take it. Please gift wrap it and send it to her sister's as well." This was turning out to be an easy Christmas shopping year. I'd still have to get a couple of little "surprise" gifts for all three, but that would be easy.

I thought that I knew just the right spot to shop for those. I quickly found it and entered with a certain amount of trepidation. After all what could one expect in a business owned and operated by the Weasley twins—Weasley's Wizard Weazes. As I entered, I found that there were very few customers in the shop.

Both Weasleys came up and greeted me, "Well, look what the dragon dragged in. Professor, you haven't come to rescind our diplomas." said Fred.

"Oh, no. We never got diplomas!" George exclaimed.

"No such luck. I'm here as a customer. And I must say that this is the only cheery spot on Diagon Alley."

"Isn't it the truth?"

"What I came for was a few small stocking-stuffers for a few young witches."

Fred smiled, "Don't tell me you're molesting the 6th years again?"

George laughed, "No. They're too sophisticated for his style."

"All I'm looking for is a few nice novelties. By the way, it looks pretty quiet in here for a Saturday afternoon. How are you boys doing?"

"Not as bad as it looks. We have a pretty thriving owl post business. People these days like the convenience," said George.

"And the safety of shopping from their homes." added Fred.

"Well, I'm glad to hear that. Now, I hope you have some non-gag gifts that would be appropriate for women of a certain age."

"Oh, yes. We cater to all parts of the trade. We have a line of household homemaker helper items. You know—things like self scouring pots and pans, Self-correcting spell-check quills, self-erasing tablets, and so on."

"And they're all on the up and up and really work and don't blow up in your face?"

"We have those varieties too if you want them." said George.

"JUST kidding." corrected Fred.

"Special discount for former teachers?"

"Yes. For you everything in the store is 25% off." said Fred.

"Of course, for everyone else, we're having a storewide 40% off sale." added George.

"Thanks. Just get me to the right corner of the store, and I'll browse. That is safe, isn't it?"

"We haven't lost a customer yet."

"Of course, we've not had any Squibs as customers yet, either."

I eyed them suspiciously, but they took me to their HHH department. I did browse and chose several small gifts. I decided that I'd not trust gift wrapping from them and would do it myself.

After leaving, it was getting close to four, so I went back to the Cauldron to meet Minerva.

A Slug Club Christmas

Things were quiet for several weeks, and with Christmas approaching, everyone was wondering if there would be a Yule ball. Last year with Umbrage in charge, there wasn't, and no one was surprised. The year before, with guests in the castle, there had been. Previous years had seen smaller Yule celebrations—nothing like the ball in the year of the Goblet of Fire.

So, it was with some sadness that week after week passed without an announcement. However, there were small compensations for the lack of a Yule ball—the new Potions Professor was going to throw a small Yule Ball of his own. And it turned out not to be not so small after all. It included all of the Slug Club, their guests (one apiece), all the Professors (sorry, no staff like Madame Pomfrey and Filch), and two student guests for each professor. Each guest of a professor could have a guest. When you added it all up, it came to a total over one hundred sixty if everyone who could invite a guest did. That isn't a majority of Hogwarts students but it's a majority of upper class (4th year and older). Minerva and I asked each other as soon as the invitations came out thus short-circuiting any plots by Sinistra.

I was terribly tempted to insist that Minerva open her Christmas gift for the party, but I chose to restrain myself. There was a lot of buzz about the party, who would be invited directly or indirectly to attend, and who wouldn't.

The day of the party arrived, and I got my dress robes out of moth balls. Minerva managed to find dress robes that I'd not seen before. How was that possible?

We arrived and found a crowd had preceded us. There was even a photographer from the *Prophet*. I managed to stay out of photos and found that Minerva wasn't any more anxious to be in them than I. Slughorn tried to get photos taken with him and all the teachers. We kept being in deep conversations when he wandered by with his pet photographer.

When he'd finally shed his photographer, we ran into him and let him introduce us to some of his guests from outside Hogwarts. One of them was a vampire named Sanguini. He later explained that he invited representatives of all minorities that he could to his larger "do's". He didn't say that in Sanguini's hearing.

I found my hand drifting down into my pocket where my purse with the Glock was. However, I said to Sanguini, 'What is your life work?"

He stared at me for a moment and asked, "What do you mean?"

"Well, how do you earn gold to have a place to live, for food, you know." As I spoke, Sanguini's eyes kept wandering away. When he wasn't looking, I glanced behind me and to the side where I could see what was attracting his attention. It was 6th and 7th year young ladies. When I realized that, I actually grasped my purse.

He answered, "Well, I work as a contractor for the Auror Office. I help to identify and trace vampires who have—how do you say it —'Gone above the edge'."

"I think it's 'Gone over the edge.'"

"Oh, yes. I have troubles with your English."

I couldn't help responding, "Funny, I have trouble with your English, too."

You'd have thought that he'd never heard a joke before. He stared blankly at me for a moment and then seemed to realize that what I'd said was funny. Then, he broke out in real laughter. "Oh, I see. Yes. That is funny.

"I also sometimes help the *Daily Prophet* and other news media understand vampires. We are very misunderstood creatures, you know."

"I'm sure you are."

Minerva asked, "What do you think of Gilderoy Lockhart's book about vampires?"

He scratched one of his long incisors and said, "Let me see. That would be *Voyages with Vampires*, right?" We agreed. "Well, it was rather superficial but he gets most of his facts right. He just doesn't have the right interpretation of them."

Just then, Slughorn grabbed his arm and led him away, saying that there was someone that he wanted Sanguini to meet and that we shouldn't monopolize him. After they were out of earshot, Minerva drew me close and whispered urgently. "I saw your right hand slipping toward your purse. What did you think you were dong?"

"I was thinking that I didn't trust that Sanguini as far as I could throw the Hogwarts castle. I was calculating how I'd fire on him without hurting someone else if he attacked one of those 7th year girls that he'd been staring at the whole time."

"You didn't read Lockhart's book, I see."

"Why, does it say that hot lead doesn't do any good against Vampires?"

"No, it says that vampires can't attack anyone who doesn't invite them—uh—in, so to speak. That wouldn't happen here."

Minerva noticed something and called my attention to it. Ms. Grainger's date appeared to be in more danger of attacking an upperclassman than Sanguini was. McKlagen repeatedly slipped his arms around Grainger's waist only to have it neatly removed before it got very far. "I see what you mean, Minerva. Should I put him out of her misery?"

"Oh, I think that she's quite capable of taking care of herself."

"I'd feel better about it if he were Ms. Weasley's date. She wouldn't brook funny business more than once."

"Right you are."

We couldn't help noticing Ms. Lovegood's party dress. Minerva commented, "Now, there's an interesting couple—Lovegood and Potter."

"Yes. You know that most students consider Lovegood to be rather 'Potty'. I admit that she has lots of loopy theories, but I think she gets them honestly from her family. If you peel that rind of the orange away, you find a clever, intelligent young woman under it, and you don't have to peel anything away to see that she's also attractive."

Minerva chuckled, "But she does her best to hide that with her somewhat bizarre clothes." She stopped a moment and went on, "Hey, do I have to be jealous of Lovegood?"

I laughed and said, "No, you're safe from Lovegood. She's way too young for me."

"Yeh, but she's closer to your age than I am."

"No, she's not. Besides, I find older women sexy—not younger ones."

She looked at me out of the corner of her eye, "Does that constitute an invite for later?"

"Why later? But first, let's dance." There was a small band. They were playing something slow–fortunately not by Celestine Warbucks. I took her hand and led her out to the small dance floor.

There was a commotion later when Filch party-crashed with Malfoy. He was dragging Malfoy over to Slughorn, complaining about how he'd found Malfoy skulking around outside. Snape covered for Malfoy, and the two left the party.

"Well, there's one more piece of abnormal behavior for Malfoy. I'm beginning to think that Potter might just be right."

Minerva answered in a distracted way, "Yes. But maybe more interesting is that Snape is covering for him. You might almost think he was a partner in crime."

"Hmmmm. Yes. What do you say that we follow them?"

"No, I don't think so. Someone else has already had the idea." It was Potter who left just a moment after Malfoy and Snape had.

"But will he share?"

"If you mean, will he tell us what he sees, I doubt that he'll dare get close enough to Snape to overhear."

"I'll take anything that I can get."

Before long Sinistra came over and asked for the dance, "And don't deny that you dance. I've seen you just a few minutes ago dancing with Minerva." She gave a polite nod of the head to her.

"I suppose I must."

We went out on the floor. She drew me as close as she politely could and looked directly into my eyes. "Well, I see that Minerva has the upper hand for tonight."

"Oh, she always does."

"Well, as long as we can talk, I should get a progress report from you on Malfoy."

"I'll submit one in writing."

"Oh, but that's not fair to Malfoy. I need to discuss his case with you—in private. How about tomorrow before the end of the term?"

I couldn't really deny her that reasonable request. The dance ended. I announced that Minerva and I were dancing the next dance. She separated from me and said, "Until later. Tata." Then she was gone with an airy wave of the hand.

The next day, Sinistra came to my office, and we had a mercifully quick discussion of Malfoy. She asked, "What are you doing over the Christmas Holiday? Do you think we could get together for a cup of cheer?"

"That is none of your business ,and any cheer that I'll be having will be with Minerva. Now, I wish you a merry Christmas, and be off."

A Cup of Kindness

The final breakfast before everyone left for the holidays was normally presided over by Dumbledore. It was a very cheery affair with Dumbledore wishing everyone a "Happy Christmas". This time, Dumbledore had apparently left for his holiday early. Or maybe he wasn't having a holiday from whatever he was doing away from school. Minerva delivered the wishes of the season to the students. I had finished my grades and was looking forward to a pleasant train trip to London.

I collected my duffel and went to find Minerva for the trip. She was in her office, not Gryffindor tower. "Come on, we'll miss the train if you don't get a move on."

"I'm not going by train, nor are you. Since you're packed and ready, let's leave by my floo."

"I know you don't like train travel, but I really do. You can go by floo, and I'll take the train, if it's not too late."

Minerva walked over to me and took my hand. "Oh, you silly man! It would be like stunning ducks in a pond. Haven't you had enough adventures on trains with Deatheaters. They'll be waiting for you for sure."

I couldn't argue with her. So, I accepted her proffered hand, and we walked into the fireplace. She spoke the name, "Leaky Cauldron." We arrived and had a drink at the bar. We never avoided our social responsibilities to pay for our use of someone's floo. Tom was morose as he always seemed to be lately. I had to admit that there was no one else in the inn.

We left. As soon as we were out of the Cauldron, Minerva took my hand, and we re-appeared outside of my sometime landlord's home. We parted. I checked in and found a small pile of correspondence waiting for me. It has always been amazing to me how long Barclays kept in mind that I had once been a customer and hoped that I might once again be one. The pile ever diminished in size each time I returned. There was one piece of mail that never failed and never would as long as I continued to buy Christmas gifts from the JCPenney Christmas book.

I tossed the rest of the correspondence in file thirteen and headed for my garret. There, after stowing my clothes, I pulled out the Christmas Catalog, a sheet of parchment, and pen (ball point, why would I struggle with quill as I do at work?). I made a list of people that I needed to order presents for in the States. I then leisurely set about finding things for them.

One of the first realizations that came to me was that I was able to afford some fairly expensive gifts. That widened substantially the selection that I had. That also made my efforts much more difficult. Not only was there the question of how much to spend for each person but also whether it was fair to spend much more for one person than another.

The resolution to that dilemma that I finally reached was that I would pick the gift for each that I really believed they'd enjoy the most, and for the most part, forget about how much each gift cost. That simplified things until I reached my parents whom I'd saved for last. Up until that point I found that my strategy had been pretty successful in finding gifts that were reasonably priced and that I was happy with.

However, when I reached my dad and mom, that scheme seemed to break down. The thing that I would choose for my dad was a fancy universal remote which would let him control the TV, cable box, and stereo system that was his pride and joy. It cost about fifty bucks— certainly no more expensive than my usual gift for him. That would have been fine except that then I had to buy for my mom.

I was stuck even coming up with ideas for her. She was a modest person with modest desires (as was really my dad), but what in the world would she enjoy? I knew that she liked to wear well-made, conservative clothes. I had a rough idea what she would consider conservative, but I didn't have sizes, and I had no color sense. I had a vague idea that women liked to co-ordinate colors in outfits, but I didn't have much of an idea of what outfits my mom had. I briefly considered consulting Minerva on the question, but rejected that idea. I wanted this gift to be my idea.

After a good bit of randomly paging through the catalog, I hit the jewelry section. She didn't have much besides her wedding ring. She didn't even have an engagement ring as far as I knew. She might or might not like jewelry in general, but I decided that I was going to buy her something nice (read expensive—I didn't have any idea how to figure out what "nice" might really be).

So, I struggled with what sort of jewelry to buy—rings? bracelets? earrings? necklaces? Come to think of it, I couldn't remember what kind of earrings my mom wore. I was pretty sure she didn't wear large showy earrings, but beyond that I didn't know.

I eventually decided on a necklace. I had the idea that a fine gold chain with a heart-shaped gold pendant with diamonds would be good. That decision made the rest easy. I only had to decide which one I liked the appearance of and make sure that they didn't want an exorbitant amount for it. Say nothing much over one thousand dollars. That was far more than I'd ever spent on any gift for anyone—even Minerva, but I thought that this would be a unique, one-time gift. Who knew? The way the world was going, it might be my last chance to do something like this —or do anything for that matter.

That took all the afternoon and stretched into the early evening. I decided that I'd go out, have dinner, then return, and make my international call to the States to place my order.

When I got back, I calculated that the time was the very early morning on the east coast and that was a good time to call to place an order. Another realization occurred to me. In the past, I would spend a good bit of time laying out the things that I wanted to buy in a very orderly fashion so that it would be easy to quickly and efficiently place my order to limit the international calling charges. Now, I realized that I didn't have to be careful about that, but I did it anyway.

The call had a couple of delays that I hadn't thought of. First, the order-taker that I was talking to had to stop me a couple of times because my order was so large. I had to give my credit card information in the middle rather than at the end so that they could authorize my large purchases. In the end, I spent more than two hours specifying items, addressees, gift wrapping, and so on. Of course, they wanted to sell me additional services. At the end, the order taker transferred me to another person who told me that I'd qualified for a special service.

"Yes, sir. We have a unique service for people who place large orders. It's a special phone # that connects you directly to someone who will have all your information available to speed the process and will make it easy to choose where to send the various parts of your order."

I was rather surprised, "But the only time of the year that I order lots of things is at Christmas."

"Oh, but you place some sort of order almost every month. You've got birthdays and anniversaries and so on that you place orders for. And we'll be here to serve you specially whether it's a large order or a small one."

He gave me the phone number, and I wrote it down so that I could put it into my phone later. I marveled at the perks that the rich and not-so famous could have in Muggle society.

Later during the holiday, I received an owl from the Diggory family. They invited me to join them later in the week. I returned the note and said that I'd be happy to. They invited me to dinner at a nice wizard restaurant and suggested that I bring Minerva. She sent an owl that arrived a little later that day to offer to come and take me to the restaurant.

When the day came, Minerva picked me up a half hour early, and we arrived at the restaurant, Gregory's, well in advance of our reservation. The Diggory's arrived shortly after us, and we were seated shortly.

After drink orders, I broached THE topic. "This is the second Christmas after Cedric's death." Minerva kicked me under the table, but I felt like we had to tackle the subject.

Diggory's mom's eyes filled with tears, and Minerva practically broke my shin bone, but Reina said, "Oh, it's good to hear someone else say his name. Yes, it is the second. You know there are times that I come down the stairs and see the Christmas tree and just feel that he'll come in the front door and give me a hug."

I nodded and said, "You know that he is my favorite student that I've ever had."

She sobbed, and Mr. Diggory put his arm on her shoulder. She gathered herself and said, "You don't have to say that."

"Well, actually, I do. It's the truth. He would have been the only student that I've ever had who would have gone on to higher education. The world is a good bit poorer since it's lost him."

We talked about traveling to tournaments together and how close he came to becoming an International Grand Master. His dad said, "You know there are times when I wonder if anyone in the world remembers him. It's good to know that other people still think about him."

I proposed a toast to Cedric. We went around the table.

His dad said, "A great son and competitor." His eyes filled for the first time that night.

His mom just said, "Dear boy."

I said, "The world was nowhere near good enough for him."

Minerva, "A cup of kindness for his memory."

We drank, and I had the irrational desire to smash the glass against the fireplace stones. It had seen the best use that it ever would have. Every other toast would be second best.

We moved on to other topics: Christmas plans, when did school start up again? did we know anyone who had gone missing and so on.

When Minerva and I left the restaurant, she patted my arm and said, "I was wrong. That was a nice thing you did, talking to them about Cedric."

"Well, he was the proverbial dragon in the room. Everyone feels better when the dragon has been acknowledged. It's painful but necessary."

We returned to my attic flat and made love that night. I reflected that all of us that night had an awful lot to be thankful for—just being alive and together.

That made me think about coming to Minerva's sister's for Christmas.

Minerva's reaction was, "Oh, heavens no. She and I haven't finished cleaning and getting ready. We'll be lucky to be ready for you by Christmas Eve."

"Great."

The next couple of days I spent traveling about town—both by bus and by Underground. It took me that much time to see the city at

Christmas. I'd not done that in several years, and I found that the lights and festivities—both great and small–to be fascinating and enjoyable. I went into neighborhoods to look at the decorations of homes at night and enjoyed it all. I didn't go to any of the many concerts. I love music, but the music of Christmas that I most enjoy is the music of the amateur singers in churches and cathedrals. It had been years since I'd attended a professional Christmas concert, and I wasn't sorry.

Minerva showed up on the morning before Christmas Eve. I'd packed and was prepared for a stay that would only be limited by the patience of her sister. We walked into a nearby alley and then disapparated to an alley near Maude's house.

Our stay would have been a completely uninteresting pleasure if it had not been for an incident that happened while I was there. One day between Christmas and New Years we were reading the *Prophet* and discovered a report of an attack on the Weasley home. It was buried in the back pages of the front section. A year before, it would have been front page news, but now it was just another incident. No one was killed or missing, so it was shuttled to the back pages between a report on international cauldron standards and a report on the choice of the venue for the 2002 Quidditch Cup final match.

Minerva found the article while I was reading *The Times*. She noted that Harry Potter had been there as a guest of the family.

"But, Minerva, I thought Potter would be spending the Holiday with the Dursleys. Isn't that the only place that he's safe outside Hogwarts?"

"Yes, that's true, but the Dursleys won't take him back for short Holidays—only the summer Holiday."

I chewed on that for a few minutes and asked, "What will happen when he leaves Hogwarts after graduation?"

No one seemed to want to answer that question. So, I decided to have a go at it, "Well, I guess there are two possibilities. One is that he and Riddle will have it out for the last time or—let's look on the bright side—maybe he won't survive that long. Riddle might just win out sometime in the next year or so."

Maude was put in a foul mood by the conversation. "Just hush. Potter will be an adult in a few months, and he will be on his own lookout then."

That sort of put an end to the conversation. The rest of the holiday was actually pretty good. Beryl, as usual, spent New Years Eve with us, and we played games, had a toast or two, and caught up on events of the last year. The catching-up mostly ignored the events concerning Riddle, although everyone knew someone who had been attacked, killed, or disappeared.

We returned to Hogwarts directly from Maude's. Minerva absolutely forbade me to ride the Hogwarts express ever again. We arrived outside the Three Broomsticks. We went in for the last hurrah before we were officially back to work. It was close to lunchtime, and there were a couple of other teachers sitting at a table, apparently waiting to be served. So we joined them. There was Snape and Madame Pomfrey. They were in a deep discussion, but I was oblivious of that until we got close. I just caught the end of a comment that Snape was making to Pomfrey.

"I've done as much as anyone could for him. That's why he hasn't confided more in. . ." Then Snape noticed us and fell silent.

I asked if they minded if we joined them. Snape replied, "I don't object. You?"

Madame Pomfrey shook her head. We sat and exchanged civilities. I said, "I've come into a bit of money recently and haven't really celebrated. Do you mind if I pick up the tab?"

No one did, but Madame Pomfrey asked what it was. "Oh, I've been doing some consulting business on the side, and one of my efforts came through very well."

Snape was interested, 'Tell us more. What sort of business are you in?"

I replied that I was under a nondisclosure agreement that forbade me to say much more than that. Then the talk turned to other topics, mostly what we did over the holidays. I asked Snape where he stayed. "I know that Minerva stays with her sister. I usually stay in a garret apartment that my landlord can't palm off on anyone else but me. Some teachers stay at Hogwarts. What do you do?"

Snape smiled, "I understand that sometimes you stay with the sister."

I smiled, 'Yes, sometimes I do. But that doesn't answer where you spend your holidays."

The food that they'd ordered arrived then, and Minerva and I ordered. Then I went back to our conversation, 'You were saying."

"Oh, yes. You wanted to know how and where I spent the Holiday. Well, are you familiar with Professor Slughorn's recent housing maneuvers?"

"Yes, but I don't know that either Minerva or Madame Pomfrey are."

He nodded, "Yes, well why don't you fill them in on his approach? I'm sure that he's not keeping it a secret if he told you."

"OK. Well, he found it inconvenient to avoid Deatheaters when he stayed at his home. So he began searching for temporary abodes. He came on the scheme of discovering Muggle homes that were temporarily unoccupied because their owners were away on holiday. He discovered them by spending time in Muggle travel agencies under an invisibility cloak, listening in on travel arrangements.

"Then he would pick a place that was to be unoccupied. He'd live there for a while and leave before the Muggles returned—always leaving the home in better shape than when he arrived."

Snape commented dryly, "Very ethical of him."

'What about you?"

"Oh, I always leave the house in at least as good a condition as when I arrived."

"Uh-huh. So, you do stay in vacationers homes during Holidays?"

"Certainly."

I pressed on, "But how do you find out about these houses? You don't have time to hang out at Muggle travel agencies."

His answer was evasive, "Oh, there are means of finding out about occupants when they're not present. Perhaps, Slughorn doesn't know about them."

I let that drop, and we talked about more mundane Holiday stories. Pomfrey had gone to visit a cousin in London, done some Christmas shopping, and went to a performance of the Nutcracker.

Snape admitted to visiting with some old friends one night at the Cauldron and staying over. I congratulated him, "I'm sure Tom was overjoyed to have you. It's pretty depressing down at Diagon Alley these days."

That ended that line of discussion, and Minerva and I told about our time together.

Academic Overture

The first couple of weeks of the new term went quietly. Malfoy was back in tutoring. At first things seemed to be going well, but it didn't take long before I noticed that he was doing poorly both in class AND in tutoring sessions. I immediately called a meeting of the ad hoc group—Minerva, Snape and I.

We met in Snape's office one evening. "Well, Wendt, what's the emergency?"

"You've been holding out. Mr. Malfoy's behavior has changed. He's become even less cooperative, and his school performance has deteriorated further."

Snape said, "Just because he's having a hard time getting restarted after the Holiday is no reason to declare an emergency."

Minerva looked back and forth between us. "He is significantly worse at transfiguration."

"Look, Snape, we can't take risks like this. Have any of the other Slytherin's been showing signs of abnormal behavior? I haven't seen any from Avery or Fischer."

"No, but that doesn't prove anything. What about the Gryffindor?"

Minerva just shook her head in the negative.

"That doesn't mean anything either. It could have been someone outside of Hogwarts altogether."

"You must admit that it would have been difficult for an outsider to have known a good candidate and when she would have been available. No one in the Broomstick was from outside Hogwarts. Or at least no one was noticed by anyone."

Snape waved his hand, 'Invisibility cloak."

"Perhaps."

Minerva objected to such trivialization of the mounting evidence. But Snape was adamant.

We parted, and as we walked back up from the dungeon, Minerva asked me if I had any ideas for next steps. "Yes, keep a careful eye on Malfoy. I have an idea, but I have to think further about it."

I really didn't need to think about it further, but I didn't want to get Minerva in trouble with her boss. So I didn't tell her what my idea was. I composed a note and left it in the pigeon hole of Professor Dumbledore.

Nothing happened for a couple of days. Then, one evening, when I checked my pigeon hole, there was a note in Dumbledore's fine round hand. "Please join me this evening after dinner for a glass of sherry."

I appeared at the gargoyle that evening and spoke the latest password—"liquorices lollipop." I found Professor Dumbledore waiting in his office, pouring two glasses of sherry. "I hope you like sherry. It's my favorite."

I had been expecting this, and I replied, "As well as most."

"Ah, well. I'm sorry, but what did you come to talk about?"

I picked up my glass and forced a swallow down, "I think that Mr. Malfoy is the man behind the poisoning of Ms. Bell. I want you to send him home before he hurts someone else or even kills someone—maybe you."

Dumbledore leaned back and looked up at the ceiling as he considered what he would say. "Professor Wendt, do you really think that Mr. Malfoy is guilty?"

"Yes. We did an investigation of the incident of Ms. Bell. You were gone at the time." Then, I worked through the logic that we'd used to come up with our short list of suspects. "We've been watching them carefully for signs of the abnormal. The only one who has shown any abnormality of behavior has been Malfoy. He's been showing it from the very beginning of the year. It's only becoming worse. He's on the verge of failing most of his classes."

Dumbledore shook his head, "It sounds like the only evidence you have is that he's not doing well at school."

I just shook my head. Then I went on, "How can you possibly take a risk with the lives of students here—not to mention your own life? Where would we be if you were gone?"

"You still have Mr. Potter."

"Oh, yes. Potter. I admit that he's faced Riddle several times, but he's been lucky several times. That can't keep going. Even you had the most difficult time escaping with your life when you were face to face with Riddle."

"You know about the prophecy?"

"That Riddle and Potter can't co-exist? Of course, but they have been for years. I think it's probably true. That day of reckoning may not come for years—perhaps decades. And who knows which will no longer exist when they meet for the final time."

Dumbledore sighed, "There is no place that students are not in risk of their lives these days. I wouldn't eject a student who has only been suspected of wrongdoing–up to now away–especially Mr. Malfoy."

"He isn't doing well. He isn't profiting from being here. He could come back next year and start over."

"I don't think he will be able to—perhaps not be able to do anything later."

I pondered a moment. What the Hell did that mean? "But your safety? You are surely taking reprehensible risks with your life."

Dumbledore closed his eyes and was silent for what seemed to be an eternity. "No, I am not going to send him away, and losing me would not be such a great loss. At least not for long."

"How can you say that!" He was making no sense at all, but I knew there must be some logic behind the seeming senselessness.

"I can say that because of this." He held up his hand. I stared and realized that between his being gone a great deal of the time and my fascination with Malfoy, I'd forgotten about his injured hand.

"Go ahead."

"It was obvious to you at the beginning of the year. I'm going to die soon. I doubt that I'll outlive the school term. I may die even sooner than that. Even if Mr. Malfoy is the guilty party, I will be dead soon, and his efforts will be for naught. He will not succeed, I am sure of it, and he will not kill anyone else either."

It was my turn to shake my head. "I wish that I could be so sure as you."

"Well, you can be sure of one thing. Mr. Malfoy will not be expelled from this school. But you should keep your watch on him. I don't want him to suffer from another accident in which someone else is injured."

"Nor, I."

I started to leave his office, but before I did, he said, "Of course, I have to insist that you keep my health status. . . "

"Yes, I know. No one should know about how little time there is left. But can you tell me, at least, who knows of your impending death?"

He looked me directly in the eye and said, 'Besides you and Minerva, Madame Pomfrey and Professor Snape."

I nodded and walked back down the spiral stairs feeling that the world had suddenly turned smaller and darker.

Gringotts Ascendant

One day, during my class with 7th years, there was a knock on the door. I walked to the door and opened it. It was one of the auror guards. He motioned me to come out into the hall. When I did, he explained the interruption.

"There's a messenger at the main entrance that has a package for you. We wouldn't bother you except that he won't release it without your signature."

Why couldn't it have been during office hours? I nodded, "I'll dismiss the class and come down to get it. Be there in a minute."

I re-entered the class, "Ladies and gentlemen, I regret to report that I have urgent business elsewhere on the grounds. I'm dismissing the class now." There was a whoop of joy throughout the class, "But, you are responsible for reading the selected poems of Ezra Pound in the next section of your text." I added with special emphasis, "Be prepared to discuss them at the next class."

The auror and I went down to the main entrance. The messenger handed over a clipboard with a parchment list of deliveries. There was a red "X" on a blank spot of one of the lines. He said, "Please sign by the 'X', guvnor."

I did, and he pulled out of a leather courier bag a large envelope addressed to me. Since I didn't have a class the next hour, I returned to my office. I sat at my desk and opened the envelope. Inside, I found a single page letter.

The letterhead was a sort of coat of arms. It appeared to be a be-jeweled circular shield with crossed swords beneath. The body of the letter said:

Professor James Wendt
3rd floor office
Hogwarts School of Witchcraft & Wizardry
Hogsmeade, Scotland

Sir;

I am pleased to announce to you that in its regularly scheduled meeting last night, the Gringott's Board of Directors voted unanimously to add a position to the Board of Directors. It also voted unanimously to appoint you as the seat's first occupant.

As soon as you send us your acceptance, you will be a member of the board with full privileges, including attending all meetings both regular and ad hoc, making motions, and voting on them.

The next scheduled meeting of the Board is May 13 at 7:00 P.M.. You will be inducted at that meeting.

Please find attached the following items:
- A list of future Board meetings scheduled this year with locations (all at the Board Room of the Gringotts bank in Diagon Alley)
- A ticket that will permit you to use the floo connection to the Waiting Room outside the Board Room
- Several copies of the form for requesting Agenda items for board meetings.
- A list of board members and brief bio's.
- A Brief History of Gringotts.
- An acceptance form of the election. (to be returned within two weeks).

Yours with best regards,

The signature was the Chairman of the Board. It was written in some sort of runes that I couldn't make out one way or the other.

I took a quick look at my bio. It was amusing. It was essentially the press release that Hogwarts had supplied when I was hired, along with a little updated history from that point forward. My contributions to Gringotts were listed briefly.

How I wished that I could show this to Minerva not just to brag, but also to get suggestions on Agenda items to be added for the next board meeting!

I got out a fresh roll of parchment and began to make notes for an agenda item that I would submit.

But then my excitement overcame me, and I hastily filled out the acceptance form. I ran out of my office to find Minerva to send the acceptance back by owl.

△

I ran to Minerva's office and had just reached it when I realized that she was in a double class at the moment. I swore under my breath and ran down to Snape's office.

He was not present. There was a schedule of his classes and office hours posted on his office door. It showed that he was in class as well. How could I be so unlucky!

It shows my excitement that I actually went to Professor Dumbledore's office. How I could have imagined that he would be there eludes me to this day.

I turned back toward my office having decided that I would just have to wait for dinner to catch Minerva or Snape to help me send my acceptance. I was trudging down the stairs with my eyes locked on my feet, lost in thought. As I reached the bottom of the stairs and started to turn the corner, I bumped into someone.

I was apologizing profusely even before I looked up to see to whom I was apologizing.

I discovered that it was Sinistra. My surprise overcame my better judgment. I said, "Oh, it's you." Then an idea occurred to me, "You're a witch."

She snickered and said, "I'm glad you noticed."

"No. NO. I just meant that you could help me send an owl." I think my eyes were a little too hopeful, so I dropped them.

427

She pulled the rolled up acceptance out of my hand and said, "Of course. Anything for you." She laughed as she spoke the words.

I was immediately regretting my haste. She took off at a brisk pace down the hall in the general direction of the Owlery. On the way, she glanced at the direction on the outside of the rolled-up up scroll. "Ah, Gringotts. I suppose they've just discovered that you're not a wizard and are kicking you out."

I only grimaced and said nothing.

We were beginning to climb the stairs to the Owlery when she unrolled the scroll a little to see the full address. She commented, "Wow, the Chairman of the Board of Directors of Gringotts. You must have really screwed up!"

Without further warning she completely unrolled the scroll and flipped it over to see what was written. I reached out with my right hand to grab the scroll, but she twisted around to keep it out of my reach.

She gasped, and I realized that I'd already failed my oath to the Board. It was too late, so I released my grip on the scroll. She whirled around and thrust her face at me. With it she planted a serious but brief kiss on my lips. "Oh, I'm so excited for you!"

She leaned back then, and the expression on her face changed from ecstatic to puzzled. She said, "I think. Who did you have to do to get elected?"

I could only open my mouth unable to reply. I'd already broken my oath once. I was not going to break it again.

Then her face changed again to wily—I swear! She asked slowly, "You haven't told HER, have you?"

My countenance dropped. She then said, "And you can't, can you?"

That woke me up! I set my jaw and said through clenched teeth, "You'd better not tell anyone! And I mean anyone! I swear, I'll get you fired if you do. AND I'll do my best to see that you don't get hired at another school!"

She nodded, apparently untroubled by what I'd just said. She continued nodding, seemingly more to herself than me, "No, no! It will just be our little secret—yours and mine."

Somehow I felt sure that she'd respect that secret. We walked the rest of the way up to the top of the Owlery together. She whistled and a large grey owl glided down to the perch near where we were standing. I wondered if it were hers. She addressed it by a name that I couldn't make out. She attached the scroll to one of its legs. She stroked its back once and said something that might have been a spell or might not have. "Go swiftly, go safely, return in haste, return to your Love."

The owl took off on the instant that the last word had left Sinistra's lips. It flew up to the opening in the Owlery roof faster than I would have imagined that a bird could.

Then we turned and walked down the stairs from the Owlery silently. As we neared the bottom steps, she said the only thing that either of us had since we'd left that spot on the way up the stairs, "Your secret and mine." I wasn't sure whether she'd said it to me or herself, it was so softly spoken.

◁▷

Over the next couple of days, I would revise and extend that agenda item until I thought it was ready to submit. I signed it, put it in a large envelope, and addressed it. After dinner that evening, when Minerva came up to my office as she frequently did to grade papers, I asked her if she would post the envelope.

She glanced at the address and smiled, "What is this?" Then she quickly added, "Oh, I know, it's tip-toppity secret, and you can't tell me." I just smiled charmingly.

"Very well, I'll get it off on my way back to Gryffindor. I suppose it's urgent."

I shrugged, not wanting to tempt fate, but then I had a thought. "Well, actually, I can tell you one thing. I have a meeting on Wednesday, May 13th at Gringotts at 7PM. Would you be willing to take me there?"

She shrugged, "Sure. That's pretty far off, but it's comfortably before finals." She turned to leave for Gryffindor, but I interrupted her.

"Oh, one more thing."

She smiled and came back to me and said, "I've forgotten something, haven't I?" And she gave me a kiss that was sure to be remembered.

After we broke, I said, "That was great, but there's actually one more thing."

Minerva squinted at me as she focused on my face while we were still in embrace. I went on, "I've requested that you attend the

429

meeting as an informal representative of the Order of the Phoenix." Her eyes popped and her caress tightened.

"What in the world for?"

I gagged involuntarily as I started to say something and then thought out carefully what I wanted to say. Treading carefully, I said, "I want to uh pitch an idea to the leadership of Gringotts that involves the Order."

She released me and took a step back, "Well, I figured that out on my own. Can you tell me what this idea is?"

I grimaced and she said, "I get it. No can do. How about twenty questions? Is it bigger than a bread box?"

I was a little miffed myself, "Well, you don't think that I like keeping you in the dark, do you? Just be prepared to . . . be an advocate for the Order."

She said, "I'll be seeing you, and I'm not at liberty to tell you when the next time will be." She closed the door to the Great Hall determinedly as she left.

When Wednesday, the 13th arrived, Minerva and I had a quick dinner at the earliest moment possible and left just as Dumbledore showed up. We said a brief hello-goodbye and went to my office to use the floo connection there. I grabbed my briefcase, and Minerva asked what floo address to use. I handed her the ticket, "Minerva, you have to use this ticket so that the floo connection at Gringotts will accept us."

She shrugged and held the ticket in the same hand that she held my hand and took some floo powder in the other. I held my briefcase in the hand that wasn't holding Minerva's. She spoke the address, "Gringott's Home Office Boardroom Reception Area." And we walked into the inner sanctum of Gringotts.

Minerva looked around and said, "Rather nice. You know, I've never been in the back offices of Gringotts."

The reception goblin stood and said, "Welcome, Mr. Wendt and Ms. McGonagall. The meeting will start in about fifteen minutes. You're the first ones here." Then he turned to Minerva and said, "To attend this meeting, you'll have to swear the Unbreakable Oath. I've got a copy of the oath for you to examine in advance. It basically just says that you agree not to reveal anything you learn in the meeting. Purely a formality."

She dropped my hand, which she was still holding. "I will not." The statement was accompanied by a very determined glare that I'd seen before. I sighed as I began to anticipate what would happen next.

The Goblin shook his head, "I'm afraid that I can't allow you to enter the meeting. You may wait here for Mr. Wendt until the meeting is over. Would you care for some tea, pumpkin juice, or coffee?"

I could tell that Minerva's sometimes short fuse was about to ignite. I took a deep breath and said, "If she can't attend, then I won't either."

The Goblin just shrugged and said, "Well, I'll talk to Mr. Glazblatt when he arrives."

We didn't have to wait long. Glazblatt was the next to arrive. The reception Goblin took him aside out of earshot and spoke with him. I couldn't make out what they were saying, but it must have been in GobbeldyGook. After this brief discussion, Glazblatt came over to me and asked me to explain why I wouldn't be attending the meeting.

"It's simple, I've brought Ms. McGonagall as a consultant to the meeting, and she's been refused admittance."

Glazblatt made a face that I was pretty sure was not a Goblin smile, "But she refuses to take the non-disclosure oath. Surely, she can see that we have a right to our meeting being treated as confidential."

Minerva stood at that, came over, and put her face in his. "Look, I have people to report to in the Order of the Phoenix, and I'm not going to keep them in the dark about what happened here!"

Glazblatt looked around, as though someone would come to his rescue, but no one seemed to be ready to do that. Just then, Ruugrat came through the door from the Board Room. Glazblatt signaled him to come over and a rapid fire conversation proceeded in GobbeldyGook. Then Glazblatt turned back to me.

"Mr. Ruugrat has suggested that Ms. McGonagall might attend just the part of the session that includes your motion. Then, she wouldn't have to be sworn to secrecy. Would that be acceptable?"

Minerva put her face in his again and said, "If you have a question for me, direct it to me."

Glazblatt rolled his eyes and said, 'All right. Ms. McGonagall, would that be acceptable?"

She turned all sweetness again and softly said, "That would be quite acceptable."

The rest of the board members had arrived, mostly by floo, while this palaver had been going on, and Glazblatt told me, "Let's go in now and start the meeting." He pointedly turned to Minerva and said, "You will be summoned when your part of the meeting comes. Please have a seat, and we'll be with you."

Glazblatt, Ruugrat and I entered the Board Room and took seats. Each seat had a triangular parallelepiped with name engraved on front and back. I sat behind mine, and the meeting was called to order.

After Glazblatt called the meeting to order, he directed the secretary, Ruugrat to record attendees and announce the agenda items as they came up. There was a page in front of each of us that listed the agenda items. Glazblatt announced that introductions weren't necessary since we'd all received the biographical material on all board members.

The first agenda item was a report on the quarterly statement of earnings. I circled a couple of figures on the handout for that item. I intended to refer to them later when my agenda item came up. In general the quarter had not been good. Vault occupancy had gone down in the European banks, most severely in the U.K., but had dropped even in the US and other continents.

In the general discussion, one of the Goblin board members suggested that vault rental should be raised to make up for the shortfall in profits. I raised my hand and was recognized, "Before you do that, I think you should do a study to see if that results in an increase in revenue or not. Some people may drop their vault lease or move to a smaller vault. Do we have competitors?"

Ruugrat shuffled through some papers and said, "There are other wizarding banks – especially in the United States. I think Mr. Wendt may be right about that market. In Europe, there are a couple of countries where we have weak competitors. In the U.K. there is no real competitor. So, it should be safe to do that in England. Less so in the rest of Europe."

I responded, "Yes, people may not completely drop their vaults, but they may go to cheaper versions–take their less valuable possessions home to enjoy them."

There was a general babble of discussion that Glazblatt cut through and tabled discussion until a study could be done. He went on to the next agenda item–a report about the extension of the virtual vault concept to other markets, "The American competitors took that idea up quickly and are already doing a thriving business in virtual vaults. I think that most of our loss of market share in the US is due to our being behind the curve on this service."

There were a couple of other lesser agenda items, dealing with special compensation for various bank officers and so on. Then the final agenda item came up – which was mine. Glazblatt sent Ruugrat out to bring Minerva in, and she found a seat across from me at the table. Glazblatt asked me to introduce Minerva.

"Thank you. Ms. McGonagall is the Assistant Headmistress of Hogwarts School of Witchcraft and Wizardry in the U.K. She is a fellow teacher with me, and she also is a founding member of the Order of the Phoenix. If you have questions about that order, I suggest that Ms. McGonagall address them."

One of the Goblin board members asked, "We thought that the Order had been disbanded after the fall of He-Who-Must-Not-Be-Named fifteen years ago?"

She looked around the table and said, "Surely, even Goblins must be aware of the return of Tom Riddle." There were confused looks around the table, even from the wizard member. She clarified, "Tom Riddle is the given name of the dark wizard that is sometimes referred to by the name you mentioned. He not only has returned, but he is reforming the alliances that he had before in his attempt to take over the government of the Magic World – not just wizards or even Muggles, but all magical creatures."

There were no other questions, so Glazblatt had Ruugrat read aloud, ostensibly for Minerva's sake, but actually for everyone's sake the motion that was contained in my agenda item. Ruugrat rose with the parchment and read,

"Title: a motion to oppose the rise to power of the dark wizard, Tom Riddle, aka The Dark Lord, etc.

"Paragraph 1: Since Tom Riddle is in the process of overthrowing the Ministry of Magic and other Magical Governing Bodies with the intent of making himself the supreme unlimited ruler of the world, the Gringotts Wizarding Bank, LLC should oppose him in every feasible way, including, but not limited to the following methods:

"Subparagraph 1: The contribution to the Order of the Phoenix of gold sufficient to fund all reasonable techniques of opposing Tom Riddle.

"Subparagraph 2: Forbidding access to their vaults of all known Deatheaters and substantial supporters of Tom Riddle.

"Subparagraph 3: Other measures that will become feasible in the course of time at the discretion of the Chairman of the Board.

"Paragraph 2: This motion will take effect immediately after its approval at the quarterly Board of Director Meeting, May 13, 1998."

Ruugrat sat and Glazblatt declared the table open for discussion of the motion. There was a tumult of responses. Glazblatt had to intervene again and ruled that each board member would have two minutes to make a statement going around the table from him clockwise and then general discussion would ensue.

The first board member, a Goblin, spoke, "This is preposterous. We are bound by contract to make the vaults of all vault owners accessible to them in ordinary business hours. If people thought that we would arbitrarily keep them from their vaults, it would be the end of our business." There were some calls of "hear, hear!"

The second board member agreed, but said, "I'm in favor of subparagraph 1. We can certainly provide gold to oppose Riddle."

The next speaker was opposed to both, "We have always been apolitical, and we should remain that way. That was the way it was the first time that Riddle rose, and we did just fine."

When my turn came, I looked around slowly at all the board members and began, "This is different. You will see first, the Riddle government forbid access to vaults of all opposed to Riddle. Then, you will see their funds and property seized by the government. Then, you will see this board packed with Deatheater members so that your votes become the minority. Then, you will see the ownership of this bank transferred to the government. Your business will be lost forever. What will happen to you personally, if you are a Goblin, I leave to your imaginations. You should not have a lot of trouble coming up with reasonable possibilities."

Speakers from that point on mostly echoed the thoughts of previous speakers. Finally when all board members had spoken, Minerva requested a voice. Glazblatt granted it. Her statement was simple, "I could not improve on Mr. Wendt's statement. However, I just want to remind you of what happened the last time when Riddle came CLOSE to having power. Goblins were *disappeared*. There were Goblins who were tortured to obtain their help in stealing from Gringotts vaults. You will see those things start to happen soon – even before Riddle takes power. That is all that I have to say."

There were a number of whispered conversations around the room which Glazblatt allowed to continue for a while. Then, he said, "Do I hear a motion for the previous question?"

Instead, one of the Goblins stood and said, "Mr. Glazblatt, I wish to offer an amendment to the motion."

Glazblatt nodded assent, and he began, "I move that the second subparagraph be stricken from the motion and the third subparagraph will become the second."

Someone seconded the motion, and Glazblatt looked to me, "Do you wish to have discussion before I entertain a motion of the previous question?"

I shrugged and said, "I've said everything that I want to on this subject. I think the two subparagraphs are the least that we could do." I looked around, and no one appeared to want to speak, so I said, "I move the previous question on the amendment."

Glazblatt nodded and asked for the vote – affirmative by raised hand, then negative by the same sign. The amendment passed by a six to four majority. Then Glazblatt accepted a second of the motion as amended from the Wizard on the board. Someone else called the previous question.

Glazblatt then was to call for the vote as before, but I objected, "Please, let's have a secret ballot on this very important motion. I don't want anyone to be influenced by fear of being in the minority." Glazblatt sighed and instructed Ruugrat to get parchment for people to vote. He instructed that everyone should mark the piece of parchment with either "Yes" or "No", fold the parchment, and give it to Ruugrat who would count the ballot.

After Ruugrat collected the ballots, he read them privately and then rose to announce the results, "The motion has five in favor." At this point, my heart fell. A tie would mean failure for the motion. I glanced at

Minerva who rolled her eyes. But Ruugrat was going on, "One abstention and four against. The motion passes."

Glazblatt was about to adjourn the meeting when I stood, "Point of order. We must decide how much gold to contribute to the Order."

Glazblatt made an expression on his face that I decided had to be disgust, "Yes, I suppose so." He then turned to Minerva, "How much can the Order use constructively."

Her eyes widened, and she kicked me under the table for being put in this spot. She thought a moment and looked at me. She started to say slowly, "Fifty." But I kicked her swiftly under the table, and she amended it to "Two Hundred Fifty thousand galleons." She lifted her eyelids in question if that were too much. I shook my head slightly.

There was a general gasp around the room, and Glazblatt rolled his eyes. Someone called out, "What can you possibly do with that much gold?"

Minerva rose and looked around the table with her best steely teacher stare, patented and guaranteed to silence any student – even the Weasley twins. "You have your secrets, and I respect that. You only permitted me to be in this meeting for the only business that concerned me directly. I ask the same courtesy from you. You must trust that as a founding member of the Order and with deep knowledge of its workings, I have good judgment of its requirements. To reveal more to you would be to put you in danger from Deatheaters anxious to learn the Order's secrets."

Glazblatt was clearly disturbed, but he shrugged and said, "So ordered. We will open a virtual vault for the Order, accessible to the members that you shall name. Its initial deposit will be 250,000 galleons, which may be replenished at the pleasure of the board.

"This session of the board is adjourned until the next scheduled meeting date, Thursday August 13." There was general discussion that followed that. However, the only person who talked to me was Minerva. "Let's get out of here." And Glazblatt, shook his head and said, "I hope you're right about this, or maybe I hope you're wrong about this, and this investment is just like most insurance payments – never to be recovered."

Minerva and I walked out, and by common unspoken consent, we didn't clasp hands until we stepped into the fireplace in the Reception Room where she threw some green powder to the hearth and spoke, "James Wendt's Office, Hogwarts."

We arrived, and we both flopped onto the couch. I said, "I'm bushed. How about going over to my desk and getting out a bottle and some glasses."

Minerva objected, "Why me? This is your office, your desk, your liquor."

I just shook my head, and she slowly rose and dragged herself to the desk and rummaged in it.

The Demand

While developments at Gringotts were developing, things were not quiet at Hogwarts. I was working in my office and a knock on my door demanded my attention. I asked the knocker to enter and was very surprised to see Mr. Potter enter.

"Well, Mr. Potter, take a chair." I indicated the red leather chair.

He did, and I gave him my full attention. "What can I do for you?"

Potter squirmed some in his chair and seemed reluctant to make his request. I simply sat and waited. Eventually, he decided that he had to say something, so he said, "Professor, I need help."

"What can I do for you?"

"Well, it's hard to talk about this." He still hesitated.

So, I decided that I had to give him as much encouragement as I could, 'Let me assure you, Mr. Potter, what you have to say—unless you're about to confess that you intend to kill someone—I will treat with the utmost confidence."

"Well, OK. Here's the thing. I need help with the Room of Requirement."

I nodded dubiously. Here was someone who would have had the Room of Requirement down "pat" if anyone did. "What do you need help with?"

"Well, you see, Professor. Someone is using the Room of Requirement, and I want to find out what he's doing."

"I assume that simply asking him isn't a reasonable possibility."

"No, sir. He wouldn't answer. He'd probably deny that he ever used it."

"And would this person happen to be Mr. Malfoy?"

Potter looked down at his feet instantly at the sound of the name, so I said, "I see that I'm right. So, tell me what you've attempted in order to find out."

It was an absolutely unique opportunity. I had never heard of Potter or hardly any other student confiding in this way with a professor. I had to tread lightly and carefully if I were to learn anything—and possibly avert a tragedy.

Potter said, "Well, I've tried to open the Room of Requirement and find what he's been doing in it."

I nodded. He went on, "I've not been able to do it. I've tried a million times, and it just won't open."

"Would you mind telling me what you've asked when you've tried to get into the room?"

Potter gave me a variety of questions. They all basically broke down to two questions: Show me what Malfoy has been doing. Show me where Malfoy goes when he's in the room.

"Well, Mr. Potter, you're not going to appreciate this, but it's ironic, don't you think?"

"What is ironic, sir?"

"Well, last year Mr. Malfoy wanted very much to find out what you were doing in the Room of Requirement and couldn't. Now you want to find out what he's doing there, and you can't find out."

Potter looked ready to explode, "Well, if you're not going to help me, I might as well go. And he did find out what we were doing."

"Wait, Mr. Potter, I didn't say that I wasn't going to help you. You can learn from that irony, if you will."

"What do you mean?"

"Well, why was it that for such a long time, despite trying as hard as you have been, he failed for so long."

That seemed to have Potter stumped. "I don't know. Why?"

"Well, he wasn't able to find out what you were doing because he didn't know what you were doing."

Potter seemed ready to walk off again, "Well, what does that mean!"

It was painful having to lead him so gently down the path. "It means that he only was able to get into the Room of Requirement when someone who already knew told him."

"You mean that I have to get him to tell me what he's doing?"

"Yes. And I've got an idea how you might be able to do that." I hesitated for emphasis. "First, let me ask you a question about the Room of Requirement that I don't know the answer to. How do you get in when you know exactly what you want? You ask the Room of Requirement for what you want. Question: Does this have to be aloud, or can it be just in your head?"

This one took Potter a moment to reflect on, "Well, I really don't pay attention. I think that sometimes I say it out loud, and sometimes, I've just thought it."

"Which do you think that Malfoy does?"

He got up and paced in concentration, "I don't know. I think he probably says it out loud sometimes."

I flourished my hand and said, "Does that give you an idea how you can find out what he wants?"

A smile broke over Potter's face. "I could wear my invisibility cloak and wait for him to ask his question." He paused a moment. "Maybe, I could plant an extendible ear there, and I wouldn't have to be close to him."

"I think that might work."

"Great. I'll have to order a couple of ears from the twins, but I should have them in a couple of days. Thanks!" Then he looked at me suspiciously, 'You were awfully quick to help me spy on a student. Why? That doesn't seem like a very 'professorly' thing to do."

"Technically, you're right, but frankly, I want to know what Malfoy is doing too. I can't ask him any more than you can.

"I expect to hear what you find out, Mr. Potter."

"If this works, you bet I'll tell you."

"One thing. Let's keep this between you and me."

"Sure, mum's the word."

"Thanks."

He left, and I pondered what Malfoy was up to in the Room of Requirement. I was afraid it was another attempt on the life of Dumbledore."

It was almost a week before I heard from Potter again. He knocked on the door as before without warning, and I invited him in.

"Professor. Bad news. I've watched Malfoy enter the Room of Requirement a couple of times from a distance. I had the extendable ears but I couldn't hear him say a word. He must be speaking in his mind."

"And do you think that you could follow him in under the cloak?"

"No, sir. He's got his two buddies—Crab and Goyle. They're all too close together. I couldn't approach the door while they were all there. Have you got any other ideas?"

"Well, let's go back to your experience last year. How did Malfoy eventually find out about what you were doing in the Room of Requirement?"

"Umbrage used Veritas serum, but Snape would never let me have any. It's probably one of the hardest to brew."

I thought about that a minute. "Could you use the Imperious spell?"

He goggled at me, "Are you crazy? Using that will get you sent to Azkaban faster than Snape running from shampoo. Besides, that would be wrong."

I nodded, 'You're right. I wouldn't recommend that. It does you credit that you reject that idea so thoroughly, but I asked you for a reason. That is the next step to take. There is nothing less drastic that you can do to find out how to get into the Room of Requirement."

Potter was clearly unhappy. He leaned forward toward me and was almost begging, "But you're supposed to be one of the smartest people in the world. Surely, you can think of something else!"

"I'm flattered, but I can't think of anything less drastic. Oh, you could try torture, I suppose."

Potter rolled his eyes, "Come on. You're not serious."

"I am perfectly serious. Maybe you can suborn one of his buddies to give you inside information. Is there any bribe you could offer Crab or Goyle?"

Potter clearly considered it seriously for a couple of minutes, "No. They can't be bribed by a Gryffindor. Don't you have anything else?"

"No. You've got to give up until you or I think of something else."

"That's crazy. Dumbledore's life is at stake. Can't you think of something?"

I threw up my hands in desperation, "Oh, Potter, I wish to God that I could, but no. I suppose that you've talked to Dumbledore about this."

Potter just shook his head, 'Yes. I see him every couple of weeks. I always ask him, but he's sure that Malfoy wouldn't do anything like that."

"Well, I won't stop thinking about it, and if I come up with anything, I'll get in touch with you. Good luck. And I really mean that. I'm as concerned about Dumbledore as you are."

Potter was clearly frustrated and left my office. I never saw him again except at meals and the rare crossing of paths in the halls. We never spoke about it again.

I did approach Minerva about the question. She didn't have ideas either.

Things remained quiet for a couple of weeks. Then, one Saturday morning, I was sleeping in for a change, but was wakened by a clamor at my door – my inner door from my office to my bedroom. I got up and slipped the Glock out of my purse. As quietly as I could, I slipped a loaded clip into it, and made sure the safety was set. I got down on the floor on the side of the bed away from the door and shouted, "Who is it?"

The voice of a disturbed Minerva came back, "Who would it be? Let me in."

"OK. OK. Just a sec." I put on a robe and went to the door. Minerva had never done anything like this before, so I thought it prudent to keep my Glock to hand. When I opened the door, she came in and dragged me back out to the office.

"It's awful. Mr. Weasley's been poisoned!"

"What the heck! How'd it happen?"

She sat down in the red leather chair, and I took one of the yellow ones next to it. "I don't know all the details, but what I got was that Weasley was actually poisoned twice. First, he ate some chocolates that were meant for Potter. They had some really strong love potion in them. He reacted violently.

"Potter, thinking fast, decided to lure him down to Slughorn's office to get him to fix up an antidote."

"And the antidote was the second poisoning?"

"No. No. The antidote worked as far as I can tell."

"Buuutt?"

"Here's where things get confusing."

"Just now?"

"OH, just shut up and listen. He—that is, Slughorn—thought that they could all use a pick-me-up. So, he proposed that they all have a drink of something that had been for Professor Dumbledore." At that name, I perked up considerably. "Anyway, the bottle of mead had been poisoned, and Ron Weasley fainted dead away after one sip. Fortunately, he was the first to drink. Anyway, Potter saved Weasley with a Beazor. Anyway." She kept speaking, but I'd pretty much lost the main points after hearing Dumbledore's name.

I interrupted wherever she was in the story. "OK. OK. Let's get down and talk to Slughorn right away before his memory fades any more than it already has. Minerva objected, but I grabbed her hand and dragged her out to the hall. We went down to Slughorn's office. He wasn't there, so we went up to the hospital wing to see if he might be up there with Weasley.

We arrived just as Madame Pomfrey was telling everyone that Weasley should be OK but needed rest, meaning NO VISITORS. We intercepted Slughorn and insisted that he let us talk with him. He was reluctant, but I was insistent. He finally agreed to let us talk with him in his office.

After we arrived there, I opened up without preamble, "OK. Tell us what happened this morning with Weasley."

He looked evasive but started. "It was early this morning. I didn't think that students got up that early in the morning on Saturdays. I think it was a little before eight.

"Anyway, there was an insistent banging on the door, and I recognized Potter's voice. I didn't want to talk to him."

That struck me as odd. Wasn't that what the Slug Club was all about? I asked, "Why not?"

Slughorn looked even more evasive, "Potter has been insistent about me talking with him about something that happened a long time ago. It doesn't matter what. I just didn't want to talk to him about it, and he's been a pest ever since.

"Anyway, he said that he had his friend Wallenby along and needed my help with something. So I decided to let him in.

"Wallenby kept talking about some girl that he was in love with. Actually, he'd been given a love potion from her that had been intended for Potter. Potter had tricked Walton into coming down to see me by claiming that she was having a tutoring session with me.

"It was obvious that he'd gotten some kind of massive dose of love potion—almost certainly Amortensia, and I agreed to brew up an antidote.

"I made an educated guess about the dosage and administered it in a glass of water. It was completely effective. He was almost instantly relieved of his slavish devotion to this girl.

"Then, with the tension relieved, I thought that it would be good for everyone to have one stiff one to get the bad taste out of our mouths. So, I pulled out a bottle of mead that I'd . . . gotten . . ." Here he hesitated and stopped, as if realizing that there were something that needed deeper consideration. Then he abruptly said, "It's been very tiring. I think I'll take a nap."

I was not going to let him go before getting a fresh account of the whole incident, and he didn't seem like he was that tired. "Look. This is important. I need to have you go over it with us now."

He wouldn't look at us. He just seemed to take an ever harder stance. He flat out refused to work with us. He finished with, "And you can't force me to. I'm too good at magic for you to force it out of me."

I was getting stubborn too. "You arrogant bastard! If you think we'd use illegal, immoral means to get it out of you, you don't know me, and you certainly don't know Minerva."

Speaking of Minerva, she was becoming distressed by the heat in both our voices. But I couldn't help that. "Look professor. Right now, no one is accusing anyone of anything. This is being treated as an accident. But let me tell you, if you don't wake up and cooperate with us, I promise you that I'm going to file a complaint with the Auror Office.

"A student has been poisoned and almost killed. By your admission the poison was administered by YOU. You say it was intended for Dumbledore. Though you claim that you were in danger, it was Weasley—and his name is W. E. A. S. L. E. Y— who WAS poisoned and you weren't. We don't know that both Weasley and Potter weren't targets of this poisoning. Maybe Potter was just lucky that Weasley drank first rather than the both of them at the same time. And that would have been convenient for you, wouldn't it."

Slughorn's eyes had been growing wider and wider as I spoke. His face turned ashen, he slumped back into a chair, looked up at us for the first time, and almost whispered, "You wouldn't."

"IF you don't start cooperating and cooperating fast, you'll be in the Auror Office telling your story to them—not to me."

He dropped his face into his hands and sobbed once. "I'm old. I shouldn't be the center of a fight with the most powerful dark wizard in history. I just want to live quietly in my retirement. Here I am."

I looked at this sad old man and thought, "He isn't bad, but he's in the center, and he can't get past that. We've got to get on with it." What I said was, "You are where you are. We have to work with the hand that we're dealt.

"Now, you have to move. Tell us what you know."

He became sullen and remained silent. "OK. You can remain silent. I can't force you to talk. But, damn it, if you don't help us, I will do everything I can to send you to the aurors. No. I'll do everything I can to send you to Azkaban. You can join your buddies there. I'm sure that they'll welcome anyone who is standing in the way of figuring out who's trying to kill Potter and Dumbledore."

He stared at me dumbfounded. "You're not serious." He resumed his truculent attitude.

I took him by the shoulders and forced him to look at me. "I spent a month being tortured in Muggle hospitals because of what Deatheaters did to me. And I am lucky to be alive.

"Now, you'd better be bloody sure that I'm going to do everything I can to send you to Azkaban if you don't start talking and talking right now!"

I could tell that he was teetering on the edge. He came down, "It was like this.

"I got this present in a brown paper wrapper. It just appeared on my desk in the potions classroom. I found it at the end of the day. It had a note attached to it. It was to be given to Professor Dumbledore for Christmas. I opened it up and found this bottle of oak-cured mead. The note wasn't signed. I didn't recognize the handwriting."

"Was there any hint of where it might have come from?"

"No."

Minerva nudged my arm and whispered, "Let him keep going. Let's come back to that later."

"OK. Keep going."

Slughorn was not happy but kept going, "Here's where it gets bad. I decided to keep the 'gift' for Dumbledore for myself. I forgot about it." He hesitated and then went on, "No. 1. . . I didn't want to remember that I'd stolen it. I didn't touch it until well after Christmas. Then I could convince myself that it was an accident, and it was too late to give it to him.

"Anyway, it seemed like this was a good day to use the gift. It wasn't just me benefiting. I just poured glasses and handed them out. We were all about to drink. Wem. . . That is, Weasley was the first to swallow. The reaction was instantaneous. Both Potter and I put down our drinks.

"Weasley was convulsing. I. . . I . . . I panicked. I didn't have time to analyze the poison and brew an antidote. Potter kept his head, found a beazor in my kit, and forced it down Weasley's throat. That saved him. At least, it gave us some time to get him to Madame Pomfrey."

I sighed and returned to the previous topic, "Do you have any evidence of where the poisoned mead came from?"

Slughorn shook his head, "No. You could get that at any good wizard liquor store. I don't remember any distinguishing marks on it."

"Where is the bottle, anyway?"

"I don't know. No, wait. I think Professor Snape took it."

"Did he say why he wanted it?"

"No. I just supposed that he wanted to make sure that nobody accidentally drank any of it."

"OK. Thanks for your help." I took Minerva's hand and started out. I turned and said to Slughorn, 'As far as I know this was just a tragic accident—on your part at least."

Slughorn just waved us away weakly.

Minerva asked after his door was shut, "You wouldn't actually have brought in the aurors, would you?"

"I'm not sure that we shouldn't still, but I don't know if I'd have filed charges against him. It's lucky for everyone that we don't have to find out, but, let's go find Snape. I want to know what he was up to with the bottle."

We went to his office and found him there. We didn't bother to knock. "Well, Professors, what brings you barging into my humble office?"

I looked around and didn't see the bottle, "We want to see if we can trace who poisoned the mead that Professor Slughorn had."

"Well, what a coincidence! That's exactly what I'm doing. I've been analyzing the potion that was added to the mead."

Minerva asked, "Any results yet?"

Snape gave her one of those penetrating stares that he seems to have patented. "Do you have any information about the mead?"

I replied, "We asked first. You tell, then we will."

Snape shrugged, "Well, I've identified the main component. It's a Muggle poison, strychnine. It included something that accelerated the reaction. I'm trying to identify that. Ordinarily, strychnine takes some time to be felt. There are several common potions that can speed the effect of other potions but have no effect themselves. I'll have that potion identified shortly. Both are pretty common and easily obtained. Whoever was the poisoner used common ingredients to make it hard to identify him."

I asked where the bottle was. Snape pointed absently in the trash basket. I looked in. It had shattered when it went into the basket. I borrowed a piece of parchment from Snape and started laying out the larger fragments on the parchment. Minerva helped me but wanted to know what we were doing.

"I'm trying to piece together the bottle label. There may be identifying marks or a batch number or something that would let us identify what store the poisoner bought it from."

Minerva found the main shard that had most of the label. Pretty soon, we had the label mostly reconstructed, "Snape, why did you throw the bottle away?"

Snape didn't answer immediately, but eventually said, "I didn't see any reason to keep it. I'd emptied it and started analysis of the poison. We didn't need it anymore, right?"

I examined the label carefully. There was no serial number or lot number or other identifying number. The manufacturer's name was printed on the bottle but not much else. Answering Snape's question, I said, "I guess not. There doesn't seem to be much unique on the label.

The bottle seems to be pretty generic too, but it's hard to be sure since you destroyed it pretty thoroughly."

He had continued his analysis and said tonelessly, "Sorry."

I weighed whether to say anything more and decided not to. "Well, unless there's some way that we can help here, let's leave, Minerva." I wrapped up the parchment containing the glass remains of the bottle. "I assume that you don't need the bottle shards further."

He turned away from his work and stared at us and the parchment package, "No. I suppose not."

We left the office, and when we were well away she asked, "Do you think that he's trying to hide something?"

"I don't know. I couldn't see any useful markings or signs on the remains of the bottle, but I sure wish that we had it intact."

"Why?"

"Well, for one thing, Muggles have a way of identifying who's touched objects by using fingerprints. It's really hard now that the bottle doesn't have any large fragments left."

She laughed, "What in the world are fingerprints?"

"People's fingers have unique patterns of ridges in them. You've surely noticed that."

"Sure, so what?"

"Well, you've probably seen fingerprints on glasses or bottles when the person's hand was dirty or very greasy. People's hands always have some grease on them, and they frequently leave traces behind. Those frequently can be detected and used to identify who had touched the objects."

She nodded with comprehension, 'You mean people like Malfoy, right?"

"Could be, but works with anyone. Slughorn might have obliterated the previous prints when he handled the bottle, but maybe they are still there. It's unlikely, but I want to hang onto the remains of the bottle just in case."

"Just in case you can find a Muggle expert in fingerprints to look at the remains, and just in case he can find some, and just in case they aren't Slughorn's, and just in case we could get everyone to give us their fingerprints, and just in case they match."

"I know it sounds like a long shot, but it's looking like all that we've got at the moment."

I asked Minerva to store them secretly somewhere in her office. I tried to think of some way to get someone to analyze the remains of the bottle for fingerprints. I didn't have much luck.

In the meantime, Minerva and I went to visit Weasley. He was being visited by his girlfriend, Lavender Brown.

When she saw us come in she got up and asked us if we knew anything about Weasley's prognosis. "Madame Pomfrey won't tell me anything except he needs rest and quiet."

Minerva smiled, "That's probably all she knows."

I asked her, "Has he been saying anything. Has he told you anything about what happened that morning?"

She shook her head forlornly. "No. He's been as quiet as the grave." She immediately gasped and said, "I didn't mean that. Really. I . I . . ."

Minerva took her by the shoulders and sat her down, "That's all right, dear. I'm sure that he'll be fine soon. Madame Pomfrey's the best healer there is."

Brown nodded mutely and resumed staring at him and holding his hand. There was nothing to learn here, so we went back to my office and mostly stared at each other. I wasn't about to offer her something to drink. Not today anyway.

After a few days with no results, I went to visit Dumbledore with Minerva. He was not in a good mood. "Well, Wendt, what brings you here?"

"I came to ask you to send Malfoy home." He started to say something but I interrupted, "Please hear me out. Malfoy may not be guilty, but he's the best suspect that we have. Another person has been attacked. Even if he was not the intended victim, that's all the more reason to do what we can that has a reasonable chance of cutting the risk for the rest of the students."

Dumbledore shook his head and simply said, "I can't do that. Malfoy's in a difficult situation. I won't make life harder for him and drive him for real to the Deatheaters without iron-clad proof."

"What do you want? Another student hurt, maybe killed?"

Minerva took my arm and said, "Really, Wendt. This isn't helpful. We just have to keep careful watch and try to catch the culprit."

I stood and paced, "Surely you can think of something, Dumbledore."

He looked at me, boring into my eyes, "Professor Wendt. You know that this can't go on much longer. It will soon be over, and it won't matter."

I swung around wishing that he'd not confided his secret to us. It would be so much easier to be righteously indignant. I looked at Minerva and said, "Let's go."

As we left, I commented, "He's right. He'll either be dead, or the assassin will make a mistake and reveal himself."

Minerva sniffed, "Cheery thought."

"Yeh."

I never figured a way to leverage having the broken bottle. Snape never turned the poison into a way of identifying the attacker.

Malfoy Invictus

The next week or so was a quiet one. Nobody died. Nobody was attacked. Nobody threatened anyone.

Then something good happened. Katie Bell, who'd been attacked the previous term returned to school. She could remember nothing of her attack. It wasn't surprising since she'd been under the imperious curse.

Then something totally unexpected happened. Malfoy and Potter got into a serious fight in a boys bathroom. Where I came from a serious fight in the boys bathroom involved fists and the occasional bloodied nose. I never found out how it got started, but by the time it was over, Malfoy was in the hospital wing recovering from multiple lacerations.

Madame Pomfrey allowed me to visit him for ten minutes. He was the only one there. Potter apparently came off without serious injuries for a change. Malfoy must have been under some light sedation because I had to say his name fairly loudly to arouse his attention, "Mr. Malfoy, I'm sorry to see you here. How are you doing?"

"Did you come to gloat?"

That remark made me take a deep breath, "No. I want to know how you're doing."

"I'm living. I hurt all through my chest and stomach. What do you want?"

"Why did you and Potter get into a fight?"

"It's none of your business."

I was losing ground with every question. "Look. You don't seem like someone who is doing well. AND, I don't just mean in this stupid fight. You're struggling in school. You're getting into fights. You maybe have done some pretty awful things."

"You've been listening to Potter, I see."

"Oh, I listen to everyone. Maybe you'd like to try me out to see how well I listen to you."

"You couldn't help me if you wanted to."

"Are you sure?"

"How are you at fighting ValdeMort?"

"Is that who you're scared of?"

For the first time, he actually did look scared. He stared at me, and I almost thought he was ready to say something, but the desire seemed to pass. I said, "Listen. I don't know what's happened with you, but no one has been seriously hurt—yet. You can still walk away from this without being on the wrong side."

His gazed turned dismissive, "You don't know what being on the wrong side is like." He rolled over to face away from me, 'Go away and don't come back."

"Think about it. It's never too late to turn around."

He didn't say anything else, and my time was almost up, so I left the hospital wing.

Malfoy left the hospital wing the next day. He never returned to my tutoring sessions.

Suddenly, Potter was perky. He hadn't been so great himself lately, but now he was happy. It didn't take long to figure out what had happened. Ginny Weasley had turned her favors toward him. He was spending his spare time basking in the ever improving spring weather with her.

$\triangle$

However, this was all the calm before the storm. One night, when Minerva and I were strolling in the moonlight, there was a strange feel in the air. Everyone that night seemed to want to be out that evening. It was as though the students had the sense that the cat was away, and the mice would play. We ended up having to shoo a lot of students back to their houses. After we'd swept the last of them back into the castle and on their way, Minerva announced, "I've got a bad feeling about this."

"No kidding. We'll probably have to patrol the halls tonight to be sure that none of them sneak out again."

She nodded and said, "And Dumbledore would be out having a nip this evening at the Broomstick."

"You can count on it."

About 11 PM when we thought that we could head for beds ourselves, something really strange happened. The third floor suddenly filled with an impenetrable darkness. Minerva and I had to feel our way back to my office.

While we were struggling back, there was a lot of commotion. Minerva tried to get her wand to light, and it became clear that, though lighted, the wand wouldn't dispel the darkness. Just as we realized that, there was a general alarm raised by the auror guards who had been patrolling outside the castle to keep it safe from attack by Deatheaters.

There was a general battle going on. I grabbed Minerva's hand more fiercely and dragged her to my office. "Damn it, I don't have my Glock with me."

I rummaged looking for it. When I found it in the bottom drawer of my dresser, I rose triumphantly and announced, "I've got it. Come on Minerva. We've got to get moving to help the aurors."

She had her wand raised and said, "You're right. Except that you're not going to be in this battle." She quickly raised her arm, pointed it at me and said, "Petrificus Totalis." I felt that all-too familiar lockjaw sensation and tipped over. I didn't hit the floor hard because her magic spell caught me and let me down slowly, face on my side.

"Sorry, Wendt. I'm not having you in danger again. This will only last a couple of hours. By then either you'll be safe, or we'll need even your help." She bent over me and kissed me on the forehead. Then she walked over my prone body and out of my office and locked the door behind her.

I tried to say, but only succeeded in thinking. "Damn, not again."

It was a long dark couple of hours. During that time, I heard bangs, shouts, cries, explosions. After what seemed like ten hours but couldn't have been because it was still dark outside, I started to feel some response in my muscles. First there was a twinge in my left foot. Encouraged, I kept working my muscles. There was no response for a while, but then there was more feeling in my right ankle. Then I found that I could crawl. I struggled to find the Glock. With no lights on, I looked for a while and decided to try to light a lamp. I struggled to rise to my knees. I fell a couple of times and finally pulled myself up to the bedside table that had a lamp.

I succeeded in lighting a match and then the lamp. Now, I could search with my eyes. I didn't find it and dropped to my knees. I looked under the bed and found that I must have kicked my Glock underneath. I found that I could stand, and I struggled to my feet Glock in hand. I kept staggering toward the door to the hall. I reached it, opened it, and found that it was pitch dark. I started walking in the direction of the entrance. I stumbled over something and thought that my control was loosening.

I discovered that I'd tripped over someone. Almost immediately, I heard bangs and shouts renew. I checked the person to see if he were alive. I detected a pulse. I went on, being able to move almost normally, but I kept tripping over bodies—thank God, still alive. I reached the main entrance. There was still fighting going on down the hill toward the forest and Haggrid's house. Outside, the moonlight and a fire somewhere in that direction provided enough light for me to move forward without tripping much.

As I proceeded, I realized that it was Haggrid's house that was on fire. There were several people ahead, one higher up the hill and there were spells crackling the air and giving rapid flashes of illumination.

I was almost half-way down the hill when I realized in the growing light from Haggrid's house ablaze that there was a student up the hill fighting with several down the hill. I dropped to my knees and brought my Glock up. It was a long shot at best, but if I didn't get it off soon, they'd be able to disapparate and would get away clean.

I steadied my gun hand with my left and tried to get a good shot or two off. I damned the dark and wished for more light. Then suddenly, there was a flare of light from Haggrid's. It clearly illuminated the figure that I was trying to hit. In that moment, my gun arm dropped as well as my jaw. I chose another target and raised the gun again. This time, I didn't have a chance to get a shot off. They had reached the limit of the area where disapparation was impossible, and they all disappeared.

I turned and ran back up the hill to the castle to see if I could help there. I saw a crowd around the Astronomy Tower, and I went to them. Minerva saw me and came to me. I threw my arms around her and whispered, "Was it, really. . ."

She finished the question for me, "Yes, it was Snape. And. And. . ." and sobbed into my ear, "It's over." I saw that she was now crying unrestrained.

I took her in my arms. "What in the world happened?"

She continued crying and between sobs got out, "Dumbledore is dead. Malfoy managed to let Deatheaters in through the Room of Requirement."

I took her to the side and pulled her down beside me. I asked her to tell me slowly and carefully what had happened. She told me the story, and I couldn't quite believe it, but I knew it must be true.

"Snape. Snape! How could he betray Dumbledore? God, I almost wish I hadn't hesitated when I had him in my sights."

"Almost?"

"Yes. Almost. I don't think I could have killed him even if I'd known about Dumbledore." I looked down at the Glock. It was as though I'd seen it for the first time. I threw it to the ground, "I should just give up on this damn gun. It betrays you when you need it the most!" Tears were on the point of welling up in my eyes.

I looked around me—at Minerva now silent beside me, at my watch—it was now after 2:30, and at the Glock that somehow I had picked up again. "Let's try to get some sleep. We'll have plenty to do tomorrow—rested or no."

She got up and started toward the castle. I said to her, "Stay with me tonight. This is a night of tragedies. No one will notice if a harried Administratrix spends the night away from Gryffindor."

She shook her head, "We have to have teachers in all the Houses. I got Slughorn to take over the male head in Slytherin. I don't have anyone to take female at Gryffindor."

I started to say, "What about Sinistra?" but I thought better of it on several grounds. I just nodded and took her in my arms, kissed her, and said goodnight.

⟁

After we'd gotten everyone sorted out and on their way back to their houses, I joined Minerva in her room in Gryffindor. I brought a bottle. She was too stunned to object, and I honestly think that no students noticed.

Once in her rooms, I got hold of myself and asked Minerva, "Did you have any idea about Snape?"

"You mean the depth of his treachery? No. Dumbledore trusted him implicitly. Everyone else trusted him because Dumbledore trusted him."

I nodded my head, "I trusted him because I knew him well. At least I thought I knew him well. If he was playing a game, he was playing a deep one."

Minerva stared at me in disbelief, "What do you mean 'IF'? You can't mean to say that you still trust him?"

"I've got this strong feeling that he's not bad. I've been trying to think about all the history that I have with him. I can't think of anything that absolutely convinces me that he's somehow still a good guy, but on the other hand, I just can't shake the feeling that he's OK."

"Well, if Potter's right, killing Dumbledore would seem to be a good starting point for shaking that feeling."

"Yeh, I know. I guess what I mean is that he's not the right profile for a Deatheater. He's passionate, and sometimes his feelings nearly break through. He hates Potter, but somehow he manages to not do anything serious to him—verbal abuse, yes, but physical abuse? Never. How many Deatheaters can you say that about?"

I looked about the room as though the real reason for my feeling were discoverable on a bookshelf or out the window or on the desk. I finally said, "Look. I met Snape before I met any other wizard or witch – excluding you and Dumbledore. The very first time that I met him was in London before I'd even decided whether or not to come to Hogwarts.

"Do you know that he tried to talk me out of coming to Hogwarts?"

Minerva stared at me a moment, "No, you never told me. What do you suppose that means?"

I reached for my liquor bottle, found two glasses, and poured two stiff shots. I needed time to think that question through and, frankly, a drink was what this night seemed to call for. Minerva objected, and then accepted the glass.

I took a swallow and had thought of what I wanted to say, "Snape tried to talk me out of it for two reasons. First, he was actually concerned for my safety. Second, he thought English Literature would be a distraction from the really important things that students would have to learn. Do you know what that was?"

Minerva started to say something, then stopped and just shook her head no.

"He was sure that the students needed to learn magical self-defense more than anything else. Do you think that those are things that a Deatheater would be concerned about?"

Minerva shook her head slowly and said, "I never understood Snape."

"Has it ever occurred to you that for someone who has strong feelings, he has never been romantically or physically in love with anyone?"

Minerva stared at me, "What does that have to do with . . ."

I rushed on, "No. Listen. Most normal people fall in love. He doesn't seem to have. Or has he? If he loved someone, wouldn't we know it?"

"I don't know. Some people aren't demonstrative."

"Is that really Snape?"

She looked glum, "No. But what does that have to do with anything."

"I think that Snape does love someone but can't express it because she. . ."

Minerva interrupted here, "OR HE."

"Don't be tiresome. You don't really think that he's gay, do you?"

"Oh, I guess not."

"Right. Either she's rejected him or she's not available for some reason. Is that something that would stand in the way of a Deatheater?" I hurried on with the answer to my rhetorical question, "NO. A real Dealtheater would move on and find someone else or maybe even force himself on that someone."

"But. He."

"BUT, BUT, but. I know. Why would he kill Dumbledore? Unless. . ."

She looked up at me quizzically, "Unless?"

I thought about how close Dumbledore had been to death. Did he decide on suicide? I decided that until I thought of a good reason to support that idea, that I should stand back from suggesting it. "Oh, I'm just drawing at straws. I don't want him to be a bad guy, so I'm trying to think of reasons that he doesn't have to be one."

Minerva took me in her arms, and I knew that we had to move on. "OK. Where do we go from here?"

She caressed my back and said, "Oh, I'm the acting Head. I'll set a teacher's meeting for tomorrow immediately after breakfast. We'll decide what to do then."

I nodded mutely. Then I said, "Malfoy. Dumbledore. Damn him. I tried to convince him to send Malfoy away. But NOOOO." My anger was building, but I realized that it was too late for anger.

The next morning, I slept the dreamless sleep of the overwhelmed and barely made it to the Great Hall in time to gulp down breakfast and head for the Teacher's Lounge. The last of the teachers were leaving as I wolfed down a buttered scone and ran after them.

The Teacher's Lounge was filled with teachers milling around aimlessly and talking loudly. I couldn't make out any conversations and didn't want to. Filch found his way to me and said, "Bloody Hell! I didn't think anyone would ever kill Dumbledore. I thought he was bloody immortal." He looked down and said, "What are we going to do now?"

Just then, Minerva came into the room, and the roar dropped to nothing.

"Please sit. I want to get this over as quickly as possible. You can ask questions after I'm done. But they'd better be damn good ones.

"Now, I've spoken with Dumbledore's next of kin, his brother Abeforth. He wants to have the memorial service here on the grounds of Hogwarts the day after tomorrow. That will give people time to arrive and mourn. His body will lie in state in a closed casket in the courtyard. You all are invited, of course, to the memorial service, and I'll ask you to volunteer to set up the chairs and a pavilion.

"We expect a very large crowd. The house elves will prepare a lunch for everyone.

"If anyone wants to speak at the memorial service, they're out of luck. The speaking opportunities will all be saved for visiting dignitaries and those extremely close to Dumbledore. Unfortunately, that's none of us." With that, there was a lot of muttered grumbling. Minerva raised her hand to request silence, and when it had fallen, she spoke.

"However, we will have our own unofficial, informal memorial service tomorrow afternoon in the Great Hall. Anyone may speak who wishes. That includes students, teachers, staff and even house elves. I'll have a notice up to that effect later this afternoon and announce it at dinner and breakfast tomorrow." She paused, looked around and said, "Questions."

There were several shouted questions. What about classes?

"Classes are canceled. Students may leave with parents whenever parents come to collect them. Any who aren't collected by parents will have to go when the Express goes, sometime after the funeral. We'll have more details about that later after the funeral. So don't bother me now."

What about finals, Newt, Owl exams?

"Those exams will be made up some time. We'll have an announcement after the funeral."

That seemed to satisfy everyone for the moment. There was a lot of discussion about what would happen after the funeral, but I wasn't interested. I worked my way through the crowd and found Minerva. "I want to speak at our memorial service."

She seemed stunned. She just said, dully, "That's fine. It's informal. Just come up to the podium and speak."

"I want to talk about how much Dumbledore did for me, a Muggle."

That seemed to wake her up. "You're going to 'come out' are you? Don't be a fool. As a Squib, you're reasonably safe—despite your experience of last summer, but as a self-avowed Muggle at Hogwarts? No, not just a Muggle, but a Muggle teacher at Hogwarts, you'll have signed your death warrant."

She shushed me and pulled me aside into an empty classroom. "Don't say that aloud again here or anywhere. I came as close as I ever want to come to losing you last summer. I will not repeat it again this summer.

"Just get up there and talk about how Dumbledore befriended you a Squibb and even gave you a teaching position."

I agreed reluctantly, and she changed the subject. She had arranged for Madame Pomfrey to take her place at Gryffindor for a couple of nights. She would stay the nights with me.

I went back to my office and started making notes for my eulogy. There was a knock on the door, and when I invited the knocker in, I was shocked to see that it was a house elf. I thought that I recognized him, but I couldn't attach a name to the face.

"Professor, I is Dobbie. We house elves are hearing that Professor McGonagall will let a house elf talk tomorrow about Professor Dumbledore. Is that being true?"

I tried to remember exactly what she'd said, and I realized that she had. "Yes. She promised that. Do you want to speak?"

"Yes. I's do. The other house elves are thinking that someone needs to talk about how Professor Dumbledore is being good to house elves."

"That sounds like a good idea. You should do that."

He looked down to his feet that were in two non-matching socks and mumbled something. I asked what he'd said.

"Dobbie is being too shy and not knowing how to talk good like any of the professors."

I smiled—probably the first time in the last 24 hours. "Dobbie. I think that good talk has to do much more with what you want to say than how you say it. Why don't you tell me what you want to say? I can help you with words a little if you get stuck."

Dobbie turned as red as a radish, but after a minute he said, "Well. House elves are having a hard time in the world. Most masters don't give them time off ever. Professor Dumbledore forced us to take one day off every week. Professor Dumbledore made us feel like he is caring about how we feel. He is never beating us or making us put our hands on the hot stove when we is making a mistake."

I realized how hard it would be for him to say those things, but I couldn't bring myself to correct a single verb or noun. I actually had a hard time holding back my tears as I said what I felt. "Listen Dobbie. That was very eloquent."

He stared at me.

I realized that he didn't know the word "eloquent." "I just mean that those are very good words. I think you should say exactly what you just told me."

"Oh, but sir, those is not good words. Everyone be laughing."

I had to turn around quickly so that he couldn't see my tears. I managed to struggle out, "No one will laugh once. As a matter of fact, there will be many tears."

Dobbie was silent. I got control of myself and turned back to him, "Listen, Dobbie. I wish I had words as good as those. Please, please come and say them tomorrow."

He still didn't say anything and after a while left my office.

Later Minerva showed up, and we sat on the sofa in my office across from the fire—the night was cool. I asked if all the arrangements for the memorial service were completed. She just nodded and took my hand in hers. Later we went to bed.

After lunch, the casket was brought into the Great Hall and placed on the dais. I looked at my notes again and shook my head in disgust. It was stupid.

The Great Hall filled with students and staff. At the very back of the hall, outside the great doors was a small group of house elves.

Minerva came forward to the podium and simply said, "This memorial service is for anyone who wishes to remember Professor Dumbledore. Come and go as you like—quietly and respectfully. Anyone may come to the podium and say whatever you like. Just before dinner, the casket will be removed back to the courtyard.

"I met Dumbledore the first day that I taught here. He was the Assistant Head under Professor Dippet. He was always kind to me and all the teachers and staff that worked for him. He occasionally played a practical joke on the teachers then.

"I remember one Hallowe'en party, he used one of his inventions —he called it a de-luminator. Anyway, he used it to put out all the lights in the Great Hall and the castle at the height of the party. People were tripping over each other and more than one couple who were dancing fell to the floor in a heap." She broke out chuckling at the memory. Then she looked up to the Head Table, having for a moment forgotten that he would not be there. The laughs turned to tears, and she was silent for a moment.

"He was always ready to see the best in people and work to help them reach their own personal goals. I'll always miss him."

There had been a line forming, consisting of students, the occasional teacher, and Peaves. Yes, it was Peaves! I wondered if a gun would have any effect on him. As I wondered that, a young boy who couldn't have been older than a second year, came up on the podium and said, "Professor Dumbledore smiled at me when I was sitting with the sorting hat on my head. I knew then that it would be OK here."

Another student, Amanda Bones, told about how her mother had had Dumbledore as an arithmancy teacher.

Peaves reached the end of the line and came up on the podium. "Peavesy is sorry that he threw a stink bomb at Professor Dumbledore once, but I's not sorry I hit him with a water balloon." Then he left the room like a rifle shot.

I got up and joined the line. When I reached the podium, I said, "Almost everyone here has been befriended at least once by Dumbledore. Before I came here, I was a struggling college graduate who was having a hard time finding a job.

"More than that, I'm a. . ." Here I paused and noticed Minerva covering her eyes as I was about to go on, "A Squibb—not really at home either in the magical world or the Muggle world. Dumbledore took a risk taking me on as a professor at a school for magic.

"I've tried to justify his risk. I never thanked him properly. I hope you all thank the people that have been your mentors and friends while you have time left. No one knows how long they've got."

I sat and realized how draining it had been saying those few words. Minerva came over and sat next to me. "Well, I was wondering if I would have to petrify you twice in as many days."

"You wouldn't have!"

"You try that again, and see if I don't."

The line of people who wanted to say a word about Dumbledore kept growing. Some of the students reached the podium and couldn't say anything, but most told simple stories of an encouraging word from Dumbledore or a second chance when they thought they had flunked out for sure.

Finally, many students had left the room and no one was in line. I got up. Minerva asked, "What are you doing? It's still not too late to be petrified."

"I have a word to say for someone who is too shy to."

I went up to the podium and looked over the scattering of faces in the hall. "I have to say a word for a friend who couldn't come up.

"Yesterday a house elf came to my office and said that the house elves were all treated kindly by Dumbledore. Dumbledore was one of the very few who did. I think that says more about Dumbledore than anything that the rest of us have managed today."

I left the podium and sat next to Minerva. She took my arm in hers, and we sat for a while and then left the Great Hall.

At supper, she announced work assignments for the next day. Teachers would have to help set up the huge number of chairs to accommodate all the guests and the pavilion. They would be assigned to be guides to and from the field where the official memorial service was to be. There would have to be teachers ready to run errands at a moments notice. Minerva had assigned everyone one or more tasks. Even the Squibbs, Filch and I, had assignments.

That evening, Minerva and I sat in my office and had a couple of shots of whiskey. On the first one, I proposed a toast. "To the only man who could find a place for me in magical society."

Minerva answered in kind, "To the man who introduced me to my lover."

We downed the shot.

I asked her THE question, "What happens to the Order of the Phoenix?"

She shrugged, "Oh, it goes on. It was never really dependent on Dumbledore. He was just the most brilliant leader. I suppose that. . . " She hesitated, "I suppose that Kingsley takes over the leadership—as much as there is a leader."

"Would you consider a Muggle member joining?"

She just frowned at me.

"I guess I can take that as a definite maybe."

"You can take it as a definite, 'I'll kill you myself before I let you do such a stupid thing.' Stop being silly and take me to bed."

"OK. That's worth toasting." And we did.

The love we made that evening wasn't great, but it was the first in a long time and we were both happy to prove that there was still love after such a great loss. Afterward, we slept peacefully for a change.

The next morning, activity started early. Breakfast for most people was abbreviated, and work, getting ready for the large influx of mourners, started promptly. There was a crew taking delivery of chairs and setting them up on the hillside approach to the lake. Another group set up the pavilion and tables for refreshments.

The house elves had been up, perhaps all night, preparing the mountains of food to be consumed.

I stood and watched. As a "gofer", I had no idea what—if anything—I'd have to do. So, I assigned myself a task. I had appointed myself to the security team. I strolled back to the area where the people disapparating in were landing. I thought I might recognize one of the Deatheaters if any dared come. It was one of the most boring times that I'd ever spent. There were a thousand guests arriving—more or less. After a while, I asked one of the aurors to conjure me a chair.

He stared at me, "First of all, my name's Michael. I know that yours is Wendt. Let's start over."

"OK, Michael, please conjure me a chair so that I can sit as I watch the endless stream of guest."

He snorted, "I can't sit. Why should you?"

"I'm a volunteer. You get paid for standing for endless hours staring at strangers." He frowned but took out his wand, and a chair appeared beside me.

"Enjoy."

I sat and watched the guests arrive. They arrived individually, in two's and three's. There were occasionally too many arriving for me to get a good look at them before they'd moved away, so I found myself getting up every ten or so minutes. I'd follow them long enough to get a good look at all of them in that group.

After nearly an hour, a man arrived who looked familiar to me, but I couldn't immediately identify why. He was tall, thin almost to gauntness and with hair so white that I wasn't sure whether he was old or young. He walked down the hill, and I got up to walk closer to see him better. I began following him slowly and then faster.

He turned around as though he felt my eyes on him. As I looked at his face again, I remembered. I'd seen him in the States on that day in July when I'd entered Hell by the back door. If I'd had to describe the people I'd seen that day, I couldn't, but seeing him in the flesh opened my eyes of memory.

I came to a trot, and he turned and speeded up. I shouted after him, "Stop!" With that he broke into an outright run. He dodged through visitors making their leisurely way down to the chairs before the lake. I heard feet behind me running as well.

Why didn't he just disapparate? I didn't know, but if I could stop him, I'd find out. He entered a clump of people and disappeared from sight for a moment. He separated himself from the crowd and was running toward the Forbidden Forest. He was alone. I reached into my pocket for my purse and the Glock. I didn't dare have it out in the crowd, but in the open, I didn't care who saw me use it. I still didn't understand why he didn't disapparate.

I worked my purse open and pulled out the Glock. I wanted to be closer. I didn't want to kill him, just threaten him and get him to stop. Just then, I was tackled from behind and fell to the ground. I rolled over to bring my Glock to bear on my attacker. It was one of the aurors. He shouted, "What are you doing?"

I shouted back. "Didn't you see the man I was chasing! He was one of the Deatheaters that attacked me in America!"

He stared a minute and said, "Oh." He looked up and around. "He's gone now—disapparated."

"Why'd he wait so long?"

"Oh, most of the grounds have the spell that prevents disapparation added to them, but the forest doesn't. That area where people are landing had the spell removed."

"Great!" I got up and dusted myself off as well as I could. I glanced at my watch and saw that the time was close to the beginning of the service. I walked back to the seating area.

Minerva came up to me, "Where the heck have you been? I've been trying to find you for the last hour. I wanted you to take the new Headmaster of Durmstrang for a tour of the castle."

I thought about trying to explain but decided that it could wait for later. That was just as well. Minerva went on, "Come on, join me for the service." She took a more careful look at me. "How did you get those grass stains on you dress robes?"

All I could say was, "I'll explain later." We proceeded to the front row where Minerva had saved two seats. We sat, and the service began.

Tears in the Rain

The funeral was over. People were working their way back to the Castle and then back through the floo network to Diagon Alley and Beaux Batons and Durmstrang and Ottery-Saint-Catchpole and the Burrow and the Castle itself. I headed for Dumbledore's old office—now Minerva's office. There was no password at the gargoyle. The gargoyle itself seemed to be permanently out of the way of the stairs to the office. As I walked up, Potter stormed down. I couldn't blame him for being in pain and angry.

I reached the door and hesitated, about to open the door when MInerva said, "Oh, just come in."

I did. She was crying, softly, almost imperceptibly. But I knew. I walked to her. She turned to me, her arms encircled me as she broke into great, heaving sobs. Then she backed away from me a little, looked me in the eye and said, "Go."

"Go?"

"Yes, Go now. Don't turn around. Go to America."

That took me by surprise. All I could do was stare and ask, "Why?"

Her voice turned truly hard, "Oh, you stupid man. You infuriate me so much! With Dumbledore gone, do you really think that you will be allowed to stay on here? And after you leave here, do you think that some Deatheater won't find you again? You were lucky the last time that happened. You were lucky to survive seeing Valdemort in the flesh. The third time WILL be the charm for the Deatheaters."

"Riddle."

The name surprised her out of her tirade, "What?"

466

"Tom Riddle."

"What?"

"You said, 'Valdemort'. You should use his real name, Tom Riddle."

She ran a hand through her hair, "That is just it. I'm talking about your survival, and you're talking about semantics."

"Look, I'm not going to leave you alone here. You're right. Things will get worse here. Even if the directors keep you on as Headmistress."

She was so angry that she couldn't speak for a moment. "I can take care of myself. But I can't take care of both of us. You've got to go."

We seemed to have reached an impasse that neither of us could get around. After staring at each other for what seemed like a half hour but was probably only a few minutes, she compromised, "We've both got to finish grades. We can never start up again next year without grades. I don't know what we'll do about OWL and NEWT scores, but we've got to end the year with some sort of scores. We'll have a meeting of the teachers as soon as I can get in touch with everyone. We'll have this out after we've closed out the year."

At that lunch Minerva, as acting Headmistress, declared the school year ended, announced that the Hogwarts express would run the next day for any students whose parents hadn't picked them up already, and announced that there would be a teacher's meeting in the Teacher's Lounge immediately following lunch. Her voice had shaking with emotion as she'd tried to imitate Dumbledore's style of dismissal. She succeeded in holding back the tears.

As we walked up to the Teacher's Lounge, the Heads of Houses, all two of them, had tried to wheedle out of me what would happen in the meeting. All I could say was, 'It's obvious that there will be announcements about how the year will be terminated—grades, etc. I've no idea what, if anything, she might want to talk about besides that." Actually, I did have one idea. It would be to announce perfectly irrevocably that I was fired. She would be sure to be rid of me then.

We arrived at the Teacher's Lounge, and I took a chair at the back. I wasn't really surprised when Filch joined me back there. He whispered, "Well, we're in for it now. Well, maybe the rest of them are in for it. You'll probably be OK."

Amazingly, there were several ghosts that entered then. Nick glided over through a few teachers and hovered beside me, "Do you know what is going to happen?"

"Well, I know that we're going to have an orderly end-of-term. I know that we've got to get grades out. Beyond that, you know as much as I do."

"Oh, come now. It's well known among the ghosts that you have a very close relationship with Ms. McGonagall. You surely know more that that."

"Oh, I surely don't. Oh, unless you mean that I'm about to be sacked."

Nick turned a light shade of red. How a ghost could do that I couldn't imagine, but he did, "Oh, surely, Professor Wendt, you're joking."

"No. I expect it any day."

"But, but you seem to belong here as much as I do!"

I thought that one over. If Minerva were right, maybe that's exactly the way that I would stay here.

"But why do you care? No one can evict you. I don't think that anyone can affect you ghosts, can they?"

Nick drew himself up and tried to look impressive, "Can you have forgotten already how I was petrified by the basilisk?"

"Oh, yes. I had forgotten, but no wizard can do anything to you can they?"

"Ghosts have feelings, like anyone else. We know when we're not wanted–when we're unwelcome. It hurts us deeply. Professor Dumbledore was very hospitable to us ghosts."

I didn't get to pursue that thought any further because just then Minerva bustled into the room. The continuing hubbub had started to settle down, but her patented throat-clearing sent the rest of the room into absolute silence.

She looked about the room with a no-nonsense expression. "We are all suffering under the loss of Professor Dumbledore. I. . ." Here she had to struggle to maintain composure. The she went on, "I as much as anyone.

"But we have to continue. The next steps are communicating with the parents to be assured that they will either pick children up before tomorrow morning or that they will pick them up in London on the Express. You all are responsible for those in your houses.

"We have to see that the remaining ones are on the Express.

"You must complete grades in all classes and forward them to me before the end of the week.

"After you've turned in your grades, you may leave for Summer Holiday. Questions?"

Nick smugly said, "See. You're not fired."

Sybill Trelawney stood, "What about Owl and Newt exams?"

Minerva sighed, "We've not gotten guidance from the Ministry of Education yet, but my suggestion, if I get to make one, is that we devote the first week of classes next term to taking those exams.

Sinistra stood, "But class assignments depend on those results— especially Owls. Are we going to wait for results to start teaching classes?"

"No, I think the vast majority of what students want to take won't be affected by them. For example, someone who wants to be an auror won't sign up for classes that they don't think they're going to be allowed to take. A few disappointed students won't be awful."

Then someone asked, "What about the contracts for next year that we signed?" Normally, midway through the second term, teachers got the next year's contract with their new salary.

Minerva just shook her head, "For now, you should assume that they will be honored next year. For my part, I'm perfectly happy with what Dumbledore has decided." Nick tried to nudge me, but that really doesn't work with ghosts.

"However," Here I would have nudged him back, if I could have, "I really don't expect to be the next Headmistress. I think the ministry will appoint someone else. They can change those contracts as they see fit. So, stay tuned, as the Muggles say."

Filch nudged me and said, "How does she know what Muggles say?"

I shrugged, and Minerva went on, "I imagine though that most of the contracts will continue as they are now.

Someone shouted out, "Those are magical contracts. They can only be changed by mutual consent."

Minerva said dryly, "Take a careful look at your contract. It was signed by Dumbledore for the school. Since," her throat caught here, "he is dead, the contract can be abrogated, and then you'd have to re-negotiate."

I stood and asked, "Do you have any hint who the new headmaster will be?"

"Your guess is as good as mine."

With that answer, no one else stood. Minerva dismissed us, and we started to wander out. She stayed to the end, and I was one of the last out. As I was about to leave, she asked me to stay. After everyone had left, she asked, "How quickly can you finish your grades?"

"Two or three days. Two if I push it. Why, are you in a hurry to get me out of here?"

She glared at me, "I most certainly am. Make it two. And if it's at all possible, one would be better. Now, off to your grading, now!"

I left immediately before she thought better of it. I worked as hard at it as I ever had.

The next day at breakfast, I sat beside Minerva. The first thing she said was, "Well?"

"I've worked a miracle, but I won't be done in time to catch the Express after breakfast. Maybe lunch."

She didn't look up from her oatmeal, "If you think that I'd let you take the Express, you're crazier than I thought. Platform 9 ¾ would be a death trap for you. I'll arrange something else for you. Just finish your grading by noon, and we'll see what we can do after lunch."

We both finished our breakfasts with our thoughts. What I wanted to say was not quite fit for the breakfast table. I went back to my office and finished my grades. It was a little after noon, but there was still plenty of time for lunch. I hadn't finished packing, but I could do it in a few minutes after lunch.

Just then, an owl flew into the room and dropped a note on my desk. I opened it. It was from Minerva, "Come to my office immediately —packed, M."

So, I finished packing. As I scanned the room, I wondered if I'd ever see it again. I looked at the bookshelf with its rows of novels and books of poetry, essays, and magazines. I wondered if I'd ever see them again. I knew that I couldn't pack them in the time I had. I hoped that I'd see them in a couple of months. I looked over my desk. There were various photos and mementos—a program from a chess tournament in Paris, a paperweight from Stanford. There was a framed photo of Minerva that showed ever-so subtle movement in the shadows of leaves in the background. I pulled that out of the frame and put it in a notebook that I kept for current business. I stuffed it into the duffel. I quickly stepped to my bedroom and glanced around. There were a couple of posters and prints on the walls. They would have to stay.

I had a small collection of lapel pins of various sorts on my dresser. I went over and picked one up. I put it in my duffel. It said, "Potter inks". It had once said, "Potter Stinks." I glanced desperately around looking for some other memento of Hogwarts that I could pack and that would be something that could remind me that I really had been a teacher here. I didn't see anything and walked through the door to my office. I locked my office door and headed for Dumbledore's office.

I arrived and Minerva held out her hand.

I asked, "You looking for my grades?"

"Of course."

I handed them over—out of my current business folder. She glanced at them and nodded. Then she looked up at me, "Look around. This will be the last you see of Hogwarts."

"I'm coming back for the next term. My contract is still good until the new Headmaster kicks me out."

She reached down to her desk but kept her eyes, cool and calm, on mine. She picked up a piece of parchment. "The original of your contract." With that she ripped it in two. "Done. Now, you don't have a job here."

My mouth tightened into a grim line. I wet my lips, "I'm not done. You may be able to eject me, but I'm not finished with you."

"We're leaving by floo." She walked over to her fireplace and held out a hand.

I crossed my arms over my chest and stood.

She was holding out her left hand toward me. She then lifted her right hand, her wand grasped in it, her index finger pointed at my eyes. "Listen to me well. If you don't come along, I'll obliviate your memory. You will never have a memory of me or Hogwarts left. I will do it thoroughly and permanently. Then, I'll put you on a plane back to the States."

"You wouldn't. That would be murder. It would kill the best part of me."

She simply said in the steeliest, most Minerva-like tone she had, "I will."

I thought of all the memories that we shared – Cedric in Paris, Minerva in the National Galleries, the boat-house on the Serpentine. These would be as tears in the rain.

"Where are we going?"

"It's better that you don't know. Now! Come!"

I did.

We stepped through the fireplace opening, green fire flaring around me. I thought about the possibility that this would be the last and only time that I walked through that fireplace. The thought occurred to me that it might not be such an awful way to travel.

We stepped out into what at first I thought might be the Cauldron, but I almost immediately started noticing differences. The windows opened on the street outside—a definitely small town outside. I took in the familiar features—a bar with bartender (NOT Tom). There were the tables that looked more like normal pub furniture—not trestle tables.

It was clearly lunch with most of the tables occupied. Most people already had their meal in progress. There was one table with a waitress taking an order. The barkeep greeted us, "Welcome ma'am, sir. Is it service of table or bar you want?"

We'd used his floo connection, so it had to be one or the other. I wasn't clear whether Minerva intended us to have lunch here or move on quickly. I definitely wanted to talk and not be overheard by the 'keep, so I said, "Table." I glanced at Minerva for guidance. She shook her head almost imperceptibly. "But we're not going to have a meal. Is that OK?"

The 'keep seemed satisfied, "Just pick one of the tables." I selected one that was further from the bar and held Minerva's chair for her. The waitress came over promptly—too promptly for me to ask her what we wanted.

Minerva seemed to want me to make the choice, so I picked my favorite, "Do you have Jack Daniels?"

She hmmed a yes, so I said, "Good and. . ." Here I wasn't sure whether I should name Minerva, but finally she said something, "The same."

"Very good ma'am. I'll have that up shortly."

The barkeep delivered it and asked, "Will you be running a tab?"

I reached for my purse, seeing what was coming. He didn't surprise me. "That'll be a galleon six."

I pulled two galleon coins out and handed them to him with my thanks. He smiled for the first time since we'd entered the pub.

After he'd gotten out of earshot I asked, "Are you planning on eating?"

She smiled for the first time today, "Yes, but not here. Let's finish our drink and move on."

"Good. Where to?"

"I'm still not ready to tell."

We both drained our glasses in silence. We didn't drink them quickly, like medicine, but not slowly and contemplatively either. That was true even though I had a lot to contemplate. What would we do next? I was sure that we'd leave the pub by foot out the front door and then go someplace secluded to disapparate but I couldn't guess beyond that.

When we had finished, we got up, waved the barman good bye. He invited us to return soon. His request was probably as sincere as my reply, "The next time we're in town for sure."

We walked out the door, and I turned immediately, hoping to catch the conversion of the door into a blank wall but missed any transition. One instant it was a closing door, and the next there was the blank cream brick wall.

I glanced around the street. It was typical of small, rural, non-suburban towns. The street had a number of storefronts—clothing, another pub (Muggle), a tea room, a post-office. In the distance I could see the spire of a church, probably Church of England. After a quick scan, we both headed without words for a side street that seemed quiet. A casual observer would probably think that we knew the town like the back of our hands.

The street was a short street with a few houses. There were a couple of cars parked in front of houses but no obvious homeowners around. We went to one side of the street. Minerva held out her hand, and we disappeared.

We re-appeared in an alley, short like the street that we'd left. It was clearly in a large town. I immediately thought London. I don't know what it was. Maybe I'd been nearby and something I'd seen before came to mind. She kept my hand in hers and led me out. I immediately recognized the locale. We were next to a hotel that we'd stayed in on several occasions.

"Well, Minerva, are we eating here or doing more?"

Her smile was impish, "More."

We walked in, and she said, "Why don't we go over to the Front Desk and reserve a room?"

"Yes!"

I held the door for her, and we entered. We went to the Front Desk. Fortunately, there was no one there whom we recognized or who would recognize us. I told the desk clerk that we wanted to reserve a room for the night.

She nodded, asked for credit card, ID for the credit card holder, and names. We'd been through it all before, but there was a new twist or two. She looked up and asked, "May we have your email ID?" When I hesitated she said, "We just want to email you a few special offers from time to time—like our special New Year's package. Like your other information, we don't share that with anyone."

I smiled and said, "Sorry. I don't use email."

She apparently got that answer quite a lot because it didn't disturb her in the least. Then I asked when we could go to our room.

"I'm afraid our check-in time isn't until 3 PM, but I can give you a key now, so long as you will respect that time. Also, you can leave your luggage here at the Front Desk."

I declined with thanks. We then went to their coffee shop, which was still serving lunch. We were seated and ordered. I looked around to be sure that there wasn't anyone close. It was toward the end of the lunch hour, so the coffee shop was pretty empty. "So. Are you going to stay the night?"

Minerva looked down toward her feet and then looked up, "Before we get to those details, let's get the uh. . . what do you Americans call it? .   . the big picture set.

"We'll have lunch, go to our room, and pretty much stay there until tomorrow."

"Sounds great to me."

"Just hear me out. No interruptions."

I shrugged.

"We can come down and have dinner. I think it would be better not to have anything delivered to our room."

I laughed, "I certainly don't want anything we'll be doing interrupted."

She frowned, and I added, "OK. OK. No interruptions."

"The next day. I want to leave with the least fuss. Can we leave without checking out at the Front Desk?"

"Sure. They have my credit card number. They'll get paid regardless what we do."

She nodded, "Good."

"Are we, at least, going to have breakfast down here?"

"I don't want anyone who doesn't have to see us to see us."

"And I suppose, no breakfast in bed."

"I told you no. . ."

"Yeh, I know. No fuss."

"And besides, if we have breakfast in bed, who knows when we'll leave."

"Right on."

"Then we'll disapparate directly from the room to your summer apartment."

She stopped for a minute and studied me as though trying to figure how to say what she needed to say next, "I wasn't kidding when I said that I wanted you back in America. I wasn't kidding about obliviating your memory."

"Look, I agreed to everything when I left Hogwarts. I said goodbye to it for good. I made a commitment. I'll keep it."

She breathed a sigh of relief, "Then you'll leave the country as quickly as you can. How long will it take you to buy plane tickets and leave?"

I thought a moment. Of course, I could do that quickly, but I thought there might be a better way. "Well, IF I were flying, I could do that in a day, two at the most."

A cloud seemed to cross her face, "What do you mean, IF?"

"I mean that flying may not be the safest way to go."

"Well, how would you go then, train?"

"Actually that's maybe not an entirely bad idea, but what I was thinking was going by boat."

Her eyes widened rapidly. "You're kidding. No one travels by boat. Do they?"

I smiled, "People who are less concerned with getting someplace in a hurry and more concerned with keeping a low profile do. No one, at least no wizard, would expect a Muggle to go by boat."

"But, do boats cross the Atlantic? I thought Muggles just cruised by boat around in circles and ended up back where they started?"

"Sure they do—answers to both. But those cruise boats sometimes have to go from one place that they travel in circles in to another place where they travel around in circles. When they do that, you can travel cheaply and nobody notices you. There are usually not many people on the boat. It's out of disapparation range most of the time. Nobody expects it."

She looked toward the ceiling as she considered it, "How long does it take to get a boat ticket?"

"Like air travel, you can get a ticket in a day or two. The key is when your boat sailing. It might be the same day. It might not be for two weeks."

"That's an awfully long time."

"It's not as bad as you think. I've agreed to your crazy demand. I'll go whole hog. I promise you that I will hole up in my garret room and not leave more than once a day – maybe not that often. I'll order out food and have it left with someone else in the rooming house. I won't be outside the house more than a total of an hour or two."

"Hmmm" she considered it. "Doesn't sound bad. I just don't like the idea of you being here in England so long."

"It will almost certainly be less. It might even be only a couple of days."

"OK. I suppose I can't complain about that."

I had my own agenda, "Now, I've got a really serious request for you."

"I suppose I owe you something."

"You sure do. I want you to stay in touch with me."

She gaped at me. "That's impossible."

"Why?"

"Well, if I sent messages to you, they could be traced."

"I could make it really hard to trace."

She sneered, "How would you do that."

"Well, first, they'd get sent to me by email. That's almost perfectly anonymous."

She looked at me as though I were playing a little joke, "Very funny. Now, how would you really do it? E-pale indeed."

"Not E-pail. Electronic mail. I can get an ID that doesn't have anything to do with my real identity. Sending it electronically makes it almost impossible to trace—even if you're a Muggle expert."

She was clearly very dubious. "I haven't even heard of this E-mail. How could I ever do it?"

"Well, you would have to have a Muggle that you could safely send messages to and who would agree to email them to me. Maybe one of your students with a Muggle parent."

"Maybe that's possible, but I would want to be sure that I didn't get them in trouble."

"Just do whatever you have to do to keep them safe. I trust you to be ingenious and not just forget about it once I'm gone."

"Well, OK. Suppose I do agree. How does it work?"

"Well, the Muggle has to know my email address. You don't have to know it unless you want to."

"Of course, I do. Especially if it's so safe."

"OK. Here is what I'll use: nwolf180286@yahoo.com."

"What did you say? Did you say you-who?"

"No. I'll write it for you."

Minerva pulled a scrap of parchment out of her purse and a quill. I spelled it slowly for her and checked what she had written, "That's right. You just give that to your Muggle. He should only have to have it once. It's not an address that you put with each message."

"This address is just random garbage."

"That's the idea. Except that it's not random to me. I'll not have any trouble remembering it."

Minerva was still not totally convinced, "What if the message is intercepted. How can we keep it safe?"

I thought a moment and said, "Yes. We'll use a code."

She actually clapped her hands together, "Oh goodee. A code. I always wanted to use codes. What kind of code—Morse Code?"

"No, that would be too easy. Even Deatheaters might figure it out. We'll use an Ettendorf code."

"What in the world is that?"

"Well, you have to have some printed material that both people have access to. So, we could work it this way. We both get a subscription to *The Times* of London. When you want to send a message you pick up a *Times of London*—it doesn't matter which one – old or recent. You turn to the sports page and find the words that you want to send somewhere on the sports page. You send them as pairs of numbers. The first number is the paragraph number that the word is in. You start counting from the first page, top left corner down columns and then left to right. The second number is the word number."

She smiled and said, "Clever. But I can think of some problems."

"Go ahead."

"How do you know which *London Times* to look in."

That was an oversight but quickly repaired, "The first three numbers of the message is the date: day then month then year. For example, 4 July 1995 is 4, 7, 95."

"OK. What if I can't find the word I want in the sports page?"

I thought about that for a minute and then had an answer, "OK. We don't limit it to the sports pages. We use the whole paper. Each word is a triplet of numbers. The first is the date of *The Times*. The rest of the triplets are—page number, paragraph number, word number."

She was getting excited. "But *The Times* has lettered sections. It doesn't have numbers from first to last."

"Yeh, yeh. OK. The page number is actually a three digit number. The first digit is the section: A is 1, B is 2, and so forth. We don't use pages from section J onward. If they have a section J. The next two digits are the page number in the section."

Minerva nodded, "I can't think of any other problems besides not being able to find the word we want in the whole paper."

"Right. One other thing. Rather than starting at the upper left corner and going top to bottom, followed by left to right, start at the bottom right corner and go bottom to top, right to left."

Minerva seemed to be focusing internally and finally said, "That's kind of complicated, can you write it down for me."

I started to hold out my hand for the parchment and quill, but then I thought better of it. "No, you should write it down. I'll dictate. You write. I'll check what you've written. Then you memorize it so that you can say it back to me and when you've got it," I paused for emphasis, "YOU BURN THAT PAPER."

She raised her hand to her head in a mock salute.

So, I dictated it again, she wrote, I checked, and she memorized. Between that and lunch, it was already past 3PM before we were done. We went directly to our room.

We arrived, and I tossed my duffel in a corner. Minerva immediately went to the window and closed the drapes. I suddenly realized that she hadn't brought her own small bag. I commented on that and asked her what she would wear to bed.

"Did you want me to wear something?"

The room had a small settee. I suggested that we sit there. She seemed happy of that, "Good. We probably should do at least some talking. This may be our last chance."

I'd kept that fact away from my mind as long as I could. "Yes. It's funny. You think that you have all the time in the world to talk. Then when you don't, you discover there are so many things that you never said."

She smiled, "Like what?"

"Like I never mentioned how much I like getting to gaze into your eyes."

She nodded. I went on, "I have always enjoyed holding you. The reason is that I just enjoy caressing your skin—all of your skin— anywhere, any time. I never said that."

"I knew it."

"But I never said it."

She smiled and said, "I never told you that I really enjoy your crazy, stupid jokes. Believe it or not, they're really sexy. I always love to hear you talk—even when you're not joking."

I remembered something from long ago. "Do you know when I first knew I was in love with you?"

"Certainly. It was one of the times that I took you to see that girl friend in Edinburgh, but that wasn't when you fell in love."

"No?"

She smiled a sly smile, "No, it was when we took the floo network for a Hogwarts visit. You took my hand, and I could feel it just as well as you did."

"What? You don't mean that it was our first meeting!"

"Yes. The first moment I saw you and talked to you, my heart was lost. I didn't realize it at the time, but while we talked about teaching, I realized how much I respected you and loved talking with you."

The conversation was strangely pleasant. It was as though we could deny the reality of what would happen the next day. This discussion was really not overtly sexy, but I could feel the strength of physical desire slowly waxing and waning, waxing and waning, always the peak was higher than before.

The conversation became more and more one of caress and whispers of love. At some point it changed from a conversation of words to a conversation of sexual fulfillment.

Sometime later, I looked down to my wrist and was shocked that it was already after 9 PM. I nibbled on Minerva's ear and asked if she wanted something more substantial to eat. Her answer, "I am a bit peckish."

We hurriedly dressed and ran down the stairs to see if the coffee shop were still open. It was. The meal was simple and eaten in silence. We returned to our room, and we found that it was way too close to the next day. We just went to bed and spooned. Minerva grasped my hand convulsively and drew it around her waist. She said nothing.

It was an unquiet night. Neither of us had more than a few minutes of fitful sleep at a time. When it began to get light outside, we got up silently and dressed. I took my duffel in hand and took Minerva in my other arm. We disappeared.

We landed in our favorite alley next to my street. We walked to my door and stood on the small stoop outside. Minerva looked at me. "Just in case we never meet again." We kissed. She stepped back, walked down the steps, turned, and disappeared.

I turned, rang the bell, and waited.

The next couple of days, I started working on getting back to the States. I bought a new cell phone. I used it to call the cruise lines and made a reservation for a repositioning cruise to Miami. It was scheduled to leave in ten days.

The next day, I went down to the Cruise Line Office intending to pay for the cruise. It all went smoothly until the agent that I was working with came to the part about paying.

She was in her early thirties and wore her blond hair short. I wasn't sure whether it was her natural color, but I suspected that it wasn't. Anyway, she asked THE question, "Will you be paying by credit card or check?"

I smiled, "Neither." I started to clarify that I was going to be using cash when she interrupted me and said, "American Express or Barclay's?"

I was puzzled, "I thought I said not by credit card."

She giggled, "Not the credit card, the traveler's checks." She leaned back and added, "You're an American, I suppose it must be American Express." She giggled again at her astute guess.

I smiled too. "Neither. I'm paying with cash."

She just made a face and said, "Really?"

"Yes." I then got out my purse. I always keep some "mad" money in my purse. Now that I was moderately rich, it was a fair amount of money. Fortunately I had enough 100's in the purse that it didn't appear strange that I had enough money in my purse to pay for the passage.

She counted the money. Ten hundreds is easy to count. Then she excused herself as she went to find change. "We normally don't keep a lot of cash in the office, but there should be enough."

She was back in about fifteen minutes with an assortment of small bills, and after counting them with me, she found she was short by seventeen pounds. She said, "Oh, bloody hell", under her breath and opened her own purse and rummaged around to come up with a fiver and six singles.

She smiled a forlorn smile and said, "I'm sorry. It looks like we don't have the proper change."

I replied, "You've put so much effort in, just keep your eleven and consider the seventeen as a tip for your sterling effort."

She was still uncomfortable, but I assured her that it was perfectly all right.

Then she filled out my receipt and printed a ticket. She threw in some brochures on the liner that I'd be on and the cruise. She profusely thanked me, and we parted company.

So, I was left with a number of days to "kill". I did my best, picking up my writing projects, choosing one to work on, and reading *The Times* of London. I experimented a bit with Ettendorf codes for potential messages to Minerva. I chose the first that I could think of, "I love you".

Two days before my trip, I decided that I'd better get money – lots of money. I didn't want someone tracing me on the "grid". I knew that I couldn't go to Gringotts–not even the smallest branch, but I could go to a normal bank and do a credit transaction.

I picked a major branch. I wanted one that would have lots of cash. I chose one in a well-to-do suburb. I walked in wearing my only suit and with a small expensive brief case that I'd just bought. I went to the first cubicle that was not occupied by a customer and asked if the banker could help me with a large credit transaction.

She smiled and said, "Certainly. Just how much money do you want to take out?"

I hesitated a moment, about to attempt the crossing of the Rubicon. I reviewed the amount that I'd had in mind and wondered if I dared name it or possibly go somewhat lower. I decided that my first intuition was right. I would need lots of money to drop off the grid for a long while, so I said, "Grasp your chair arms." I hesitated a moment, and she frowned. "I want one hundred thousand pounds."

Her mouth dropped and she leaned back. "You aren't shy, are you?"

All I could do was shake my head.

She shrugged and held out her hand, "I need your passport and your credit card, please."

I had anticipated that. "I'll allow you to look, but I hold at all times. You can copy all the information you need onto a piece of paper."

She wrinkled her brow and then said, "OK. We can do it that way." She pulled a legal tablet from a desk drawer and asked me to place the card and the passport flat on the tabletop. She wouldn't touch either. I did, and she started copying information. When she'd finished, she took a long look at me and said, "I need to get the branch manager. I'll be back in a few minutes."

It was indeed a number of minutes before she returned with him. She introduced us, and we all sat. The manager, a Mr. Broderick, asked, "We need to know why you want that much money."

"Well, it's simple. I've lived here in England for several years, only visiting my family's home in the US on rare occasions. I don't have a bank account there that I could transfer funds to. And, to be honest, I've a certain distrust of banks. I'm sorry."

He stared at me for a couple of minutes. I returned the gaze – not offensively. I'd had plenty of practice with Minerva and especially Snape. Eventually, he said, "You realize that you'll have to fill out some government forms as well as sign the charge receipt. Since you intend to leave the country with that much money, you realize that you'll have to declare it when you go through customs–both here and wherever you end up?"

"Yes, I do realize those things."

"And you will also have to sign a statement, releasing the bank of all responsibility for what happens after you go through our front door?"

"That's perfectly acceptable."

He continued to stare at me for a while. Then he said, "Ms. Hastings, please get the routine parts of this started–validating that the credit card company will accept this large a transaction and so on. I'll get the government forms and start with those."

They both left the cubicle, and I leaned back to wait. I didn't have to wait long. Ms. Hastings returned first, picked up her phone, and pressed a button. She said into the handset, "I have Mr. Wendt here in my office. He can talk to you in a minute." She pressed another button and then turned to me. "This is a representative of your credit card company. He has a few questions for you." She then pushed the button again and handed the handset over to me. I stood and accepted the handset.

"Hello, this is James Wendt."

The voice on the other end had a certain tension in his voice, "First, I need to validate that you are our Mr. Wendt. Would you please give me the maiden name of your mother's mother?"

I thought a second and then remembered, "It's Dent."

"Thank you. Now, I need assurance that you are not under any undue influence to make this transaction. If you are under duress, please give me the maiden name of your Mother. If not, make up a name."

I replied, "Davies."

"Thank you, Mr. Wendt. Please return the phone to Ms. Hastings."

I did. She accepted it and talked for several minutes. Then she wrote something down on her legal pad and hung up the phone. "Very impressive, Mr. Wendt. You're approved for the amount you requested. We don't have enough cash to satisfy that here, but we'll arrange for a courier to bring the rest from another branch. They should be here before we've finished."

Then Broderick returned and looked a question at Ms. Hastings. She said, "It's set." His eyebrows raised, and he sat next to me at the desk. He laid a small sheaf of forms on the desk and said, "We need you to fill out this, this, and this. And then when you receive the money, you'll have to sign this acceptance and release form."

I nodded and started the lengthy process of filling out the forms. I finished, and then Ms. Hastings apologized that the money wasn't quite assembled yet. I sat back, and she told me, "I've never had a complete stranger walk into this office and walk out the same day with so much money. This is rather exciting."

All I could do was smile. Shortly after that Broderick returned with a small brief case. He silently opened it toward me. He was on the other side of it blocking view from the hallway outside with his body and the top of the briefcase as he opened it. I whistled. He then asked, "Do you want to count it?"

There were ten stacks of bills. Each was banded with a piece of paper labeled, "100 X 100". I picked one up and riffled it next to my ear and then riffled it under my eyes."

Ms. Hastings giggled, suppressed it, and asked, "Can you actually count that stack that way?"

I laughed, "No. I've just always wanted to do that." Then I added, "But, I think I could tell if the occasional tenner had snuck in among the hundreds." She giggled again. I chalked it up to tension, but Broderick looked disapproving. I did that to the rest of the stacks and lifted my brief case to the desktop.

Broderick said casually, "You can have the briefcase if you like."

"No thanks. It's nice but I like mine better." I then transferred the bills to my briefcase.

Broderick said, "Now, please sign the receipt and release. Ms. Hastings will notarize it, and we can all be off about our businesses."

I nodded, read the release, and signed it. Broderick signed it, and Ms. Hastings notarized it and went off to make a copy for me. She quickly returned with it. We all shook hands. Ms. Hastings patted the back of my hand with her free hand and smiled a warm smile at me. I bid them farewell and left the bank branch.

By this time it was late in the afternoon. I took the Tube back to my neighborhood, just another tired commuter returning home from a hard day's work. The whole trip I wondered if I shouldn't pop into a loo someplace and transfer my money to my purse, but decided the fewer unusual things I did, the better.

I exited at my normal stop of the Tube and walked the few blocks home. As soon as I arrived, I ran up the stairs to my garret and quickly pulled out my purse. I transferred the stacks of bills to the purse and pulled out my Glock. I looked around for someplace to hide the purse. I ordinarily wouldn't have done that, but since it contained over 100,000 pounds, I now felt differently about it. I looked around the room. There was always the loose floorboard. I looked at it a minute and thought, "Way too obvious."

Then, I noticed the sole window in the room. I wondered about putting it outside the window–maybe wedged under the sill. That thought didn't last long. As I was staring at the window, I noticed something. The window was an old design. It had a counterweight that was supposed to make it easy to raise or lower the window. Then, I noticed something that I'd seen a couple of hundred times but hadn't really thought about.

There was a little door that gave access to the pulley and counterweight. I opened the window and got out my Swiss Army knife. I opened the small screw driver blade and unscrewed the lone screw that held the door in place. I opened the door and, sure enough, there was a cavity there where the weight was. I took my purse and squeezed it in. Then, I opened and closed the window several times to see if it would still work with the purse inside. It worked fairly well. Someone who was familiar with the action might have noticed, but I was the only person who used it enough to notice.

I quickly put the door back in place, screwed it tight, and raised and lowered the window several times as a final test. I then ordered out dinner and went down to eat in the kitchen when it arrived, quite confident that my purse was safe from discovery.

I went to bed that night quite satisfied. In two days, I'd be on the boat, and I'd enjoy a leisurely trip back to America. Maybe I could get some writing in. The purse was hidden. My Glock was under my pillow. All was right with the world.

There was a tremendous crash that would have waked the dead. I felt like I knew a little bit about being dead–or at least near dead. This was definitely a wake-the-dead crash. There was some sort of shouting going on. Something like, "DID, DID", the letters being spelled. Then the room was flooded with light, and I could make out the shouting quite clearly. "Hands up. Don't move. This is the CID."

I lifted my head from my pillow and looked around to see my bed surrounded by three burly men, carrying some sort of assault rifles– all pointed squarely at me. They stripped off my sheet and saw that I was only wearing a pair of briefs. I had my hands up.

Someone shouted, "Clear." Then a business-suited man entered my garret, holding a piece of paper forward. He spoke, "This is a warrant for the arrest of one James Wendt for questioning under the Official Secrets Act. Please get dressed and come with us peacefully."

I looked around me and shrugged, "OK. My clean clothes are in that wardrobe. May I get them? And, you really don't need all the firepower."

The officer with the warrant said, "OK." I walked over to the wardrobe, and one of the armed officers opened it and asked, "What do you want?"

"The blue shirt. A pair of jeans. I've got underwear and socks in the top drawer." He pulled them out and checked them efficiently for concealed items. Then he tossed them to me.

In the mean time one of the other armed officers said, "Hello, hello, hello! Oh, I don't know about not needing the firepower." He had my Glock held up by a pencil run through the trigger guard. "This looks like a nine, no a ten mm. Glock to me."

I finished dressing. The plain clothes detective asked, "Where's your ID."

I thought furiously. I couldn't let them see the purse or its contents. But my passport was there. I decided to pretend ignorance. "It's over there on the dresser."

They rummaged through the items that I had there—a few pounds, a galleon, keys, my pocket knife, and a resident alien card—all of which I might have to use frequently enough that I didn't keep them in my purse. One of the officers put them in an evidence bag and then reported. "No passport."

The plain clothes detective looked at me and asked, "Where's the passport?"

I made up a lie, "In my safety deposit."

He thought a moment and said, "You admit to being James Wendt, a citizen of the United States?"

"Yes."

"Good enough. We'll go."

The detective preceded me down to the main floor and out onto the street. The armed men followed me. There was a plain step lorry there and a black sedan. One of the officers opened the door for me and made sure that my head didn't hit the door frame as I sat down. There was a driver, and the detective took the front seat beside him. There was a glass partition between me and the front seat. They drove off without another word.

About the Author

William Wilkin lived in a small Southern Ohio town until he began his college career. He has a Bachelor's degree in Physics from The Ohio State University and a Master's degree in Physics from The University of Chicago. He had a career in corporate Information Technology and currently lives in Nashville, TN.

He enjoys music, both "serious" and "classic Rock". He reads classic Detective fiction and Science Fiction & Fantasy as well as trying to stay current in Physics.

He began writing seriously about 2005. He has a blog, in-mid-world, where he writes about Science Fiction & Fantasy and remotely related topics.

www.ingramcontent.com/pod-product-compliance
Lightning Source LLC
Chambersburg PA
CBHW051056030726
47504CB00006B/1648